Thomas Jackson

The Life of John Goodwin

Comprising an Account of his Opinions and Writings

Thomas Jackson

The Life of John Goodwin
Comprising an Account of his Opinions and Writings

ISBN/EAN: 9783337415761

Printed in Europe, USA, Canada, Australia, Japan

Cover: Foto ©Raphael Reischuk / pixelio.de

More available books at **www.hansebooks.com**

THE LIFE

OF

JOHN GOODWIN,

SOMETIME FELLOW OF QUEEN'S COLLEGE, CAMBRIDGE, AND VICAR OF ST. STEPHEN'S
COLEMAN STREET, LONDON, IN THE SEVENTEENTH CENTURY:

COMPRISING

AN ACCOUNT OF THE CONTROVERSIES IN WHICH HE WAS ENGAGED

IN DEFENCE OF UNIVERSAL TOLERATION IN MATTERS OF RELIGION, AND OF
THE UNIVERSAL REDEMPTION OF MANKIND BY THE DEATH OF CHRIST:

WITH A REVIEW OF SEVERAL PUBLIC TRANSACTIONS IN GREAT BRITAIN,
DURING THE CIVIL WARS AND THE COMMONWEALTH.

BY THOMAS JACKSON.

He had a clear head, a fluent tongue, a penetrating spirit, and a marvellous faculty
in descanting on Scripture; and, with all his faults, must be owned to have
been a considerable man.—CALAMY.

This was all thy care,
To stand approved in sight of God, though worlds
Judged thee perverse.   MILTON.

SECOND EDITION, GREATLY IMPROVED.

LONDON:

LONGMANS, GREEN, READER, AND DYER,

1872.

PREFACE.

It will probably excite surprise that an extended biography of a man comparatively unknown, and one of the most abused men that England ever bred, should appear more than two hundred years after his death. The statement of a few facts, therefore, relative to the origin and composition of the narrative, may not be inappropriate.

Through a long life the author has found one of his highest pleasures in the perusal of old books, especially of books written in the seventeenth century; which he cannot but regard as the golden age of English theological literature. Among the numerous writers of that eventful period, no one excited his attention more than John Goodwin. The fine temper of this remarkable man as a controversialist,—the general raciness of his style,—the originality of his thoughts,—the clearness and force of his argumentation,—the native humour with which he repelled the hard sayings of angry opponents,—the surprising facility with which he elicited the meaning of the sacred writers,—his elevated views of the Divine Philanthropy, and of the extent of human redemption effected by the death of

A 2

Christ,—the unrivalled clearness with which he unfolded the evangelical method of a sinner's justification before God,—the earnestness and ability with which he defended the doctrine of universal toleration in matters of religion,—all conspired to excite his admiration.

Under the impulse of this feeling the author was led to inquire into the personal history of this gifted man. But here he was met by difficulties which appeared insuperable. He could find no record of Goodwin's life written by any one that knew him personally; and the Puritan contemporaries of Goodwin in general spoke of him in terms of the strongest censure, imputing to him almost every heresy that has disturbed the peace of the Church; such as Arianism, Socinianism, Pelagianism, scepticism. They charged him with denying the inspiration of the Holy Scriptures and the conscious existence of the souls of men in the separate state. Yet in his printed works it was clear that, with respect to the doctrine of the Holy Trinity, he was as orthodox as Athanasius, or as any of the fathers of the Nicene Council; and that no man has expressed himself in stronger language on the subject of original sin, or on the necessity of the grace of the Holy Spirit in the process of human-salvation. At the same time, he published the best book on the Divine authority of the Scriptures that his age produced.

After being perplexed for a while the author discovered a way by which these contradictory statements might, at least in part, be reconciled. The Puritan ministers believed their own theological opinions to be orthodox, and such as were opposed to them they regarded as heretical. They believed that the Lord Jesus died to redeem only a part of the human race. Goodwin believed that He died to redeem the whole. They contended that the doctrine of universal redemption was a heresy, connected with other heresies of equal magnitude, such as free will, and the possibility of falling from a state of grace. He was an avowed and uncompromising advocate of universal toleration, and most of his contemporaries regarded this tenet with equal, if not even greater horror; some of them, the Independents, for example, believing that such as held the fundamental doctrines of Christianity might be tolerated; but the more rigid Puritans contending that the incorrigible abettors of heresy ought to be visited with nothing less than capital punishment, even in the form of hanging and burning. In opposition to these narrow views, Goodwin held that all classes of people who are otherwise obedient to the laws, and live in an inoffensive manner, are entitled to the protection of the civil power; the only appropriate antidote to mental error being, not civil pains and penalties, but Scriptural argument, proposed in the spirit of meekness and charity. On this account, and on this account only, could he be justly chargeable with being an abettor of error in all its varieties of form. So that hitherto no just charge was proved against him; although the London clergy united in a public "testimony" against him, and repeatedly requested the government to subject him to a State prosecution as a most dangerous man; and other persons openly urged the members of his church to deliver him up to the devil on account of his perilous opinions.

After the death of this persecuted man accusations of a still more formidable kind were preferred against him than any that he had personally encountered, or had even anticipated. In his time there arose a body of religionists, who expected the immediate appearance of the Lord Jesus, to set up in the earth a universal monarchy, which was to be the fifth in the order of succession; and were therefore denominated, "Fifth Monarchy men." They meditated the overthrow of every existing government in the world; formed a plan for the assassination of Cromwell, as the Lord Protector; and after the Restoration some of them sallied forth into the streets of London, vociferating, " No king but Christ!" killing various persons in their frenzy. The ringleaders were apprehended and executed; and thus ended the delusion of the fifth universal monarchy.

In the history of his " Own Times" Bishop Burnet says, " John Goodwin headed these;" and then goes on to state, that "he filled all people with such an expectation of a glorious thousand years speedily to begin, that it looked like a madness possessing them." The truth, however, is, that John Goodwin was as innocent of all connexion with the Fifth Monarchy men as Burnet himself. He was indeed contemporary with them, but he was their open and avowed adversary; warning the people both against their tenets and their proceedings. The question is, how came a respectable prelate to write such a series of bare-faced falsehoods? It was not, we believe, that he intended to deceive his readers, but that he was negligent. He did not come to reside in England until many years after the death of Goodwin. He probably heard some vague reports concerning him and the Fifth Monarchy men, and, without taking any trouble to ascertain the truth, identified the one with the others; thus compromising his character as an historian. He would hardly have committed a greater blunder, if, in writing his History of the Reformation, for which he received the thanks of both Houses of Parliament, he had said that Gardiner and Bonner were Protestant Reformers, the innocent victims of Papal cruelty; and that Cranmer and Latimer were their cruel persecutors, who condemned them to be burnt alive. Yet Burnet's untruthful record has been believed, repeated, amplified, and exaggerated for two centuries; and John Goodwin, who in some respects was one of the ablest men of his times, has been held up to public scorn as an incendiary, a fanatic, and a fool!

The author confesses that the minute researches into which he has been led when prosecuting inquiries respecting John Goodwin have produced in him a considerable amount of scepticism with respect to our popular histories and traditions. It cannot be said of every writer of history, as it is said of honest John Strype, that he never misrepresented a fact for the sake of rounding a period; and that he never injured the character of any man in his eagerness to produce a sensational paragraph. Historians, like other persons, have their favourites, and the men and parties whom they dislike; and they some-times flatter the one, and unjustly disparage the other, without intending to mislead their readers. Yet they do mislead them by substituting fiction for truth, and by a false colouring of facts. Even the eloquent pages of Lord Macaulay, which have been so greatly admired, are not immaculate. As a Whig and an historian of the Revolution of 1688, it was not to be expected that he would admire the Nonjurors; but he has passed an unjust censure upon an eminent man belonging to that party. A small volume, entitled "The Predestinated Thief," was published in London anonymously, containing a severe satire upon the doctrine of absolute predestination. This publication his lordship ascribes to the pen of Archbishop Sancroft; and accuses the archbishop of meanness in writing a caricature of the tenets of the Puritan ministers, and then requesting them to afford their aid in resisting the attempts of James the Second to subvert the Protestantism of the National Church. But the volume charged upon Sancroft was not even of English origin, having been published in Holland before Sancroft had learned to write his own name. Ample proofs of the facts now stated relative to Burnet and the noble lord will be found in the ensuing volume; showing that even popular historians are to be read with reserve and caution.

But, however unjustly Goodwin may have been treated by his intolerant contemporaries, and by a gossiping prelate, it cannot be denied that he wrote in defence of the men who brought his unfortunate sovereign to the scaffold. This is acknowledged and regretted, and regretted by no man more than by his biographer. Let the case, however, be fairly stated; and then let him endure all the blame that is due to him,......and no more. After many years of mal-administration both in the Church and State, the king drew the sword against the other branches of the legislature, thus involving the country in the miseries of civil war, and drenching the soil with blood. He was beaten in the conflict, and in fact reduced to the condition of a subject. After a while two powerful parties, the Episcopalians and the Presbyterians, earnestly proposed that he should be restored to the exercise of his regal prerogatives; these parties, with the King at their head, being decidedly opposed to a general toleration in respect of religion. In the event of his restoration, a renewal of the cruelties which had been practised in the former years of his reign was apprehended; and perhaps even worse; for some of these royalists contended for the infliction of capital punishment in cases of alleged heresy. In this sad emergency, the heads of the army interposed, controlled the civil power, and slew the king, under forms of law which they themselves constituted; and of these acts John Goodwin, with other eminent men living at the time, among whom was John Milton, attempted a vindication.

It has been said by Solomon that "surely oppression maketh a wise man mad." But it is difficult for those who never either felt or feared the iron rod of the oppressor to form a correct judgment concerning the irregular proceedings of even a "wise man" in such a condition. John Goodwin was led into this practical error by his passion for religious toleration. His ears had been stunned, and his heart wrung with anguish, by the cries of the oppressed in the ecclesiastical courts, where noses had been slit, checks branded with hot irons, ears cut off, and godly men condemned to spend their days in filthy prisons; and he dreaded a repetition of these horrible barbarities, especially after so many of his countrymen had sacrificed their lives for the attainment of liberty, religious as well as civil. He was no republican; but openly enforced subjection to every form of civil government under which in his time the nation was placed. Yet he demanded liberty of conscience, as the inalienable right of every human being; and had it been his privilege to live in our times, there can be no doubt that he would have been as loyal as any subject in the realm; for all classes of people, both at home and in the colonies, now enjoy the liberty for which he contended, and more than he even hoped to witness. Could he have taken his stand in St. Paul's cathedral on the memorable 27th of February, 1872, when the Queen, as the head of the nation, rendered public thanks to Almighty God for the recovery of the Prince of Wales from a dangerous illness, John Goodwin would have joined in singing the national anthem with as hearty a voice as any one in the vast assembly; and from the ground of his heart would have prayed, "God save the Queen." He never opposed royalty, as such; but when royalty claimed authority over the consciences of Christian communities, and inflicted upon them civil pains and penalties, he thought it was their duty to obey God rather than men.

There are, however, parties who will never forgive him for the pamphlet which he wrote on the fate of Charles the First. His defence of the High Court of Justice, it is confessed, has

left a blot upon his memory which time will never efface. Yet
it is but just to him that his claims upon the national gratitude
should be duly appreciated; and these will perhaps serve to
moderate the censures that will still be passed upon him. The
greatness and prosperity of England at this day are unquestionably to be ascribed, under the blessing of a bountiful Providence,
to that liberty of religious thought and action which all classes
of the community now enjoy. Such liberty is by no means
coeval with Protestantism, which was long hampered in its
operations by the impertinent interposition of the secular
power. In the time of the civil wars, under the Long Parliament,
it became a subject of discussion and of earnest inquiry, and was
asserted not as a question of mere policy, but as a most sacred right
of human nature. Some godly men of the Baptist denomination led the way in this momentous controversy; but they
failed in their attempts to gain general attention. To this
question John Goodwin turned his earnest thought, studied it
in all its bearings, and then came forward as the unflinching
advocate of universal toleration, claiming for Jew and Gentile,
Christian and Mahometan, the right of free thought and action
with respect to the worship of God. When he introduced the
doctrine of religious liberty, in this its true latitude and form,
the generality of his Puritan brethren stood aghast, and raised
such outcries against him as would have terrified any man of
less firmness of nerve; but he stood his ground, strong in the
armour of righteousness and truth.

Jeremy Taylor and Milton next took up the subject, and
afterwards Locke; adding nothing indeed by way of argument,
but presenting the doctrine in new aspects, and carrying it into
quarters where Goodwin could not obtain a hearing. The
doctrine at length triumphed over all opposition, and full
religious liberty was secured to every British subject by statute

law. But what, in all probability, would have been the state of Great Britain at this day but for the noble stand in behalf of oppressed humanity made by the four men just mentioned? Let any man contrast the peaceful and happy state of England and Scotland in the reign of Queen Victoria, under the laws of toleration, with the wretched condition of those countries in the time of the First and Second Charles, when Acts of Uniformity were in unmitigated force; and then say what is due to the memory of Goodwin, Taylor, Milton, and Locke; especially to Goodwin, who led the way in this noble enterprise, so as to expose not only his reputation, but even his liberty and his life, among the furious advocates of religious coercion; who would not have hesitated to impose silence upon him by imprisonment or by death, could they have had their will: whereas Taylor, Milton, and Locke wrote in the absence of public clamour, and when the minds of men were prepared for a free and calm consideration of the subject. Yet Goodwin was a host in himself, resembling Ajax in the Grecian camp, and Samson among the Philistines. When one of the hot spirits of the age said that he would make the very name of Goodwin "an abhorring to that and future generations," on account of what he had written and published in favour of universal toleration, Goodwin answered, "I say to Mr. Edwards, and I say it upon good grounds, that for those very opinions shall I be had in honour. For when the madness of error shall be made known unto all men, it shall prevail no longer; and truth only shall be exalted in that day: and those that have stood by her, and fought her battles, when she had many enemies and few friends, shall partake with her in her triumphs."

Well said, venerable old man! It is high time that this prophecy should be fulfilled. Indeed your name would long since have been among the most honoured in British history,

but for the pamphlet you wrote on the death of your unfortunate king, and the scandalous libel upon you, which was
written by a careless prelate when you and your friends were
sleeping in your graves. The bishop's libel is proved to be an
absolute untruth; and it may be hoped that the good people of
England will now condone your pamphlet, as they have long
condoned the more faulty pamphlets of Milton on the
same subject. Take then your place among the enlightened
divines and philosophers of your country, with whom on many
accounts you richly deserve to be associated!

There is another ground on which it is thought John Goodwin
is entitled to public gratitude. He found the doctrine of redemption by the death of Christ held in bondage by the unauthorized
restrictions and limitations of the Puritan clergy, and he undertook its emancipation. What he undertook he accomplished
by exhibiting the Scripture doctrine on this great subject in its
true latitude and extent; and it is worthy of observation that
the doctrine advocated by him is now so generally held, that
ministers who do not fully agree with him, when addressing
their hearers on the subject of salvation, speak *as if* they were
all redeemed, and *as if* every one of them might be saved through
the blood of the cross. This, indeed, if it is not all that is desired,
is a movement in the right direction; and to bring about this
result no man rendered more efficient service than the brave vicar
of Coleman Street.

It is only requisite to add, that the present volume was first
published just fifty years ago. It has been revised throughout,
and many additions have been made to it, chiefly relating to
contemporary events; and it is again submitted to the public
as a chapter of ecclesiastical history. It will be observed that
an attempt has been made to render Goodwin, as much as possible, his own biographer, by inserting copious extracts from his

writings. These are mostly given in an abridged form, but
always in the author's own language. Fidelity is the object at
which the biographer has aimed; and in reference to the
entire volume he trusts he may say, without hesitation,

> "These things are true, though facts of distant times."

It may be hoped that this record of Goodwin's life and
labours will, soon or late, lead to the republication of more
of his volumes, which are at present extremely scarce, and
among which are some of the choicest specimens of old English divinity, practical as well as controversial. The four small
volumes which he published at the beginning of his literary
career, together with his treatise on Justification, and that on
the Divine Authority of the Holy Scriptures, are especially
worthy of being placed within the reach of general readers.
It may be fairly doubted whether there ever appeared in the
English language a specimen of more thoroughly argumentative divinity than Goodwin's treatise on Justification. It
would afford a fine intellectual exercise for a theological
student. His practical pieces would serve no less to stir up
the minds of devout people by way of remembrance.

LONDON, *July* 29*th*, 1872.

CONTENTS.

CHAPTER IX.

CHAPTER X.

CHAPTER XI.

THE LIFE

OF

JOHN GOODWIN.

CHAPTER I.

THE time of the civil wars and of the Commonwealth is one of the most interesting periods of British history. The extraordinary occurrences of that age brought into public view a number of individuals, who would otherwise, in all probability, have lived and died unnoticed and unknown, except by the narrow circle of their own immediate connections. The peculiar circumstances in which they were placed, not only called into exercise their great intellectual powers, but gave birth to a series of actions by which their characters were fully developed, and the influence of their religious principles distinctly exhibited.

Among the personages thus distinguished, the celebrated JOHN GOODWIN is entitled to no small share of attention. His abilities were of a high order, and his integrity unimpeachable ; but, unhappily, his sentiments and conduct have been ill understood, and therefore subject to gross misrepresentation.

This learned man was born in the year 1593. He was a native of Norfolk; but of what particular place in that county we are not informed. In a local history, it is stated, on the testimony of a descendant from Mr. Goodwin, that he was born at Newcastle-under-Lyme, in Staf-

B

fordshire : * but this is manifestly a mistake ; since Granger mentions a manuscript in the library at Lambeth, in which he is denominated, "Johannes Goodwin, Norfolc ;"† and he himself, after a residence in London of twenty-six years, speaking of Norfolk, calls it " my country."‡

Concerning the family of Mr. Goodwin, I have not been able to obtain the slightest information. During the reign of Queen Elizabeth, a clergyman named Vincent Goodwin, residing in or near the city of Norwich, was suspended for nonconformity to the rites of the Church.§ Doctor Thomas Goodwin also, the noted champion of Independency and of Calvinism, was born at Rolesby, in Norfolk; ‖ but whether any relationship subsisted between them and the subject of these memoirs, remains to be decided.

John Goodwin received his academical education at Cambridge, where he took his degree as Master of Arts, and was elected Fellow of Queen's College, Nov. 10th, 1617, in the twenty-fourth year of his age.¶ On his admission into holy orders, his sermons are said to have displayed an elegance and an erudition which excited general admiration.**

One of the most censorious and quarrelsome men that ever lived, accused him of holding his Fellowship after his marriage.†† What truth there might be in the allegation, I have no means of knowing. Mr. Goodwin treated the charge with indifference, as unworthy of a direct reply.‡‡

After his removal from the University, having preached occasionally for some time at Raynham, Lynn, Yarmouth, and Norwich, he went to London in the year 1632 ; and on the 18th of December, 1633, was presented to the Vicarage

* Pitt's Hist. of Staffordshire, p. 367, Edit. 1817.   † Biog. Hist. of Eng. Vol. III p. 42, Edit. 1804.   ‡ Goodwin's Triumviri, p. 247, Edit. 1658.   § Brook's Lives of the Puritans, Vol. I. p. 39.   ‖ Dr. Goodwin's Works, Vol. V. p. 5, Edit. 1704.   ¶ Kennet's Register and Chron. p. 935, Edit. 1728.   Nonconformists' Memorial, Vol. I. p. 196, Edit. 1802. ** Aikin's General Biog. Art. Goodwin.   †† Edwards' Gangræna, Part II. p. 84, Edit. 1646.   ‡‡ Inexcusableness of that Grand Accusation, Preface.

of St. Stephen's, Coleman Street, upon the choice of the
parishioners.* This living was vacant through the voluntary resignation of Mr. John Davenport, who, from conscientious motives, declined all further connection with the
Ecclesiastical Establishment; and who, to escape the vengeance of Archbishop Laud, soon after left his native country, and spent the greater part of his remaining days in
exile.†

When Mr. Goodwin commenced his ministerial labour,
examples of clerical delinquency abounded on every side.
Not a few of those who held livings in the Church never
attempted to preach, were scandalously immoral in their
lives, and destitute of every qualification for their office,
except that of ability to read. Of those who had learning
and talents, some employed their strength in the support
of ceremonial observances, which, to say the least, are
not essential to true religion; and others, in contending
for the simplicity of Christian ordinances, manifested as
much zeal against the use of the ring in marriage, the sign
of the cross in baptism, and other things of a similar description, as if they were actually defending the most important doctrines of revelation, or guarding the Church against
the sin "which hath never forgiveness." Comparatively few
seemed so to enter into the spirit of their work, as to employ
their time and energies in one laborious and prayerful effort
to turn men from darkness unto light, and from the power
of Satan unto God.

While these evils were extensively prevalent, the style of
preaching which was generally adopted, was far from being
judicious. In fact, the eloquence of the pulpit was vicious
and corrupt. Several of the most popular preachers, though
men of piety and of extensive literary acquirements, were
notorious punsters; their sermons were plentifully inter-
larded with scraps of Greek and Latin, and disfigured by an
almost incalculable number of doctrinal propositions, divisions, sub-divisions, objections, solutions, inferences, uses

---

* Newcourt's Repertorium, Vol. I. p. 537, Edit. 1708. Edwards' Gangræna, Part II. p. 84. Kennet's Register, p. 454.   † Brook's Lives of
the Puritans, Vol. III. p. 447.

of instruction, of comfort, of reproof, of exhortation, and
so forth. Such discourses, how admirably soever they might
be calculated to exhibit the learning and display the logical
dexterity of the preacher, were ill adapted to the mental
habits of the great mass of mankind. The " shrewd and
severe animadversion of a Scottish lord " upon Bishop Andrews, addressed to King James the First, was applicable
to many a "painful preacher" in those times : "He was
learned, but he did play with his text as a Jack-an-apes
does; who takes up a thing and tosses and plays with it;
and then he takes up another and plays a little with it :
here's a pretty thing, and there's a pretty thing." *

Scarcely any of Mr. Goodwin's discourses were committed to the press as they had been delivered from the
pulpit : it is therefore difficult to ascertain how far they
were conformable to the prevailing practice. But if a
judgment may be formed from his practical writings,
nearly all of which consist of sermons melted down into
treatises, he rose as a preacher above the pedantic and
unedifying fashion of his age. In the life of one who had
been a regular attendant upon his ministry, his public
discourses are designated as "elegant and learned." †
Indeed his intellectual and moral qualifications as a
Christian pastor were far above the common standard.
His deep and comprehensive knowledge of the Holy
Scriptures, which must have been the result of incessant
and unwearied application, enabled him to produce in the
course of his ministry an endless variety of the most interesting and useful matter. He bore no resemblance to
those theologians, whom a distinguished prelate has
characterised as the "apes of Epictetus." Deeply impressed with the high importance of the peculiar doctrines
of Christianity, to the latest period of his life he never lost
sight either of the atoning Saviour, or of the quickening
and sanctifying Spirit : fully persuaded, that when they
are either systematically discarded, or practically for-

---

* Letters from the Bodleian Library, Vol. II. p. 207, Edit. 1813.
† Life of Thomas Firmin, p. 6, Edit. 1698.

gotten, the teacher of religion is not only guilty of a flagrant breach of trust, as a steward of the mysteries of GOD; but is spending his strength as uselessly as those philosophical speculatists, whom the poet describes as

————dropping buckets into empty wells,
And growing old in drawing nothing up.

Mr. Goodwin's mode of preaching was never loose and declamatory. With the laws of reasoning he was well acquainted; and by the practised habit of his mind he appears to have been rendered incapable of expatiating upon any subject except in an argumentative manner. In the establishment of his various positions, his arguments are all deduced from pertinent texts of Holy Scripture; and the simple, natural, and striking manner in which the meaning of those texts is unfolded, affords as fine an illustration, as the whole compass of English theological literature can furnish, of the just and beautiful remark of Lord Bacon; that, "As wines which, at first pressing, run gently, and yield a more pleasant taste than those where the wine-press is hard wrought; (because these somewhat relish of the stone and skin of the grape;) so those observations are the most wholesome and sweet, which flow from scriptures gently expressed, and naturally expounded, and are not wrested and drawn aside to common-places of controversies."*

In expressing his own views of the peculiar business of a Christian preacher, Mr. Goodwin says, "Aristotle, in setting out the work of a rhetorician, asserting it to be, *Not to persuade, but to speak things pertinent and proper to persuade,*—drew with the same stroke of his pencil a happy character of the proper work of a minister of the Gospel. To overrule the judgments and consciences of men, in the great things of eternity, appertaineth to Him that rideth upon the heavens: they who dwell in houses of clay quit themselves to the utmost point of their line, by proposing and pressing such things upon them, [as]

* Advancement of Learning, Lib. IX.

have a sufficient potency of reason and argument to persuade, where there is no bar of wilful neglect, froward-
ness, or resistance in the way." *

As a clergyman Mr. Goodwin did not eat the bread of
idleness : but giving himself wholly to the duties of his
office, he laboured night and day to promote the salvation
of the people committed to his care. After he had been
resident in London fifteen years, a contemporary writer,
speaking of him, says, He is a man "whose innocency and
integrity in the cause of Christ, and great work and labour
of love to Christ and His churches, I doubt not but in due
time will be cleared and rewarded abundantly."†   In consequence of his personal virtues, and ministerial abilities
and fidelity, he lived in the affections and esteem of all
who were able to appreciate his worth ; many of whom
acknowledged with gratitude, that they regarded their
attendance upon his ministry as one of the highest privileges of their lives.‡

When Mr. Goodwin officiated in the national church,
Christianity as taught by the Inspired Writers, and re-
vived by the pious Reformers, was far from being in a
prosperous condition in Great Britain. The Roman
Catholics were somewhat numerous, and were very active
in making proselytes. Though laid under severe restrictions by existing laws, yet, the Queen being of their community, by her influence they obtained considerable indulgence. This circumstance excited great alarm in the
minds of many, who regarded Popery not only as a per-
version of revealed truth, but as directly hostile to the
liberty of mankind. The Puritans also abounded in different parts of the kingdom ; and though they held discordant
sentiments among themselves on various subjects, they
agreed in hostility to the government of the church, and
to its mode of public worship. The Brownists contended,

* Divine Authority of the Scriptures, p. 377, Edit. 1648.   † Bartlet's
Model of the Congregational Way, p. 126, Edit. 1647.   ‡ Apologetical
Account of some Brethren of the Church, whereof Mr. John Goodwin is
Pastor, 1647.

that the system of ecclesiastical polity, which was sanctioned by law, was Antichristian; and conformity to its injunctions, a violation of religious duty. The Presbyterians, though less violent, meditated the complete subversion of diocesan episcopacy, and the substitution of the "Genevan platform," as the national establishment. Both these classes of religionists were immoderately attached to the peculiar doctrines of Calvinism, and not unfrequently spoke and wrote against the sacerdotal vestments, the authority of the bishops, and the ceremonies of the hierarchy with the utmost bitterness.

While some valid objections may be made both to the sentiments entertained by these parties, and to the spirit in which they were too often defended, some of the clergy manifested a considerable defection from the principles of genuine Protestantism. Many of them have been accused of departing from the authorized creed of the national church, by a partiality for the doctrinal sentiments of Arminius. But the justice of this charge is not very apparent. There is nothing in any of the standard writings of the Church of England, that can be considered as favouring the *peculiarities* of Calvinism, except the Seventeenth Article of Religion; and even that article is silent on the precise question at issue between the followers of Calvin and those of Arminius. That question is not, Whether there is any such doctrine taught in the Holy Scriptures, as God's predestination of some men to eternal life, and of others to eternal death? for this is acknowledged on both hands; but, Whether such predestination is absolute or conditional? Whether it is a predestination of individuals *personally* considered, or of individuals regarded as *believers* in Jesus Christ, or as obstinate and voluntary *unbelievers?* The former opinion was held by Calvin; the latter by Arminius, and by several eminent men before him; and on which side the truth lies, the compilers of the Seventeenth Article took not upon themselves in that document to determine. At the same time it is worthy of remark, that the Formularies of the Church contain various passages which no ingenuity can ever reconcile to the principles of

strict Calvinism. According to the general complexion of
the Liturgy, redemption is universal, the mercy of God
unlimited, and the actual bestowment of salvation suspended upon the performance of certain specified conditions
on the part of man. Of the truth of this remark, the following sentences afford ample proof. They are only a small
specimen of what might be adduced on the same subjects
from that incomparable and truly evangelical manual of
devotion: " Almighty God, the Father of our Lord Jesus
Christ, *who desireth not the death of a sinner*, but rather
that he may turn from his wickedness and live." *—" Almighty and everlasting God, who, of Thy tender love
towards *mankind*, hast sent Thy Son our Saviour Jesus
Christ, to take upon Him our flesh, and to suffer death upon
the cross, *that all mankind* should follow the example of His
great humility." †—" O merciful God, who hast made all
men, and *hatest nothing that Thou hast made*, nor *wouldest
the death of a sinner*, but rather that he should be converted
and live; have mercy upon ALL Jews, Turks, Infidels, and
Heretics; and so fetch them home, blessed Lord, to Thy
flock, that they may be saved among the remnant of Thy
true Israelites." ‡—" Almighty God, our heavenly Father,
who of Thy tender mercy didst give Thine only Son Jesus
Christ to suffer death upon the Cross for our redemption;
who made there (by His one oblation of Himself once
offered) a full, perfect, and sufficient sacrifice, oblation and
satisfaction *for the sins of the whole world*."§ In the Catechism every child is taught to say, " I learn to believe in
God the Son, who hath redeemed me *and all mankind*."
The Thirty-first Article states, that " the offering of Christ
once made is that perfect redemption, propitiation, and
satisfaction, for *all the sins of the whole world, both original
and actual*." And to every communicant who approaches
the table of the Lord, the officiating minister is required,
on presenting the sacramental elements, solemnly to declare, " The BODY of our Lord Jesus Christ was GIVEN for
THEE;" and " the BLOOD of our Lord Jesus Christ was

* Absolution.   † Collect for Sunday before Easter.
‡ Collect for Good Friday.   § Prayer of Consecration.

SHED for THEE:" a practice which it is difficult to justify
upon the principles of particular redemption, and of Calvinian reprobation. An Arminian member of the Church
of England, therefore, to say the least, has as just ground
of complaint against his Calvinistic brother, as his Calvinistic brother can possibly have against him. The truth is,
the theological sentiments of Arminius were in substantial
agreement with those of Melancthon, to whose judgment
the English Reformers paid a profound deference.

One of the most learned of the episcopal divines of that
age, against whom this charge had been unjustly preferred,
expresses himself in the following dignified language: " I
disavow the name and title of Arminian. For my faith
was never taught by the doctrine of men. I will not pin
my belief unto any man's sleeve, carry he his head never
so high. A Christian I am, and so glory to be; only denominated of Christ Jesus, my Lord and Master; by whom
I was never as yet so wronged, that I could relinquish willingly that royal title, and exchange it for any of his menial
servants.—I protest, before God and His angels, the time
is yet to come that I ever read word in Arminius. The
course of my studies was never addressed to modern epito-
mizers: but from my first entrance to the study of divinity,
I balked the ordinary and accustomed by-paths, ...
and betook myself to Scripture, the rule of faith interpreted
by Antiquity, the best expositor of faith, and applyer of
that rule: holding it a point of discretion, to draw water
as near as I could to the well-head, and to spare labour in
vain in running off to cisterns and lakes. I went to *enquire,*
when doubt was, *of the days of old,* as God himself directed
me; and hitherto I have not repented. If Arminius in
tenets agreeth unto Scripture, plain and express; if he hath
agreeing unto his opinions the practice, tradition, and consent of the ancient Church, I embrace his opinions; let his
private ends, if he had any, alone. If Calvin, so far in
account and estimation before Arminius, dissenteth from
antiquity, and the universal ancient Church, I follow him
not. No private man, or peculiar spirit, ever did or ever

shall tyrannize upon my belief. I yield only unto God and
the Church." *

On other points, however, the characters of these ecclesiastical dignitaries were far from being invulnerable.
Though decidedly opposed to several of the peculiarities of
Popery, yet, apparently desirous of effecting a union between the Churches of England and Rome,† and hoping to
induce the English Catholics to conform to the ecclesiastical
Establishment,they contended for the lawfulness of images
in places of religious worship, for the real presence of Christ
in the consecrated elements of the Lord's Supper, and spoke
of the monstrous doctrine of transubstantiation as a nicety
of the schools. They also pleaded for auricular confession,
and for priestly absolution; and not only denied the morality of the Christian Sabbath, but peremptorily required
the inferior clergy publicly to read the King's Book of
Sports, encouraging the common people, on the Lord's Day,
after the celebration of divine worship in their respective
churches, to amuse themselves with dancing, archery, leap-
ing, vaulting, morrice dances, and other sports of a similar
nature.‡

An excellent man, who had himself been a spectator of
those scenes of profane and noisy riot, thus excited, says,
" I cannot forget that, in my youth, in those late times
when we lost the labours of some of our conformable godly
teachers, for not reading publicly the Book for Sports and
dancing on the Lord's Days, one of my father's own tenants
was the town-piper, hired by the year, for many years together, and the place of the dancing assembly was not a hundred yards from our door; and we could not, on the Lord's
Day, either read a chapter, or pray, or sing a psalm, or cate-
chise or instruct a servant, but with the noise of the pipe
and taber, and the whootings in the street continually in
our ears. And, even among a tractable people, we were the
common scorn of all the rabble in the streets, and called
Puritans, Precisians, and Hypocrites, because we chose

* Mountagu's Appello Cæsarem, pp. 10–12, Edit. 1625.   † Heylin's
Life of Archbishop Laud, p. 390, Edit. 1671.   ‡ Neal's Hist. Purit. Vol.
II. pp. 123, 247, 249, Edit. 1733.

but to read the Scriptures, than to do as they did; though
there was no savour of non-conformity in our family. And
when the people by the Book were allowed to play and
dance out of public service-time, they could so hardly break
off their sports, that many times the reader was fain to stay
till the piper and player would give over: and sometimes the
morrice-dancers would come into the church in all their
linen and scarfs and antic dresses, with the morrice-bells
jingling at the legs: and as soon as the Common Prayer
was read, did haste out presently to their play again."*

The conduct of some of the Bishops was particularly
cruel and unchristian towards the Puritans, many of whom
were pious and conscientious men, though of narrow and
illiberal principles. Goaded by persecution, multitudes of
them left their native land, and fled, some to Holland, and
others to the wilds of America, that they might enjoy that
common right of human nature, liberty of conscience.
Irritated also by the restraints which were arbitrarily
imposed upon them, the Puritans, in defending their own
sentiments and in exposing their oppressors, not unfrequently overstepped the boundaries of decorum, and
expressed themselves in language highly insulting and
inflammatory. In such cases the offenders were sentenced
in ecclesiastical courts to endure the most painful and
degrading personal mutilations, to stand as objects of
public infamy on the pillory, were reduced to absolute
beggary by heavy fines, and doomed to spend their days
in the horrors of a prison.†

Mr Goodwin had not been long settled in his living
before he was called to endure a portion of those troubles
which awaited such clergymen as could not satisfy themselves with a rigorous conformity. At this time, Archbishop Laud enjoyed the See of Canterbury, and ruled
the king's subjects with a rod of iron. As a munificent
patron of sacred literature and of learned men, this
celebrated metropolitan is entitled to high praise. But

* Baxter's Divine Appointment of the Lord's Day, p. 116, Edit. 1671.
† Chandler's Hist. of Persecution, p. 364, Edit. 1736. Clarendon, Vol. I.
p. 94, Edit. 1707.

he was inordinate in his attachment to religious ceremony and parade; and his vindictive spirit towards such as were Puritanically inclined, prompted him to acts of cruelty, the recital of which inspires terror and disgust. With him it appears to have been a favourite maxim, that ecclesiastical discipline should be *felt* as well as spoken of; and hence, in the enforcement of canonical obedience, many useful ministers, who scrupled at the observance of all the ceremonies which he introduced, were, at his pleasure, admonished, suspended, or deprived of their livings.* According to the archbishop, Mr. Goodwin's clerical conduct, at one period, was not perfectly regular. In the account which his grace presented to the king concerning the state of his province after his visitation in the summer of 1637, among other ministers who had been "convented" before their diocesan for "breach of the canons of the church, in sermons, or practice, or both," mention is made of "Mr. John Goodwin, Vicar of St. Stephen's, Coleman Street." But as he and his fellow-delinquents "promised amendment for the future, and submission to the church in all things;" it is stated, that "my lord very moderately forbore further proceedings against them."†

Early in the year 1639, Mr. Goodwin was brought into collision with a man of some notoriety among his parishioners, who has been generally known by the name of "Cobbler Howe." He was employed on the week-days in mending shoes, and on the Sabbath preached to a company of people who did not like the form of worship which was practised in the Established Church. Goodwin having said, on some occasion or other, that learning is a necessary qualification for a preacher of Christ's Gospel, the sentiment was immediately called in question, and a reference made to Howe; who, it was alleged, could preach from any text in the Bible, after a short time allowed him for reflection. "Then request him," said

---

* Wilson's Hist. and Antiq. of Dissenting Churches, Vol. II. p. 404, Edit. 1808. Clarendon, Book First. † Hist. of the Troubles and Trial of Archbishop Laud, Vol. I. p. 536, Edit. 1695.

Goodwin, "to preach on the following text, and I will come to hear him : " "As also in all his epistles, speaking in them on these things; in which are some things hard to be understood, which they that are unlearned and unstable wrest, as they do also the other Scriptures, unto their own destruction." (2 Peter iii. 16.) This proposal being reported to Howe, he readily accepted it, and engaged to deliver a sermon on St. Peter's words the next day, when Mr. Goodwin and several other ministers were present. At the conclusion of the service, being pressed to give his opinion of the sermon, Goodwin said, "You have set up a calf, and danced around it." Being further urged to specify the things to which he objected, the preacher's friends intimate that he was silent; and they add, "Mr. Goodwin went away in a huff."

Howe and his friends, being grieved that the sermon was stigmatized as a "calf," resolved to print it, and thus appeal· to the judgment of the public; but when they applied to the London printers, not one of them would pass it through the press; the disappointed parties laying the blame upon Mr. Goodwin, thinking that the printers acted under his control. Yet resolved not to be beaten, they sent the sermon to Holland, where it was printed by an honest Dutchman, and then returned to London, where it was put into circulation, "numbering good intellects," like Milton's treatise on Divorce. It has often been since reprinted, but never as it was orally delivered; some things being omitted, and others added; so that it is in reality no criterion as to Howe's abilities as an extemporary speaker. It is entitled, "The Sufficiency of the Spirit's Teaching without human Learning;" and is a singular farrago of ignorant declamation and devout feeling, setting at defiance all the rules of logic and the canons of scriptural interpretation, placing ordinary Christians upon an equality with the inspired apostles of our Lord, and learned men in general in the same category with heathen philosophers and soothsayers. With regard to the Gospel ministry, Howe gives the preference to pious ignorance before pious learning. "Suppose two men," says he, "both alike endued with the grace of God, and alike gifted by His Spirit, the one learned, and the other an unlearned man; which of these two should be chosen into the ministry of Christ in His church? I answer, The unlearned man; for these reasons: First, because God respects no man's person. Secondly, this is indeed most suitable to the Gospel, which is in itself simplicity, and appears to the wisdom of man so to be; and it is not meet, our Saviour saith, to put contraries together, as a new piece into an old garment, nor new wine into old bottles. Thirdly, God chooses such things in opposition to others, to astonish the wisdom of man: as when the Council perceived Peter and John were unlearned men, and without knowledge, they marvelled, and were amazed."

The Rev. Daniel Neal, in his History of the Puritans, gives a brief notice of this publication, and says that Howe "was a man of learning;" a clear proof that he had never read the pamphlet, nor even the introductory advertisement, which was written by one of the author's friends, who expressly states that "he had no school learning." This is not the only case in which Neal, with all his excellencies as a writer of history, makes bold and unqualified statements concerning subjects which it is clear he had never carefully examined.

As to Howe, there is no reason to doubt that he was an upright and godly man. He wrought daily at his craft, with his Bible open before him; and being possessed of a ready apprehension, of fluent speech, and of personal courage, he was able to speak on religious subjects so as to edify people of the same rank in life. But when he deemed himself qualified to preach on any text in the Bible, and to decide upon the nature and value of what is called "learning," in its connexion with revealed truth and personal religion, he forgot his providential calling, and "the cobbler went beyond his last." It was his misfortune to live before the rights of Englishmen were properly defined. He was forced by the hand of violence from his shop and his stall, where he obtained an honest livelihood, and did nobody any harm, was excommunicated,

shut up among thieves and murderers, and at length died
in prison, a martyr to nonconformity. His friends wished
to bury him in the churchyard of Shoreditch, but were
refused, a grave in consecrated ground being deemed too
great an honour for an excommunicated man; and therefore Howe was buried in one of the highways in the
neighbourhood of London, where some of his friends also
found their final resting-place. Yet, it is very possible
that these oppressed people, when the trumpet of the
judgment shall sound, may appear quite as glorious as
their judges. Before the Divine tribunal the persecutor
will appear stripped of his robes of office, and his victims
divested of their prison dresses.

In respect of Mr. Goodwin, it is but just to say that the
account which we have given of his conduct towards
Samuel Howe is supplied by his adversaries; that if we
had his own version of the affair, it would probably present a very different aspect; and that he at length became
a decided advocate of lay-preaching. When Episcopacy
was abolished in England, and he was no longer under
the control of canon law, certain gifted men of established piety, and of competent qualifications otherwise,
though engaged in secular business, and destitute of an
academical education, occasionally occupied his pulpit in
Coleman Street, preaching under his sanction, and to the
edification of their co-religionists, as will appear in a subsequent part of this narrative.

In the same year (1639) Mr. Goodwin published, with a
recommendatory preface, a small volume of posthumous
sermons, under the title of "A Gleaning of God's Harvest." These discourses were written by Mr. Henry
Ramsden, who, in the latter part of his life, was vicar of
Halifax, in Yorkshire; but who had formerly been a
minister of considerable repute in London. This very
excellent man was born at Greetland in the parish of
Halifax, and admitted a commoner of Magdalen Hall in
Oxford, in the year 1610. At the University he was greatly
celebrated for his proficiency in theological learning, and
after he became a preacher in the metropolis "was

much resorted to, for his edifying and Puritanical sermons."*

In this elegant and well written preface, Mr. Goodwin says, " The author of these sermons having fallen asleep before their time came to do service in the world, I conceived it might bear the construction of some light charity to lead them out, in their orphan-like condition, by the hand of a recommendatory epistle. Men for the most part desire in books to know first what is said of them, before they care to know what they say : and sometimes an author, worthy of prime inspection, for want of an agent to make his worth his harbinger, may lie as long neglected and unread, as the cripple at the pool of Bethesda lay uncured, for want of one to cast him into the water."

Having presented to the world the sermons of Ramsden, Mr. Goodwin assumed the character of an author himself. The first work which he appears to have committed to the press was a small volume entitled, " The Saints' Interest in God opened, in several Sermons preached anniversarily upon the Fifth of November," and bearing the date of 1640. The feelings with which he commenced his career of authorship are not unworthy of notice : they form a perfect contrast to the hardihood of those who palm their indigested lucubrations upon mankind, and the false modesty of such as withhold from the world that fruit of their genius and industry, which would add to the general stock of knowledge, or contribute to the mental gratification and improvement of society. "I am not conscious," says he, "either of forwardness or backwardness of being made public. The judgments of men, if they could agree, may easily overrule me either way. It argues some distemper of spirit, to be importunate upon the world with a man's private conceptions : neither is it the best posture to put the world upon importunity with us, to purchase them, if they have a mind to them."

Mr. Goodwin thought, that the signal interposition of Divine Providence, in the discovery of the Gunpowder

Plot, was worthy of special attention; and that the people of England were not sufficiently observant of its annual commemoration. The occasion upon which the discourses contained in this book were delivered, he remarks, " was the anniversary remembrance of that great battle fought between Hell and Heaven, about the peace and safety of our nation, on Nov. 5th, 1605 ; when Hell was overthrown, and Heaven and we rejoiced together. I have not, to my present remembrance, met with any thing published of late, of any special influence or tendency, to maintain the life and spirit of the solemnity and joy of that day and deliverance. And pity it is, that such a plant of Paradise should wither or languish for want of watering."

This pious and instructive manual is dedicated to "Mr. Isaac Pennington, Alderman of the City of London," together with the rest of the author's "loving parishioners, and dear friends, the inhabitants of St. Stephen's, Coleman Street." The address to these persons, which is of considerable length, appears to have flowed from the fulness of a generous heart. It shows the high esteem in which the author was held, and displays that ardent love to the souls of men, which is essential to the character of every " good minister of Jesus Christ."

" Though I have no ground of confidence," says he, " to put any such question to you, as Paul did to the Galatians : What hath your felicity been since my coming and preaching the Gospel to you? Yet this I cannot but testify to the praise of the grace that hath been given to you, by my dispensation of the Gospel towards you, (let the tree of interpretation fall which way it will, it shall neither hurt you nor me by the fall,) that you have rejoiced in my light, and have been ready, many of you, in the best way of Christian expression, to signify the truth, life, and power, which you have seen, tasted, and felt, in my ministry.

" My confidence is, concerning you that are spiritual, that you, by the light, partly of my labours amongst you, (having served you near seven years,) partly by my manner of life, can read it in my heart, how dear you are to me, and how high my comforts are in such amongst you

c

whose faces are set towards heaven, and are resolved to take nothing in exchange for your souls. I will not be importunate with you, in pleading the cause of my endearments to you upon this occasion: I had rather give you an account of my heart towards you in deeds than in words. Neither shall I ever be troublesome to you, for any greater measure of esteem, than my carriage shall be reasonably valued at, between a pastor and his people. If you will please to interpret this dedication as a testimony of mine especial love and respects to you, the burden shall not need to lie more upon your affections than your judgments: and those actions ever come off with best satisfaction to sober men, that are so divided.

"The great and mighty God of heaven and earth make these meditations as the cloud of the latter rain to you, to drop fatness upon your souls, that they may be felt by yourselves, in renewing and strengthening your inner man; be seen upon you by others, in an unstained excellence of life and conversation; and found also in your accounts at the great day, as having contributed their share towards that joy, which is the promised reward of all those that know God to be the true God, and Him whom He hath sent, Jesus Christ. Which crown of blessedness there is not a man of you but shall most assuredly obtain, if you will run for yourselves with as much faithfulness, as he is ready to run for you night and day, who here, in the presence of heaven and earth, giveth it under his hand, that he is your loving and truly affectionate pastor."

Mr. Goodwin's "Saints' Interest in God" appears to have been well received by the religious world; and hence, in the following year, he published three other small volumes of a similar description. The first of these bears the title of, "The Christian's Engagement for the Gospel; opened in Four Sermons on Part of the third Verse of the Epistle of Jude. Also, Christ's Approbation of Mary's Choice; a Sermon preached at the Funeral of Mrs. Abbot, in St. Stephen's, Coleman Street, London." The "four sermons" are given in the form of a continuous treatise, divided into thirteen chapters, on the duty of Christians to contend earnestly for " the faith which was once delivered unto the saints," but which is liable to be corrupted by various classes of people whose characters are here described. The volume, which is dedicated to " the Right Worshipful and much honoured John Pymme, Esq.," doubtless referred to the abuses which had been introduced into the Church of England, and into which the House of Commons had begun to inquire. The sermon on "Mary's Choice" relates to the death of a young married lady, the daughter of a London merchant ; and is an earnest defence and recommendation of that supreme regard for heaven which the conduct of Mary indicated, when she placed herself at the Saviour's feet, from which He refused to remove her. The character of the lady is beautifully drawn ; and the sermon is dedicated to her father, who appears to have been a personal friend of Goodwin, whose next publication is entitled, " God a Good Master and Protector ; " and the fourth, "The Return of Mercies ; or, the Saints' Advantage by Losses." The latter of these publications is dedicated to " Lady Clark, of Reading ; " and the former to " Mrs. Elizabeth Hampden, of West-minster," the mother of the celebrated patriot of that name. From the dedicatory address to Mrs. Hampden, it should seem that our author had been under considerable personal obligations to that distinguished lady. " I acknowledge myself," says he, " a debtor to you for many expressions of love, which very slender engagements on my part have drawn from you. I have nothing wherewith to recompense your kindness, but my prayers, and the travail of my soul for yours. A minister's thankfulness to his friends, is to show them the way to heaven ; and to enable them, if he can, to walk from strength to strength, that they faint not till they come there."

Lady Clark also appears to have had a high respect for Mr. Goodwin, and to have commanded his gratitude by her generous defence of his character. " Your ladyship," says he, " by many expressions of love and kindness, hath drawn me into bonds of thankfulness above my substance, and before I was aware: especially that noble charity of yours, in so constant a relieving of my reputation, with the adventure and exposal of your own, is a courtesy of entire and universal obligement alone. But I know it is more easy for you to show kindness, than to hear of it again: therefore I spare you and your praises together; and will tender my respects in that which I know you love and will approve: I mean, in prayer for you."

The four small volumes just mentioned are all written in a strain of pure and fervent piety; and are distinguished by a depth and originality of thought, as well as by a delicacy and elegance of manner, very uncommon in the theological productions of that period. They also contain many graceful allusions to scriptural facts and phraseology, together with many happy illustrations of different passages of Holy Writ, which render the reading of them highly edifying and delightful.

When these works were in a course of preparation for the press, Mr. Goodwin was called to oppose the proceedings of some of his ecclesiastical superiors, and to show his regard for civil and religious liberty. The promptitude and decision which he and others his co-adjutors displayed on this occasion, were highly honourable to themselves, and have laid posterity under great obligations. When British freedom had received a thousand wounds from the hands of guilty statesmen and divines, and was actually bleeding at every pore, anxious to perpetuate her existence, they marshalled themselves around her lovely form, and presented their shields to her numerous and inveterate assailants.

The king having allowed the Convocation to continue its sittings after the dissolution of Parliament, that reverend assembly passed several resolutions, the substance of which was afterwards published under the title of, "Constitutions and Canons Ecclesiastical, treated upon by the Archbishops of Canterbury and York, Presidents of the Convocation for their respective Provinces, and the rest of the Bishops and Clergy of those Provinces, agreed upon with the King's Majesty's License, 1640." In this official document the divine right of kings, and the absolute unlawfulness of resistance, under any circumstances, are strongly asserted, in opposition to those principles of constitutional liberty which at that time were prevailing in different directions. Threatenings also, of a most alarming nature, are held out, not only against "Popish recusants, who came not to church," but against "all Anabaptists, Brownists, Separatists, and other Sectaries;" concerning whom it is determined, that if they should persist in their non-attendance upon the religious services of the establishment, they should be excommunicated : and if neither persuasions nor censures could avail to remove their scruples, the "Reverend Justices of Assize" are solemnly adjured, in the name of Almighty God, to execute the laws against them. At the same time, all School-masters, Lawyers, Physicians, and the Clergy in general, are peremptorily required to declare upon oath their entire approbation of the doctrines and government of the church as by law established, and their determination never to consent to any alteration in either. *

When these injunctions were made public, they excited great dissatisfaction; many pamphlets were therefore written against them, and dispersed through the kingdom. "The exception of exceptions against these Canons is," says Fuller, "because they were generally condemned as illegally passed, to the prejudice of the fundamental liberty of the subject..........Mean time some bishops were very forward in pressing this oath, even before the time thereof. For, whereas a liberty was allowed to all, to deliberate thereon, until the feast of Michael the Archangel, some · presently pressed the ministers of their dioceses, for the taking thereof; and, to my knowledge, enjoined them to take the oath kneeling : a ceremony, to my best remembrance, never exacted or observed in taking the oath of supremacy or allegiance ; which some accounted an essay of their activity, if Providence had not prevented them."†

* Sparrow's Collection of Articles, &c. p. 345. Edit. 1684.   † Church History, Cent. XVII. Book XI.

Mr. Goodwin was neither a timid nor an indifferent spectator of these intemperate and impolitic proceedings. He did not oppose them by the publication of anonymous and libellous tracts; but, in conjunction with some of his brethren, the London clergy, he drew up a petition against them to the privy council; and, to render it the more effectual, they procured a large number of signatures. The ministers, schoolmasters, and physicians, in most of the counties of England, followed their example; and so great was the outcry against the conduct of the bishops, that the king deemed it requisite to issue an order to his grace of Canterbury to relax his severity.*

It was Mr. Goodwin's misfortune to witness the prevalence of confusion and disorder in the State, as well as in the Church. His sovereign, Charles the First, was educated in high and extravagant notions concerning the regal power. He was taught to believe, that monarchy and lineal succession are of divine institution, and consequently sacred and inviolable; that all the privileges and liberties of the subject are so many concessions or extortions from the crown; that the king is not bound to his people by his coronation oath, but only to God; that his subjects ought either actively to obey his commands, or passively to submit to his will; and have no other refuge left, under the most cruel tyranny, but prayers and tears.† He had unhappily received these principles, not as subjects of abstract speculation, but as maxims of government: and hence, under his reign, the most alarming encroachments were made upon the liberty of the subject. Within the space of one year, two parliaments were summoned and dissolved in displeasure, for presuming to complain of grievances, and to investigate the conduct of his majesty's ministers. In the fourth year of his reign, another parliament was dismissed for the same reasons, with a reproachful and threatening speech; and such members as had given offence were imprisoned and fined. After this, the king governed nearly twelve years without

* Wilson's Dissenting Churches, Vol. II. p. 405.   † Tindal's Continuation of Rapin, Introduction.

a parliament: during which time, the bulwark of national freedom, the power of raising money, was not only assumed and vigorously exercised by the crown, but methods used for this end were pronounced legal by the judges, and declared to be obligatory on the subjects' conscience by some of the dignified clergy. In consequence of these proceedings, and especially of the king's tacit renunciation of the constitution by the disuse of parliaments, jealousy and discontent spread among all classes; and while many, who had suffered in their persons or their families, no doubt meditated the deepest revenge, all who were alive to the interests of the nation anxiously waited for the period at which these grievances should be redressed. This at length appeared, and they exulted at its arrival. An attempt having been made to impose Bishops and a Liturgy upon the Scottish Church, the people of that country appeared in arms to defend their ancient ecclesiastical usages, and actually drove the English army back again into the heart of their native land. The king's embarrassments, at this crisis of his affairs, were insupportable. Defeated by the Scots, in consequence of the disaffection of the English, and in the midst of political gloom which was hourly growing darker, he was compelled, averse as he might be from the measure, to have recourse in earnest to a parliament; the assembling of which constitutes a new era in British history.*

Several of the leading members of the House of Commons "were greatly versed in ancient as well as modern learning, and were enthusiastically attached to the great names of antiquity; but they never conceived the wild project of assimilating the government of England to that of Athens, of Sparta, or of Rome. They were content with applying to the English constitution and to the English laws, the spirit of liberty which had animated and rendered illustrious the ancient republics. Their first object was to obtain a redress of past grievances, with a proper regard to the individuals who had suffered; the next, to prevent the recurrence of such grievances, by the

* Symmons's Life of Milton, p. 178, Edit. 1806.

abolition of tyrannical tribunals, acting upon arbitrary
maxims in criminal proceedings, and most improperly
denominated courts of justice. They then proceeded to
establish that fundamental principle of all free government, the preserving of the purse to the people and their
representatives." *

The king inadvertently resigned a large portion of that
power which is essential to monarchy, but which he had
unhappily abused in former instances, by consenting that
this parliament should never be dissolved without the concurrence of its members; and thus rendered them little
less than absolute. Having also, in other respects, complied with their wishes, he became indignant at their
proceedings, and expressed his resolution to maintain the
royal prerogative in opposition to their further demands,
which he contended were exorbitant and unconstitutional.
Exposed at the same time to popular insult in the
metropolis, his majesty retired to York, and prepared for
war; while the queen pledged the jewels of the crown in
Holland, and with the money thence arising furnished
him with arms and ammunition. Mean time the parliament, resolved to defend what they regarded as the rights
of the subject, prepared for resistance.† Thus was the
country involved in civil discord, and witnessed through a
series of years a lamentable effusion of human blood.

Mr. Goodwin, who seems never to have espoused a
cause except from principle, and who was therefore always
in earnest, expressed a decided predilection for the parliamentary interest, and threw the whole weight of his influence into that scale. To maintain any thing like neutrality in his public situation, had he been so disposed,
was impossible; and he espoused the side which his judgment and conscience recommended: the side which was
avowedly that of practical godliness, and of civil and
religious freedom. Milton, who was just returned from
his travels on the continent, is said to have been the first

* Fox's History of the Early Part of the Reign of James the Second,
p. 9, Edit. 1808.   † Ludlow's Memoirs, Vol. I. p. 26, &c. Edit. 1722.—
Clarendon, Book Fifth.—Husband's Exact Collection, passim.

who availed himself of the change of the times to plead, through the medium of the press, the cause of general liberty.* Mr. Goodwin appears to have been the first clergyman who, on this occasion, followed the example of our great epic bard. To stimulate the inhabitants of London and its vicinity to co-operate with the parliament in heart and hand, he wrote a small pamphlet, which he entitled, "The Butcher's Blessing: or, The Bloody Intentions of Romish Cavaliers, against the City of London, demonstrated by Five Arguments, to the Right Honourable the Lord Mayor, the Sheriffs, and other the religious and worthy Inhabitants of the said City, 1642:" and, during the same year, to afford satisfaction to the consciences of the scrupulous and the doubtful, he published another tract under the title of "Anti-Cavalierism: or, Truth pleading as well the Necessity as the Lawfulness of the present War." Whether the parliament might not have reduced the power of the crown within its just limits, without having recourse to the sword, is a question which must be referred to the general historian. Many persons, however, thought, that, after the actual commencement of the war, every thing that was dear to the friends of liberty depended upon its vigorous prosecution. Should the king be ultimately successful in this momentous struggle, holding the sentiments which he did concerning the extent of the regal authority, and surrounded as he was by men who were actuated by the same principles, they feared, according to all human probabilities, that the yoke of national slavery must be perpetual, and all hope of general freedom in matters of religious opinion and worship abandoned for ever. Mr. Goodwin appears to have felt the full force of this impression, in writing the tracts before us. They contain an animated and powerful appeal to the judgment and feelings of those who were able duly to appreciate what he calls "the benefit and sweetness of this blessing of liberty."

Several passages in the latter of these publications were warmly controverted by Williams, bishop of Ossory, in a

* Symmons's Life of Milton, p. 180.

tract which he entitled, "Vindiciæ Regum: or, The Grand
Rebellion: that is, A Looking Glass for Rebels, 1643."
In this work, the Right Reverend author contends, that
"a king hath power and authority to do what he pleaseth;"
and that, while the parliament were opposing the will of
Charles, they were involved in the guilt of a "grand rebellion."   In reply to his lordship, Mr. Goodwin published
another pamphlet, the title of which proves that, like
many of his contemporaries, he was not unacquainted with
the art of punning: " Os Ossorianum: or, A Bone for a
Bishop to pick, 1643." In these tracts our author expresses
conscientious respect for the person of the king, laments
that he was in the hands of evil counsellors, and pleads
for nothing but just and equal liberty founded upon the
basis of law.   His political creed, at this period, appears
to have been in perfect unison with that of our great
patriotic statesmen, who, under the auspices of Divine
Providence, effected the Revolution of 1688.   The following beautiful passage will be read with approbation by every
genuine Protestant.   Happy would it have been for Mr.
Goodwin, and for the cause of true religion, had he and
his contemporaries always adhered to the principles which
are here expressed with such elegance and force.   "As
for offering violence to the person of a king, or attempting to take his life, we leave the proof of the lawfulness of this to those profound disputers the Jesuits, who
stand engaged by the tenor of their professed doctrine and
practice, either to make good the lawfulness thereof, or
else to leave themselves and their religion an abhorring
and hissing unto the world.   As for us, who never travailed
with any desires or thoughts that way, but abhor both
mother and daughter, doctrine and practice together, we
conceive it to be a just prerogative of the persons of kings,
in what case soever, to be secure from the violence of men,
and their lives to be as consecrated corn, meet to be reaped
and gathered only by the hand of God himself.   David's
conscience smote him, when he came but so near the life
of a king, as the cutting off of the lap of his garment." *

* Anti-Cavalierism, pp. 7, 8.

In active and zealous co-operation with the parliament Mr. Goodwin followed the example of the great body of the Puritan clergy; the reasons of whose conduct are thus represented by Richard Baxter, who lived in those unhappy times:—"Many were much set against the bishops by observing men of parts and piety silenced, while insufficient and vicious men were preferred among the clergy, and many thousands of the people were perishing in ignorance and sin. And it not a little disturbed them to see fasting and praying, and other religious exercises, so strictly looked after, and punished in the High Commission and Bishops' Courts: as if more perilous than common swearing and drunkenness. And it added to their disturbance, to have a Book published for recreations on the Lord's day, with the bishops' approbation, as if they concurred with the profane; that afternoon sermons and lectures, though carried on by conformable men, were put down in divers counties; that so great a number of conformable ministers were suspended or punished, for not reading the Book of Sports, or about altars, &c., and so many thousand families, and many worthy ministers, driven out of the land; that bowing towards altars, and other innovations, were daily brought in by the hyper-conformists, none knowing where they would end; and finally, that the bishops proceeded so far as to swear men to their whole government by the *Et Cœtera Oath,* and that they approved of ship-money, and other such encroachments on their civil interests. These were the causes why so many of those who were counted most religious, fell in with the parliament." *

Under the influence of these views Baxter himself entered into the army as a chaplain, and was equally distinguished by his religious zeal and his efforts for the success of those political measures in the prosecution of which his masters were professedly engaged. On a calm review of this part of his conduct, several years after the termination of the civil wars, this upright and conscientious man expressed himself on that subject in the follow-

* Calamy's Abridgment of Baxter's Life, p. 48, Edit. 1713.

ing manner:—"The hatred of strife and war, and love of peace, and observation of the lamentable miscarriages since, have called me oft to search my heart, and try my ways by the Word of God, whether I did lawfully engage in that war or not?—which I was confident then was the greatest outward service that ever I performed to God; and whether I lawfully encouraged so many thousands to it?—and the issue of all my search is this, and never was any other but this: The case of blood being so dreadful, and some wise and good men being against me, and many of their arguments being plausible, and my understanding being weak, I shall continue with self-suspicion to search, and be glad of any information that may convince me if I have been mistaken; and I make it my daily earnest prayer to God, that He will not suffer me to live and die impenitently, or without the discovery of my sin, if I have sinned in this matter; and could I be convinced of it, I would as gladly make a public recantation as I would eat or drink: and I think I can say that I am truly willing to know the truth. But yet I cannot see that I was mistaken in the main cause; nor dare I repent of it, nor forbear the same, if it were to do again. In the same state of things, I should do all I could to prevent such a war; but, if it could not be prevented, I must take the same side as I then did: and my judgment tells me that if I should do otherwise, I should be guilty of treason, or disloyalty against the sovereign power of the land, and of perfidiousness to the commonwealth, and of preferring the offending subjects before the laws and justice; and the will of the king above the safety of the commonwealth, and consequently above his own welfare; and that I should be guilty of giving up the land to blood, (as Ireland was,) or to much worse, under pretence of avoiding blood, in a necessary defence of all that is dear to us."*

Such were the views of the great body of the Puritan ministers of that age, and the motives by which they were actuated in supporting the parliamentary interest. Their conduct has often subjected them to the severest censures,

* Holy Commonwealth, p. 486, Edit. 1659.

as a race of incendiaries. Far be it from the writer of this work to attempt a defence of all their proceedings, or a reconciliation of their principles and spirit with the example of Jesus Christ, and the precepts of His word. Many of them were anxious to gain ecclesiastical dominion, and to introduce the most serious innovations in the church; and others of them, no doubt, were prompted by revenge occasioned by the wrongs they had previously suffered. At the same time it must be confessed, that the Episcopal clergy, who adhered to their royal master, were equally culpable for their warlike character, and the absence of kind and conciliatory dispositions. It is difficult to say which party was more deeply involved in "blood-guiltiness." These general remarks will of course admit of many exceptions. Several pious and excellent men, on both sides, should rather be viewed as objects of commiseration than of blame. The legislature was divided; and two powers, both claiming the supremacy for the time, were engaged in actual conflict. To join the parliament was to countenance that which many considered to be "rebellion;" and to be identified with the royalists was to support a party, many of whom had sanctioned the open profanation of the Sabbath, had persecuted some of the best men in the nation, and were hostile to practical godliness.—"Say not that the former days were better than these;" but rather be thankful to Divine Providence, that in the present age of civil and religious freedom the consciences of British subjects are not liable to be entangled in snares so destructive of peace and tranquillity.

CHAPTER II.

SCRIPTURE DOCTRINE OF A SINNER'S JUSTIFICATION BEFORE GOD.

In tracing the personal history of Mr. Goodwin it is with pleasure that the mind turns from his pamphlets on secular politics, to survey his pastoral labours, his patient sufferings, and his theological discussions. His writings on the subject of Justification, had he published nothing more, would have been sufficient to immortalize his name, and to command the unceasing gratitude of all lovers of sound argument and of evangelical truth.

Nothing can be more deeply interesting to the human mind, when awakened to a discovery of its fallen condition, than the method of a sinner's justification before God, as it is laid down in the gracious counsels of the Divine mind, and revealed in the Gospel of Jesus Christ. This method, so simple in itself, so worthy of the God of wisdom and love, and so admirably adapted to the condition of mankind, was lamentably obscured by religious teachers in the times which preceded the Protestant Reformation. In those days of mental darkness, when the sinner inquired of his spiritual guides, where he was to find the expiation of his crimes, and deliverance from their dreadful consequences ; the answer he generally received was, " In the merit of penitence, a merit capable of annihilating guilt and of appeasing the anger of incensed Omnipotence."

The abettors of this doctrine argued, " He who, having disobeyed the laws of heaven, is desirous of being restored to the favour of God, must not expect *free forgiveness ;* but previously by unfeigned sorrow of heart must *deserve* the restoration of grace, and with it the obliteration of his offences. In order to this, he is bound strictly to survey and detest his former evil conduct, accurately to enumerate his transgressions, and deeply to feel them; and, impressed with a due sense of their magnitude, impurity, and consequences, to condemn his folly, and deplore those faults which have made him an outcast of heaven, and exposed him to eternal misery. "So far," said they, "he can proceed by that operation of the mind which is denominated ATTRITION;" and which, being within the sphere of his natural powers, they regarded as congruous piety, meritorious of justification; as a preparation of soul, more or less necessary to receive and merit justifying grace. When he has arrived at this point, attrition ceases, and contrition commences; the habit of sin is expelled, while that of holiness is infused in its stead, and with the infusion of charity, which is the plastic principle of a new obedience, justification becomes complete.*

In opposition to these mysterious refinements, the Protestant Reformers, holding the Apostolical Epistles in their hands, maintained, that "We are justified FREELY by His GRACE, through the REDEMPTION which there is in CHRIST JESUS: whom God hath set forth to be a propitiation through FAITH in HIS BLOOD." This point they regarded as a vital article in Christianity: and, however they might differ on other subjects, they were careful to embody this in all their public confessions of faith: nor can any one justly claim alliance in theological opinion with that illustrious body of men, who holds that a sinner can be justified from personal guilt by the merit of good works, or by any other means than that of Faith in Christ crucified.

Among those, however, who consider themselves close copyists of the Reformers, a diversity of opinion has obtained on a point intimately connected with this important subject: some avowing their belief, that in the justification of a sinner there is an imputation made of the active righteousness of Christ, (using the term imputation in the sense of *transfer*;) while others contend that the apostle is to be literally understood, when he says, "Faith is imputed for righteousness;" understanding the word IMPUTED as signifying *reckoned* or *accounted*. The former of these opinions, which contradicts the very letter of Sacred Writ,

* Laurence's Bampton Lectures, p. 120, Edit. 1805.

and is the soul of the Antinomian delusion, has been contended for with as much eagerness and animosity as if the salvation of the world depended upon its establishment and reception.

Mr. Goodwin's life was devoted to the study of the Holy Scriptures; and in his conscientious endeavours to form a deep and extensive acquaintance with "the truth as it is in Jesus," he was led, almost immediately after his settlement in the metropolis, to entertain and advance sentiments concerning the doctrine of justification, different from those which were held by some of his Puritanical brethren : men who neither understood the right of private judgment, nor seem to have been at all aware that the exercise of candour and forbearance is a Christian duty. Considerable animosity was therefore manifested towards Mr. Goodwin, both by ministers and laymen, in London and its vicinity. He was nevertheless well able to defend himself, both from the pulpit and the press : but alas, in those days of ecclesiastical tyranny all freedom of public discussion was strictly prohibited, and a silence imposed upon persons of opposite sentiments, somewhat resembling that oppressive stillness in the atmosphere, occasioned by an excess of electric matter, which usually precedes a thunder-storm. Mr. Goodwin and his opponents were cited to appear before their diocesan in the year 1638; and charged, on pain of episcopal censure, to desist from all further discussions, in the pulpit, of the points at issue between them. Concerning this business archbishop Laud presented the following account to the king :—

" In the diocese and city of London, there was like to be some distraction, both among the ministers and the people; occasioned at first by some over-nice curiosities, preached by one Mr. Goodwin, vicar of St. Stephen's, Coleman Street, concerning the imputation of Christ's righteousness in the justification of a sinner. But the differences arising about it were timely prevented by convention of the parties dissenting. And so, God be thanked, that business is at peace." * How degraded must the nation have been,

* Hist. of the Troubles and Trial of Archbishop Laud, Vol. I. p. 553.

when a few theologians were not at liberty to inquire, whether faith, or the active righteousness of Christ, is imputed to believers for their justification; and when it was deemed necessary to make a formal representation of such a dispute to his Majesty, as an affair of State!

While Mr. Goodwin had reason to complain of the hostility of several contemporary ministers and private Christians, he was happy in the testimony of a good conscience, and in the undeviating friendship and encouragement of the pious among his own parishioners. They had voluntarily chosen him as their pastor, and were too well acquainted with the various excellencies of his character, to suffer their attachment to be weakened by popular clamour. Their conduct, in this respect, made a deep impression upon his heart, and drew from him the following grateful acknowledgment:—

"That which I know not how to draw aside to any other construction, but only to make a demonstration of the naturalness of your affection towards me, and towards the truth itself delivered by me, though the iniquity of many hath abounded against both, is, that your love to neither hath waxed cold. Which crown of praise I could willingly enrich yet seven times more, and set it upon your heads, if I knew how to work upon it, without seeming at least to soil others by way of complaint, and to make men offenders for personal wrongs: which is a strain of too much effeminateness in a Christian, and little less than an acknowledgment of the strength of other men's weakness, or of the weakness of a man's own strength. Howsoever, my silence will be found no treason either against the life or the dignity of your Christian and worthy deportment therein: there is One greater than all the world besides, that will see that righteousness of yours fully rendered to you in due time. Truth is honest in her deepest poverty and distress; and whatsoever she borroweth or taketh from any man for her support in prison, she will pay double and treble when she recovers her liberty, and entereth into her glory. And fear not: He that would not leave the soul of His Son in hell, nor suffer His Holy One to see corruption,

D

will be as tender over His daughter Truth, and will give her beauty for ashes in due season." *

The satisfaction arising from obedience to the dictates of conscience, and from the approbation of wise and good men, was not the only consolation which Mr. Goodwin enjoyed, while he was an object of popular animosity, and of the clamorous invectives of his Puritanical contemporaries from the pulpit, in consequence of the open avowal of his sentiments concerning the imputation of faith for righteousness. He had the high gratification of finding, that what he advanced on this subject was a means of correcting dangerous error. One remarkable instance of this kind, related by Mr. William Allen, the individual concerned, is still upon record. This gentleman, who was well known to Mr. Baxter, and whom that excellent man has characterized as a person " of extraordinary sincerity and understanding," † says, "I was taken in the snare of Antinomianism, about thirty-seven or thirty-eight years ago, not being able to withstand the insinuations of it, and yet to retain the opinion of the imputation of Christ's righteousness, in that notion of it in which I had been instructed; and never recovered myself till I heard Mr. John Goodwin. The experience of what I suffered myself, and occasioned others to suffer, by my running into those errors, hath put me upon doing more to warn others against them, or recover them out of them, than otherwise I should have thought fit for me to have done." ‡ This statement is given in a letter which bears the date of 1672: thus, it appears that Allen was convinced of his error, and delivered out of the snare of speculative Antinomianism, by the preaching of Mr. Goodwin, soon after this able minister had entered upon his vicarage in London.

None of Mr. Goodwin's contemporaries distinguished themselves more by their opposition to him on this occasion, than Mr. George Walker, rector of St. John the Evangelist, Watling Street, London. Prior to this contest, that theologian and some of his friends had charged Mr.

* Saints' Interest in God, Dedication.   † Reliquiæ Baxterianæ,
p. 181, Part First, Edit. 1696.   ‡ Ibid. p. 98, Appendix.

Anthony Wotton, "a very learned and godly divine of London," with Socinianism, heresy, and blasphemy, on account of his sentiments concerning justification. This charge was investigated by several London ministers, at two separate meetings; and a verdict was given in favour of Wotton.* "This very eminent man," says Baxter, "wrote a Latin treatise *De Reconciliatione*, one of the learnedest that hath ever been written on that subject; in which he laboureth to disprove the rigid imputation of Christ's holiness and obedience to man, and showeth that he is righteous to whom all sin of omission and commission is forgiven, and confuteth these three assertions: (1.) That a sinner is reputed to have fulfilled the law in and by Christ: (2.) And, being reputed to have fulfilled the law, is taken for formally just as a fulfiller of it: (3.) And being formally just as a fulfiller of the law, eternal life is due to him by that covenant that saith, *Do this and live.*" †

To prefer a charge of "Socinianism, heresy, and blasphemy," in a serious and formal manner, against a person of Wotton's elevated character, shows a lamentable want of Christian meekness and moderation.

With the bold man who advanced and attempted to support this accusation, Mr. Goodwin was involved in a controversy, the occasion of which is thus stated by himself: "Upon the clamorous, uncessant, and insulting importunity of some, who were confident it seems of finding shelter under Mr. Walker's wing, for some opinions they held and loved dearly, (though they little deserved it,) and would not trust so bad a cause in the hand of any other champion, (their own word and style they gave him;) I was much pressed, from time to time, by some of my acquaintance, that if I could spare a day, I would go over to Mr. W. to consider and reason some points depending in sharp dispute among themselves. Why Mr. W., amongst all the divines in city or country, should have been so importunely pitched upon by those men, I leave to those that know him to consider: only thus far they discovered themselves, that they little thought I either would or durst

* Brook's Lives of the Puritans, Vol. II. p. 347. † Treatise of Justifying Righteousness, p. 19, Edit. 1676.

look such a champion in the face. In which conceit of my unwillingness and fearfulness to appear before him, Mr. W. himself was partaker with them, and lost a wager of five shillings, as himself confessed, upon it. Whereby it appears these men had an opinion that there was some property in him, which should make men of few words afraid to come near him in a way of disputation; which, whether it be the depth of his learning, the sharpness of his wit, acuteness in disputing, or some other thing, I will not divine; but had rather that others should conjecture, than I determine. At last, not without much gainsaying from my other employments, I sacrificed a day upon the service of Mr. Walker's reputation, and went to confer with him about the points in question between his friends and mine, and to receive further information from him therein, if he had any of this commodity in his hand. But my going to him was with the like success that Christ went to the fig-tree; who found no fruit thereon, but leaves only. The conference between us being managed in a tumultuous and issueless manner, the one of us still carrying aside the state of the question, and hiding it in a thicket of words, I was desired at last by Mr. Walker's own brother, (the minister of the place in whose house we were,) and by divers others unknown to me, (well-wishers as I conceived to peace and truth,) to leave something in writing, whereby the state of the question might be more distinctly known. The day being far spent, and opportunity otherwise wanting for setting down what I judged necessary for such a purpose, and having casually about me a paper of some collections I had formerly made concerning such passages in the fourth chapter to the Romans as concerned the business between us; this I left behind me, with a promise, that if either Mr. W., or any other, could give me a clear account how those passages might with any tolerable congruity of reason, and consistence with other scriptures of like argument, be carried in their interpretation to comply with the opinion held against me, I would willingly acknowledge such satisfaction, and let my present opinion fall."

Walker had not long been in possession of the papers which Mr. Goodwin had left in his hands, before he produced a reply; and as the press was then under severe restrictions, manuscript copies of this rejoinder were put into circulation among religious people in the metropolis. Mr. Walker has been highly praised, not only as a man "well skilled in the Oriental tongues," and as "an excellent logician and divine;" but also, as a "man of a holy life, and humble spirit."* These qualifications, however, are not at all discoverable in his tract against Mr. Goodwin. His mode of writing is so confused and incoherent, as to render it extremely doubtful whether he really understood the question at issue between his opponent and himself; and the temper which he displayed is execrable. The following are some of the epithets which he applies to the man whose sentiments he deemed it his duty to oppose:— "Socinian—liar—lying sophister—impudent fellow—heretic—blasphemer—man of a satanical spirit," &c. &c. &c. On the receipt of this scandalous production, Mr. Goodwin addressed the following epistle to its angry author:—

"SIR,

"A FEW days since, there was sent to me, from a gentleman, a friend and neighbour of mine, a manuscript of about twenty-one leaves in quarto, which, though I have not yet had time fully to peruse, yet, casting my eye here and there, I conjecture to be yours. Wherein also I am further confirmed, by the common rumour abroad in the city, and which came to my ears several weeks before I received the writing, that your answer to my reasons was in the hands of many. Yet two things there are, that make me at some stand, whether the discourse be yours or no; at least whether it be come to me as it came from you; or whether it be not some libel, wherein both you and myself may be abused together. The one is, there is no name of any author put to it; which, you know, is libel-like. The other is, the many veins of unsavoury and foul language which run through the body of the discourse.

* Fuller's Worthies of Lancashire, p. 118, Edit. 1662.

If the piece be yours, I cannot but suspect that the scribe
to whom you committed it hath wronged you, by mingling
your milk with blood, and defacing your intellectuals with
his patheticals.   It will not readily enter into me, that so
uneven and coarse a thread should be of Mr. Walker's
spinning.   Wherefore my request in love to you is, that
you will please to signify, either by writing or otherwise,
whether the discourse be yours or no, whole and entire,
good and bad together, as it came to my hands ; or
whether only that which is somewhat rational and Christian in it be yours; but for the rough Turkey dialect, as
Socinian, Arminian, liar, lying sophister, impudent fellow,
heretic, blasphemer, a man of a satanical spirit, with other
terms of the same kind, you are willing to disavow? Because,
if there be a necessity, that for the truth's sake I must have
wars with you, I desire they may be Christian and fair; such
as may tend to settle the truth in peace, with as little
bloodshed of the names and reputations of the combatants
as may be.   Thus desiring you to send me back the paper
I left in your hands, with the tender of my respects and
love to you, I recommend you to the grace and love of
God in His Christ:

Your loving brother,

In the work of Jesus Christ,

JOHN GOODWIN."

This letter was conveyed, by some of Mr. Goodwin's
friends, to his antagonist. "But," says Mr. Goodwin,
"when I was for peace, he was for war; and entertained
the messengers that were sent to him, with such magnifi-
cent presents of further railing, reviling, and horrid imputations against me, as if he had been newly returned from
the slaughter of Rabshakeh."

As Mr. Walker's manuscript excited considerable attention, Mr. Goodwin deemed it his duty to write a reply,
which he put into the hands of his friends, for the purpose
of being transcribed and circulated.   Both these tracts,
with an account of the circumstances which had led to
their production, were published in the year 1641, by a

person who denominates himself "a lover of the truth and
peace." In this controversy Mr. Goodwin appears to great
advantage. His comprehensive knowledge of the subject
in dispute, his singular acuteness in argument, and his
calm unruffled temper, enabled him to defend his own
thesis, and to expose the mistakes of his antagonist with
superior effect.

"If Mr. Walker had an intent," says he, "to have
gained ground upon me, or led me away in triumph, he
was quite mistaken in the method of his war. Five sober
words, well balanced with reason and understanding,
would have wounded me deeper than a thousand crackers.
If any man speaks reason, I am ready to tremble and do
him reverence. Therefore, Mr. Walker might have kept
his earthquake, and whirlwinds, and fires, and sold them
for bugbears to scare children ; his small still voice would
soon have laid me at his feet. I dare not indeed deal
with him at his own weapon, I mean railing, however
provoked. The yoke that Christ hath put about my neck,
to keep me in compass this way, I dare not break nor cast
from me : neither do I know of any example in all the·
history of heaven, that would bear me out in such a practice. And therefore I here promise him, that in all my
reply I will neither call nim Socinian, nor Arminian, nor
heretic, nor blasphemer, nor liar, nor lying sophister, nor
impudent fellow, or the like. It may be I may now and
then administer the infusion of some of these simples, but
will never give him the gross substance. I hope that,
having taken a liberty, *in folio,* to speak evil of me
undeservedly, he will not be a man of so hard a conscience as not to give me leave, *in decimo sexto,* to make
merry with him. If he gives me gall and vinegar, and I
requite him with pleasant wine, I trust he shall have no
cause, in the judgment of any reasonable man, to complain.
Though I cannot meet with any faithful servant of God,
in all that long road that lieth between Genesis the first
and the first, and Revelation the last and the last, in a
reviling posture ; (but only Shimeis, Rabshakehs, and
such like sons of Belial ;) yet I find that holy prophet

Elijah in pleasant discourse with the sleepy Baal, and his zealous and slashing priests. And David, we know, had many troubles, trials, difficulties, dangers, pressures, Doegs, Achitophels, tongues as sharp as razors, and that cut like swords, upon him from time to time, yet he contrived all into matter of music and song, and played them off upon his harp.—The great God, by whom I must be judged, as well concerning my carriage in this business, as the other acts of my life, knoweth that I stand clear and free in my spirit to the man, notwithstanding his sevenfold provocation, wishing him no more evil than I do to myself, and am ready at an hour, upon the acknowledgment of his oversight, to give him the right hand of fellowship."

Walker soon prepared another tract against Mr. Goodwin, which he published under the title of " Socinianism in the fundamental point of Justification, Discovered and Confuted." To this piece Mr. Goodwin wrote no direct reply ; having pledged himself, at the conclusion of his former tract, " never more to anti-pamphlet " with Mr. Walker, nor to " envy him the glory and privilege of a scold." Nevertheless, in a succeeding treatise, of which we shall now proceed to give a circumstantial account, he answers every thing which the publication of his antagonist contained in the shape of argument, though without making any mention of his name, except in the preface.

On the assembling of the Long Parliament, the press was freed from its " horrid silence ; " and as a natural consequence, the nation was inundated with books on politics and religion. Availing himself of the liberty then granted, Mr. Goodwin published, early in the year 1642, one of his most important and valuable theological works : " IMPUTATIO FIDEI : or, A Treatise of Justification ; wherein the imputation of faith for righteousness (mentioned Rom. iv. 3–5) is explained, and also the great question largely handled, Whether the active obedience of Christ, performed to the moral Law, be imputed in Justification, or no, or how it is imputed : wherein likewise many other difficulties and questions, touching the great business of Justification, viz., the matter and form thereof, &c., are opened and cleared; together with the explication of divers Scriptures which partly speak, partly seem to speak, to the matter herein discussed." In this inestimable work, the learned author largely explains and defends those principles which had excited so much attention when they were advanced from the pulpit and partially argued in the tract against Walker.

This is a small quarto volume, the title-page of which is an elegant copper-plate engraving, executed by Glover, and containing some ingenious devices illustrative of the doctrine contained in the work. In one compartment is a person elevated above the earth by an angelic figure, and stretching himself to the utmost limit of his power, to lay hold upon a circle; the well-known emblem of immortality. On the opposite side some enormous masses of metal or of stone are suspended by an attenuated thread; while a man appears gazing upon them in an attitude of astonishment and alarm. Underneath these figures are the following expressive lines:—

" Small wires, sometimes, massy weights do carry ;
And on poor faith hangs great eternity."

As no man was more perfectly acquainted with the subject of Justification, and with every question connected with it, than Mr. Goodwin, so no man has written upon it with greater command of temper or force of argument. Indeed, his logical acumen, his critical and familiar acquaintance with the Holy Scriptures, and his vast reading, all of which he has brought to bear upon this subject, qualified him to write upon it with such accuracy and depth of thought, as have seldom been equalled and perhaps never surpassed. At the commencement of this most elaborate and instructive treatise, the author premises:

"First: That the terms justifying, justification, &c., are not to be taken in this question, nor in any other usually moved about the justification of a sinner, (1) in a physical sense; as if to justify signified to make just, with

any habitual or inherent righteousness. Nor (2) in a
judiciary sense properly so called, where the judge hath
only a subordinate power, and is bound to give sentence
according to the strict rule of the law; as if to justify
were to pronounce a man just, or to absolve him from
punishment, according to the precise rule of that law,
whereof he was accused as a transgressor. But (3) in a
judiciary sense, less properly so called; when he that
sitteth judge, being the supreme magistrate, hath a
sovereignty of power to dispense with the law, as reason or
equity may require. So that to justify, in this question,
imports the discharging or absolving of a man from the
guilt, blame, and punishment of those things whereof he
either is or justly might be accused: not because he is
clear of such things, or justifiable according to the letter
of the law; but because the judge is willing, upon weighty
considerations, to remit the penalty of the law, and to
discharge him as if he were a righteous man.

" As for the sense of making just by inherent righteousness, though Bellarmine and his angels earnestly
contend for it; yet, till Scriptures be brought low, and
etymologies exalted above them ; till use and custom of
speaking deliver up their kingdom into the Cardinal's
hands, that sense must no ways be acknowledged in this
dispute. Yet it is true, that God, upon a man's justification, begins to infuse inherent righteousness into him.
But here the Scriptures and the Cardinal are as far out in
terms, as in a thousand things they are in substance.
That which he will needs call justification, the Scriptures
will as peremptorily call sanctification.

" Concerning the other sense of a judiciary justification,
usually and strictly so called, wherein the justifier proceeds
upon legal grounds to absolve the party accused, neither
can this be taken in the question propounded, except the
Scriptures be forsaken; because the Scriptures constantly
speak of this act of God, not as an act whereby He will
pronounce him legally just, or declare him not to have
offended, and hereupon justify him; but as of an act whereby
He freely forgives him all that he had done against the

law, and acquits him from all blame and punishment due
by the law unto such offences. So that in that very act of
God whereby He justifies a sinner, as there is a discharge
from all punishment due to him, so there is a profession
withal of the guiltiness of the person, and that he is not
discharged upon any consideration that can be pleaded
for him according to the law; but that consideration upon
which God proceeds to justify him is of another order;
the consideration of somewhat done for him in this case,
to relieve him out of the course or appointment of the
law. He whose justification stands, whether in whole or
in part, in the forgiveness of sin, can in no construction
be said to be justified according to the law; because the
law knows no forgiveness of sins, neither is there any rule
for any such thing there. The law speaks of the curse,
death, and condemnation of a sinner; but for the justification of a sinner it neither takes knowledge nor gives any
hope thereof.

"SECONDLY: That Jesus Christ, the natural Son of God,
and the supernatural Son of the virgin, ran a race of
obedience with the law, and held out with every jot and
tittle of it, as far as it any way concerned Him, during the
whole continuance of His life in the flesh, no man's
thoughts ever rose up to deny, but those that denied Him
His Godhead. 'Which of you convinceth Me of sin?'
was His challenge to the nation of the Jews, whilst He was
upon earth, and remains through all ages as a challenge
to the world. He that can cast the least imputation of
sin upon Christ, shall shake the foundations of the peace
and safety of the world.

"THIRDLY: That Christ offered up Himself as a Lamb
without spot, in sacrifice upon the cross, to make an
atonement for the world, and to purge the sin of it, I
know no spirit at this day abroad in the Christian world
that denies, but that which wrought in Socinus formerly,
and still works in those that are baptized into the same
spirit of error with him.

"FOURTHLY: I can conceive it to be a truth of greater
authority amongst us, than to meet with contradiction

from any man, that Jesus Christ is the sole meritorious
cause of every man's justification that is justified by God;
or that that righteousness or absolution from sin and condemnation, which is given to every man in his justification,
is a part of that great purchase which Christ hath made for
the world. Justification is *for Christ's sake*. He is worthy
to be honoured by God with the justification of those that
believe in Him, whatsoever He is worthy of more.

"FIFTHLY: It is a truth that hath every man's judgment
concurring with it, that Faith is the condition appointed
by God, and required on man's part to bring him into
communion and fellowship of that justification which
Christ hath purchased; and that, without believing, no
man can have part in that great and blessed business.

"SIXTHLY: It is evident from the Scriptures, that God,
in the act of every man's justification, doth impute or
account righteousness to him; or rather, somewhat for or
instead of a righteousness; by means of which imputation
the person passeth in account as a righteous man, and is
invested accordingly with those great privileges of a man
perfectly righteous,—deliverance from death and condemnation, and acceptance into the favour of God. The
reason of which imputation, or why God is pleased to use
such an expression, seems to be, the better to satisfy
the scruple of the weak consciences of men, who can
hardly conceive of being justified by God, without an
express, literal, perfect, legal righteousness. Now the
purpose of God in the Gospel being, to justify men without
any such righteousness, (being a righteousness whereof
any man in his lapsed condition is wholly incapable,) the
better to salve the fears of the conscience touching such a
defect, and prevent all troublesome thoughts that might
arise in the minds of men, who, when they hear of being
justified, are ready to ask, But where is the righteousness?
conceiving a legal righteousness to be necessary to justification,—God is graciously pleased so far to condescend to
men in scripture-treaty with them about the weighty business of justification, as in effect to say to them, That
though He finds not any proper righteousness in them, yet

if they truly believe in Him, as Abraham did, this believing shall, in the consequences of it, be as good as a perfect righteousness to them ; or, that He will impute righteousness to them upon their believing.

" So that the question is not, (1) Whether faith without an object, or as separated from Christ, be imputed for righteousness? For such a faith, in the point of justification, was never dreamed of by any man that kept his wits company. Men may as well fancy a living man without a soul, or a wise man without his wits, as faith without an object. Neither, (2) is it any part of the question, Whether faith be the meritorious cause of justification? For both they that affirm and they that deny the imputation of faith for righteousness deny the meritoriousness of faith every way. Neither, (3) is it the question, Whether faith be the formal cause of justification? that is, Whether God doth justify a man with his faith, as a painter makes a wall white with whiteness, or a master makes his scholar learned with knowledge? For both parties make the form of justification to be somewhat differing from faith. Nor yet, (4) Whether Christ be the sole meritorious cause of justification? For both they that go on the right hand of the question, and they that go on the left, are knit together in the same mind concerning this. Neither, (5) doth the question intend to dispute at all, Whether the active obedience of Christ, falling in with the passive, and considered in conjunction with it, contributeth any thing towards the justification of sinners? This also is acknowledged on both sides.

" But the question is this, Whether the FAITH of him that truly believes in Christ, or the RIGHTEOUSNESS OF CHRIST, (that is, the obedience which Christ performed to the moral law, consisting partly of the righteous dispositions of His soul, partly of those several acts wherein He obeyed,) be, in the letter and propriety of it, that which God IMPUTES TO A BELIEVER FOR RIGHTEOUSNESS in his justification? so that he that believes is not righteous only by account, or by God's gracious reputing and accepting of him for such ; but as rigidly, literally, and peremptorily righteous,—constituted as perfectly, as completely, as legally righteous as Christ Himself, no difference at all between them *quoad veritatem*, but only *quoad modum*, both righteous with the self-same righteousness, only the justified wears it as put upon him by another, the Justifier as put upon Him by Himself. That the Scriptures no where countenance any such imputation of the righteousness of Christ as this, I trust, the Spirit of truth assisting, to make manifest in the sequel of this discourse; and to give good measure of this truth to the reader, heaped up by testimonies from the Scriptures, pressed down by the weight of many arguments and demonstrations, running over with the clear approbation of many authors, learned and sound, and every way greater than exception.

" When we affirm, that faith is imputed for righteousness, our meaning is simply this: That as God, in the covenant of works, required absolute obedience to the whole law, for every man's justification; which obedience, had it been performed, had been a perfect righteousness to the performer, and would have justified him; so now, in the covenant of grace, God requires nothing of any man for his justification, but Faith in His Son: which faith shall be as available to him, for his justification, as a perfect righteousness should have been under the first covenant.

" That which we deny is this: That God should look upon a believing sinner as one that had himself done all that Christ did in obedience to the moral law, and hereupon pronounce him righteous. Or, which is the same, that God should impute to him those particular acts of obedience which Christ performed, in the nature and propriety of them, so that he should stand as righteous before God as Christ Himself; and God make Himself accountable to him for such obedience imputed, in matters of reward, as he would have been for the like obedience personally performed.

" In a word, this is that which we deny, and which we affirm, concerning the righteousness of Christ in the justification of a sinner: That God clothes no man with the letter of it, but every man that believes with the spirit of it:

that this righteousness of Christ is not that which is imputed to any man for righteousness, but that *for which* righteousness is imputed to every man that believeth. A justified person may, in such a sense, be said to be clothed with Christ's righteousness, as Paul's necessities were supplied by his own hands. ' *These hands,*' says he, ' *have ministered to my necessities.*' Paul neither ate his fingers, nor spun the flesh of his hands into clothing; and yet was both fed and clothed with them. So may a believer be said to be clothed with the righteousness of Christ, and yet the righteousness of Christ itself not be his clothing, but only that which procured his clothing to him. So Calvin calls the clothing of righteousness wherewith a believer is clad in his justification, *Justitiam morte et resurrectione Christi acquisitam:* A righteousness procured by the death and resurrection of Christ."

Our author has answered every objection against this view of imputed righteousness, that had come under his notice, and has confirmed it not only by an almost incredible number of scriptural arguments, but also by apposite and striking testimonies from the writings of the following eminent men : Tertullian, Origen, Justin Martyr, Chrysostom, Augustine, Œcumenius, Ambrose, Primasius, Beda, Haymo, Anselm, Luther, Bucer, Peter Martyr, Calvin, Musculus, Beza, Olevian, Ursine, Zanchius, Piscator, Parœus, Melancthon, Zuinglius, Œcolampadius, Bullinger, Hyperius, Gualter, Aretius, Pelicanus, Illyricus, Hunnius, Junius, Tremellius, Preston, Forbes, Bishop Abbot, &c., &c.

That any man professing to derive his creed from the Bible, should have imbibed the notion of the imputation of Christ's personal righteousness in the justification of a sinner, is a singular circumstance, and affords a striking proof of the liability of even good and upright minds to erroneous impressions. It is repeatedly said by the sacred writers, that faith is imputed for righteousness; but it is never said that Christ's obedience to the moral law is imputed to any man. In the language of Scripture, the terms justification, forgiveness of sin, the non-imputation of sin, and the imputation of righteousness, are manifestly employed to express substantially the same blessing; and that blessing is uniformly represented not as the fruit of Christ's obedience to the moral law, but of His Death considered as a propitiatory sacrifice for sin. "To him that worketh not, but believeth on Him that *justifieth the ungodly*, his *faith is counted for righteousness*. Even as David also describeth the blessedness of the man unto whom *God imputeth righteousness* without works, saying, Blessed are they whose *iniquities are forgiven*, and *whose sins are covered*. Blessed is the man to whom the Lord will *not impute sin*." (Rom. iv. 5–8.) "Through this man is preached unto you the *forgiveness of sins*: and by Him all that believe are *justified from all things*, from which ye could not be *justified* by the law of Moses." (Acts xiii. 38, 39.) "Being now *justified by His blood*, we shall be saved from wrath through Him." (Rom. v. 9.)

It should also be observed, that there are several moral duties imposed upon mankind in their relative situations, as husbands and wives, parents, masters and servants: relations these in which Jesus Christ never stood, and the duties of which therefore cannot be placed to the account of any people as having been performed by Him in their stead. To say nothing of the violence offered to the apostolic term λογίζομαι, when understood as signifying any such imputation as that in question; and of the absurdity of supposing that when it is so peremptorily asserted, that "by the deeds of the law shall no flesh be justified" in the sight of God, (Rom. iii. 20,) in every instance men are actually justified by an imputation or transfer to them of those very "deeds," performed by the Lord Jesus!

Upon this subject a very learned and accurate divine has made the following pertinent observations:

Abraham believed; that is, as the Chaldee Paraphrase turns it, in the Word of Jehovah: in that Word which, being in the beginning with God, was God; by which the world was created, who was made flesh, and to whom the Lord said, "Sit Thou on My right hand, till I make Thine enemies Thy foot-stool."

It was reckoned to him for righteousness; that is, his faith, or in that he believed in that eternal Word, Christ Jesus, to be incarnate. The plain meaning is, that He judged him, believing in Christ, to be righteous by Christ.

To him that worketh, that is, to him that so worketh or obeyeth, as not to disobey or sin at all, the reward of righteousness is adjudged to him, as perfectly righteous; as of debt by the law of works, not of grace by the law of redemption.

God justifieth the ungodly, the sinner, the guilty person; not as such, but as believing on Him that justifieth the guilty; yet as penitent and believing.

The imputation of righteousness is the forgiveness of sin: for to have faith counted or imputed for righteousness, is explained by David, to have sin forgiven, covered, or not imputed.

The state of the party justified even in this life is blessed, and very happy.

That the party to whom righteousness is imputed, is he that believeth on Him that raised up Christ from the dead; not he who believeth that Christ performed perfect obedience active to the law in His person. For though He perfectly obeyed the law, as without which He could not have offered Himself an unspotted sacrifice for us; yet He did it not that that active personal righteousness should be imputed to us. Though God in His absolute power might have done so, yet His wisdom did not think good to do it. The thing to be specially noted is, that Romans iv. is the principal, if not the only place, that speaks of the imputation of righteousness; and this imputation consists in the remission of sins by a sentence of the Supreme Judge.

Remission of sin, justification, and eternal life, are ascribed to the sacrifice of Christ's Death, as their meritorious cause, in many places. Christ is said, by one offering, to have perfected, that is, consecrated, the sanctified, for ever. To be consecrated for ever, is to be made a complete priest, to serve the living God in the temple of heaven, and to be eternally glorified. And this is ascribed to the Death and Offering of Christ.*

* Lawson's Theo-Politica, p. 432, Edit. 1705.

E

To his views of justification Mr. Goodwin attached considerable importance; but he had too much charity and
good sense to consider them essential to salvation.
"Though I have no commission from heaven," says he,
"to judge that opinion touching the imputation of Christ's
active obedience, which I oppose, to be inconsistent with
the favour of God; yet I humbly beseech those that build
their peace upon that foundation, seriously to consider,
that the bridge of justification, by which men must be
conveyed over from death unto life, is very narrow, so
that a careless step may be the loss of their precious souls
for ever :—That to promise ourselves justification upon
any other terms, than the express Word and Will of God
revealed, is to build upon the sand, and ought to be
trembled at by us as the first-born of presumptions :—
That to seek justification by the law, is, by the determination of Scripture itself, no less than a rendering of Christ
of none effect to salvation :—And that the distinction you
commonly make, between the works of the law as performed by yourselves and as performed by another, to
salve the danger as you conceive of being justified by the
law, is but a device of human wisdom, and nowhere
warranted by the Scriptures; and therefore must be a
dangerous principle to hazard the everlasting state of
your souls upon." *

Past experience had fully convinced Mr. Goodwin, that
to write strongly and explicitly against the imputation of
Christ's righteousness to believers, whatever might be
the clearness and force of his arguments, or the mildness
of his temper, would rouse the indignation of his Puritanical brethren, many of whom could ill bear the slightest
contradiction. In reference therefore to this work, he
says, "I can expect no better than to see it vexed from
all quarters; with a spirit of zeal in some, of learning in
others, of wisdom in a third, and of indiscretion in a fourth
sort of men. The first will cry out against it, 'Heresy!
Blasphemy! Socinianism! Arminianism! What need we

* Preface.

any more witnesses?' The verdict of the second, it is like, will be, 'Error and Novelty!' The profound and sage remark of the third, 'Uselessness, and non-necessity.' The sober and soft expression of the last, 'Unseasonableness: and, better at another time.'" To each of these objections the author gives an ingenious and satisfactory reply in his introduction.

It would be difficult, in the whole range of didactic and controversial theology, to find a piece of more dispassionate, acute, and convincing argumentation than this treatise. It contains not a single sentence that appears to have been written under the influence of an unkind spirit, or that is at all calculated to excite an unholy passion. At the same time, the cogency of reasoning by which the author has endeavoured to establish his position reflects the highest honour upon his talents, and can only be duly appreciated by those readers whose minds are free from prejudice, habituated to close thinking, and familiar with the science of logic. The attempt which has since been made by the affected author of "Theron and Aspasio," to recommend the contrary opinion, will bear no more comparison with the learned and argumentative work of Mr. Goodwin, than the pretty "Reflections in a Flower Garden," with the profound disquisitions of Butler in his "Analogy of Religion Natural and Revealed." Violent are the outcries which have been raised against this work, but nothing like a refutation of its arguments has ever been presented to the world. In the year 1643 a weak and inefficient tract was published by Mr. Henry Roborough, under the title of "Justification cleared, by Animadversions on Mr. John Goodwin's Animadversions upon Mr. George Walker's Defence, &c. Together with an Examination of both Parts of his Treatise of Justification;" but Mr. Baxter, than whom perhaps no man was more competent to judge, says, "John Goodwin, not yet turned Arminian, preached and wrote with great diligence about justification, against the rigid sense of imputation; who being answered by Mr. Walker and Mr. Roborough, with far inferior strength, his book had the greater success for such answerers." *

After his opponents had tried their powers, both in railing and argument, and had actually accused him of Socinianism, Mr. Goodwin was emboldened to express himself in the following confident and decisive tone : " I may say, without offence, that I challenge all the Presbyterians, one after another, assembled or not assembled, in England, Scotland, France, and Ireland, to prove by the Scriptures, or by dint of argument, either that Faith is not imputed in a proper sense, or that the Active Obedience of Christ is, in the formality of it, imputed in Justification." † This challenge was extorted by the unmeasured calumnies which were heaped upon our author ; and since it was given, though several writers have attempted to establish that doctrine, every one of them appears to have thought it advisable to take little or no notice of Mr. Goodwin's book. Indeed, if any man were able to refute the objections urged by Mr. Goodwin against the imputation of Christ's personal righteousness, it was Dr. Owen : but this task he declined, although Mr. Goodwin's treatise had been in circulation upwards of thirty years, when the Doctor published his defence of " Justification by Faith, through the Imputation of the Righteousness of Christ."

Mr. Goodwin's admirable work was abridged by the Rev. John Wesley, and published in the year 1763, for the benefit of the religious societies under his care. In the preface to his abridgment, that eminent man says, " Perhaps I should not have submitted, at least not so soon, to the importunity of my friends, who have long been soliciting me to abridge and publish the ensuing treatise, had not some warm people published a tract entitled, ' The Scripture Doctrine of Imputed Righteousness Defended.' I then judged it absolutely incumbent upon me to publish the real Scripture Doctrine. And this I believed I could not either draw up or defend, better than I found it done to my hands, by one who, at the time he wrote this book,

---

* Treatise of Justifying Righteousness, p. 21, Edit. 1676.   † Brief Answer to an Ulcerous Treatise, p. 11, Edit. 1646.

was a firm and zealous Calvinist. This enabled him to confirm what he advanced by such authorities, as well from Mr. Calvin himself, as from his most eminent followers, as I could not have done, nor any who had not been long and critically versed in their writings."

Speaking also of this work, in his "Remarks" on one of Dr. Erskine's publications, Mr. Wesley says, " I desire no one will condemn that treatise before he has read it over; and that seriously and carefully, for it can hardly be understood by a slight and cursory reading. And let whoever has read it declare, whether the author has not proved every article he asserts, not only by plain express scripture, but by the authority of the most eminent Reformers. If Dr. E. thinks otherwise, let him confute him; but let no man condemn what he cannot answer." *

Mr. Wesley's abridgment, which was evidently intended to be placed within the reach of the poor, contains about one-third of the original work. The abridgment is an invaluable treasure; but, if possible, the whole treatise should not only be read, but carefully studied, by every man who wishes thoroughly to understand the evangelical method of the justification of a sinner before God. This work is useful in another respect: it shows upon what slight grounds even wise and good men will sometimes tenaciously adhere to favourite doctrines; and the consequent necessity, in all our religious inquiries, of a constant reference to the Records of Inspiration, rather than to mere human compositions.

When men professing godliness consider it their duty to correct what they conceive to be the mistakes of their brethren, they ought to abstain from all sarcastic and provoking language; recollecting that "the wrath of man worketh not the righteousness of God," and that the purest orthodoxy forms but an inadequate compensation for the loss of Christian meekness and love. In his "Treatise of Justification" Mr. Goodwin has conformed to this rule beyond almost every other controversial writer, and has therefore with an admirable grace recommended its

---

* Wesley's Works, Vol. XIII. p. 115, Edit. 1812.

adoption to others. "If any man shall please," says he, "to write against what is here published, I have two requests to make to him: First, that he will bend the main body of his discourse against the main of mine, and not browse or nibble upon twigs or outward branches; but strike at the root or main body of the tree; or at least, at some of the principal arms and limbs. * A tree may stand firm and be choice timber, and yet the smaller boughs, being tender, easily broken. It is no prejudice to a discourse, though some sentences may be picked out here and there, which, being separated from the stem, seem weak and capable of opposition.

"My other request to such a man is, that he will please to interdict his pen of all passionate language and expression, and return no worse measure in this kind, than is here measured unto him. Truth is not to be drawn out of the pit were she lieth hid, by a long line of calumnies, reproaches, and aspersions upon him who is supposed to oppose her; but by the golden chain of solid demonstrations, and close inferences from the Scriptures. The readiest way to overtake her, is to follow her in love. When men are fierce and fiery in their disputes, it is much to be feared that they want the truth; or at least, the clear and comprehensive knowledge of the truth, to cool and qualify them."†

In a dedicatory address to his "dear brethren, the reverend and faithful ministers of the Gospel, in and about the city of London," prefixed to this work, Mr. Goodwin says, "I presume you have all taken special knowledge of a book not long since presented to you by a Levitical hand, entitled, 'Socinianism Discovered and Confuted.' What quarter the divinity of the said discourse hath in your approbation, I do not yet so well understand as I desire I

* "If any man shall have a mind to publish any thing against that I have written, I shall desire it may be done fairly, not....by nibbling upon the twigges and utmost branches, but by striking at the root or body of the tree, or at leastwise some of the principal limbs thereof."—Hakewill's Apology of the Power and Providence of God. Preface, 1635. Goodwin had evidently read the elaborate volume of the learned Hakewill, and perhaps quoted it unconsciously.   † Introduction.

might; but for the morality of it, I make no question but you have done justice upon it, as well to mine, as to other men's satisfaction. Ἱκανὸν τῷ τοιούτῳ ἡ ἐπιτιμία αὕτη ἡ ὑπὸ τῶν πλειόνων.* I do not here offer to you any formal answer to that piece; because if I could do the truth and myself right otherwise, I would willingly decline all personal contention. I only lay down more fully and at large mine own judgment concerning those things about which the question is still depending between my antagonist and me; conceiving it a special duty lying upon me, to give an ingenuous and fair account to yourselves especially, and from you to all men, of what I hold therein; as well by making known what scriptures, reasons, and grounds otherwise, have commanded my judgment to that point whereat it now stands, as wherefore I judge those scriptures and arguments impertinent, and insufficient to prove the contrary, which have been produced for that purpose, either by my adversary in the mentioned discourse, or any other I can meet with. Nor do I make the least question, but that when you have examined the particulars of my account, you will give me your *quietus est.* Or in case you deny me this, that you will give me in the stead, that which will be of superior consideration, better reasons for the contrary opinion than I here deliver for mine. It is sweet and comfortable to be accompanied in the way of a man's judgment by those that are learned and religious; yet it is much more desirable to be turned aside out of a way of error, by a high hand of evidence and truth.

"Since God engaged me in these and some other controversies, and the oppositions of men grew strong and thick upon me, I have bestowed some time to possess myself thoroughly of such considerations as might make me rejoicingly willing to exchange error for truth. And if God hath not given me darkness for vision herein, I apprehend a marvellous beauty and blessing in such a frame of spirit as makes a man willing and joyful to cast away even long-endeared opinions, when once the light of

* "Sufficient to such a man is this punishment which was inflicted of many." 2 Cor. ii. 6.

truth hath discovered them to be but darkness. I look upon ignorance and error in the things of God, as that region in the soul, wherein only doleful creatures, as owls, and satyrs, and dragons,—spiritual tumults, storms, and tempests are engendered. Therefore, to me it is no more grievous to abandon any opinion whatsoever, being once clearly and substantially evicted for an error, than to be delivered out of the hand of an enemy, or to take hold of life and peace. But, on the other hand, it argues childishness of understanding, and folly bound up in the heart, to be baffled out of a man's judgment with any light and loose pretence."

With the same sentiment our author concludes this justly-celebrated treatise : "We have at last," says he, "fully answered all those arguments which, to my knowledge, have been insisted upon for the up-bearing of the imputation of Christ's righteousness, in the letter and formality of it. If any man, yet unsatisfied, will vouchsafe, in the spirit of meekness and love, either to discover the insufficiency of these answers, or further to object what he conceives to be of greater weight than the arguments already answered, I shall willingly and unpartially consider of either : and if I find any thing of pregnant and solid conviction, shall soon turn proselyte, and be glad to be delivered of an error. I had much rather be employed in cancelling mine own errors, than other men's ; and desire to make it my daily occupation to exchange darkness for light, crooked things for straight, errors for truth."

The cultivation of this ingenuous temper prepared Mr. Goodwin for important changes in his religious sentiments; and ultimately led him, as will appear from the sequel of this narrative, to renounce the bold and daring school of Calvinian theology, and avow himself a convert to the mild and moderate system of the amiable, pacific, and learned Arminius.

CHAPTER III.

To conciliate the favour of the Scots, and engage them to assist in the prosecution of the war, the Long Parliament passed an Ordinance, in the month of September, 1642, for the abolition of Episcopacy in England. This measure, however, was not actually to take place till after a lapse of somewhat more than twelve months.[*] " Our masters," says Lord Hollis, " finding themselves to be mortal, began to be afraid ; and now the Scots must be called in. So in all haste they send for them to come and help, with open cry, *Save us, we perish!* They promise any thing, do any thing, for the present, that the Scots would have them do : the honour of England is not thought of; liberty of conscience and the godly party are not mentioned :. but all that was heard was, *The Covenant, Uniformity of Church-government, uniting the two nations, never to make peace without them;* and a solemn treaty for all this closed there, and was presently ratified by the parliament here." [†]

For the gratification of their northern friends, the parliament also issued an Ordinance, requiring British subjects in general to enter into a " Solemn League and Covenant; " binding themselves in the name of Almighty God, that they would " sincerely, really, and constantly endeavour, in" their " several places and callings," to secure " the preservation of the reformed religion in the Church of Scotland, in doctrine, worship, discipline, and government, against" their " common enemies ; the reformation of religion in the kingdoms of England and

* Neal's Hist. Purit. Vol. II. p. 583, Edit. 1733.　　　† Memoirs of Denzil Lord Hollis, p. 12, Edit. 1699.

Ireland, in doctrine, worship, discipline, and government, according to the Word of God, and the example of the best Reformed Churches ;—and to bring the Churches of God, in the three kingdoms, to the nearest conjunction and uniformity in religion, confession of faith, form of church-government, &c."*

From the abolition of Episcopacy, till June, 1646, there was no properly established mode of ecclesiastical government in England. During this interval the different bodies of religious people were desirous of bringing themselves into notice, and of obtaining the patronage of the higher powers. On behalf of the Independents, five of their most noted ministers published, in the year 1643, "An Apologetical Narration, humbly submitted to the honourable House of Parliament;" explaining their scheme of church-polity, the steps by which they had been led to its adoption, and soliciting protection in their religious exercises. "We believe," say they, "the truth to lie and consist in *a middle way*, betwixt that which is falsely charged upon us, *Brownism*, and that which is the contention of these times, the *authoritative Presbyterial government*, in all the subordinations and proceedings of it." †

This publication, which was the joint production of Thomas Goodwin, Philip Nye, William Bridge, Jeremiah Burroughs, and Sidrach Simpson, excited considerable alarm among the Presbyterian clergy, most of whom contended, that, as their system of ecclesiastical discipline was of *divine origin*, it should be established to the exclusion of every other. Dr. Adam Stewart and Mr. Thomas Edwards were especially distinguished by their angry writings on this occasion. With equal vehemence they opposed Independency and the toleration of its adherents.

Mr. Goodwin had no part in drawing up this "Narration," but he approved of its contents, and defended it against the attacks of these gentlemen. His defence of

---

* An Ordinance, &c. for the taking of the League and Covenant, p. 10, printed for E. Husbands, 1643. † Page 24.

Independency against Stewart is entitled, "A Reply of two of the Brethren to A. S. &c.; with a Plea for Liberty of Conscience, 1644." In this tract Mr. Goodwin not only answers the objections of Stewart against the Congregational scheme; but also contends for Universal Freedom in all affairs of a purely religious nature. He maintains, that magistrates are so far from possessing legitimate authority to lay the consciences of Christians under restraint, that on the contrary they ought to allow a free toleration even to Jews and Mahometans, so as not to subject them to pains and penalties on account of their religious opinions and modes of worship, nor to employ any means in order to their conversion, except such as are of a persuasive kind. He avows his unhesitating conviction, that all descriptions of people who conduct themselves in a peaceable and orderly manner, are entitled to the full protection of the civil power, whatever may be the peculiarities of their creed. In the composition of this important pamphlet, another person, whose name does not appear, was associated with our author for the sake of expedition; but Mr. Goodwin states, that the part which treats of religious liberty was the production of his own pen.*

The design of church-discipline, in Mr. Goodwin's apprehension, is the improvement of Christians in knowledge and holiness: and as the Congregational plan appeared to him, after a careful examination of the subject, more conducive to this end, and more accordant with the Scriptures, than the Presbyterian, it obtained the preference in his mind. The formidable powers with which the law invested the English prelates, having, in several instances, been exercised rather to the obstruction than the advancement of civil and religious freedom, and of sound spiritual religion; and the Presbyterians being equally hostile to general liberty of conscience; it was natural for Mr. Goodwin, as the zealous friend of universal toleration, to pass into the tents of Independency. And hence, in recommendation of this system of ecclesiastical

* Innocency's Triumph, p. 4.

polity, he employed both the pulpit and the press, and exemplified its principles during the remainder of his life. The truth is, the Independent scheme at that time promised general liberty of conscience; although some of its disciples, as we shall afterwards perceive, when they got into power, could play the tyrant as well as others.

The Independent mode of church-government, though sanctioned by the practice, and defended by the talents of men of high respectability, is open to serious objections, which must be felt by its most ardent admirers. It certainly has an unfriendly bearing upon the liberty of the pulpit, which it is of the utmost importance to preserve sacred and inviolate. When a minister is dependent upon a few opulent individuals, and is in fact at their disposal, he is under a strong and perpetual temptation, instead of following the convictions of his own mind, to accommodate his preaching to the taste of his benefactors. In such a state of things it should seem that the apostolical injunction, " *Obey them that have the rule over you, and submit yourselves,*" were more applicable to the pastors of the church, than to the flocks committed to their care. Among the Congregationalists of England we often find ministers without any pastoral charge, and churches without a stated pastorate. A man of independent property and of powerful and commanding talents may occupy the same pulpit for life; but a poor man of ordinary ability is liable to frequent changes, his position being any thing but independent. This system appears also to be defective in cases of disagreement. When a spirit of faction happens to prevail in any church, as all foreign authority is disclaimed, there is no tribunal to which the contending parties can appeal : and hence, they are left to erect altar against altar, and to indulge themselves in all the bitterness of strife. "In the Independent way," says Baxter, "I disliked the lamentable tendency to divisions and sub-divisions, and the nourishing of heresies and sects. But above all I disliked, that most of them made the people, by majority of votes, to be church-governors, in excommunications, absolutions, &c., which Christ hath made an act of office and so they governed their governors and themselves: and their making a minister to be no minister to any but his own flock, and to act to others but as a private man." *

Whatever may be thought concerning the correctness of Mr. Goodwin's judgment on this subject, the motive by which he was actuated in adopting the Independent scheme, must command the approbation of every candid mind. " I here make open profession," says he, "in the presence of heaven and earth, that if any of my brethren of opposite judgment shall give me any reasonable account how I may build up myself in holiness better (or if it be but as well) in the way of Presbytery, than in that wherein I am for the present engaged, I will pull down what I have built, and devote all my strength to the service of that way which, for distinction-sake, is called Presbytery. I make no question but that way which hath the richest sympathy with the edification of saints in holiness, is the way which Jesus Christ hath sealed." †
—" I know that I am looked upon as a man very deeply engaged for the Independent cause against Presbytery. But the truth is, I am neither so whole for the former, nor against the latter, as I am generally voted to be. It is in my '*spirit*' only that '*I serve the law*' of Independency, but with '*my flesh I serve the law*' of Presbytery. And if the cause of Presbytery could be so pleaded as to legitimate her pedigree in my judgment and conscience, it would be as a resurrection from death into life to my flesh, yea, my spirit would rejoice also, that gain and godliness are so well agreed. And if I apprehended nothing more desirable in Independency than matters of accommodation for the outward man, I would cut all the cords by which I am bound to her, and let myself and mine drive upon the providence of God for our maintenance. So prepared am I to take the impression of any rational plea either for Presbytery, or against Independency, without prejudice. If I had liberty in my conscience to pass into the tents of the one, the taber-

* Reliq. Baxterianæ, Part Second, p. 143, Edit. 1696.   † Innocency and Truth, p. 29.

nacles of the other should no longer be my habitation. Yea, if I could meet with any thing that had strength enough to make me doubt of my way, I would interdict my pen from dealing further in the controversy, and stand still upon the watch-tower of inquiry, till God [should] show me the way in which He would have me to go.

" Some things I have written in favour of the Congregational way, and some against Presbytery; but I may truly say, that my great design was, the glory of God, in bringing the churches of God, in the three kingdoms, to the nearest conjunction in religion and form of church-government; being fully assured, that if ever the people of God in these kingdoms be conjoined in either, it must be in the truth, not in error. And therefore being fully persuaded in my judgment and conscience, that the way of the Congregation is the truth, I conceived a possibility that the churches of God in the three kingdoms might be drawn into a near conjunction in this, when the beauty and truth of it should be fully manifested; but had no hope of procuring any such conjunction of them in the other.

" As for those who by ' the churches of God in the three kingdoms,' understand ' all the inhabitants of these kingdoms, good and bad,' and swear unto the Most High, that they will endeavour to bring these into the nearest conjunction in religion and form of church-government; what do they, in effect, but swear that they will endeavour to bring day and night, Christ and Belial, into the nearest conjunction they can? Wolves and tigers, bears and lions, are as capable of civil conjunction with men, as wicked and profane men are, without the change of their natures by grace, of spiritual communion with the saints.

" In case that desirable end I speak of, should be too great for me, together with those who are partakers of the same design, to perform ; my next proposal was, to bring the people of God who differed in judgment about church-government, into the nearest conjunction of spirit and affection that might be, under this difference. Where-

unto I could not but judge this a promising expedient,—
to show what might be said for the way of the Congregation, and what to render the way of Presbytery suspected;
considering that they were the sons of Presbytery, not
the Congregational men, that stood in need of that allay
of spirit, without the mediation whereof there was no
hope of conjunction between them. As for any design of
making parties, increasing strife, countenancing persons
erroneous, hindering reformation, or the like, the ever-
blessed God knows, that such virtue is gone out from His
Spirit as hath made these the disdain of my soul; and
hath brought my life, and whatsoever I have or am, into
my hand, where it is all ready at a moment to be offered
up upon the service of the peace of His Churches and
prosperity of his Gospel whensoever these shall call." *

While his mind was occupied with the theory of church
government, he did not lose sight of questions more strictly
theological; and in the year 1643 he published an elaborate pamphlet of twenty-one quarto pages, entitled, "The
First Man; or a Short Discourse of Adam's State: viz. 1.
Of his being made a Living Soul: 2. Of the Manner of his
Fall." On the subjects here discussed, he reasoned in a
more satisfactory manner a few years afterwards, when he
had renounced the dogma of absolute predestination. He
here maintains that Adam, created in the image of God,
received from his Maker a power to stand; that this power
was afterwards withdrawn; and hence the original transgression with all its consequences to him and his posterity.
He resolves the whole into the mere will of God, which he
describes as the supreme law that renders actions good or
evil as the case may be. After he had embraced the views
of Arminius, he laid great and just stress upon the fact
asserted by St. Paul, (Eph. i. 11,) that God "worketh all
things," not after mere will, but, "after the *counsel* of
His will:" His will being in all things as it were counselled and guided by His goodness, justice, holiness, and
truth. To this tract he prefixed only the initials of his
name.

* Inexcusableness of Antapologia, Preface.

In the year 1644 Mr. Goodwin published a tract under the title of "The Grand Imprudence of Men running the Hazard of Fighting against God, in suppressing any Way, Doctrine or Practice, concerning which they know not certainly whether it be from God or no." In this work, which is the substance of two sermons preached in Coleman Street, our author applies the well-known caution of Gamaliel, (Acts v. 38,) to the case of the Independents, who were then comparatively few in number, and for whose suppression by parliamentary interference many religionists were exceedingly clamorous. In the prefatory address to his readers Mr. Goodwin says, "We have an English saying, 'That a burnt child dreads the fire.' I have oft been cast into the fire of men's indignation by an unclean spirit of calumny and slander. Some have reported, that I deny justification by Christ: that is, that the sun is up at noon-day. Others, that I deny the immortality of the soul: that is, that I murdered my father and mother. Others, that I have preached against the Parliament and Assembly: that is, that I am out of my wits, weary of my present life, and careless of that which is to come. Others, again, that sometimes I stood for Presbytery, but am now fallen to Independency: that is, that once I was so wise as to think that six and seven made nineteen, but now am become so weak as to judge they make thirteen and no more.

"I confess I do not much dread this fire, made of the tongues of asps and vipers, because I have a long time been accustomed to such burnings, and have found them rather purifying than consuming. Nevertheless I had rather give an account of mine own words, than of other men's pretending to be mine; and so keep out of the fire as far as the peace and safety of my own soul and other men's will suffer me. This is the true account of the publishing of these sermons. Understanding that the foul spirit which hath for years haunted my ministry, was beginning to practise upon these sermons, I thought it the safer course of the two, to put myself into the hands of the truth, than to expose both it and myself to be rent and torn by him.

What good or hurt they will do now they are gotten abroad, is not easy for me to conjecture. When the danger of the disease runs high, there is little hope but in that physic whereof there is some fear. We are under a bondage of misery, and it is only the truth that can make us free. And yet there is cause to fear lest the truth should increase our bondage and misery, by being rejected and opposed when it comes to visit and to bless us. God hath made me a lover of men in such a degree, that I can willingly consecrate myself to their service, through any sufferings from them. If this world fail me, I know God hath prepared another which will not fail."

In this pamphlet Mr. Goodwin answers several objections against the Independents, and solemnly admonishes those in authority, not to attempt by the hand of violence to suppress the congregations of Christians who bore that name, "lest haply" they should be found to be "fighting against God." He also introduces the subject of the right of private judgment, and argues against all interference of the civil power in the concerns of conscience.

By this publication he had the misfortune to excite, in no ordinary degree, the ire of the celebrated William Prynne. This noted barrister was one of the most singular characters the world has ever seen. He possessed considerable learning, both in law and divinity, and was indefatigably diligent in his application to books. Entering completely into the views of the Puritans of the old school, both in regard to doctrine and ecclesiastical discipline, he was decidedly hostile to Episcopacy and to Arminianism; and by his writings on these subjects rendered himself highly offensive to Archbishop Laud and his friends. Having incurred the displeasure of the court by his *Histrio-Mastix*, a book against theatrical amusements, and in the index of which dishonourable mention is made of " women actors; " he was sentenced by the Star-Chamber to pay a fine of five thousand pounds to the king, to be expelled the University of Oxford and Lincoln's Inn, to be degraded and rendered incapable of following his profession as a lawyer, to stand twice on

the pillory, at each time to have one of his ears cut off,
to have his book burned before his face by the common
hangman, and to be imprisoned during the remainder of
his life. Unsubdued by these disasters, he persevered
with undaunted courage in his career of authorship, and
from the place of his confinement published some severe
reflections upon his Grace of Canterbury and several of the
bishops. In consequence of this additional offence, the
incorrigible delinquent was once more brought into the
Star-Chamber, and sentenced to pay five thousand pounds
to the king, to stand on the pillory, to have the stumps
of his ears cut off, to be branded with a red-hot iron on
both cheeks with the letters S L, for a Seditious Libeller,
and to be perpetually imprisoned in the castle of Carnarvon. The execution of this horrible sentence the sturdy
offender bore with his characteristic firmness, and even
composed Latin verses when returning from the pillory
with the blood oozing from his wounds. From Carnarvon
he was removed to the castle of Mount Orgueil, in the
Isle of Jersey; and, on the assembling of the Long
Parliament, an order was issued by the House of Commons for his emancipation. On regaining his liberty, he
entered London in triumph, accompanied by Henry
Burton, another of the archbishop's exiles; while many
thousands of people, several in carriages, some on horseback, and others on foot, carrying rosemary and bays,
hailed his return and welcomed him into the city.*

Prynne, however, derived not the smallest intellectual
or moral advantage either from the sufferings he had
endured, or from the state of misery and confusion into
which he saw the nation plunged by a system of ecclesiastical oppression. His temper retained all its original
violence, and his principles continued perfectly intolerant.
Could his wishes have been realized, the sword would
have been drawn to convert the whole nation to Presbyterianism. Never was the peace of the Christian church
disturbed by the learned and incoherent ravings of a more
furious and bitter enemy of religious liberty. Contending

* General Dictionary, Vol. VIII. p. 564, Edit. 1739.

for the *divine right* of Presbyterianism, and unwilling that any who refused to bow to its authority should be tolerated, he attempted to refute the arguments which Mr. Goodwin had adduced in behalf of the Independents. Not satisfied with this, he made an attack upon Mr. Goodwin's personal character, attempted to render him odious to the secular power, and to expose him to a state-prosecution. In reply to this ungenerous assailant, Mr. Goodwin published two tracts, in one of which, entitled "Innocency's Triumph," he defends his own conduct; and in the other, entitled, "Innocency and Truth Triumphing Together," vindicates his principles against his formidable antagonist.

In reference to Prynne, our author says, "If the learned gentleman would vouchsafe that courtesy to himself and to me, that we might reason the points in difference between us, without aspersing one the other, or wresting the sayings one of the other, or exasperating those that stand by, he were a man with whom I could willingly live and die; and could make treasure of the last interest that should be vouchsafed to me in his acquaintance. For my part, I trust that through His grace who hath commanded me ' not to be overcome of evil, but to overcome evil with good,' I shall be able to carry along my answer without any of those miscarriages.

"He incenseth the parliament against me," continues Mr. Goodwin, "as one that hath ' presumptuously undermined the undoubted privileges thereof;' chargeth me with ' several anti-parliamentary passages, diametrically opposite to my vow and covenant; and, which is the first-born of all his bitter insinuations, preacheth this doctrine to the parliament, ' That they cannot, without perjury, permit any wilfully thus to violate their privileges in the most public manner.'" These tremendous charges, which were manifestly intended to expose Mr. Goodwin to the vengeance of the civil power, were preferred against him, because he had denied that the parliament possessed any legitimate authority over the consciences of British subjects. In repelling these accusations our author says, "I have no ways undermined (least of all presumptuously) any undoubted privilege of parliament; but have, from first to last, with singleness of heart, as in the presence of God, with all my might, endeavoured to assert and vindicate the authority, power, and privileges of parliament, to the utmost height I was able to discern their altitude. If I am not so quick-sighted to take their true altitude as some others, I trust this incapacity may be atoned with a more gentle sacrifice than to be arraigned as a presumptuous underminer of the undoubted privileges of parliament, or to suffer under the insupportable weight of this charge. If I have denied the least drachm of that power which is truly parliamentary, and consistent with the Word of God, (of which I am not conscious,) I most solemnly profess, I did it out of a loving and affectionate jealousy over the Parliament, lest they might dash their foot against that stone, by which all rule and all authority and power will one day be broken to pieces. So that, if either my tongue or pen have miscarried upon this point, I may truly say, that it was *error amoris*, not *amor erroris*, which caused that miscarriage. I confess I am, in the habitual frame of my heart, tender and jealous over all the world, and much more over those who are dear to me, but most of all over those who, being dear to me, are more exposed than others to temptation and danger, lest they should touch with any claim the sacred and incommunicable royalties of Heaven, and so count it no robbery to make themselves equal to God; knowing most assuredly, that this is a high provocation, and, if continued in, will kindle a fire in the breast of Him whose Name is Jealous, which will consume and devour."

In attempting to prove that the civil magistrate has a coercive power in the affairs of private conscience, Prynne adduced the example of Cyrus, Artaxerxes, and Darius, who all made statutes and decrees in reference to the Jews and to their peculiar mode of religious worship. To which our author justly replies, "Whatsoever maketh for the safety and honour of the whole community of persons fearing God, within the limits of their jurisdiction, without the pressure and just grievance of others, the civil magistrate I conceive hath not only a power, but a necessity by way of duty, lying upon him to interpose for the establishing of such things. Of this nature were those statutes and decrees of Cyrus, Artaxerxes, Darius, and other heathen princes for the building of God's temple, and advancement of His worship, which Mr. Prynne insisteth upon, but quite besides the point. For these princes did not impose any thing upon the people of God in point of worship, under mulcts and penalties; much less did they impose anything upon the generality of them, which was controversial and matter of conscience; by means of which one half of them should have been gratified, and the other half ruined and oppressed. Those statutes and decrees equally respected the good of all, and contained nothing oppressive to the judgments or consciences of any; nor any new determination of anything appertaining to the service of God, under mulcts and penalties."

"Besides the grand and bloody suggestion," continues our author, "that I presumptuously undermine the undoubted privileges of parliament, (a crime which my soul abhorreth,) there are others of a like nature wherewith the gentleman hath stained his paper here and there. He chargeth me, 'That instead of my parishioners, I have gathered an Independent congregation out of divers parishes:' and that I 'neglect my parishioners, preaching seldom to them, though I take their tithes.' If these things be true, let Mr. Prynne keep his honour and place at the bar, and let me be hoisted: but if otherwise, *contrariorum contraria sint consequentia*. I am so far from neglecting my parishioners, that it will be acknowledged by some hundreds of them, that scarce any minister in the kingdom has been more laborious or constant in the work of the ministry than I have been amongst them, from my first coming to them unto this day. For several years together, without some special hindrance, I preached constantly thrice, often four times, sometimes five or six times a week to them. Their agreement with me was, upon my preaching two expository lectures weekly, to find me an assistant to preach once on the Lord's Day; this assistant, after some short continuance, departed to a place of better accommodation; [yet] whilst I was able I both continued my two weekly lectures, and preached twice on the Lord's Day: myself, when I was able; by the ablest I could procure, when I was not able. Notwithstanding, I never received so much as a penny, to my knowledge, from any of them, for a whole year's labour in preaching those two weekly lectures; nor did I receive above twelve pounds ten shillings a year for them at any time. Since I was necessitated to discontinue these two weekly lectures, I have, upon the request of some of them, and that without either promise or hope of any pecuniary consideration, engaged to expound some part of Scripture, before sermon, on the Lord's Day. Nor did I ever diminish my parishioners' portion in my ministerial labours, for that congregation's sake, which the gentleman is pleased to baptize by the name of Independent: nor did I ever preach to this congregation apart from my parishioners. Sometimes I prayed with them, and now and then debated a question in mine own house; but ever with the door open, and liberty given to any of my parishioners to come and partake with us in those exercises; which several of them have accepted of, and been present with us.

"I am charged with 'receiving their tithes:' my answer is, that I demand no tithes of any of them, nor ever had any right to do it. Nor have I ever received anything from them in the nature of tithes, but as their voluntary contribution. The parsonage is impropriate in the parishioners' hands: the vicarage is only endowed with eleven pounds per annum. For the last half-year I have received little above twenty pounds, excepting one half of the yearly rent of a small house, let sometimes but for twelve pounds, [and] never for above fourteen pounds a year. Out of which sum, twelve pounds ten shillings being deducted for the rent of my house, the remainder is of as low a proportion as envy herself can desire, for the maintenance of a minister, his wife, and seven children in such an expensive place as this city. If Mr. Prynne knew how small a proportion of subsistence I receive, and what my labour and pains are, I verily believe that, instead of upbraiding me with ' receiving tithes,' he would pity me that I receive no more.

"He chargeth me [with having] gathered an Independent congregation to myself, out of divers parishes: I answer, If his meaning be, that I have gone about to persuade any man or woman to be of my congregation, I utterly deny the truth of this charge. I never opened my mouth to any person whatsoever, to any such purpose, save only what I have preached in the face of my parochial congregation. And what I have here said, there are many hundreds, if not some thousands, to testify. If by gathering such a congregation as he speaks of, he means, the receiving of persons upon their Christian requests into a church-relation, and so as to become a pastor to them; in this sense, which is very improperly called a 'gathering,' I confess the charge, or commendation rather, to be true. I have, with the consent of my parishioners in a public vestry, received some out of other parishes in such a way; who yet have liberty at any time to withdraw themselves to any other pastor or congregation, for their better accommodation in spiritual affairs. Of what I have done in this, I am ready to give an account with meekness to any man that shall require it."

In this unhandsome and illiberal attack upon the character of Mr. Goodwin, Prynne was seconded by an anonymous writer, who published a pamphlet entitled, "Faces About: or, A Recrimination charged upon Mr. John Goodwin, in the Point of Fighting against God, and Opposing the Way of Christ." This tract, which is very short, appears to have been the production of a zealous Presbyterian. The author expresses the greatest consternation and alarm at the doctrine of general toleration, as taught by Mr. Goodwin; and intimates that the parliament ought to watch over him with a jealous eye, since the principles advanced by him concerning religious liberty, were replete with the greatest mischief to the

community! In reference to this assailant, Mr. Goodwin
says, "As for that empty pamphlet, called FACES ABOUT,
the author of it, whatever face or faces he had, (for it
may be he carries two in a hood,) it seems he dares show
none. He fears his name would have suffered, if it had
been in the company of such a piece. Yet the paper is a
glass; and there is the face of a man, such as it is, to be
seen in it. The man that looks out from behind the lattices,
is ignorant that the Lord of Glory was numbered amongst
transgressors, and crucified between two thieves; or he
would never have thought to disparage me, by putting me
into the same account with Socinians. Jesus Christ being
crucified with malefactors, hath spoiled their market that
think to sell men's reputations under disgrace, by coupling
them with names of infamous resentment." *

Mr. Goodwin's defence of his own character, and
attempt to guard his brethren from persecution, exasperated the irritable Prynne more than ever. Fired with
indignation, he soon produced another pamphlet, the
title of which was, "Truth Triumphing over Falsehood,
Antiquity over Novelty: or, A Seasonable Vindication of
the undoubted Ecclesiastical Jurisdiction, Right, Legislative and Coercive Power of Christian Emperors, Kings,
Magistrates, Parliaments, in matters of Religion, Church-
Government, &c., in Refutation of John Goodwin's Innocency's Triumph," &c. This intemperate publication,
which was intended for ever to confound the advocates
of religious liberty, contains a repetition of the charges
against Mr. Goodwin's character, heightened by all the
colouring of angry rhetoric. As he had contended that
those who called the principles of Presbyterianism in
question, were nevertheless entitled to toleration; and
denied that God has given magistrates authority to
punish mankind merely on account of their religious
sentiments, he is again represented as an enemy to the
government; and the parliament is indirectly invoked
to pour its vengeance on his head. Conceiving it to be a
duty to himself and his brethren, Mr. Goodwin published

* Innocency's Triumph.

a reply, entitled, "Calumny Arraigned and Cast: or, A Brief Answer to some extravagant and rank Passages lately fallen from the pen of William Prynne, Esquire."

"Because the crown for which Mr. Prynne runs," says he, "in this and his other lucubrations against me, is to transform me into a man of a 'rancorous and disaffected heart against parliaments,' and to couple me with the 'worst malignants, royalists, cavaliers,' yea with the 'Arch-Prelate himself;' I shall specify what I have done, and continue to do, for the parliament, and solemnly profess, that if any man can say to me wherein I may do more for them, (provided that what shall be required doth *really* tend to the benefit of the parliament,) I am ready, and bind myself, to perform it. I have once and again in print, with the utmost of my abilities, asserted the parliamentary cause against the Oxfordian; yea, as far as I understand, I was the first among my brethren who serve at the altar, that rose up in this kind for the parliament; with what exposal of myself to danger, and advantage of the cause undertaken, many there are that know, and are ready to declare. How frequently, for many months together, when the parliamentary occasions were most urging, with what fervency I laboured by preaching to advance the service;—how many young men and others, as useful in the army as any of their rank, were, through the blessing of God, armed with courage and resolution by me for the wars, there are more than a few that can inform. Nor is it unknown to thousands, with what earnestness of supplication I have without ceasing, in my public prayers, commended the Parliament with all their affairs to God. There hath no proposition for advance of monies been at any time recommended by the Parliament to the city, that I know of, but hath been entertained by me with a full proportion of my estate. What I have been in public, the same have I been in private: strengthening the hands of some which began to be feeble, resolving the doubts of others; so setting them at liberty to serve the Parliament who before could do nothing. Nor have I quitted myself at this rate in the parliamentary service in the city only, but have been as faithful an agent for them in the country also, where I have come, and that not without considerable success. I am a *fool* to speak all this of myself, but Mr. Prynne hath compelled me. If I be yet defective in my duty to the parliament, if there be any service wherein I may further express myself for them, all the powers of my soul stand ready to fall upon the work. If for all this I must be numbered amongst men of rancorous and disaffected hearts to the parliament, I shall congratulate the felicity of those who are better thought of, and yet shall think mine own the more princely portion. A good conscience is never at her full of sweetness, light, and glory, but when uprightness suffers and is eclipsed."

It was for maintaining the sacred rights of conscience that our author became involved in this controversy; through the whole of which he faithfully copied the example of his Lord and Master, "who, when He was reviled, reviled not again." At the conclusion of this contest, though much injured, and though his antagonist displayed the deepest malignity, Mr. Goodwin addressed Prynne in the following affectionate and pious language: "Mutual discontentments now and then are a tribute which men must look to pay for the commodity of living together in the world. If we have offended one the other, happy shall we be in forgiving one the other, and circumvent him whose design was to have circumvented us. If I have offended you otherwise than by speaking the truth, so as the defence of it required, you shall not long complain of want of satisfaction, as far as I am able to do or speak any thing that may accommodate you, if you will make your demands in a Christian and loving way. And if your heart will answer mine in these inclinations, the storms of our contestations shall end in a sweet calm. If you reject the motion of a Christian compliance by the way, I can very patiently and with comfort enough await the decisions of the great Tribunal, whose awards will shortly seal all the righteousnesses and unrighteousnesses of men against all further disputes or inquiries to the days of eternity."

Such was the manner in which Mr. Goodwin poured forth the feelings of his heart towards one, who, without the slightest provocation, had wantonly endeavoured to destroy his reputation, and even to endanger his life. It is easy to perceive from these extracts, that in this contest he gained a complete triumph over his opponent, both by the nature of those facts to which he appealed, and by the mildness of his temper. To Prynne, however, this was a matter of no moment. Ever prompt

> To pour the torrent of opprobrious speech,

and glorying in an ostentatious display of learning, this most unamiable man was no sooner repulsed in his attack upon one character than he commenced hostilities against another ; and through the whole of that turbulent period in which he lived, was the most active agent in the immense host of pamphleteers who scattered over the country polemical tracts on almost every subject,

> Thick as autumnal leaves, that strew the brooks
> In Vallombrosa.

" I verily believe," says Anthony Wood, " that, if rightly computed, he wrote a sheet for every day of his life, reckoning from the time when he came to the use of reason and the state of man. His custom when he studied was, to put on a long quilted cap, which came an inch over his eyes, serving as an umbrella to defend him from too much light ; and seldom eating a dinner, would, every three hours or more, be *maunching* a roll of bread, and now and then refresh his exhausted spirits with ale, brought to him by his servant."* It has been further said, that he published nearly two hundred treatises of all sorts and sizes, against all persons, and parties, and all offices and governments ; and most of them written with all the rage and fury, and all the smoke and dust, that can well be imagined. Weary at length with

* Athen. Oxon. Vol. II. col. 439, Edit. 1721.

engaging all his enemies and antagonists, to keep him out of further mischief, he was put upon vast labours among the records in the Tower, where he did the most service.*

On the publication of his "Innocency and Truth Triumphing Together," Mr. Goodwin presented a copy to the noted John Vicars, of Hudibrastic memory, and usher in the Hospital of Christ-Church, London: a zealous Calvinist, and author of several works both in prose and verse. "In the beginning of the civil wars," says the Oxford Historian, "he showed himself a forward man for the Presbyterian cause, hated all people that loved obedience, and did affright many of the weaker sort and others, from having any agreement with the king's party, by continually inculcating into their heads strange stories of the wrath of God against the Cavaliers."† Having read Mr. Goodwin's tract, Vicars addressed a private letter to its author, expressing the highest admiration of Prynne, censuring Mr. Goodwin with great severity for writing against such a man, even in self-defence, and reflecting upon the people who had placed themselves under his pastoral care. Mr. Goodwin does not appear to have taken any notice of this letter; but Mr. Daniel Taylor, a member of his church, a man of property, of eminent piety, of strong sense, and of great moderation, addressed to Vicars a few lines in reply. Vicars immediately published his own letter, and was very diligent in the distribution of copies among his friends. Desirous of furnishing an antidote to this intemperate and unseasonable production, Taylor also presented his epistle to the world, accompanied by the following advertisement:

"The author of this Letter did not intend it for the press, but sent it to Mr. Vicars in a private way: but Mr. Vicars's Letter coming forth in print, and divers copies thereof being dispersed into several hands by himself, it was thought fit that this Letter should be published also."

---

* Peck's Desiderata Curiosa, p. 547, Edit. 1779.　　　† Athen. Oxon.
Vol. II. col. 153.

This scarce and curious document, which was equally honourable to Taylor and to his Pastor, was as follows:

" SIR,

" WHETHER it was my good or hard hap to meet with your Letter, directed and sent to Mr. Goodwin, I cannot easily determine: for though all manner of knowledge, either of persons or things, be in some kind or other beneficial; it being an undoubted maxim, that *verum et bonum convertuntur;* yet some knowledge may be so circumstantiated, that it may prove more burthensome and offensive, to the party knowing, than commodious. I confess, from the reading of your lines, I have gained thus much, to say I know you: but this gain hath occasioned such a considerable loss in the things of my joy, that I do even wish for my former ignorance; and could be well contented, to have met with no other description of your frame and temper, than what the promise of your countenance, and the report of your friends, have made of you. Indeed it cannot but deduct somewhat from the comfort of a reasonable man, to see one whom one would think grey hairs should have taught the language of soberness, shooting with his tongue at rovers, and speaking sharp and devouring words against persons and things which he knows not. Sorry I am, that Mr. Vicars should break the fair face of his reputation upon this stone, against which this besotted world is dashing itself in pieces, from day to day. I have some hope, that though your zeal for Mr. Prynne's glory did cast you into such an ecstasy of passion, that you scarce knew what you writ; yet, by this time, you have pretty well recovered yourself again: and lest the sense of your miscarriage should too much oppress you, I give you to know, that you are fallen into soft and tender hands, and have discovered your nakedness to such only who rather pity than deride it. For my part, I love not to disport myself at the weakness of any man, or to turn his folly into laughter: for what were this, but to reflect dishonour upon the same nature, wherein he partakes with myself? Rather I could mourn over the vanities of your

pen, and weep to see you so far intoxicated, as to call the
most injurious dealing one.can lightly meet with, by the
name of candour and ingenuity.   The truth is you have so
foully bewrayed your paper with bold and untrue assertions
[and] imputations,—that I thought, even for modesty's
sake, to have drawn over them the veil of silence, and to
have contested with that spirit that breathes in them no
further, than by speaking to it in a secret wish, *The Lord
rebuke thee !*   But I considered with myself, that perhaps
you might communicate in the nature of such persons who,
as Solomon saith, (Prov. xxvi. 5,) are apt, being un-
answered, to be wise in their own conceits : and if I shall
hereby demolish, or at least weaken, this conceit of yours,
I presume I shall do you a very charitable and Christian
piece of service.

"Think not I am become your enemy, because I tell
you the truth : you have injured me no otherwise than by
trespassing upon your own credit, and by making thereby
a sad breach in that holy profession, wherein you stand
engaged with myself.   Whatever your intentions were, I
conceive you have done me no more wrong in clapping the
title of an *Independent Proselyte* upon my back, than Pilate
did to Christ, in affixing this superscription over His head,
This is the King of the Jews.   I think the name to be full
as honourable as that of a *poor and unworthy Presbyterian*,
wherewith you have pleased to baptize yourself; and conceive that herein only you have followed your own rather
than the apostle's counsel, *In honour to prefer others before
yourself.*   But had you been minded to suppress your
name, your very dialect had been enough to betray you :
methinks you write just like such a one as you say you are.
Did I not hope for better things from the hands of more
worthy Presbyterians, your unworthy dealing had set me off
ten degrees further from your way, than now I stand.   But
I will not take the advantage of any man's misdemeanor,
though more gross and absurd than yours, to render
Presbytery odious to the world.   To clothe any opinion or
practice with the garments of men's personal distempers,
thereby to fall upon them and beat them with the more

applause, is a method which I as much abhor, as the
gentleman you admire delights in: and if this property
in him were one of those beauty-spots which ravished
you into a passionate adoration of him, you need not fear
that I should ever become your cor-rival: and yet I love
and honour Mr. Prynne for whatever you can find lovely
and honourable in him. I cannot deny but that in some
of his works he hath acquitted himself upon commendable
terms: but to say, that in all things he writes after the
rate of a god, when in many things he falls beneath the
line of a man, is to make him and myself obnoxious to the
wrath of God, and the scorn of man. I acknowledge that,
for a time, he ran well: but who hindered him? Questionless, he who is ever and anon hindering the saints in the
race of holiness. The prince of darkness owed him a fall,
for his sharp contesting with his prime agents, and now he
hath paid the debt. But if Mr. Prynne will be ruled by
the advice of his best friends, he may rise again to his
greater glory; and, notwithstanding his fall, triumph over
the envy and malice of the devil.

"Concerning Mr. John Goodwin, over whom you shake
the rod of your reproof, as if he were one of your scholars,
I could speak as high and excellent encomiums, as you have
spoken of your *precious gentleman.*'—I could compare him
even with Mr. Prynne himself: but such a comparison as
this would be to me most odious. I could tell you what
he hath done, what he hath writ, how deeply he hath
suffered from unreasonable men; yea, I could give you such
a lively and bright description of him, as would dazzle
your eyes to look upon, and make you blush for shame, to
have grappled with such a person as he is, upon such rude
and unmannerly terms as you have done. For you, who
are but a *teacher of boys*, so haughtily to correct a great
master in Israel, is such an absurdity, as cannot but rend
a more patient soul than mine into disdain and grief. It
is a wonder to me, that, whereas at the beginning of your
Letter you confess yourself to be but *a poor and unworthy
Presbyterian*, you should so far forget yourself, before you
come half-way, as to take upon you, like the Doctor of the

Chair, to censure the best of men and ways, with as much
confidence as if your pen had dropped the Votes of a
General Assembly with its ink.   Had a poor and unworthy
Independent done . the like, you would have cast his boldness into a basilisk, and used it to batter down the way of
his profession, and to lay the glory of it even with the
ground.   But I well perceive, though you have escaped the
snare of *gifts and parts*, in which you fear Mr. Goodwin is
taken, yet you are fallen into the pit, not of divine but
natural simplicity; and have verified the old proverb : *A
rash man's bolt is soon shot.*

"As for that book of Mr. Goodwin, called 'Innocency
and Truth Triumphing Together,' though you are pleased
to triumph over both, and to cast it out as an arch-rebel
to reason and morality; yet, I must tell you, it hath found
joyful and bountiful entertainment in the judgments of
sober and intelligent men.   But certainly it was the
unhappiness of this treatise to fall into your hands, when
you stood upon the mount of Mr. Prynne's honour, and
when the vision of his transfiguration wrought so strongly
in you, that you did not wot what you spake; no, nor what
you did neither : for you laid about you, with such regardless fury, that you broke the head of your friend Priscian ;*
of whose safety men of your profession should be most
tender.   I thought to have argued the case with you,
whether your exceptions against this treatise and its
author will hold in the court of reason and equity; but
perhaps you are not so well skilled in the rules of this
court ; and I am loath to take the advantage of you.   I
shall only propound a few queries; peradventure the
strugglings of your thoughts to give them satisfaction
may dissolve the enchantment that now is upon you.
What persons did ever most *learnedly declare* Mr. Goodwin
to be justly censured for Socinianism?   When, or in what
public place, did they make this declaration?   How call

* "The words in the written copy of his letter are these, and thus
spelled : *qui in alterum paratus est dicere, ipsum vicio careat oportet*, as may
appear from the original in Mr. Goodwin's custody.   But it seems the Cor-
rector, being the better Grammarian, transformed them into good Latin in
the printed copy."

you that brother of his, who will *justify* against him the charge of *holding a most damnable opinion about justifying faith?* I suppose you must strain, not so much your memory, as your invention, in shaping your answer. You had done well to remember, that though *fools*, as Solomon speaks, *believe every thing;* yet *wise* men will question such assertions as these.

"Alas, Sir, the best course you can run to gain credit with the prudent, is to cut your allegations and your proofs just of one and the same length. To clothe large and broad sayings with curtailed arguments, reflects as much shame upon such sayings, and him that speaks them, as Hanun did upon the servants of David, in cutting off their garments to their buttocks. You cannot but know, how that many grave, sober, godly, and learned men have fallen into that way you call Independency. Now your only method to have brought over these to your party, and to have filled their mouths with the cry of a confederacy against this way, had been this: Not barely to have affirmed it to be a *novel* and *disturbant way,* as you have done, but to have poised the lightness of your affirmation with the weight and substance of a demonstration. I assure you, Sir, whatever you may think, I approve of this way no further than I see the footsteps of those sweet sisters, truth and peace, printed in it. I have narrowly viewed it, and I can find no drops of blood, no strewings of the liberties, estates, names, comforts of the saints, scattered in it; and yet some travellers affirm, they have seen such things as these in that way, which the ignorance of thousands lust after.

"But to conclude, I beseech you, Sir, be more watchful over the extravagancies of your tongue and pen for the future: since you are in part acquainted with their infirmities, let it be your wisdom to seek their cure. I reverence you for age, piety, and some services you have done for the public; and I should rejoice to see such an ancient standard in the garden of God, as you are, carrying your hoary head with honour to the grave. Which that you may do, as I have, you see, in part, endeavoured, so I shall

G

further prosecute with my prayers to HIM, who is able to
keep you to the end: in whom, though I am unknown to
you, yet with all sincerity I profess myself,

　　　　Sir, a cordial well-wisher to your peace and credit,
January 27th, 1644.　　　　　　　　　　　　D. T."

During the progress of the civil war, and the residence
of the king at Oxford, his majesty, learning that the Presbyterians and Independents were ill agreed,—the Independents claiming for themselves liberty of thought and action,
and the Presbyterians clamouring for the suppression of
every sect but their own,—sent an agent to London to
exasperate these differences, and, if possible, persuade the
Independents to espouse his cause; promising them liberty
of conscience, against which the Presbyterians protested,
with other favours of a like kind.　His agent, whose name
was Ogle, had an interview with Philip Nye and John
Goodwin, to whom he disclosed the king's purposes and
plans; which they immediately exposed to the men in
power, and thus rendered the scheme abortive.　For this
service the houses of parliament tendered to these two
Independent ministers a vote of thanks, January 26th,
1643-4;* and yet this same parliament, within a short time,
suffered one of its own committees to inflict an irreparable
injury upon Goodwin, by turning him out of his living,
and putting a Presbyterian in his place!　Well therefore
might he say, at a subsequent period of his life, that he
adhered to the parliamentary side under "disobligements
not a few."

It is a trite, but correct observation, that troubles seldom
come singly.　Scarcely had Mr. Goodwin repelled the
calumnious attack of Prynne, when he became more eminently an object of Presbyterian vengeance, and was called
to suffer "the loss of all things."　During the progress of
the war, several of the Puritan clergy in different parts of
the country, being driven from their cures by the army of
the royalists, fled with their families to London; and being

* Stoughton's Ecclesiastical History of England from the Opening of the
Long Parliament to the Death of Oliver Cromwell, Vol. I. pp. 305, 306.

reduced to great distress, represented their case to the parliament. The House of Commons first ordered a charitable collection to be made for them at their monthly fast; and to afford more permanent support, in December, 1642, appointed a committee to consider the most proper means for "the relief of such godly and well-affected ministers as have been plundered;" and to inquire, "What malignant clergymen have benefices in and about the town, whose benefices being sequestered may be supplied by others who may receive their profits." The persons invested with this authority were called THE COMMITTEE FOR PLUNDERED MINISTERS. By the royalists, however, they were denominated *The Committee for Plundering Ministers:* a designation which was highly appropriate. In the month of July, 1643, they were empowered to receive information against scandalous ministers, and to deprive them of their livings, though no *malignancy* with regard to the parliament were proved against them. From this time the Committee for Scandalous Ministers, and that for Plundered Ministers, were united, and continued so to the end of the Long Parliament.*

This Committee made terrible havoc among the regular clergy. It excluded from the church many comparatively worthless ministers, whose faults it was careful to emblazon before the world, to the scandal of religion and public morals; but it treated not a few upright, learned, and pious men with great severity, because of their conscientious attachment to episcopacy and to their king. Who can repress the feeling of indignation, on finding that such men as the ever-memorable Hales of Eton, and Dr. Brian Walton, the editor of the London Polyglot Bible, were by this committee deprived of their ecclesiastical preferments, and left to starve, or subsist by the kindness of their friends?

The praise of Walton " is in all the churches," and Hales was one of the greatest and most excellent men of whom any age or nation can boast. He was a man of

* Neal's Hist. Purit. Vol. III. p. 29, Toulmin's Edit.—Walker's Sufferings of the Clergy, p. 73, Edit. 1714.

liberal principles, of the most extensive learning, and possessed of every virtue that can adorn and exalt human nature. His modesty was as remarkable, as his knowledge was deep and various; he therefore withstood the importunity of his friends, who were perpetually urging him to give the world some lasting proof of his genius and acquirements.

> "FAME is the spur that the clear spirit doth raise,
> (That last infirmity of noble minds,)
> To scorn delights, and live laborious days."

But from this infirmity the mind of Hales was unhappily free. A small number of fugitive pieces were snatched from him during his life-time, and these with a few of his imperfect papers were published after his death; but he suffered his immense treasures of learning, which might have instructed the world and immortalized his name, to descend with him to the grave. This eminent man, because he was an episcopalian, a royalist, and an Arminian, was expelled from his fellowship of Eton College, and from the canonry of Windsor, and reduced to such needy circumstances as compelled him to submit to a measure, painful in the extreme to a man of letters— the last resort of a scholar enduring the severities of hunger—the sale of his extensive and valuable library. Having generously distributed among his fellow-sufferers a considerable part of the money thus obtained, he at length took up his residence under the roof of a poor widow, whose deceased husband had formerly been his servant; and from that humble retreat was removed to those peaceful abodes "where the wicked cease from troubling, and the weary are at rest."* "I reckon it not the least ignominies of that age," says Andrew Marvel, "that so eminent a person should have been, by the iniquity of the times, reduced to those necessities under which he lived; as I account it no small honour to have grown up into some sort of his acquaintance, and conversed awhile with the living remains of one of the

* General Dictionary, Vol. V. p. 702.

clearest heads and best prepared breasts in Christendom."*
The fate of this consummate scholar and amiable man
most amply shows, if any proof were necessary, that the
bare expulsion of men from ecclesiastical benefices, by
this committee, implies neither moral delinquency, nor a
want of ministerial qualifications.

To Baxter's allegation, that the episcopal divines
whom the Long Parliament deprived of their livings
were generally ignorant men of lax morals, and incom-
petent preachers, Dr. Thomas Pierce replied:—

"Did Bishop Hall never preach? or Bishop Duppa
preach worse than they that were never called preachers?
Did not Bishop Davenant understand his catechism? nor
Bishop Morton his creed? Yet how were they spoiled of
their estates, and clapped up prisoners in the Tower, whilst
the most ignorant and the most scandalous had both their
livelihoods and liberties indulged to them? Of those that
preached in the great city, the first occurring to my mind
were Dr. Holdsworth, Dr. Howel, Dr. Hacket, Dr. Heywood,
Dr. Westfield, Dr. Walton, Dr. Featley, and Dr. Rives, Dr.
Brough, Dr. Marsh, Mr. Shute, Mr. Hall; and besides, the
Rev. Dr. Fuller, now Dean of Durham; since the naming
of whom I think of the Rev. Mr. Udall. These did not live
more in the alehouse than in the church. The fame of
their piety and their learning is long since gone throughout the churches : yet Mr. Shute was molested and vexed
to death, and denied a funeral sermon to be preached by
Dr. Holdsworth as he desired. Dr. Holdsworth was cast
out of his mastership in Cambridge, sequestered from his
benefice in the City of London, a long time imprisoned at
Ely House, and the Tower. Dr. Walton, who hath put
forth the late *Biblia Polyglotta*, was not only sequestered,
but assaulted also, and plundered, and forced to fly. Dr.
Rives, Dr. Howel, Dr. Hacket, and Mr. Hall, were sequestered and plundered, and forced to fly for their lives.
Dr. Marsh was sequestered, and made to die in remote
parts. Dr. Brough was plundered, as well as sequestered,
his wife and children turned out of doors, and his wife

* Rehearsal Transprosed, p. 175, Edit. 1672.

struck dead with grief. Dr. Westfield was sequestered, abused in the street, and forced to fly. Dr. Featley was sequestered and plundered, and died a prisoner. Dr. Fuller was sequestered and plundered, and withal imprisoned at Ely House. Mr. Udall was not only sequestered himself, but his bed-rid wife was also cast out of doors, and inhumanly left in the open streets. Dr. Heywood was sequestered, and tossed from prison to prison, put in the Counter, Ely House, and the Ships; his wife and children turned out of doors. Could the ejection of a few scandalous and unlearned men (supposing them really such, and regularly ejected) have made amends for such riots as were committed upon men of exceeding great worth? Go from the city to the country, and you will find the case the very same. Such venerable persons as Dr. Gillingham, Dr. Hinchman, Dr. Mason, and Dr. Ranleigh, Mr. Sudburie, Mr. Threscross, Mr. Simmons, and Mr. Farrington, and a very great multitude of the like, (whom nothing but want of time, and love of brevity, doth make me forbear to reckon further,) were used like dunces and drunkards, (by your Reformers,) though powerful preachers, and pious men; men so eminent for learning, and so exemplary for life, that it is scandalous to be safe when such men suffer as malefactors. To let you see briefly what it was by which they were qualified for ruin, I will tell you a story of Mr. Simmons, the most exemplary pastor of Rayn, in Essex, who, being sent for up to the House of Commons by a pursuivant, was told that being an honest man, he did more prejudice to the good cause in hand than an hundred knaves, and therefore would suffer accordingly. So he did in great plenty his whole life after. And who should be sent in his place but a scandalous weaver, who cannot seemingly be named! Do but read that sober and useful book entitled *Angliæ Ruina*, and then you will be likely to change your style. If none had been thrown out of Oxford but Dr. Sheldon, Dr. Mansell, Dr. Sanderson, Dr. Hammond; or none out of Cambridge but Dr. Lany, Dr. Brownrigg, Dr. Cosins, and Dr. Collins, Mr. Thorndike, Mr. Gunning, Mr. Oley, and Mr. Barrow; no excuse could have been made for so great a dishonour to religion. But, above all, let me recommend a famous passage to your remembrance. Dr. Stern, Dr. Martin, Dr. Beale, men of eminent integrity, exemplary lives, and exceeding great learning, and heads of several colleges in the University of Cambridge, were carried away captives from thence to London, there thrust up into the Tower, thence removed to another prison. They often petitioned to be heard, and brought to judgment; but could not obtain either liberty or trial. After almost a year's imprisonment, they were by order from the Houses put on shipboard. It was upon Friday, August 11th, 1643. No sooner came they to the ship, called the 'Prosperous Sailor,' but straight they were put under hatches, where the decks were so low, as that they could not stand upright, and yet were denied stools to sit on, yea, and a burden of straw whereon to lie. There were crowded up in that little vessel no less than eighty prisoners of quality: where, that they might stifle one another, the very auger-holes, and inlets of any fresh air, were very carefully stopped up: and what became of them after, I have not heard." *

To that lawless and oppressive power by which so many eminent men were ruined, Mr. Goodwin was constrained to bow. When episcopacy was abolished by the parliament, and the clergy were at liberty to govern their parishes at discretion, Mr. Goodwin, following the example of several of his brethren, refused to administer the ordinance of baptism and of the Lord's Supper to his parishioners in a promiscuous and indiscriminate manner. Complaint was made against him on this account, and he was summoned to appear before the Committee for Plundered Ministers, where he underwent several examinations, and was treated with great harshness. His accusers were caressed, and those friends who appeared with him were brow-beaten and censured. In reference to the charges preferred against him, he says, " I confess, that since my coming to this place, which wants but little of eleven years, I have refused the baptizing of two or three

* Pierce's New Discoverer Discovered, pp. 142-145, Edit. 1659,

children of my parish; but upon grounds, the opening whereof, were it meet to publish them, would, I verily believe, make all complaint against me ashamed. I fear I have made myself, a far greater transgressor by *not* refusing, than by refusing in this kind. Besides, if my intelligence will bear that confidence which I lay upon it, as I think it will, in case such refusals be just matter of offence, the Assembly itself will not in all the Presbyterian members thereof be found innocent."

With regard to his having refused to administer the Lord's Supper to some individuals, he says, "I have done nothing but what hath been done by many godly ministers, in and about the city, as is known to thousands: most of them, if not all, of a different judgment from mine, in the point of church-government; yea, some of them, if my memory deals faithfully with me, of the assembly itself.— I proffered to that honourable committee, that if either themselves or any other would assign me a rule by which I might safely walk in that administration, I would willingly take up again what I had laid down, and accommodate with my parishioners in that ordinance. As for the rule prescribed in the Book of Common Prayer, themselves seemed not satified with it.

"Whereas several ministers in and about the city, of good report and esteem,—nor should I mistake for matter of truth, whatever I may do in point of good manners, if I should say, some very nearly related to the assembly,— have *demanded* and *had* pretty considerable sums, some twenty, thirty, yea, forty pounds a year, of their parishioners, only for their *consent* that the Gospel might be preached to them out of their pulpits, by such minister or lecturer as they should choose: I have been so far from tying my parishioners to this apple tree, that I not only gave my consent freely to them, to choose what minister they pleased, either to preach or deliver the sacrament to them, but offered them forty pounds a year out of mine own allowance, (in case they would continue it to their former proportion, for otherwise I could not be able,) toward making up a valuable consideration to him whom they should choose in such a way."*

Mr. Goodwin's reasonable and liberal proposals made to the committee, were seconded by one of its members, who pleaded, on his behalf, his great zeal and success in promoting the parliamentary interest.† And at the same time forty-five of his parishioners, who were well known to be religious persons, and strongly attached to the parliament, presented a petition in his favour; in which they attested his fidelity in discharging the duties of his office, and earnestly prayed that he might be continued among them as their spiritual pastor. ‡ After repeated examinations before this committee, Mr. Goodwin remained in possession of his vicarage several months, during which he received no official information that his expulsion was intended. When Prynne, therefore, intimated to him in the spirit of malignant triumph, that such an event was contemplated, Mr. Goodwin replied with all the frankness of conscious integrity, " It will not enter into me to conceive a thought so dishonourable to that committee, as that they should suspend or sequester a minister of Jesus Christ, who hath in all things approved himself faithful to them, and to that cause wherein they are engaged, for preaching his judgment and conscience in a point of doctrine, having such substantial grounds, (which I in part accounted to them, and am ready to perfect the account if called to it,) to conceive it none other but the very truth of God." § The "point of doctrine " here referred to by Mr. Goodwin as having been preached by him, and which Prynne stated to be the ground of his meditated expulsion, was, That civil governors have no legitimate authority either from God or man, to use coercion in the affairs of private conscience. "Besides," continues he, "a friend of mine inquiring of some that are members of the Committee, concerning that sequestration Mr. Prynne speaks of, received this answer, 'That they knew no such thing.' I suppose it is not ordinary, that a sentence should pass in a

* Innocency's Triumph.   † Calumny Arraigned, p. 21.   ‡ Innocency's Triumph, p. 15.   § Calumny Arraigned, p. 40.

court of justice against any man, and he not have any knowledge of it for several months together : but if it be so, God's will and Mr. Prynne's wish are fulfilled together." *

While Mr. Goodwin's cause was still pending before the committee, Samuel Lane, a young man who was under considerable obligations to him, made an attack upon his orthodoxy, in a pamphlet which he entitled, "A Vindication of Free Grace." In this publication, which was mightily praised by the Presbyterians, Mr. Goodwin is charged with having repeatedly advanced an "Arminian position" in the course of his ministry in the parish church. The appearance of this production, though insignificant in itself, formed an important era in the life of Mr Goodwin. He wrote a reply to it, which he circulated in manuscript among his friends ; and was thus led into such a train of thought on the Quinquarticular Controversy, as afterwards gave birth to those distinguished defences of Arminianism for which his name has been so deservedly celebrated: Of Lane's book a more particular account will be given in a subsequent part of these memoirs.

In the mean time Mr. Goodwin's incredulity concerning the design of the committee was effectually removed. No means could avail to secure his continuance in his living. He was in the hands of men who deemed it their interest to effect his ruin ; and therefore, though destitute of property, in May, 1645, he was expelled from his vicarage with a wife and seven children dependent upon him. Nor was this the only hardship he was called to endure. A part of the salary due to him for his faithful labours was withheld.† No formal reason was ever assigned by the committee for this sentence : ‡ for many of the boasted champions of liberty in that age, like several of their successors in the present, when invested "with a little brief authority," were consummate tyrants. That Mr. Goodwin had done nothing to merit such a sentence, is

* Calumny Arraigned, p. 6. † Goodwin's Postscript to the Scourge of the Saints Displayed.—Edwards's Gangrœna, Part First, p. 194, Second Edition. ‡ Goodwin's Peace Protected, Preface.

abundantly manifest. No malignancy in regard to the parliament could be proved against him, even by the eager and disingenuous Prynne. And though several tracts were published after his ejectment, for the avowed purpose of destroying his good name, the most watchful and bitter of his enemies could not fix a stain upon his moral character. It is not difficult, however, to account for his sequestration. The Presbyterians had gained the ascendancy in the management of both civil and ecclesiastical affairs, and were loud and incessant in their clamours for the suppression of every other sect. Mr. Goodwin had confuted their favourite notion concerning the imputation of Christ's righteousness, and was understood to have advanced principles favourable to the theological system of Arminius. He had written against their plan of church-government; and, above all, had defended universal liberty of conscience, by arguments which not one of them could refute. He was also a man of deep learning, of ready wit, of invincible courage, of great diligence, and of extraordinary polemical talents; so that to crush such an opponent was a desirable object. Professing the deepest abhorrence of the tenet, "that no faith is to be kept with heretics," Mr. Goodwin's oppressors appear to have thought, that those whom they deemed heretical were not entitled to either justice or mercy.

The conduct of the persons then in power, towards Mr. Goodwin, was the more abominable, as many of the Puritan ministers of that age, having obtained parliamentary patronage, held a plurality of ecclesiastical benefices : a circumstance which they had strongly censured in the Episcopalians, and had represented as a scandalous offence. Speaking of the ASSEMBLY OF DIVINES, Milton says, "The most part of them were such as had preached and cried down, with great show of zeal, the avarice and pluralities of bishops and prelates ; that one cure of souls was a full employment for one spiritual pastor, how able soever, if not a charge rather above human strength. Yet these conscientious men (ere any part of the work done for which they came together, and that on the public salary) wanted not boldness, to the ignominy and scandal of their pastor-like profession, to seize into their hands, or not unwillingly accept, (besides one, sometimes two or more of the best livings,) collegiate masterships in the Universities, rich lectures in the City, setting sail to all winds that might blow gain into their covetous bosoms: by which means these great rebukers of non-residence, among so many distant cures, were not ashamed to be seen so quickly pluralists and non-residents themselves, to a fearful condemnation doubtless by their own mouths."[*]

The same practice appears to have been carried on during the Commonwealth. According to Doctor Pierce, Mr. Hickman, a writer and divine of the Calvinian school, held the fellowship of a college, the vicarage of Brackley, and the parsonage of St. Towles: and Mr. Tombs, the celebrated Baptist, was parson of Ross, vicar of Lempster, preacher of Bewdley, and master of the hospital at Ledbury.[†]

Ordinary men, when treated as Mr. Goodwin then was, lose all control over their passions, and stun the world with the noise of their complaints. But his magnanimity was eminently conspicuous upon this trying occasion. Conscious of the purity of those motives by which his conduct had been governed, he submitted to the sentence which was pronounced against him with the dignified firmness and meekness of a Christian. And though the parliament, unmindful of his services, or rather, desirous of gratifying a party to whom he was obnoxious, permitted their own servants to reduce him to poverty and want; yet he declares, that his attachment to them, and to that cause in which they were engaged, suffered no diminution on this account: a convincing proof that his political conduct was not the result of secular considerations, but proceeded from principle.

In an address to the "Lords and Commons," two years after his expulsion, he says, "It is a memorable saying of an ancient heathen, 'He is the bravest man that best

---

[*] Prose Works, Vol. IV. p. 84. Edit. 1806.   [†] Impartial Inquiry into the Nature of Sin, p. 220, Edit. 1660.

knows how to be injured.' The slightest working of the spirit towards revenge, though upon the sharpest provocation, being discovered, suffereth not a man to be seen in his glory. In the mean time, it is a crown of glory upon the head of men in power, and of divine parallel, to suffer such men to be least injured who best know how to suffer. The anointed ones of God know how to suffer, far above the wisdom or patience of other men; and yet these must not be put to suffer : ' *Touch not Mine anointed, and do My prophets no harm.*'—To me, I speak the truth and lie not, it is more easy to suffer than to complain. I am not conscious of the least wrong I have ever done, either to man, woman, or child ; nor of any refusal of subjection to any just law or imposition of men. If my memory or conscience herein deceive me, I stand forth and humbly offer myself before your honours and all the world, to make satisfaction with the best of my substance or otherwise, as far as I am or ever shall be able.—I reverence the great concernments of the kingdom in your hands, wherein I have served you with all faithfulness and simplicity of heart. The great and blessed God, whose is the kingdom, the power, and the glory, fill your assemblies from day to day with the presence of His glory ; that so the whole nation may rise up before you and call you blessed ; and your name be ' the repairers of the great breach, and the restorers of paths to dwell in,' through many generations." *

While Mr. Goodwin was in possession of his vicarage, as has been already stated, several pious persons residing in different parts of London, formed themselves into a church, and voluntarily placed themselves under his pastoral care, after the manner of the Independents. These people had long esteemed and loved him, as a minister of talents and worth; and his expulsion from his living, together with his behaviour on that occasion, only tended to strengthen their attachment to him, and to enhance their admiration of his virtues. When they saw him driven from his pulpit, they were unwilling either

* Divine Authority of the Scriptures, Dedication.

that their relation to him as their pastor should be dissolved, or that they should be deprived of his ministry: with their approbation and concurrence, therefore, he rented some buildings in Coleman Street, which he converted into a meeting-house, and opened for public worship and evangelical instruction.*

It is worthy of remark, that Mr. Goodwin was not so thorough-paced an Independent, as to divest himself of the ministerial character, for the purpose of receiving it from the people.† Nor had he at any time much intercourse with the great body of the Independents, either when they were few and despised, or after they had gained the ascendancy in the nation under the patronage of Cromwell. "They that have any competent knowledge of my spirit," says he, "and of the course I have steered in the world all the days of my vanity hitherto, will testify on my behalf, that undue compliance with any faction or party hath been none of my visible sins. It is well known, not only to my friends and acquaintance, but to thousands more, how faint a correspondency I have with the faction which dogmatizeth with me about matters of church-government. My interest with these men, though it was never much considerable, yet was it much more whilst they were the tail, and the high Presbyterian faction the head, than it hath been since the turning of the wheel." ‡

Between Mr. Goodwin and his church a union of the closest kind, a union founded upon mutual esteem and love, subsisted, and was expressed on both sides in language highly interesting and impressive. Addressing them as his "Beloved flock, the sons and daughters of God, who first gave up themselves unto the Lord, and then unto us by the will of God," he says, "The days of mine abiding with you in the flesh, neither you nor myself can expect should be many. The law of mortality established in heaven, and daily put in vigorous execution on earth, cutteth off this hope. But the comfort is, the

* Brief Answer, p. 37.   † Reliquiæ Baxterianæ, Appendix, p. 65.
‡ Obstructors of Justice, p. 102.

hole of this pit is not only levelled, but a mount is raised upon it, by the law of life in Christ Jesus our Lord. If our forlorn of ministerial accommodations be scattered and defeated by the hand of death or otherwise, our reserve in heaven will advance and bring us off with honour and peace. The great and precious promises of life and salvation to those who believe, for the making good whereof Jesus Christ Himself, with all His glory, are given in pledge, are not suspended upon the presence of a mortal man, but glory in the truth and power of Him who hath made them, and are ready to swallow up in victory whatsoever shall oppose their performance.

" God is able, without His earthen vessels, to convey His vessels of honour into their blessedness and glory, yet He graciously accepteth the faithful service of His earthen vessels in making one shoulder with Him to carry on His great design. And for you, though I am abundantly confident, at least of many of you, that your anointing is such, that you stand in as little need of any man's teaching as any other people; yet I know that no people whatever will more thankfully accept the labour of any man for their edification or establishment. Upon these considerations, in conjunction with the longing desire of my soul, that your whole spirit and soul and body may be preserved blameless to the coming of our Lord Jesus Christ; I shall endeavour, whilst I remain with you, to prevent, as much as may be, any supposed inexpediency in my departure. This I shall attempt, by seeking to leave as much of my spirit with you as I know how, when my bodily presence shall be disposed of otherwise. In order hereunto, not knowing how near the laying aside of this earthly tabernacle may be, I have thought it meet not only to leave the ensuing treatise* for your perusal, but also to incorporate with it the express mention, and that dear remembrance of you which I have in my soul; that so in one and the same monument the entire spirit of your pastor may be preserved for your converse, and to make company for your minds when you please.

* Divine Authority of the Scriptures.

" You are my present joy, and will be, I hope, my future crown. For neither hath your faith, hitherto, presumed to ascend into heaven, to bring down some other Jesus, besides Him whom Paul preached; nor have you suffered your minds to be corrupted from the simplicity of the Gospel; nor yourselves to be baptized into any other spirit, than that which speaketh ῥητῶς, *expressly* in the Scriptures. You have neither presumed to be wise above, nor been satisfied to be ignorant beneath, what is written. Whilst many professors have compassed themselves with sparks of their own kindling, you have warmed your hearts with faith and love at that fire which Jesus Christ came from heaven to kindle on the earth; and so have kept yourselves out of that sore judgment which the Scripture calls, a delivering up to an injudicious mind.

" I commend you to God, and to the word of His grace, which speaketh in the Scriptures, and which is able (so you pervert it not with mystical interpretations, making it to become your own instead of His,) to build you up, and to give you an inheritance among them that are sanctified; and implore, with all humble and unfeigned ardency of soul, that great Shepherd of the sheep, so to prosper you in the hand of that poor under shepherd, whom he hath set over you, that you may be found in Him at the last great day." *

Such was the language in which this Christian pastor expressed his attachment to his flock, the estimate which he formed of their religious character, and his affectionate solicitude for their spiritual and eternal welfare. Nor were they less ardent in their love to him. " We cannot," say they, " but bless the hand of that Providence, which planted us by the waters of his ministry, the streams whereof refresh our souls with the refreshings of the Almighty. As for his life, we have seen 'HOLINESS UNTO THE LORD' written in fair and convincing characters upon the forehead of it. Verily the signs of a true minister of Christ, and of an elder indeed of His church, hath he wrought among us, in all wisdom, temperance, gravity,

---

* Divine Authority of the Scripture, Dedication.

humbleness, patience, faithfulness, and love. In the presence of angels and men, we call God for a record upon our souls, that we know nothing by him which deserves the lightest censure of a church; all his deportments among us calling for love, reverence, honour, and imitation. And our prayer to God is, that He would, by the influence of his doctrine and example, make us so abundantly fruitful in well-doing; that, as he is our glory and rejoicing for the present, so we may be his glory and the crown of his rejoicing in the day of the Lord Jesus." *

Mr. Goodwin's ejectment from his vicarage was quickly succeeded by the loss of two of his children, who died of an epidemical disease then prevalent in London. About the same period he was also assailed in one of the most scandalous publications that ever disgraced the Christian Church: "GANGRÆNA : or, A Catalogue and Discovery of many of the Errors, Heresies, Blasphemies, and pernicious Practices of the Sectaries of this Time, 1646." The author of this work was THOMAS EDWARDS, who calls himself a "Minister of the Gospel;" but who was apparently as destitute of its spirit as any man that ever lived. He was indeed rather a personification of bigotry, than a human being; and ought, for his own benefit, and for the public good, to have been put into some place of confinement. Before the wars he appears to have officiated as a lecturer at Hertford, and at some places in London and its vicinity; and to have incurred the rebukes of his ecclesiastical superiors by his Puritanical style of preaching, and by offences against the rules and orders of the church. When the parliament declared against the king, he became a zealous advocate for the changes which were then introduced, and supported with all his influence the ruling party. He defended the Presbyterian discipline with equal zeal, when the Independents began to gain ground; and in several tracts expressed himself in language bitter and intemperate almost beyond example.† His avowed design in "Gangræna" was, to cover with odium all classes

* Apologetical Account of some Brethren of the Church whereof Mr. John Goodwin is Pastor.   † Wilson's Dissenting Churches, Vol. II. p. 407.

of Christians who differed from the Calvinistic Presbyterians, and to stimulate the civil power to suppress them. In the prosecution of his purpose, he not only furnished long catalogues of what he calls "errors and heresies;" but ransacked the kingdom for scandal, and published a vast number of idle tales respecting individuals. While he was violating every principle of justice and charity, and bellowing against religious toleration with all the fierceness of a Dominic, he was encouraged by his Presbyterian brethren in almost every part of the land, and weakly imagined that he was doing God service. He therefore gravely requests his readers to unite in prayer for him, that, being favoured with supernatural assistance in his lucubrations, his labours might be rendered extensively beneficial to the cause of Christianity!

In the first part of "Gangræna," the author attacks Mr. Goodwin without ceremony, and without provocation. "If such things," says he, "had befallen some of us, which have to many of the Sectaries, (which I name not to upbraid them with, but to show them their own folly,) as that, by the plague of pestilence, our children, two at a time, had been taken away; as Mr. Goodwin's was upon his making his house a meeting for the Sectaries, &c.; we might have expected as bad books written against us, as were written by the Papists against Luther and Calvin." * He also accuses "Mr. John Goodwin and several of his church," of going "to bowls and other sports, on days of public thanksgiving;"† and is mightily offended, that Mr. Goodwin had called Henry Burton his "brother," and that Burton had neither "made a sermon," nor "writ a book," to "wipe off the aspersion."‡

To a few passages in the first part of this infamous publication Mr. Goodwin wrote a reply, which he entitled, "A brief Answer to an ulcerous Treatise, 1646." In this pamphlet Edwards's mode of supporting Presbyterianism is animadverted upon with just severity; and, in a few instances, his folly is exposed by merited ridicule. "I crave leave," says Mr. Goodwin, "to say, or at least to think,

* Page 70. † Page 73. ‡ Page 160.

that it is a most insufferable presumption, for a poor weak thimble-full of dust, that knows not how to put the nominative case and verb together regularly in English, nor how to frame a period according to the common rules of grammar, to advance himself into a paper throne; and from thence, with confidence enough for an emperor, pronounce the sentence of ' Error and Heresy' against all opinions which will not comport with his fancy as the standard of truth."*

" Touching the providence about my children," continues Mr. Goodwin, " whether I should look upon it as having more of mercy or of judgment I am not satisfied. Though the children were dear to me, and their lives very desirable; yet considering that the best part of that livelihood which I had, was, by a strong hand, taken from me; I could not so much look upon the taking of them away by God, as a taking them away from *me,* as from that *misery,* whereunto the injustice of my Presbyterian neighbours had exposed them. Men took away my means; and God made up the breach in part, by diminishing my charge. Neither were they taken away alone : there was a greater number of children taken away out of a Presbyterian family near to them, where there was no ' meeting-place for Sectaries.' Besides, I could soon be out of Mr. Edwards's debt, by telling him of three grave men, and two of them great, who were principal actors in my ejection, taken away by death, since that transaction. God hath cut off those adversaries : but I leave Mr. Edwards to make reflections; I make none." †

The first part of Edwards's work was speedily followed by a second and a third; and the whole forms a thick quarto volume : the most singular farrago of intolerance and defamation that ever issued from the British press. Never was a half-famished vulture more eager for his prey, than Edwards for the ruin of Goodwin's character. If his own salvation had depended upon this object, he could not have pursued it with greater assiduity and perseverance. Passing by whole pages of unmixed slander,

* Brief Answer, p. 10.　　† Ibid. p. 37.

the following paragraphs will afford a sufficient specimen of his mode of writing :—

"As for Cretensis the Cretian, alias Master Goodwin, he is a man who expresses so much pride, arrogancy, malice, wrath, jeering, and scoffing, not only at me and my books, and some few faithful ministers and servants of God, but against all Presbyterians, assembled or not assembled, in England, Scotland, France, and Ireland, coming forth just like Goliah, railing and defying the armies of the living God, that I have much ado to keep myself from answering him according to his folly, and beating him with his own weapon : *Difficile est satyram non scribere :* and my indignation to see the unworthiness and insolency of the man, much provokes me. But I consider what becomes me, as a minister of the Gospel, to do in such a case, rather than what he hath deserved ; and therefore shall pass by his railings and scoffs, not rendering evil for evil, nor railing for railing, but contrariwise blessing, knowing that I am thereunto called : and instead of railing and vilifying Mr. Goodwin, I will a little expostulate with him. Mr. Goodwin, will you never leave your scoffing and scorning, your reviling and reproaching of all men, stuffing your pages with great swelling words, and filling whole leaves with nothing but jeers and multitude of six-footed words, instead of reasons and arguments ? Will you, by all your writings and preachings, make good that title, which, by way of reproach, was first given to you, namely, The great red Dragon of Coleman Street ? Will you still speak as a dragon, and, dragon-like, fly fiercely in the faces of all ; spitting your poison and venom against all ? casting fire-brands everywhere ?...... For my part, instead of re-proaching and scoffing you, (though not for want of matter, Cretensis being a very fruitful subject for a man to exercise his wit upon,) all I will do, either in this brief, or in my full and large reply, shall be to draw to one head all the errors and strange ways Cretensis holds, and hath walked in ; by which, if God will, he may be ashamed and truly humbled, and his spirit saved in the day of Christ : or, however, that godly weak Christians may know him as a dangerous erroneous man, and avoid him. All I will say now shall be this: That Cretensis hath an heretical wit, and holds many wicked opinions; being an......and a compound of an Arminian, Socinian, Libertine, Anabaptist, &c." *

"The Christian reader may observe Cretensis,.........in all his preachings and ways, to have all the characters and marks of false prophets and false teachers, not only in his hands but upon his forehead; so that, if I would here enlarge, I might clearly show all that Christ and the apostles spake of false prophets, are to be found in Cretensis: but I will only instance in a few, laid down by Peter and Jude in their Epistles ; and upon the propounding of them, I know the reader will say, As face answereth face in glass, so doth Cretensis answer these scriptures...............I do appeal to any man, who knows Cretensis, whether he be not a man that speaks great swelling words of vanity ; whether he doth not promise his followers liberty, yea, a universal liberty ? whether he be not a cloud without water? flourishes and shows without substance ? Whether he be not a raging wave of the sea, foaming out his own shame ? witness his Answer : a wandering star, wandering from one opinion and religion to another ? And lastly, whether he be not a separatist, and sensual person, without the spirit of love, meekness, humility, zeal for God's truth, and of a sound mind ? In one word, I do not think there is any man in the kingdom hath a more heretical head and heart than Cretensis; and unless God give him repentance, and recover him out of those snares of death wherein he walks, I fear, if the man lives but one seven years, he will prove as arch an heretic, and as dangerous a man, as England ever bred ; and that he will be another David George, Francken, Socinus, and be canonized for a saint amongst those of Munster, Racconia, &c."†

" There is Cretensis, alias Master John Goodwin, a monstrous Sectary, a compound of Socinianism, Arminianism, Libertinism, Antinomianism, Independency, Popery, yea and Scepticism ; as holding some opinions proper to each

* Part Second, pp. 30, 31.　　　† Part Second, p. 44.

of these.—As some men discover a natural inclination and a disposition to one evil more than another; some to theft, being given more to stealing; some to lying; so is Master Goodwin to heresy and error: [he] seems made for a heretic.—I have not done with Cretensis: and I have no doubt but that, as I have now, by God's assistance, made a good beginning, both defensive and offensive; so by the same good hand upon me, I shall give so good an account, that I shall deal with this daring enemy as little David with Goliah; stand upon him, and triumph over him, and give you his head upon the top of my sword. I intend to dress him up, and set him out, in all his ornaments and flowers; in his practices and opinions, and ways of promoting them: in all which I shall render him and his name an abhorring to this and the following generations." *

After the most insulting provocation from Edwards, of which only a small sample is here given, Mr. Goodwin says, "I am not conscious of the least ill-will towards the man, but am perfectly free in my spirit to lick the dust of his feet for his good. I had rather meet with an opportunity of showing Christian love and respects to him, than of very good accommodation to myself. Yea, I can willingly seek a favour at his hand, and be beholden to him for my gratification in it. Of the reality of this disposition I think I shall ere long give an account, in desiring him to procure me an IMPRIMATUR for a small treatise, which I have drawn up by way of answer to those aspersives which were lately published by Samuel Lane against me."

Before the publication of his "Gangræna," Edwards had written an inflammatory pamphlet entitled, "Antapologia: or, A Full Answer to the Apologetical Narration, &c., 1644;" the design of which was to disprove the principles of Independency, and to convince the parliament that the men who held them ought not to be tolerated in a Christian country. As this was not only an attack upon Mr. Goodwin and many others, but was intended to expose them to persecution; he drew up a reply, under the title

---

* Part Second, p. 136. Part Third, p. 114.

of, " The Inexcusableness of that grand Accusation of the Brethren called Antapologia, 1646."

With regard to the charges of his persecutor, Mr. Goodwin says, "There is never a stain that Mr. Edwards hath made in my reputation, but will be found a precious gem in that crown of righteousness, which the Lord shall give me in that day. And for those opinions, which he threatens to dress up to my perpetual infamy; the very mention of them as to my disgrace, is to me like the salutation of Mary to Elizabeth. I am very jealous lest many tenets which I hold, should deceive me ; but this jealousy chiefly lies in relation to opinions wherein I accord with Mr. Edwards in the beaten road of unsuspected divinity. But for those wherein I differ from Mr. Edwards, I have bestowed so much labour of soul to satisfy myself in the truth of them, and have received such abundant satisfaction from God for what I hold, that if light be light, reason reason, scripture scripture, I suppose I shall never be unsettled in them though the world should rise up to oppose me. For it hath always been a commanding principle with me, never to dissent openly from the united judgments of sober, pious, and learned men, but upon the most irrefragable demonstrations whereof I am capable. I never declare myself opposite in judgment to any received doctrine, except the reasons that war against it are like armed men, against which no reasonable resistance can be made.—I say to Mr. Edwards, and I say it upon good grounds, that for those very opinions by which he thinks to render me ' an abhorring to the present and future generations,' shall I be had in honour. For when the madness of error shall be made known unto all men, it shall prevail no longer ; and truth only shall be exalted in that day : and those that stood by her and fought her battles, when she had many enemies and few friends, shall partake with her in her triumphs. The breath in my nostrils, I conceive, is as a cloud before the eyes of many, which keeps them for the present from seeing the brightness of those truths which are held in dissent from them. But when God shall have disposed

of this breath otherwise, and scattered the mist of it by
the hand of death, (which yet a little while and it will be
done,) there will be a way opened for a more free intercourse between the truths now contested with, and the
understandings of men.

"Yea, I should forbear to give testimony to the grace and
providence of God, if I should not say, that the regions
already begin to look white towards the harvest; and that
many godly and inquiring men, Presbyterians as well as
others, begin to acknowledge truth in those opinions for
which Mr. Edwards threatens to make me an abhorring
to this and the following generations." *

Edwards completely failed in his endeavour to fix a
stain upon Mr. Goodwin's character; and of course all his
reproaches recoiled upon himself. The sum total of the
charges which he could at all substantiate against the
object of his hatred, was, a predilection for the doctrinal
sentiments of Arminius; the adoption of the Independent
mode of church-government; and avowed hostility to all
coercive interference in the affairs of private conscience.

One cannot contemplate this part of Mr. Goodwin's
history without sympathizing with him under the compli-
cated trials by which he was exercised. Expulsion from
the pulpit which he had long occupied, and around which
thousands had listened to him with deference, respect,
and delight, was immediately succeeded by an afflicting
domestic bereavement; while the press was teeming with
pamphlets, replete with misrepresentation and calumny,
threatening to overwhelm him with reproach. In his
situation, to take away his good name, was to prevent the
success of his ministry, and to expose his children to that
overwhelming calamity—the want of bread. Under the
pressure of these circumstances, no doubt, "some natural
tears were dropt" by him; but, supported by the consola-
tions of religion, and by the testimony of his own conscience, he "wiped them soon," and resumed an equanimity
which was highly exemplary. "I am able," says he,
"through Christ strengthening me, to be abased in name

* Inexcusableness of Antapologia, Preface.

and credit, as well as otherwise. Dishonour, disparagements, defamation, are the element wherein I have lived, and my soul prospered through the goodness of God, these many years. The yoke is little or no offence to me, my neck having been so long accustomed to it. I look upon sufferings for righteousness' sake, (and sufferings from men upon any other terms I fear none,) as the best earnings I can make of mortality. My name is better able to bear the burden of my reproaches, than my soul to want the benefit and blessing of them."*

With Mr. Goodwin it was not unusual, in the course of his ministry, to deliver a series of discourses in defence of some particular doctrine of religion, the truth of which happened to be called in question. He defended at large the Godhead and Personality of the Holy Ghost, and proved the reality of His operations upon the human mind, in opposition to the notions of Socinus, which some of his contemporaries endeavoured to propagate in this country. He also delivered several sermons on the Divine Authority of the Holy Scriptures, which were made a signal blessing to multitudes. This "labour of love" appears to have been performed soon after his ejectment, and was regarded by him as the most useful act of his life. "If I have done any service," says he, 'for the world, since my entrance into it, or if the souls of men have any cause at all to bless me, it is because I have clothed them with confidence of the royal parentage of the Scriptures, and have subdued their fears and jealousies in that kind ; or rather, that I have attempted with all my heart and soul to do them."† The members of his church express themselves to the same effect : "He hath," say they, "engaged more thoughts, spent more hours, preached more sermons for the vindication of the Divine Original of the Scriptures, than any of his profession that we know. And were his labours in this kind transmitted to public view, if we may judge of the fruits of it by what we have found in ourselves, it would bless the world,

* Divine Authority of the Scriptures, p. 30.   † Scourge of the Saints Displayed, Appendix.

and be the establishment of the hearts of thousands in
this great truth."*

The person who succeeded Mr. Goodwin in the vicarage of St. Stephen's, was William Taylor, a minister of
the Presbyterian denomination: a man who was not at
all inclined to moderate counsels. His name is appended
to most of the violent documents published by his
brethren against religious toleration. Some time after
he had obtained possession of Mr. Goodwin's living, he
joined several of his brethren in a public testimony
against him as a heretic, and one that denied the inspiration of the Scriptures: thus adding insult and falsehood
to injury.

* Apologetical Account.

CHAPTER IV.

PROTESTANTS HAVE BEEN PERSECUTORS—GOODWIN'S MANFUL AND HEROIC
DEFENCE OF UNIVERSAL TOLERATION—OPPOSITION RAISED AGAINST HIM—
GENEROUS VINDICATION OF HIM BY THE MEMBERS OF HIS CHURCH.

During the civil troubles which agitated this country,
one of the principal subjects of dispute among ecclesiastical
men was the doctrine of Religious Liberty, or of toleration, as it was then usually designated. "Nothing makes
more stir amongst us at this day," said a theologian of
that age, "than the principle of absolute liberty in matters of religion."* In this contest, so interesting to
every upright and conscientious man, and the results of
which have been so immensely important, Mr. Goodwin
took a very decided part, and was more eminently distinguished than any one of his contemporaries.

Religious liberty is, liberty to choose our own religion,
to worship God according to our conscience, guided by
the best light we have. Every man has a right to this,
because he is a rational creature, whom the Creator has
placed under moral government, and made responsible
for his personal conduct: for nothing can be more clear,
than that every man ought to judge for himself, because
every man must give an account of himself to God. This
is therefore an indefeasible right, and not one of those
which we have even the power to surrender when we enter
into a state of society. This right was clearly implied,
when our Lord said, "Search the Scriptures," and when
an inspired apostle declared, "Every man shall bear his
own burden." What a melancholy reflection therefore it
is, that the civil and ecclesiastical governors of almost every
nation, and in almost every age, should have assumed
authority to rob all under their power of this liberty!†

The flames of Smithfield and of the Inquisition, which

* Burroughs's Heart-Divisions, p. 18, Edit. 1646. † Wesley's Works,
Vol. XV. p. 281, Octavo Edit.

were kindled by Popish bigotry, and consumed so many friends of God and of the Bible, can never be forgotten. Protestants also have stained their hands with blood, in their attempts to realize uniformity in religion. Calvin, who secured the banishment of Bolsec, and endeavoured to ruin the character and take the life of the learned and virtuous Castellio, actually brought Servetus to the stake, and in cool blood published a defence of the horrid act, both in the Latin and French languages. Melancthon, proverbial for his moderation, expressed his approbation of this murderous deed. Luther contended that any punishment, short of death, might be inflicted upon those whom he denominated " obstinate heretics." Cranmer had his victims among the Baptists; and the generous heart of honest Latimer could bear the contemplation of their fate without a sigh. "The Anabaptists," says he, "that were burnt here in many townes in England, (as I heard of credible men, I sawe them not myselfe,) went to their death even intrepide, as ye will say, without any fear in the world, cheerfully. Well, let them go."* During the reign of Queen Elizabeth, British subjects were condemned to die at Tyburn, and to suffer in various other ways, because they presumed, contrary to her royal pleasure and the counsel of her advisers, to follow the convictions of their own consciences in the worship of Almighty God.

James the First twice rekindled the fires for the suppression of reputed heresy, and, in effect, left it in charge to his son and successor to persecute the Puritans. "Take heede therefore, (my Sonne,)" says he, " to such Puritanes, verie pestes in the church and common-weale, whom no deserts can oblige, neither oathes or promises binde; breathing nothing but sedition and calumnies; aspersing without measure, railing without reason, and making their own imaginations, (without any warrant from the word,) the square of their conscience. I protest before the great God, and since I am here as upon my Testament, it is no place for me to lie in, that ye shall

* Sermons, fol. 56, Edit. 1570.

never finde with any Hie land or Boarder thieves greater
ingratitude, and moe lies and vile periuries, then with
these phanaticke spirits: and suffer not the principals of
them to brooke your land, if ye like to sit at rest; except
ye would keepe them for trying your patience, as Socrates
did an euil wife." *

Entering into the spirit of this charge, Charles the
First sanctioned the arbitrary and cruel proceedings of
Laud and his associates, in the Star-Chamber and High
Commission Court, till the nation was convulsed to its
centre, and many thousand families left the kingdom for
ever. In consequence of these measures, the unhappy
primate was brought to the scaffold, and the Episcopal
Church of England, which had been reared by the labours,
and cemented by the tears and blood of the Reformers,
and which had long stood as a barrier against Popery,
and an asylum of learned men, was delivered into
the hands of implacable enemies, who exulted in its
demolition.

The Presbyterians, who had long groaned under the
rod of oppression, and sighed for power, had the high
gratification at length of seeing their system of ecclesiastical polity receive parliamentary sanction, and adopted
as the national establishment. But instead of "remembering the wormwood and the gall," which they and their
forefathers had been made to drink, and of treating with
lenity their brethren who differed from them in religious
opinion, they rivalled the greatest tyrants in systematic
opposition to the rights of conscience. Had not these
sons of intolerance been restrained from the execution of
their purpose by the army, they would unquestionably
have left their names written in characters of blood. They
contended for the *divine right* of Presbyterianism, and
protested, in the genuine spirit of fanaticism, against the
toleration of " sectaries." The inflammatory prayers,
sermons, and tracts of their clergy, not unfrequently
excited popular tumults in London, and stimulated their
admirers to assemble in mobs, and annoy other congrega-

* Works of the Most High and Mighty Prince James, p. 160, Edit. 1616.

tions of Christians by showers of stones.*   They imagined that the sacred truths of revelation would soon become extinct, unless guarded by penal statutes; and that the ministers of Christ, even with the inspired volume in their hands, could do little in the defence and propagation of Christianity, unless, in the enforcement of their arguments, they could command the services of constables, and justices of the peace.   Their determined opposition to that liberty of conscience which others claimed, after their own example, proves them unworthy of the deference paid to them by the Long Parliament, and has left an indelible stain upon their memory.   It would be easy to produce some hundreds of extracts from their printed works, in which they not only avow the principles, but also display the spirit, of persecution.   In this place, however, a few must suffice.

" The magistrates should remember," says Dr. Bastwick, " that they are called pastors : now no godly and faithful pastors will suffer wolves to come into their folds, and worry and destroy their sheep.   How diligent ought they likewise to be, to keep out these ravenous wolves, though they come in sheep's clothing, out of their several pastures, that would destroy the souls of all their sheep ?   All these things, I say, all magistrates should lay to heart and duly consider ; for their place it is, to whom God hath committed the SWORD, and who ought to watch over the people for good, and whose neglecting of their duty will be laid to their charge, and who are to answer for it before God, if, through their connivance or negligence, any evil happen to the people.   But if they should wilfully suffer the corruption of the true religion, and allow of a Toleration of all religions, how would this provoke the Lord to anger against the nation? "†

In defence of these principles the notorious Prynne wrote several books, one of which is entitled, " The Sword of Christian Magistracy Supported : or, A Full Vindication of Christian Kings' and Magistrates' Authority under the

* Bates's Elenchus Motuum Nuperorum in Anglia, p. 58, Edit. 1685.
† Utter Routing of the Independents and Sectaries, p. 506, Edit. 1646.

Gospel, to punish Idolatry, Apostasy, Heresy, Blasphemy, and obstinate Schism, with Corporeal, and, in some Cases, with CAPITAL PUNISHMENTS, 1647." In this work, which was dedicated to the House of Commons, and intended to stimulate them to shed blood in favour of Presbyterianism, the author produces arguments, authorities, custom, decisions of doctors, confessions of faith, &c., to prove that the "sword" should be employed in the suppression of mental error; by which was meant any doctrine contrary to Prynne's own Presbyterian and Calvinistic opinions. This work was so highly esteemed by the author's own party, that scarcely had it been in circulation two years, before it was translated into Latin by Wolfgang Meyer, a Protestant Minister of Switzerland, and published in that language for the general benefit of the Christian world. And when Lewis the Fourteenth, having repealed the Edict of Nantz, was banishing and murdering his Protestant subjects with the malignity of a fiend, in answer to their complaints, Father De Sainte Marthe contended that such proceedings were perfectly *orthodox;* and, in proof of this, appealed to the "Vindication" of Prynne, which had been received with approbation by the Presbyterians themselves, both in England and on the continent of Europe.*

Samuel Rutherford, professor of divinity in the university of St. Andrews, published "A Free Disputation against pretended Liberty of Conscience," in the year 1649; of which the following accurate account is given by Bishop Heber: "Rutherford's work is perhaps the most elaborate defence of persecution which has ever appeared in a Protestant country. He justifies it from the law of nature, the Mosaic law, the analogy of the Christian religion, the practice of the patriarchs and godly princes of old time; the prophecies which foretel that the kings which have sometimes served the Babylonian harlot shall, on their repentance, burn her with fire and eat her flesh; and the commandment of St. John, that a true believer is not to say God speed to a false teacher. They who condemn the burning of Servetus would have con-

* General Dictionary, Article Prynne.

demned, he tells us, on the same principles, the slaughter
of the priests of Baal ; and though he seems, in one place,
to have some compunctious doubts as to the propriety of
fire as the instrument of conversion, and, on the whole, to
give the preference to hanging, yet he elsewhere urges
that, as stoning was the punishment of idolatry under the
Mosaic law, and as the despisers of the Gospel are, unquestionably, worthy of a much sorer punishment,—so it
may be thought that burning hath something in it mar-
vellously suited to the occasion, and to the necessities of
Christendom. To invade a foreign nation of idolaters
with a view to apply such instruments and means of grace,
he, indeed, confesses to be of doubtful morality ; but it
may be, he says, a most interesting and curious question,
whether, such a conquest having been effected on other
grounds, it is not the duty of the believing conqueror to
force away the children of his new subjects, to the end
that they may be brought up in the true religion." *

The author of this very remarkable volume may be
justly considered as a type of the Presbyterian sect, to
which he belonged.   He was a scholar, and a man of unquestionable piety, but of narrow views ; and could he have
had his own way, he would have slain Christian men for
denying the truth of Calvin's doctrine of election and
reprobation, and for refusing to submit to the Presbyterian form of church government. He cherished as deep
a conviction of the divine right of Presbyterianism as
Laud did of Episcopacy ; and his spirit was not a whit
more tolerant than was the spirit of that rash and unfortunate prelate.   The advocates of religious liberty
against whom his book was specially directed were the
Dutch Arminians, John Goodwin, and Jeremy Taylor.
Goodwin he denominates, " This learned and sharp-witted
divine." †

Thomas Edwards published a treatise expressly against
religious toleration. It is entitled, " The Casting Down
of the Last and Strongest Hold of Satan ; or, a Treatise
against Toleration, and Pretended Liberty of Conscience.

* Heber's Life of Bishop Taylor, p. 318, Edit. 1822.   † Page 64.

By Thomas Edwards, 1647." It is a quarto tract of two hundred and eighteen pages. The following extract from another of his books explains his views on this subject with sufficient clearness : " A toleration is the grand design of the devil, his master-piece, and chief engine he works by at this time to uphold his tottering kingdom. It is the most compendious, ready, and sure way to destroy all religion, lay all waste, and bring in all evils : it is a most transcendent, catholic, and fundamental evil for this kingdom, of any that can be imagined. As original sin is the most fundamental sin of all sin, having the seed and spawn of all sin in it; so a toleration hath all errors in it, and all evils : it is against the whole stream and current of Scripture, both in the Old and New Testament, both in matters of faith and manners, both general and particular commands : it overthrows all relations, both political, ec- clesiastical, and economical. And whereas other evils, whether errors of judgment or practice, be but against some one or few places of Scripture or relation, this is against all : this is the Abaddon, Apollyon, the Destroyer of all religion, the Abomination of Desolation and Asto- nishment, the Liberty of Perdition; and therefore the devil follows it night and day; working mightily in many by writing books for it, and other ways : all the devils in hell, and their instruments, being at work to promote a toleration."*

The Commissioners of the Kingdom of Scotland, who were deputed to give advice on ecclesiastical subjects to the British parliament, were equally hostile to religious liberty. " We do," say they, " from our very souls, abhor such a general toleration. And if the houses (which God forbid !) shall adhere thereunto, and insist that it may be established, we do protest against it; as that which is expressly contrary to the Word of God, utterly repugnant to the Solemn League and Covenant, destructive to reformation and uniformity in religion, altogether incon- sistent with the declarations and professions of the houses, against the treaty between the kingdoms, directly opposite

* Gangræna, Part First, p. 153.

I

to the example and practice of the best Reformed Churches,
and as that which will unavoidably subvert all order and
government, and introduce a world of confusion. Our
minds are astonied and our bowels are moved within us,
when we think of the bitter fruits and sad consequences
of such a toleration."*

Sentiments similar to these were avowed by the whole
body of the Presbyterian clergy residing in the metropolis,
in a tract entitled, "A Letter of the Ministers of the City
of London, presented, the first of January, 1645, to the
Reverend Assembly of Divines sitting at Westminster by
Authority of Parliament, against Toleration." After assigning a considerable number of what they call reasons,
to prove that "the desires and endeavours of Independents
for a toleration" were "extremely unseasonable and pre-
posterous;" they add, "These are some of the many considerations which make deep impression upon our spirits,
against that great Diana of Independents and all sectaries,
so much cried up by them in these distracted times, viz.,
A Toleration! a Toleration!—We detest and abhor the
much-endeavoured toleration. Our bowels, our bowels are
stirred within us, and we could even drown ourselves in
tears, when we call to mind how long and sharp a travail
this kingdom hath been in for many years together, to
bring forth that blessed fruit of a pure and perfect
Reformation; and now at last, after all our pangs and
dolors and expectations, this real and thorough Reformation is in danger of being strangled in the birth by a lawless toleration, that strives to be brought forth before it."†

Nor were the generality of the Assembly of Divines at
Westminster, who were convened at the public expense as
the counsellors of the parliament on subjects relating to
the church and religion, less intolerant in their principles
and spirit. "The main doctrine," says Milton, "for which
they took their pay, and insisted upon with more vehemence
than Gospel, was but to tell us in effect, that their doctrine

* Answer of the Commissioners of the Kingdom of Scotland, to both
Houses of Parliament, upon the new Propositions for Peace, p. 17. London,
1647.   † Page 6.

was worth nothing, and the spiritual power of their ministry less available than bodily compulsion; persuading the magistrate to use it, as a stronger means to bring in conscience, than evangelical persuasion: distrusting the virtue of their own spiritual weapons, which were given them, if they be rightly called, with full warrant of sufficiency to pull down all thoughts and imaginations that exalt themselves against God. They taught compulsion without conviction, which not long before they complained of as executed unchristianly against themselves. They endeavoured to set up a spiritual tyranny by a secular power, for the purpose of advancing their own authority above the magistrate, whom they would have made their executioner to punish church-delinquencies."*

The following indignant lines, from the same pen, were addressed to these "new forcers of conscience under the Long Parliament:"

> " Because you have thrown off your Prelate Lord,
>   And with stiff vows renounc'd his Liturgy,
>   To seize the widow'd whore Plurality
>   From those whose sin ye envied, not abhorr'd,
> Dare ye for this adjure the civil sword
>   To force our consciences that Christ set free,
>   And ride us with a classic hierarchy .
>   Taught ye by mere A.S. and Rutherford?
>
> Men whose life, learning, faith and pure intent
>   Would have been held in high esteem with Paul,
>   Must now be nam'd and printed Heretics
> By shallow Edwards and Scotch what d'ye call;
>   But we do hope to find out all your tricks,
>   Your plots and packing worse than those of Trent,
>   That so the Parliament
>   May with their wholesome and preventive shears
>   Clip your phylacteries, tho' bauk your ears,
>   And succour our just fears,
>   When they shall read this clearly in your charge,
>   New PRESBYTER is but OLD PRIEST writ large."

The hope here expressed, that the parliament would discover the real character of the Presbyterians, and withstand their exorbitant claims, was never realized. This renowned parliament, while professing to execrate the

* Prose Works, Vol. IV. p. 84, Edit. 1806.

persecuting spirit of the prelates, whose property they had seized, in their ordinance for putting the directory in execution, not only prohibited the use of the Book of Common Prayer in all places of public worship; but also subjected those who should use it in their families or in secret, to the penalty of five pounds for the first offence, of ten pounds for the second, and, for the third, to one whole year's imprisonment, without bail or mainprize.* This parliament also issued an ordinance for "Punishing Blasphemies and Heresies;" in which it is determined that the "maintaining and publishing" of certain specified opinions, such as Deism, Socinianism, &c., shall be "adjudged felony;" and in case the delinquent should refuse to abjure his errors, he was to "suffer the pains of death, without benefit of clergy."   In regard to errors of a less atrocious character, such as, "that man by nature hath free will to turn to God,—that the soul of man sleepeth when the body is dead, that the baptizing of infants is unlawful, &c.," the ordinance requires the reputed heretic to recant his sentiments before a public congregation; and in case of refusal, directs that he shall be committed to prison, and remain there till he can produce two sufficient sureties, that he will not divulge his error more.†

On this subject it would be easy to enlarge: but enough has been said to display the intolerance of the Puritanical Presbyterians, after they had subverted the Episcopal Church, and were attempting to establish their own upon its ruins.

If the men who expose themselves in the field, and succeed in guarding their country against invasion, are entitled to public gratitude: if those who have taught mankind the arts of agriculture and of commerce, are regarded as the benefactors of their species: then are those persons entitled to high and general esteem who, disregarding the clamours of aspiring ecclesiastics, and rising above the fears of weak though good men, first brought the doctrine of religious liberty fairly before the world, and established it upon scriptural and rational principles. The honour of

* Scobell's Collection, Part First, p. 97, Edit. 1658.   † Ibid., p. 149.

having done this, has been challenged on behalf of three distinct classes of religious people : the Baptists,* the Dutch Arminians,† and the English Independents. ‡ The claim of the Dutch Arminians appears to be the best founded; but the Independents have been the most loud and urgent in demanding their meed of praise for their services in this cause. The erection of a " statue of gold " to their memory, it has been suggested, would be but an imperfect payment of the debt which is due to them from this country.§ Among their eminent men who have distinguished themselves by writing in its defence, the preference has usually been given to Dr. Owen ; of whom it has been said, that he was "one of the first of our countrymen who entertained just and liberal notions of the right of private judgment and of toleration ; which he was honest enough to maintain in his writings, when the times were the least encouraging ; for he not only published two Pleas for Indulgence and Toleration in 1677, when the Dissenters were suffering persecution under Charles II.; but took the same side much earlier, pleading very cogently against intolerance, in an essay for the practice of Church-government, and a Discourse on Toleration, both of which are printed in the Collection of his Sermons and Tracts ; and clearly appear to have been written, and probably were first published, about the beginning of 1647, when the parliament had arrived at full power and he was in much repute."‖

The late Rev. David Simpson has also observed, when speaking of religious toleration : " Dr. Owen was the first I am acquainted with, who wrote in favour of it in the year 1648 ; Milton followed him about the year 1658, in his Treatise of the Civil Power in Ecclesiastical Causes. And the immortal Locke followed them both with his golden Treatise on Toleration in 1689."¶

* Ivimey's Hist. of the Baptists, p. 6, Edit. 1811. † Tucker's Letters to Kippis, p. 32, Edit. 1773. ‡ Bogue and Bennett's Hist. of the Dissenters, Vol. I. p.138, Edit. 1808. § Ibid. ‖ Palmer's Nonconformists' Memorial, Vol. I. p. 204. ¶ Plea for Religion, p. 202, Edit. 1815.

With all deference, however, to the admirers of Dr. Owen, we presume that his merits as a friend and advocate of religious liberty· have been greatly over-rated. It does not appear that he renounced the narrow and intolerant views of the Presbyterians on this subject, till about the year 1645 ;* and for a considerable time after that period, his principles, compared with those which had been avowed by many of his contemporaries, were not at all remarkable for liberality and catholicism. While he held the Vice-Chancellorship of the University of Oxford, he was concerned in condemning two Quaker women to be publicly whipped for addressing a congregation in one of the churches, after the celebration of Divine service; notwithstanding they had been already treated with more than brutal violence by some of the students, in consequence of which one of them died soon afterwards.† The conduct of these females, however, may be considered as a civil offence; they certainly had no right to occupy the church for any such purpose, and they may have cast unwarrantable reflections upon the officiating minister; a case which was not uncommon in those times. Yet, considering their sex, their conscientious motives, and the treatment they had just received, it would have required no very singular stretch of forbearance in the Doctor, to have been satisfied with the infliction of a punishment less severe; especially as the mayor absolutely refused to interfere, expressing his conviction that the women, though mistaken, were sincerely religious, and had no evil intention. Besides, the execution of such a sentence was illegal, when unsanctioned by the chief magistrate of the city. But waiving this circumstance, the Doctor did not publish any thing *expressly* on the subject of toleration till the latter end of the year 1648, when the army had dispersed the parliament, and put the king to death; and when every man was at liberty to write what he pleased against religious persecution with perfect impunity. But even then, speaking of what he conceived to be the duty of the civil magistrate, he says, "Outward

*Orme's Memoirs of Dr. Owen, p. 51, Edit. 1820.   † Gough's History of the Quakers, Vol. I. p. 147, Edit. 1789.

monument s, ways of declaring and holding out false and idolatrous worship, he is to remove : as the Papists' images, altars, pictures, and the like ;....... Prelates' Service Book : "* that is, the Book of Common Prayer. In another publication, which bears the date of 1655, though he expresses his disapprobation of capital punishments in cases of heresy, he intimates that the burning of Servetus was an exception, and coolly thinks that "*the* ZEALE *of them that put him to death may be* ACQUITTED."† Now if Dr. Owen's views of religious freedom were so liberal and correct as his friends have represented them, how is it that he should have expressed himself in language so highly objectionable? If liberty of conscience is one of the most sacred rights of human nature, it is a universal right. A Protestant magistrate therefore can have no legitimate authority to interfere with the peculiarities of Papal worship, any more than a Romanist has to interfere with those of a Protestant. And on what ground could Dr. Owen justify an Independent or a Presbyterian magistrate in wresting from an Episcopalian the Book of Common Prayer, which would not equally justify an Episcopalian in the prohibition of extemporaneous worship? If the unhallowed "zeal" of those men who burnt Servetus alive may be "acquitted," upon what principle shall the "zeal" of Gardiner and Bonner be condemned ? The sentiments of Servetus could not be more revolting to Calvin, than those of a Protestant are to a zealous member of the Church of Rome. These remarks are not introduced for the purpose of detraction, but to illustrate a matter of fact : and surely historic truth ought not to be either violated or suppressed, to raise the honour of any man, whatever may be the elevation of his rank or the splendour of his talents. To Dr. Owen the Christian Church is under some obligation for his writings on the subject of religious liberty, but he certainly was not " one of the first of our countrymen who entertained just and liberal notions of the right of private judgment and of toleration ; " much less can he be ranked

* Collection of Sermons, p. 309, Edit. 1721. † Vindiciæ Evangelicæ, Preface, p. 44, Edit. 1655.

among the first of those by whom they were openly avowed and consistently defended. What would be thought in the present age, if the principles of Dr. Owen were reduced to practice? If the officers of the civil power were to enter every Roman Catholic place of worship for the purpose of destroying all the images, altars, and pictures? and to remove by violence the Book of Common Prayer out of every Protestant church and chapel in the land? Would the projector of such measures be entitled to the highest eulogies for the liberality of his spirit, and for enlightened views concerning " the right of private judgment?" Suppose the mob of Birmingham, who burnt the house of Dr. Priestley, to have burned him alive; had they been charged with murder at the ensuing assizes, would they have been entitled to a sentence of " acquittal " from an English jury, because the Doctor held the opinions of the man who suffered at Geneva?

The doctrine of religious liberty became a subject of public discussion early in 1644, and several very able tracts in its defence issued from the British press, during that and the three succeeding years. In this important contest Mr. Goodwin appeared in the front rank, and had this merit, —that, while most of his co-adjutors, as if ashamed of their cause or afraid of consequences, concealed their names and fought under a mask, he was so impressed with the truth and importance of his principles, as to risk his reputation, his property, and his life for their advancement: he therefore fairly and openly met his antagonists on the great question then at issue. An ecclesiastical establishment which furnishes the people with the pure Scriptures in the vernacular tongue; which supplies them with every requisite help in the exercise of public worship; which makes provision for the evangelical instruction of all classes of society, and at the same time allows a liberal toleration of such as prefer a different mode of worship and of church-government, does not appear liable to any serious objection, and is unquestionably a blessing to any nation. To such an establishment Mr. Goodwin manifested no hostility; but he justly thought that a system of ecclesiastical polity, especially one of doubtful origin, enforced by the civil magistrate, and unaccompanied by toleration, was an enormous and insupportable tyranny. This was the high claim of the Presbyterian party : he therefore employed all his energies in demonstrating its impolicy and injustice. Liberty of conscience, he contended, is a natural right, both antecedent and superior to all human laws and institutions whatever : a right which laws never gave, and which laws can never take away. His tracts and sermons on this subject, more than those of any other man, annoyed his intolerant contemporaries of the Presbyterian denomination, and, like the touch of Ithuriel's spear, led to a complete discovery of their real character. Most of his brethren, the Independents, pleaded for a toleration on behalf of all who held what they called " the fundamental doctrines of Christianity ; " whereas he maintained that all coercion in matters purely religious, doctrinal, as well as ecclesiastical, was antichristian ; and that to attempt to frighten men into orthodoxy by fines, prisons, or the gallows, was but to make them hypocrites, and expose them to deeper misery for ever. Hence, many of those who hated both him and his doctrine, with a perversity of mind that cannot be too strongly condemned, represented him as the great patron of error in all its diversified forms ; and declared that he especially ought to feel the weight of the secular arm : as if a man were an enemy to truth, because he protests against the use of unlawful means for its support. "If good Nehemiah were now living," says Dr. Bastwick, " and should hear not only the language of Ashdod,......but see the abominable practices of the sectaries of our times,.........how would he bestir himself in cudgelling these fellows into the true religion ? Without all controversy, good Nehemiah would baste them to the purpose, and all such as should side with them; and especially he would belabour all such well, as should write books in defence of such.......I say I am most confident, were good Nehemiah in our times, and had he the authority he had in Jerusalem, he would baste them all to some purpose ; and make and force them, by cudgelling of them,

to be conformable to wholesome words. And I am most
assured, he would pluck off Cretensis's blue beard, and
knock him soundly about his hairy scalp."*   Cretensis was
a nick-name given to John Goodwin by the advocates of
religious coercion. It appears to have been understood in
the sense of " the liar."

In his reply to Dr. Adam Stewart, a second edition of
which was published in the year 1644, Mr. Goodwin explains his sentiments concerning religious liberty, and
argues in their defence in a manner worthy of his talents
and learning. "The grand pillar of this coercive power,
in magistrates," says he, " is this angry argument : ' What,
would you have all religions, sects, and schisms, tolerated
in Christian Churches ?   Should Jews, Turks, and Papists
be suffered in their religions, what confusion must this
needs breed both in Church and State !'   I answer,

"If, by a toleration, the argument means either an approbation, or such a connivance which takes no knowledge
of, or no ways opposeth such religions, sects, or schisms as
are unwarrantable, they are not to be tolerated : but orthodox and able ministers ought, in a grave, sober, and inoffensive manner, soundly from the Scriptures to evince
the folly, vanity, and falsehood of all such ways.   Others
also, that have an anointing of light and knowledge from
God, are bound to contribute occasionally the best of their
endeavours towards the same end.   In case the minister
be negligent, or forgetful of his duty, the magistrate may
and ought to admonish him that he fulfil his ministry.
If a person, one or more, being members of a particular
church, be infected with any heretical or dangerous
opinion, and after two or three admonitions, with means
of conviction used to regain him, shall continue obstinate,
he ought to be cast out from amongst them by that church.
If it be a whole church that is so corrupted, the neighbour-
churches, in case it hath any, ought to admonish it, and to
endeavour the reclaiming of it.   If it be refractory, after
competent admonition, and means used for the reducing
of it, they may and ought to renounce communion with it,

* Utter Routing, p. 599.

and so set a mark or brand of heresy upon the forehead of it.

"If by a toleration the argument means, A non-suppression of such religions, sects, and schisms, by fining, imprisoning, disfranchising, banishment, death, or the like, my answer is, THAT THEY OUGHT TO BE TOLERATED: *only upon this supposition,* THAT THE PROFESSORS OF THEM BE OTHERWISE PEACEABLE IN THE STATE, AND EVERY WAY SUBJECT TO THE LAWS AND LAWFUL POWER OF THE MAGISTRATE." * In proof of this position our author proceeds to urge ten powerful and unanswerable arguments.

From this extract it will be seen, that Mr. Goodwin does not contend for the absolute innocence of mental error, as some latitudinarian theologians have done. He was aware that some religious errors take their origin from human depravity, and, so far as their influence extends, are injurious to the spiritual interests of men ; and that a denial of the distinguishing truths of the Christian Revelation, amidst ample means of instruction, involves a high degree of criminality in the sight of God, and therefore ought to be visited by marked animadversion. The obstinate abettors of dangerous opinions, however, he would not deliver up to the vengeance of the civil power, but would subject them to the more appropriate punishment of ecclesiastical censure. Solemn exclusion from a Christian Church on account of heretical pravity, he considered to be much better adapted to secure the religious and moral improvement of the individual concerned, and to operate as a salutary warning to others, than civil pains and penalties ; and, in cases of this nature, the only punitive infliction warranted by the New Testament Scriptures. "God's design," says he, "as well as ours, is Unity amongst the saints in matters of faith and knowledge. But by what means hath He projected the obtaining of this desire? Mark, he doth not say, that He gave some kings, and some princes, and some judges, and justices of the peace, some pursuivants, and some jailors, to bring men into the unity of the faith; but 'He gave some Apostles, and some

* Reply of two of the Brethren to A. S. p. 55.

Prophets, and some Evangelists, and some Pastors and
Teachers,' to bring this desirable end to pass.   And if we
would make more use of these *instruments of God*, of
Apostles, Prophets, Evangelists, Pastors, and Teachers,
and less of those other, which are our own, for quenching
those divisions that are amongst us; we might, in all
likelihood, see our desires in this, many years sooner than
by any other course we are like to do.   The word of God,
especially in the hand of an able minister, is given for the
conviction and stopping of the mouths of gainsayers; and
therefore will do it, when a thousand other means, not
having this anointing oil upon them, though never so
promising in the eye of human wisdom, will rather open
them wider.

"External compulsion in matters of religion is of a
direct tendency to make men two-fold more the children
of sin and wrath than they were before, or would be otherwise.   Suppose the state-religion, and manner of worship-
ping God the magistrate professeth, be agreeable to the
truth; yet if I, having no such faith of either, but judging
in my conscience, that both state and magistrate are
polluted in both, should make profession of either, I should
be a notorious hypocrite and dissembler before God,
wounding my conscience, and condemning myself in what
I allow.   And yet such a profession as this, is that which
the compulsive power of the magistrate seeks to extort
from me.   In which case I must suffer because I will not
sin to the ruin of my soul.

"If the civil magistrate hath an actual coercive power
to suppress heresies, &c., because he is truly Christian,
which he had not before, then Christianity alters the
property and tenor of magistracy, and that for the worse,
in respect of those that are in subjection to it; yea, and
possibly in respect of the best of those that are in such
subjection.   Before he was truly Christian, he had, say
the Presbyterians generally, no power to punish, fine,
imprison, banish any of his subjects for the exercise of
their conscience towards God: but by virtue of that great
mercy vouchsafed to him by God, in giving him fellowship

with the saints in Jesus Christ, he is invested with a new power to persecute the saints, to make them pay dearly for having consciences, it may be, better than his own ; at least better than to comply outwardly with what they cannot inwardly digest and approve. If this be the case between a Christian and the civil magistrate, under whom he lives, he hath small encouragement to pray for the conversion of such a magistrate to the truth, in case he were heterodox or Pagan : it being far better for him to live under such a magistracy, which hath no power to misuse him for his conscience-sake, than under that which hath, and is made to believe that it ought to use it accordingly.

" That power which was never attributed to the civil magistrate, by any Christians, but those that had good assurance that it should be used on their side, is not likely to be a power by divine right, or conferred by God· It is no ways credible, that within the compass of so many ages, no man of that conscientious generation of saints, which hath been wont to deny itself even unto death, should acknowledge such a power in the civil magistrate, as did by divine right belong to him, only because such an acknowledgment was likely to make against himself. That coercive power in matters of religion, for suppressing errors, heresies, &c., was never attributed to the civil magistrate by any Christian, but only by those that were very confident, that it would be used for their turns, and to effect their desires. A[dam] S[tewart] himself is wary and tender above measure, in conferring it upon him ; distinguishing once, and again, and a third time also upon it, before he dares let him have it ; and in the close doth as much as tell him, that except he be Presbyterian right down, and will accommodate him and his party with it, he ought not to claim it.

" That power which, in the exercise of it, directly tends to hinder or suppress the increase of the knowledge of God and Jesus Christ, in a church or state, and the reformation of such things in doctrine or discipline as are unwarrantable therein, is not questionless of any divine right

or institution. Such a power in the civil magistrate as
we speak of, directly tends to all the mischief and inconvenience mentioned. When men are obnoxious to the
stroke of the civil power, for any thing they hold or
practise in religion contrary to him, it must needs be a
great discouragement upon them from searching and
inquiring into the Scriptures, after a more exact knowledge of the good and holy and perfect will of God.
Because, in case he should discover any thing contrary to
what the magistrate professeth, he must run the hazard,
either of withholding the truth in unrighteousness, and so of
having God and his own conscience his enemy, or of having
his bones broken by the iron rod of the civil magistrate,
for making profession of any thing contrary to that which
he professeth.

"That power which directly tends to defile the consciences of men, by destroying the tenderness of them, or
by disturbing the lawful peace and comfort of them, is a
power from beneath, not from above. Such is the coercive
power in matters of religion, wherewith A[dam]
S[tewart] would fain befriend himself in the civil magistrate. When the conscience of a man hath once broken
the bands of its own light, and prostituted itself to the
pleasures of men, against its own judgment and inclination, (whereunto it is sorely tempted and urged, when the
man is threatened deep, in case he shall not comply with
the state in religion, his judgment and conscience being
wholly averse to it,) one of these two great evils commonly
befalls him : Either God takes no more pleasure in such
a conscience, but, withdrawing Himself, leaves it unto
itself; whereupon secretly, as it were, resenting the
departure of God, it falls upon a course of hardening
itself, and contracts a boldness and desperateness in sinning : Or, by reflecting upon what it hath done, and
feeding night and day upon the sad thoughts of its own
act, and casting it up between God and itself, how
grievous a sin it is, to trample upon its own light,
for any man's sake; it brings itself into grievous

agonies of perplexity and horror, out of which it never recovers."*

Mr. Goodwin resumed the same subject in his sermons on "Fighting against God," which he published within the same year; and further illustrated and confirmed his opinions in two of his tracts in answer to Prynne. In defence of the same correct and liberal principles he also made an appeal to the good sense of the nation, in an admirable pamphlet which he entitled, "Twelve serious Cautions, very necessary to be observed in a Reformation according to the Word of God, 1646." To make arrangements for such a Reformation in the national church, was the professed design of the parliament in calling the Assembly of Divines at Westminster. The result of their grave and long-continued deliberations was, that the parliament should establish Presbyterian uniformity, by the suppression of every other sect. In pointing out the inconsistency of such a project with the Word of God our author, in the tract before us, has given a happy delineation of what ought to be the character of every church which is patronized by the state. "That reformation," says he, "which is froward, peremptory, imperious; will gather where it hath not strewed, and reap where it hath not sown; exact obedience and subjection from those whom it hath not effectually taught or persuaded; nor give any tolerable account to conscientious and disinterested men, why it should be submitted unto; but rather obstruct its access to the judgments and consciences of such men, by advancing itself by practices that savour more of the subtlety of the serpent than the simplicity of Christ:—A reformation which commends itself to the world upon no better terms than these, cannot be judged a reformation according to the Word of God, by any, except those who either suppose gain to be godliness, or the resolutions of a synod the Word of God."‡

"Reformers who say unto men excellently gifted and inclined by God, and ardently desired of men, for the work of the ministry, 'Preach not in that name, except

* Reply to A. S. pp. 56–63, Edit. 1644.

you will preach in our name also, except you will acknowledge in us a power to give you leave to preach, and a
power to restrain you, and be willing to receive neither
you nor we can tell what, by our imposition of hands : '—
Reformers that model their reformation upon such terms,
that either the souls of thousands must starve, or the
consciences of those that should feed them be brought into
a snare ; well may they reform by some other rule, but their
ACCORDING TO THE WORD OF GOD they leave for others."

"The Apostle Paul, by commission from heaven, saith,
'I will that men pray every where, lifting up holy hands
without wrath and doubting.' So then God having sanctified the whole world, and every corner of it, for His saints
to worship Him in ; they that by a strong hand seek to
bring them back again, either to this mountain or to Jerusalem, to worship ; that will allow the saints no other
places as lawful to worship God in publicly, but those only
concerning which the greatest question is, whether they
be sanctified or no ; these without all controversy shape
their reformation rather *secundum usum Sarum* than
according to the Word of God.

"A reformation that would not be flattered, and yet be
styled 'a reformation according to the Word of God,' must
give leave to the wind to blow where it listeth ; give liberty
to the Spirit of God to do with His own what He pleaseth ;
to make what discovery of truth, and to what persons, and
when, and where He pleaseth; and not compel Him to traffic
only with councils and synods for His heavenly commodi-
ties. That reformation which asserts the authority of
councils, synods, assemblies, as infallible ; that restrains
the ministers of the Gospel from declaring to men the
whole counsel of God concerning their salvation; that con-
demns as heretical the tenets of sober, learned, pious, and
conscientious men, only because an inconsiderable number
of men imagine (it may be only dream) them to be inconsistent with the Scriptures ; that shall subject the world
to such hard terms, that men shall not publicly taste of the
precious fruit of the gifts which God hath bestowed upon
thousands in a nation, but only according to discretion,

and at the allowance of a small parcel of men, and those (it may be) not of the greatest abilities for discerning : when the Alcoran of the Turks or the Missal of the Papists shall appear to be 'according to the Word of God,' then may such a reformation as this hope to partake of the same honour."

When the "Ordinance for the Punishing of Heresies and Blasphemies" was drawn up for the purpose of receiving parliamentary sanction, Mr. Goodwin published a tract under the title of "Some Modest and Humble Queries concerning a late printed Paper, &c., 1646." There are few publications in the whole compass of English literature better adapted to expose intolerance, and to recommend universal liberty of conscience, than these Queries. They never received a satisfactory answer, and the principles upon which they are grounded can never be refuted. The following are a sample :

"Whether it be agreeable to the Spirit of Christ, who came into the world not to destroy men's lives but to save them, to make snares of any of His doctrines, for the destruction of the lives of men ?

"Whether it is Christian, to maintain that religion by putting others to death, which, as Lactantius saith, 'ought to be defended, not by slaying others, but by dying ourselves for it?'

"Whether it is not evident from ancient and authentic writers, that the heathen sought to maintain their idolatrous religion by the same methods which the Ordinance proposeth for maintaining the religion of Christ ?

"Whether our best records of later times do not clearly show, that the papacy and antichristian party have gone about to uphold that false religion which they profess, by the very props wherewith the Ordinance seeks to support the religion of Christ ?

"Whether are errors and heresies any other things than some of those strongholds and imaginations in men, which, as the apostle saith, exalt themselves against the knowledge of God ? Or can they be better thrown down, than by those weapons which are 'mighty through God'

K

for that purpose? And are those weapons carnal or spiritual?

"Whether to enjoin ministers and others, upon pain of death, imprisonment, &c., not to teach anything in religion, contrary to the present apprehensions of the said enjoiners, be not in effect to say to the Holy Ghost, 'Reveal nothing more to others than Thou hast revealed to us? Or if Thou hast not revealed the truth to us, reveal it not unto any other men?'

"Whether a mistake in judgment, joined to a public profession, be more sinful, or more deserving of imprisonment, death, &c., than an open and manifest denial in works of such truths as men profess in words?

"Whether ministers, truly faithful and conscientious, being fully persuaded that many of the opinions asserted in the Ordinance for truths, are errors, (of which persuasion there are many in England,) shall do well to comply with the Ordinance against their judgments, and publicly hold those things for truths, which they are absolutely persuaded are nothing less? Or whether the Ordinance, threatening them with imprisonment or death in case they declare themselves otherwise, be not a dangerous temptation upon them to draw their foot into that snare of death?

"Whether twelve simple countrymen, such as our juries usually consist of at country assizes, (who, alas! are far from being versed in the profound questions in divinity, and who are generally incapable of such proprieties and differences of words, upon the understanding whereof the innocency or guiltiness of the person is likely to depend,) be of any competent faculty to pass upon the life or liberty of a studious, learned, and conscientious man, in cases where the ablest professors of divinity are not able, with any competent satisfaction to the scrupulous, many times to determine?

"Whether an ordinary judge of assize, who either doth *not* pretend, or in most cases doth *but* pretend, to any thoroughness of search into the deep things of God, in the abstruse points of religion, be a competent judge in such questions over such men, (to the bereaving them of life or liberty,) who are known to be men of able parts, and to have made the study of divinity their sole employment all their days; being grave, sober, and conscientious men in all their ways?

"Whether did God ever give any authority to civil magistrates, or others, either in the Old Testament or the New, to make any controverted exposition of any clause in the law; controverted between priest and priest, scribe and scribe; or any matter of doubtful disputation between learned, pious, and conscientious men; punishable either with imprisonment or death? And are not many points, condemned by the ordinance, matters of this nature? controvertible, and actually controverted, between persons of equal worth, parts, learning, judgment, conscience, on both sides?"

The publication of these Queries, and of others of a similar kind, to the number of thirty-eight, though pacific in their nature and design, and proposed in this modest and humble manner, like the application of fire to inflammable matter, produced such an explosion among the Presbyterian advocates of persecution as would have terrified any man of less mental energy than Mr. Goodwin. The ebullitions of passion and intolerance of which they were the innocent occasion, resembled a volcanic eruption of fiery lava. Puzzled, confounded, and mortified by this seasonable production, poor Edwards, of waspish memory, was thrown into a state bordering upon distraction; and expressed the feelings of his disordered mind in the following manner: "Concerning the author of these Queries, I may say, as the Holy Ghost doth of Herod's imprisoning John; *He hath added yet this above all!* to write such a wicked pamphlet, and at such a time! there being not a more desperate, ungodly, atheistical piece written by any man since the Reformation. I have had occasion to read many discourses and tractates of libertines and sceptics, that have been writ within the last hundred years; and have seen much wickedness in them, both in those of other countries and our own; especially those written and newly printed within five years last past:

but in none of them do I find such a spirit of libertinism, atheism, profaneness, and laying waste of all religion, breathing, as in those Queries. For beside those other evil spirits of error, scoffing, disorder, confusion, irreligion, that works in all the other Queries, there is a legion of wicked and unclean spirits, sevenfold worse than those which have been cast out, in that second Quere.

"How hath the Lord left him to himself, to write such Queries! I remember that in my second part of Gangræna I write thus: 'That I feared, if he lived but one seven years, he would prove as arch an heretic, and as dangerous a man, as ever England bred; and that he would be another David George, Francken, Socinus.' And behold, within a few months, not giving God glory to repent of his evil deeds, but going on to write, he hath by these Queries made good what I prophesied of him, and hath filled up the measure of his iniquities: so that I believe he hath justified Cornbert, Sebastian Franck, Francken, Socinus, David George, with all the rest of that rabble : and I do not think it lawful for Christians to receive such a one into their house, or to bid him God-speed; but rather, if they come where he is, to fly from him."*

Scarcely had Edwards poured forth these effusions of unhallowed zeal, when he published his tract against religious toleration. He then stood pledged to prepare a large work against Mr. Goodwin, in which he hoped to present to his readers the "head" of his antagonist "on the top of his sword," and render "his name an abhorring to future generations." "Alas!" said Mr. Goodwin, "the top of the sword he speaks of, I believe will be broken off, before his time comes of doing the execution. *Nescia mens hominis fati, sortisque futuræ.*"†
Such was the fact. The power of the Presbyterians began to decline; and Edwards, to escape the vengeance of the sectaries, against whose toleration he had written with such unmeasured violence, fled to Holland, where he died soon after his arrival, in the year 1647.‡

* Gangræna, Part Third, p. 117.   † Inexcusableness of Antapologia, Preface.   ‡ Wilson's History of Dissenting Churches, Vol. II. p. 407.

Edwards was not the only advocate of religious coercion, whose indignation was roused by the Queries of our author. An anonymous writer, of similar principles and spirit, undertook the defence of that ordinance concerning which Mr. Goodwin had instituted so many pertinent inquiries, in a tract entitled, "A Vindication of a printed Paper, &c., against the Irreligious and Presumptuous Exceptions called, Some Humble and Modest Queries." This *brave advocate* of Christianity contended that its doctrines were insecure, unless guarded by penal statutes; and that the civil magistrate was bound to inflict the punishment of DEATH upon the abettors of what he called "heresy." This book drew from the pen of Mr. Goodwin another excellent defence of religious liberty entitled, "Hagiomastix: or, the Scourge of the Saints Displayed in his Colours of Ignorance and Blood, 1646." On the publication of this very able book, a number of Presbyterians, both ministers and laymen, united in an urgent application to the parliament, that it might be burned by the hands of the common hangman, and that a prosecution of the author might be immediately instituted, in order that some exemplary punishment might be inflicted upon the man who dared to plead for a universal toleration. Disregard of truth is a general characteristic of informers; and these officious men wickedly perverted Mr. Goodwin's words, and represented him to the parliament as one who denied the inspiration of the Sacred Volume.*

In the parliamentary Ordinance for the Suppression of Heresy, the denial that the Holy Scriptures are the Word of God is made a capital offence, and rendered punishable with death. The apologists of this edict attempted to justify that severe sentence, by saying, that an error of such magnitude should be thus visited, because it overthrows the foundation of the Christian religion. In his reply Mr. Goodwin inquires, What was meant by "the Holy Scriptures;" whether "an English translation," or "the original Greek and Hebrew?" If the former,

* Postscript to the Scourge of the Saints, Preface.

which of the several English translations was intended? If the latter, what judgment could unlettered men form on the subject? And where was the equity of putting men to death for a denial of that with which they were totally unacquainted? By " the Word of God," which is the foundation of Christianity, Mr. Goodwin thought, should rather be understood " the distinguishing doctrines of Divine revelation; " which are indeed embodied in the Holy Scriptures, but may be held by persons who entertain doubts concerning the inspiration of some of the sacred books; and he mentions, as instances, those ancient Christian churches who at first refused to acknowledge the canonical authority of the Revelation of St. John, and Luther, who at one time rejected the Epistle of St. James. These remarks occasioned a mighty clamour against him, as a man who attempted to subvert the faith of the unwary. To vindicate himself from so foul a charge, he drew up a short piece of four pages, under the title of " A Candle to see the Sun; " in which he says, " Understanding that offence had been taken at some passages in the twenty-eighth section of a treatise lately published, as if the author intended to deny the Scriptures to be the Word of God, or at least, to scruple others about believing them so to be; (both which are the great abominations of his soul;) though he be fully assured, that there is no word or syllable in the said section which is capable of such a sense, yet it being the first-born desire of his soul to give no offence either to Jew or Gentile, or to the meanest member of any of the churches of God, he is willing to light up this candle to that sun; that such who understand not language of a more scholastic import, may be made apprehensive of the truth delivered therein by more plain and familiar terms. His intent therefore in the said section is none other, his words bearing him witness, than to require of his adversaries a distinct explication, what they mean by the word *Scriptures*, when they assert the denying of them to be the Word of God, as worthy of death. Of this demand he gives this double reason: first, because he supposeth it no foundation of Christian religion to believe that the English translation of the Scriptures is the Word of God: that is, that God spake to His prophets or apostles in the English tongue; or that our English translation doth agree in *all things* with the originals: neither of which he presumes will be affirmed by any person of competent understanding. Secondly, because concerning the original Hebrew and Greek copies, the far greatest part of men in the kingdom being ignorant of the said languages, he conceives it very unreasonable, that it should be required of them under pain of death to believe these copies, the contents whereof they no ways understand, to be the Word of God. This is the entire sum of the whole section contested against. He is not able to conceive, what expression there is throughout the section that ministers the least occasion of offence to any. Nevertheless, if any such shall be made known to him, no man shall be found more ready than he, to make his pen do penance for any error or delinquency in this kind. Meantime, what construction soever either weakness or a worse principle in men may make of his words, he conceives this to be an abundant purgation from the guilt of unsettling any man in his belief about the Divine authority of the Scriptures; that there are many hundreds of persons, in and about the city, who have known the course of his ministry for the space of thirteen years, who can testify on his behalf that the main bent and tendency of his ministerial engagements all this while have been the confirmation of the testimony of Christ, as the apostle calls the Gospel, in the hearts and consciences of men; together with the building up of the Divine original of the Scriptures with both hands. With what integrity he hath laboured in this vineyard of the Lord, God and his own soul are conscious: with what fruit in the souls of men, he leaveth to the testimony of others. He only craveth leave to say, without the least touch of vanity, or self-assuming, that in the said argument, he hath laboured more than all his brethren in the ministry in or about the city; and that he is at this very time in a serious prosecution of the same in the ordinary process of his ministry."

With respect to the charge of scepticism, preferred against him to the civil authorities, Mr. Goodwin declares his readiness to die rather than deny the Scriptures or the momentous truths they contain ; and in reference to his accusers, he exclaims, "Miserable men! who know not how to refrain from making themselves more miserable than they are, by making sin of innocency in other men, and innocency of sin in themselves. I am so far from denying the Divine authority of the Scriptures in the said book, that I assert the same as demonstrable by many grounds and arguments. But I remember, that He that glorified God more than all the world besides, was charged with blasphemy by those who thought they knew what blasphemy was, and judged themselves as holy, just, and zealous men, as far from the abomination of condemning the innocent, as were to be found among all the living ; yea, He was at last, notwithstanding His faithfulness to both worlds, sentenced by such men as worthy of death, as a blasphemer. I cannot but comfort myself with these words."*

The anonymous writer who attempted to answer Mr. Goodwin's queries, and to vindicate the parliamentary Ordinance, in the true spirit of his undertaking, solemnly adjured Mr. Goodwin's church, in the name of the Holy Trinity, to deliver their pastor up to the devil, as having not only pleaded for universal liberty of conscience, but published the following query, which according to his apprehension contained a "complication of blasphemy : " "Whether it be agreeable to the mind of Christ, for men to inflict the heavy censure of Death upon their brethren, for holding forth such doctrines or opinions in religion, suppose contrary to admonition, which, for aught the said inflictors know, unless they make themselves infallible, may be the sacred truths of God ? "

This outrageous charge induced twenty persons in religious connexion with Mr. Goodwin, on their own behalf and that of their brethren, to publish a defence of their minister's character. This piece is entitled, "An Apolo-

* Appendix to the Scourge of the Saints, Preface.

getical Account of some Brethren of the Church whereof
Mr. John Goodwin is Pastor, why they cannot execute
that passionate and unchristian Charge of delivering up
their Pastor to Satan, which is imposed upon them in a
late printed Book, 1647." A copious extract from this
very rare and interesting document, which is equally
honourable to Mr. Goodwin and to his friends, cannot be
unacceptable to the intelligent reader of these memoirs.

"It was a general observation," say they, "among the
heathen, that envy was an inseparable companion to
virtue. And truly, if Christians would but consult the
experience of all ages, they would find that holiness hath
been always haunted with a like or worse spirit: the former being but a slight provocation to flesh and blood, in
comparison of the latter. Our blessed Lord and Saviour,
who spake as never man spake, and acted for the glory of
His Father at a higher rate than the angels themselves
can attain to, was stigmatized by the rulers of the Jewish
church with those odious titles of blasphemer, devil, friend
of publicans and sinners. And such as have followed Him
closely in the regeneration, hath the world forced to drink
deep with Him of this bitter cup. The apostle Paul, who
drew the most perfect resemblance of his heavenly pattern, had much ado to uphold the honour of his name,
even in the churches of Christ, against the suggestions
of false teachers. We conceive it a work of no great
difficulty, to produce out of every century since the coming
of our Lord variety of examples of this nature, and to
show how, in all times, such as have been the most richly
furnished from heaven to do service to the God that dwells
therein, have deeply suffered in this kind, and that from
those who have been zealous pretenders to the same sacred
employment with themselves.

"But is not the counsel of God and the hand of Satan in
all this? Yea, doubtless, though the one be founded in
wisdom and love, the other stretched forth in hatred and
revenge. The devil, through the enmity which is in him
to the glory of the Creator, and the everlasting peace of
the creature, burns with jealousy against all those who

are best appointed with courage and skill to practise upon his vassals, and to make the widest breaches upon his territories; and because he knows there is no way more likely to render their attempts fruitless, and to lay their highest achievements in the dust, than to cast dead flies into the pot of their ointment, he provokes the tongues and hearts of men to wound their names; that, if it be possible, the credit and reputation of them might bleed even to death. But wherein this 'accuser of the brethren' thinks he deals wisely, God is above him, and compels this stratagem against His servants to become contributory to His own ends and to their good. Knowledge and abundance of revelations are apt, through the weakness of the flesh, to puff up even the best of men; yet buffetings by these messengers of Satan prove excellent corrections of such swellings, and are proper means to keep their hearts in an humble posture; which posture, as it renders them capable of the largest effusions of grace, so doth it qualify them to become instruments for God's hand. Whereas if they wanted this qualification, though accommodated in all other respects for His service, He would soon lay them by as useless. For in the election of means for His own ends, He passes by proud and high persons, with as much neglect as high things.

"The consideration hereof, amongst other things, as it had, we doubt not, a sovereign influence upon our dearly beloved pastor, for strengthening him against the assaults of the powers of darkness and this world; so had it a like operation upon us also, who otherwise could not have borne the cruel and malicious dealings of men towards him, with that equanimity of spirit we have done. To see a beautiful visage causelessly deformed by the talons of cruelty, is a sight which cannot but afflict nature: but to see innocency suffer for the truth's sake, O how grievous is it to an ingenuous spirit! This was our case in respect of him. Our strict observation of him for some years together, filled us to the very brim with assurance of his integrity both to God and man; and this made us so tender in our affections to him, that the loud and furious outcries against him were as a sword which pierced our bowels through and through. Nevertheless it came not into our thoughts to move for his vindication beyond the sphere of those companies whither our private occasions led us. Yet ignorant we were not what advantage his accusers had of us in this respect. We knew full well, that the line of our opportunities was too short to traverse the circumference of the press; and consequently, that it was impossible for us to gather up by our apologies and defence, what they had scattered in the minds of men. Our hope indeed was, that through our private testimonies, and his public vindications of himself, and the blessing of God upon both, the wise and sober part of the world might have been antidoted against the poison of their informations. However we persuaded ourselves that the day was not far off, when those ways and truths for which he suffered, would rise out of their graves, ascend their throne, and draw his name out of its dust, to partake in their glory. Under this expectation we possessed our souls in patience : only we could not but weep in secret over the astonishing wickedness and folly of this age, which spits its venom in the faces of such as most industriously promote the peace and welfare of it.

"But the breaking forth of a late treatise, or rather, the breakings out of an unchristian spirit in that treatise, have forced the pen into our hands, and laid a necessity upon us to let the world know why we cannot obey the voice of this spirit, speaking in blackness, smoke, and fire. We cannot but judge concerning the author or authors of that ' Vindication,' that when they imposed upon us that direful charge, they were under the same inspiration with the Jews, when they cried, *Crucify Him! Crucify Him!* And doubtless Pilate had as much reason to gratify the bloody desires of this people, as we have to deliver up to Satan him whom we know to be a most faithful minister of Jesus Christ: there being no reason for either one or the other. That blasphemy for which we are commanded to throw the thunderbolt of excommunication against him, being inquired into, will be found to be of the same nature with that for which this Just One was put to death; that is, no blasphemy at all.   If to vindicate the truths of God from the false imaginations of men—to maintain the royalties of Christ, and the privileges of His subjects, against the encroachments and tyranny of the world—to stand in the gap, and endeavour to keep out the horned beast of persecution from the societies of the saints—if this be blasphemy, we confess him to be one of the greatest blasphemers under heaven.   But though such practices as these are arraigned and condemned under the names of heresy, blasphemy, and the like, in the consistories of men; where carnal interests sit as judges, the sentence shall be reversed in the court of heaven, and all engagements of this nature shall be rewarded as loyalty to the King that rules there.

" We have fully known his doctrine, life, and conversation; and as far as we are able to judge of them, they are according to truth, and as becomes the Gospel of the Lord Jesus.   Those streams of light which have run through his ministry, have been as pure and unmixed as the vessel whence they issued could well permit.   The doctrines of the Father and of the Son, the involving whereof in clouds of uncertainty the said 'Vindication' most falsely chargeth upon him, hath he brought into so clear and open view, that we have seen the peace and everlasting salvation of our souls in them.   Every one of those fundamental principles of Christian religion, which this gangræned pen would persuade the world he denies or doubts of, hath he not only asserted in our hearing again and again, but proved them with such evidence and demonstration of the Spirit, that our consciences were forced to fall before them, and confess that of a truth God was in them.   Sure we are, he hath laid amongst us that true and everlasting foundation Jesus Christ, other than . which no man can lay without extreme peril of himself and his disciples.   It is possible, that the structure he hath set upon this foundation, is not all of 'gold, silver, and precious stones;' perhaps somewhat of 'wood, hay, and stubble,' will be found in it: yet of this we are strongly possessed, and that not upon light grounds, that his 'works' in this kind shall suffer as little loss by fire in the day of purgation, as the 'works' of any of his fellow-labourers.

"Whether the publishing of 'some modest and humble queries,' or in particular that query upon which these men fall so foul, will amount to wickedness and blasphemy, we presume all intelligent men may receive satisfaction from a pen far more able, and in some respects more interested than ours. We have looked upon this query; we have searched into it with all possible exactness and impartiality, and cannot find that cursed treasure in it over which they insultingly rejoice. Certainly they had never found a 'complication of blasphemy' in a query so innocent and inoffensive, had they ploughed with the fair heifer of Love; which, as the apostle speaks, 'thinketh no evil, beareth all things, believeth all things, hopeth all things.' And yet, we are persuaded, that they triumph in face more than in heart; and are conscious that those *great spoils* which they boast, like emperors, to have taken from the querist's name, are but *cockles*—mere flourishes and bubbles. Had they been able to make good their charge of blasphemy, in all likelihood he had felt the heat of their zeal, and been convented before rulers and magistrates long ere this. To think otherwise, were to conceive that they are less zealous for truths than for tithes—for the cause and glory of God, than for their own greatness and domination.

"But is it not a sad thing, and of portentous consequence, that such great pretenders not to the office only, but also to the qualifications of an elder, should act so diametrically opposite thereunto? should become public brawlers and revilers; smite their fellow-servant in a place more tender than his eye—in his name and honour; arraign, judge, condemn him to hell, for no other crime than the publishing of a naked query?—the nature whereof, every body knows, is neither to assert any thing nor deny: nay, should conjure a whole church to be co-partners with them in their sin, and help them to pour the dregs of unrighteous wrath upon their own pastor!

What temper shall we call this? If they will call it zeal, we will call it so too; but it is a zeal from beneath, and symbolizeth with that wisdom which comes from the same place. If he had dropped any sentence, the face whereof might have been forced to look towards the borders of blasphemy, it became elders to take that to be the meaning which it gave out freely and without torture: a Christian method, from which others have. likewise deviated, in perverting his sayings, and thereupon reporting that he denies the Scriptures to be the Word of God.

"Suppose he had published something which struck point blank at a main principle of the Gospel, it had been their office, if they would needs intermeddle, to have advised us to admonish him, and endeavour in love and patience to convince him, before we proceeded any further; but to command us, in such peremptory terms, at the very first dash, to excommunicate him, without trial, admonition, or means of conviction; what does this argue, but that they have more of Christ's spirit, mind, and government in their lips, than in their hearts and ways? Such overtures of their great sufficiency to rule, we think are sufficient cautions to the state, to deny them that royal crown which they so earnestly desire. Were they accommodated in all things to their heart's content, they would soon make the best to feel, what most do fear, that the little finger of their discipline would be thicker than their predecessors' loins. The soundest Christians in the land could not escape their rods and scorpions, had they as good authority to punish heresies and blasphemies *how* they please, as they have a faculty to make heresies and blasphemies of *what* they please.

"One thing further we desire the reader to notice: They press us with the most prevailing motives, to do that which they judge to be unlawful for us to do. The power of the keys by *Divine right*, is a chief royalty of that sacred empire for which they, with others of their order, contend so strenuously as to make the foundations of the land to tremble under them. For any to intermeddle herein, with unconsecrated hands, is the abomination of their souls.

And yet, though they cannot but know that not one drop of their consecrated oil hath touched our heads, they charge us, as we regard the honour of God, and the Lord Jesus Christ, and the authority of the Spirit, to execute the highest censure not only against the consent, but upon the person of our only elder. Whether they have not hereby insinuated, that they can speak any thing, do any thing, command any thing, *to serve a turn,* we leave themselves to determine. They can find in their hearts to shake a main pillar of their Babel, or suffer their *jus divinum* to fall to the ground, so the man of their hatred might fall with it.

"We have turned their injunction upside down; we have viewed it on all sides; and find it in every respect abhorrent to all principles of ingenuity, civility, reason, and religion. To perpetrate such a deed of darkness against him whom God hath made more precious to us than our lives, is far more grievous than to cut off our right hands, and to pluck out our right eyes. We could open our mouths yet seven times wider on his behalf, but are unwilling to provoke his enemies any further, in reflecting shame upon their weakness and folly, by the light of his life and conversation."[*]

Such was the manly ardour of Mr. Goodwin in the sacred cause of religious liberty, the formidable opposition he had to encounter, and the generous promptitude of his friends to shield him from those poisoned arrows which intolerance discharged by a thousand hands. It is to the operation of the principles which he expounded and defended with such disinterestedness, perseverance, and ability, that we are indebted for the abolition of those persecutions that were formerly practised in this country under the sanction of law, and were so immensely injurious to commerce, morals, and religion. To the same cause must be attributed those legislative enactments, by which the rights of con-

[*] This important document bears the following signatures: Robert Smith, Mark Hildesley, Robert Saunders, Thomas Davenish, William Montague, William Allen, Joseph Gallant, Thomas Lamb, William Godfrey, John Dye, Daniel Taylor, James Paris, Thomas Norman, Bartholomew Lavender, Richard Priece, Thomas Morris, John Price, Richard Arnald, Henry Overton, Philip Webberly.

science are guarded, and in consequence of which the
nation has gradually risen to an unprecedented elevation
of wealth and power.   Under the protection of toleration
laws, this country has been the theatre of a revival of vital
Christianity, such as the church has hardly witnessed since
the earliest ages : a revival that has given birth to pious
and charitable institutions unexampled in the history of
man, and which bid fair to introduce the universal reign
of righteousness and peace.

> "'Tis liberty alone, that gives the flower
> Of fleeting life its lustre and perfume ;
> And we are weeds without it. All constraint,
> Except what wisdom lays on evil men,
> Is evil : hurts the faculties, impedes
> Their progress in the road of science ; blinds
> The eyesight of discovery ; and begets
> In those that suffer it a sordid mind
> Bestial, a meagre intellect, unfit
> To be the tenant of man's noble form."

While British Christians therefore are happy in the enjoyment of religious liberty, and in the delightful anticipation of its final results ; and while they justly cherish the
memory of the Miltons and the Lockes, who have demonstrated this blessing to be the birth-right of every human
being, let them not forget to pay a small tribute of respect
to the name of JOHN GOODWIN.   He not only belonged to
the same honourable fraternity, but was an elder brother.
Nor would it be easy to produce any English writer, who
understood the doctrine of religious freedom better than he,
or who has argued in its defence with greater consistency
and zeal.   The grand principles contained even in Locke's
far-famed Letters concerning Toleration are clearly developed and ably supported in the writings of Mr. Goodwin.
It is also a fact, that he had published at least six tracts
in which he had defended universal liberty of conscience,
two years before Dr. Owen sent into the world his first
piece on Toleration, for which he has been so highly
praised.

" The persecution of saints," says he; " the rough hand-
ling of tender consciences ; the lifting up of religion upon

a sword's point; violenced conformities; uniformities
enforced; quenching of proceedings in the knowledge of
truth; binding up of judgments in synodical decrees;
standing upon ceremonies to the prejudice of the substance,
as when the Gospel must not be preached because such and
such hands have not been imposed; the lording over the
heritage of Christ; these have been the abhorrencies of
my former years as well as of my latter."*

When Mr. Goodwin first published his views on these
topics, and found the world up in arms against him on this
account, commiserating their folly and sin, he remarked,
" It is matter of sad contemplation, to see what commotions, tumults, and combustions are presently raised in the
minds of men upon the birth of any truth into the world,
concerning which there is the least jealousy that, in case it
should reign, it would rack them from off their old customs:
to see what hurryings up and down; what engaging of parties; what inquiring after parts and abilities; what ram-
bling over authors old and new; what incensing of authority; what straining of wits and consciences; what slighting of solid arguments; what evading of substantial and
clear interpretations of Scripture; what magnifying of
those that are strained and far-fetched; what casting
abroad of calumnies and reproaches; what misrepresentations of opinions, sayings, actions; what shiftings, what
blendings, what colourings, what disgracings, what persecutions; what appealings to fire, sword, prisons, banishment, confiscations; and all to turn a beam of light and
glory into darkness and shame—to keep a new-born truth
from ruling over them. As soon as Herod the king heard
that Christ was born, and that wise men from the East
were come to worship Him, inquiring after Him as a King,
he was troubled and all Jerusalem with him."†

* Inexcusableness of Antapologia, Preface. † Innocency and Truth.
Preface.

CHAPTER V.

THE circumstances in which men are individually placed
are so greatly diversified, and so variously are their minds
constituted, that on almost every subject upon which their
reasoning faculties can be exercised, they have entertained
opposite and conflicting opinions. In the most enlightened
state of society, both in ancient and in modern times, discordant sects of philosophers have existed, and contended
with each other; and in the Christian church, men of
equal learning, talents, and piety, have differed in their
views concerning several of the doctrines of divine revelation : nor are the instances few in which men of high
mental endowments have been compelled by the power of
conviction to retract sentiments to which they had yielded
their cordial assent, and to embrace a creed to which they
were once strongly averse. If a judgment may be formed
from the past, there is no reason to believe that Christians
will ever be brought to think exactly alike on all subjects,
during their present imperfect state of existence. The
wisest and best of men "know but in part," and "see
through a glass darkly." These facts, so humiliating to
the human intellect, are replete with instruction, especially
to those religionists of every class, who, although they possess few requisite qualifications for a calm and profound
investigation of any branch of knowledge, either human or
divine, weakly imagine that truth is confided to them alone,
and that wisdom will become extinct when they cease to
dogmatize.

Of all the controversies which have agitated the Christian
church, there is not one which is more deeply interesting
in itself, or in whose range greater difficulties are compre-
hended, than that which respects the nature and order of

the Divine Decrees. In the discussion of these topics several of the greatest theologians in Europe have spent a considerable part of their lives, without bringing their respective parties nearer to each other in their modes of thinking. Among the English divines who have taken an active part in this controversy, Mr. Goodwin is eminently distinguished. In command of temper, depth of learning, comprehension of thought, and cogency of reasoning, he is scarcely inferior to any polemical writer whatever; and in all these respects is vastly superior to a large majority of theological combatants.

It has been already observed, that, in the early part of his life, he held the doctrine of the absolute predestination of some men, personally considered, to eternal life, and of others to endless misery; as taught in the writings of Calvin, and especially in his "Institutes of the Christian Religion." This celebrated reformer and learned man says, " Predestination we call the eternal decree of God, by which He hath determined in Himself, what He would have to become of every individual of mankind. For they are not all created with a similar destiny; but eternal life is fore-ordained to some, and eternal damnation for others. Every man, therefore, being created for one or the other of these ends, we say, he is predestinated either to life or to death."*

" Many indeed, as if they wished to avert odium from God, admit election in such a way as to deny that any one is reprobated. But this is puerile and absurd, because election itself could not exist without being opposed to reprobation. God is said to separate those whom He adopts to salvation. To say, that others obtain by chance, or acquire by their own efforts, that which election alone confers on a few, will be worse than absurd. Whom God passes by therefore He reprobates, and from no other cause than His determination to exclude them from the inheritance which He predestines for His children." †

" Foolish mortals enter into many contentions with God, as though they could arraign Him to plead to their accusa-

* Institutes, lib. iii. cap. 21. Allen's Translation. † Ibid. lib. iii. cap. 23.

tions. In the first place they inquire, by what right the Lord is angry with His creatures who had not provoked Him by any previous offence; for that to devote to destruction whom He pleases, is more like the caprice of a tyrant, than the lawful sentence of a judge; that men have reason, therefore, to expostulate with God, if they are predestinated to eternal death without any demerit of their own, merely by His sovereign will. If such thoughts ever enter the minds of pious men, they will be sufficiently able to break their violence by this one consideration, how exceedingly presumptuous it is only to inquire into the causes of the divine will; which is in fact, and is justly entitled to be, the cause of everything that exists."*

"If, therefore, we can assign no reason why He grants mercy to His people but such is His pleasure, neither shall we find any other cause but His will for the reprobation of others. For when God is said to harden or show mercy to whom He pleases, men are taught by this declaration to seek no other cause beside His will."†

"That the reprobate obey not the word of God, when made known to them, is justly imputed to the wickedness and depravity of their hearts, provided it be at the same time stated, that they are abandoned to this depravity, because they have been raised up by a just but inscrutable judgment of God to display His glory in their condemnation."‡

"When the impious hear these things, they loudly complain that God, by a wanton exercise of power, abuses His wretched creatures for the sport of His cruelty. But we who know that all men are liable to many charges at the divine tribunal, that of a thousand questions they would be unable to give a satisfactory answer to one, confess that the reprobate suffer nothing but what is consistent with the most righteous judgment of God. Though we cannot comprehend the reason of this, let us be content with some degree of ignorance where the wisdom of God soars into its own sublimity."§

* Ibid. † Ibid. lib. iii. cap. 22. ‡ Ibid. lib. iii. cap. 24.
§ Ibid.

Various attempts have been made by the disciples of Calvin, to modify their master's doctrine, so as to render it less revolting to the minds of those who have not been initiated into its mysteries, and whom he was accustomed to denominate "dogs" and "swine:" but such was the frank and ingenuous manner in which he expressed his sentiments on the awful subject of predestination. It was his full conviction, that Almighty God has from eternity appointed the endless destiny of every human being, by an absolute and irrespective decree. Such an appointment, he contended, was perfectly compatible with the moral attributes of the blessed God; though he confessed his inability to reconcile the decree of reprobation with the divine equity and mercy, and therefore resolved the whole into the sovereign and inscrutable Will of the Almighty.

Calvin's system of theology, which was the *orthodoxy* of Mr. Goodwin's Puritanical contemporaries, gained such an ascendency over his mind, through the influence of education, that, like many others of the same school, he applied the doctrine of absolute reprobation not only to adult persons, but even to children who die in their infancy. There are men, says he, "who teach, that there are some reprobates, and these not a few neither, towards whom God showeth no patience or long-sufferance at all; imagining that many infants of days, yea and many immediately from the womb, are sent to the lake that burneth with fire and brimstone for evermore. My soul hath once been in the secret of these men, but let it never enter thereinto more."*

Having been taught to regard the Calvinian doctrine as a part of the intellectual bread provided by God for the spiritual nourishment of His intelligent offspring, Mr. Goodwin endeavoured so to feed upon it as to "grow thereby" in personal religion. "But the truth is," says he, "I found it ever and anon gravellish in my mouth, and corroding and fretting to my bowels. Notwithstanding, the high esteem I had of many of those who prepared it, and fed upon it themselves, together with a raw and

* Exposition of the Ninth Chapter to the Romans, p. 265, Edit. 1653.

ill-digested conceit that there was no better bread to be
had, prevailed upon me to content myself therewith for a
long time, though not without some regret of discontent-
ment." *   It is not therefore surprising, that, as he
advanced in years and knowledge, and his judgment
became more matured, like several of the greatest divines
in Europe, he abandoned those opinions concerning predestination in which he had been educated, and which
he had taught in the early years of his public ministry.

Considering every Christian preacher as a steward, to
whom the doctrines of salvation are committed in trust
for the benefit of his hearers, and taking the Apostle of
the Gentiles as an example of ministerial fidelity, Mr.
Goodwin resolved to " declare the whole counsel of God,"
so far as he was acquainted with it, and to " keep back "
from the people committed to his charge nothing that was
profitable.   All the doctrines of Christianity he regarded
as designed and adapted to promote the moral improvement as well as the personal happiness of mankind; and
he was too deeply impressed with the awful responsibility
attached to his office, to imagine himself at liberty to
conceal any branch of revealed truth, either in compliance
with the wishes of his friends, or on any account whatever.   His faithfulness in this respect was exemplary, and
worthy of universal imitation.   Among other rules by
which he was guided in the interpretation of the sacred
oracles, and in the consequent formation of his creed,
there is one which is worthy of deep attention, and is thus
stated by himself: " I shall make my reader so far of my
council, as to give him to know, that when the letter of
Scripture hath for a time left me in a strait between contrary opinions, (a condition that hath more than once
befallen me,) that brief periphrasis or description of the
Gospel, which the apostle delivers, calling it ἀληθείας τῆς
κατ᾽ εὐσέβειαν, _the truth which is according to godliness_, hath,
upon serious consideration, oft delivered me, and brought
me to such a clear understanding of the letter itself,
wherein before I was entangled, that I evidently, and with

* Redemption Redeemed, Preface.

the greatest satisfaction I could desire, discerned the mind
of God therein; and that with full consonancy to the
ordinary manner of speaking in the Scripture upon a like
occasion. Having this touchstone by an unerring hand
given unto me, that the Gospel is a *truth according to godli-*
ness, that is, a body of truth calculated and framed by God,
in all the veins and parts of it, for the exaltation of godliness in the world, I was directed hereby, in the case of
doctrines incompatible between themselves, to own that as
the truth the face whereof was in the clearest and directest
manner set for the promotion of godliness amongst men,
and to refuse that which stood in opposition hereunto.
Nor did I find it any matter of much difficulty, especially
in such cases wherein I most desired satisfaction, to determine which of the opinions, competitors for my consent,
was the greater friend to godliness. That knowledge
which God hath given me of the Scriptures,—the experimental knowledge I had of mine own heart,—that long
observation I had made of the spirits, principles, and ways
of men,—their ebbings and flowings, risings and fallings,
advancings and retreats, in matters of religion,—in conjunction with that light of reason and understanding
which I have in common with other men; these were
sufficient to teach me, and that with a plenary satisfaction
in most cases, what doctrines are of the most cordial
sympathy and compliance with godliness; and what, on
the other hand, are but faint and loose in their correspondency with her, or secret enemies to her." *

In the application of this principle, and in the study of
the Holy Scriptures, Mr. Goodwin proceeded with the
utmost caution; but still with a fixed determination to
follow the light of truth, in whatever direction it might
lead him. "I learned this Christian principle," says he,
" from a heathen philosopher: διὰ τὴν ἀλήθειαν δεῖ καὶ τὰ
οἰκεῖα ἐναίρειν : *A man must be content to sacrifice even his*
own sayings and opinions upon the service of the truth."†
When therefore it had become the full conviction of his
mind, that the Calvinian doctrine of election and reproba-

* Redemption Redeemed, p. 268, Edit. 1651. † Water-Dipping, p. 68.

tion was not only destitute of scriptural authority, but,
when received as a principle of action and applied to practical purposes, was unfriendly in its influence upon personal
religion; he did not hesitate to renounce it, and to maintain with Arminius, That whatever partiality the blessed
God may display in the gratuitous distribution of talents
amongst men, and in the bestowment of religious advantages, during their probationship in this world; his
Decrees, according to which their *Eternal States* will be
appointed, though absolute and unchangeable in themselves, *are Respective of Character*, and therefore conditional
in their application to individuals.   According to his
apprehension, God has immutably decreed to elect or
choose to eternal life all that believe in Jesus Christ, and
to reprobate or abandon to endless misery all that neglect or refuse to believe in Him : graciously affording them,
at the same time, every requisite assistance for the acquisi-
tion and continued exercise of that faith upon which their
everlasting happiness is suspended.   In the open avowal of
these sentiments he repeatedly declares, that nothing but
a solemn conviction of duty could possibly induce him to
contradict opinions which so many of his brethren regarded
as the sacred truths of revelation.   " My love to the souls
of men," says he, " is such, that I cannot knowingly suffer
any suspicious doctrine, or loose opinion in the things of
God, to pass through the world near to me, unexamined ;
especially when any considerable number of men are like
to suffer: which, though it be a thankless engagement, and
very obnoxious to those who love ease or honour more than
clearness of judgment and pureness of mind, is a proper
and effectual course to preserve the Gospel from that inter-
mixture of error, which commonly issueth from supine
incogitancy and sloth in those who are entrusted with the
ministry of it." *

It is scarcely possible for British Christians in the present
age to form an adequate conception of the magnanimity
displayed by Mr. Goodwin in the open renunciation of the
Calvinistic system, and in the avowed adoption of Armini-

* Divine Authority of the Scriptures, Dedication.

anism. To divest the mind of principles which were imbibed in early life as incontrovertible truths, and have been associated with the best feelings of the heart during a series of years, is at all times a difficult task. Such a procedure generally excites a suspicion of mental imbecility and a want of decision, and thus raises "the world's dread laugh," the magic of which few men are able to withstand. The anticipation of this must be extremely revolting to the mind of a minister whose labours are confined to one congregation : for how strong soever may be his conviction in his study, that some of his theological principles are untenable ; yet as they have been identified with evangelical truth in the constant tenor of his ministry, frequently applied to the purpose of personal godliness, and enforced by the authority of Scripture ; how can he bear the thought of retracting and opposing them in the pulpit ? especially when the probability is, that his judgment will thus be brought into disrepute among his hearers, and the tone of his ministerial authority considerably lowered. In reference to this subject, the peculiarity of Mr. Goodwin's circumstances should also be taken into the account. He was twenty-five years of age when the Dutch Arminians were condemned as heretics by men reputed orthodox, who constituted the Synod of Dort ; when the clergy of that denomination in Holland, who refused to abjure their creed or to renounce their office, were sent into banishment, as unworthy of a place in civil society ; when those of them who returned to their native land were condemned to perpetual imprisonment, and such as were found attending their ministry, though but in a private house or in a forest, were plundered of their property, and in some cases put to death. Such was the representation given of the dangerous tendency of Arminianism, by the predestinarians of that age, that neither the piety of the venerable Uitenbogaert, nor the talents and integrity of Corvinus and Episcopius, could secure those excellent men and their associates from the vengeance of the ecclesiastical and the civil power. Mr. Goodwin had indeed seen some of the Arminian doctrines patronized by dignitaries of the English church; but the character of those men had covered their religious sentiments with odium. Those dignitaries had been distinguished as the friends of arbitrary power, had treated the Puritans with great severity and injustice, and were vehemently accused of a design to subvert the Protestant religion, and to introduce a system of refined Popery in its stead. After the subversion of the hierarchy, there were also several divines of great learning and talents, who held most of the distinguishing tenets of Arminianism; but as they were inflexible loyalists, they were stigmatized as "malignants," and driven into obscurity by the scourge of persecution. The great body of Mr. Goodwin's Puritanical friends and connexions viewed Arminianism, at the period when he adopted that system, as a deadly east wind, which, when permitted by angry heaven to blow upon the garden of the church, withers every flower, and produces a general blight. Or rather, they regarded it as a region

" Where all life dies, death lives, and nature breeds,
Perverse, all monstrous, all prodigious things,
Abominable, unutterable, and worse
Than fables yet have feign'd or fear conceiv'd,
Gorgons, and Hydras, and Chimœras dire."

Hence in the language of several of the old Puritans, prelacy and Arminianism are not unusually associated with blasphemy, profaneness, and Atheism! Such however was the power of conviction in the mind of Mr. Goodwin that, with all these difficulties and discouragements before him, at the advanced age of fifty years, he abandoned the school of Calvinian theology, and boldly preached Christ as the infinitely gracious Redeemer of all mankind.

The manner in which he was led to the adoption of the Arminian system is not unworthy of attention. While he was in possession of his vicarage, he delivered a series of discourses in defence of the peculiar doctrines of Calvinism. The discourses were numerously attended, and excited considerable interest in London. In the last of them, which was delivered on the 12th of April, 1644, he was understood to advance a principle favourable to those tenets, which it was his avowed object to confute. This circumstance roused the feelings of one of his auditors, a warm young man, recently returned from the army, of the name of Samuel Lane ; who attacked him in a pamphlet, entitled, " A Vindication of Free Grace, in Opposition to this Arminian position : *Natural men may do such things as whereunto God hath, by way of promise, annexed Grace and Acceptation ;* first preached, and after asserted, at Stephen's, Coleman Street." This tract, which bears the date of 1645, is dedicated to the members of Mr. Goodwin's church, who are represented as having made a remarkable proficiency in Christian knowledge.

Lane appears, before his entrance into the army, to have been a regular attendant upon Mr. Goodwin's ministry, and a passionate admirer of him in every respect. Having however become, as it should seem, more zealous in his attachment to the peculiarities of Calvinism, by attending the ministry of military chaplains and officers, he imagined on his return, that he was wiser than his teacher, whom he considered now as not quite orthodox. Deeming himself also qualified to handle a pen as well as a musket, and able to decide the quinquarticular controversy, he assumed the character of a theological combatant, and entered the lists with his vicar. His conduct was the more reprehensible, considering that he had derived his religious knowledge and impressions from Mr. Goodwin's preaching, and had received from him many tokens of " respect," which he acknowledges to have been "utterly undeserved." The publication of his rhapsody against his spiritual pastor, his friend, and the guide of his youth, he nevertheless deemed to be amply justified by three considerations : "First," says he, " because his disputings upon this matter have been highly approved of by many ; whereof divers give this testimony, *that he hath cut the hair between other divines and Arminians.* Yea, Mr. Goodwin told me, he was much desired to print his disputes against the Arminians, so highly are they esteemed ; in the last of which disputes, the ensuing error was pleaded for.

"But secondly, and specially, there are, as it is conceived, thousands now amongst us, who hold that grand error, *That God hath promised grace upon man's doing.* Two of that sect, discoursing with a reverend divine of this city, told him, that in holding this tenet, they held but that which Master John Goodwin maintains; in whom they greatly glory. Now it is not easy to conceive how great mischief the preaching and arguing of so eminent a person for that error may do, to the confirming of men therein; especially if we consider how highly he hath gratified the maintainers thereof in another way also, as namely, by his earnest pleading for a toleration of any sect whatsoever.

"Thirdly, I might add the consideration of his so often pressing that error, not only three several Lord's-Days, ... but also in some of his last exercises against the Arminians. ...... Yea further, it hath been often acknowledged, by a known member of Mr. Goodwin's church, that about seven years ago he preached the same matter; and that then divers able divines of this city did affirm to Mr. Goodwin, that he preached Arminianism. Seeing then this error, together with its defensive arguments, have been with great zeal so often inculcated, for a more sure and thorough distilling the same into the minds of the hearers, hence it is necessary not only to declaim against it, but *tanquam digito monstrare,* so distinctly and directly to point it out, as that all such hearers may have peculiar admonishment hereof, and that by mentioning the publisher of it."

Summoned to the bar of the public, to answer for an imputed error, Goodwin was prompted to a more minute investigation of the controversy concerning "the five points;" the deliberate and conscientious study of which gradually led to that revolution of sentiment which has been already stated. To these facts he alludes in the following passage: "That which first turned to a sharp engagement upon me to search more thoroughly than I had done into [these] controversies was, a pamphlet published by a young man about five or six years since, under the title of 'A Vindication of Free Grace;' which, though libellous enough, and full of broad untruths; yet being fiercely set against me, and my doctrine, it was lifted up as near to heaven as Herod's oration, by the applause of persons in and about the city, whose ways in matters of discipline, and thoughts in more weighty points of religion, my understanding would never serve me to make mine. Being for a time under a conscientious resentment of a necessity lying upon me, to publish some answer to the said pamphlet, as well the person as the doctrine therein stigmatized being innocent of the crimes charged upon them; I drew up a competent answer as I supposed, with the perusal whereof I was willing, upon request, to gratify some private friends, amongst whom it lay dormant for a time. In the interim, perceiving that the noise which the pamphlet had made, was like the crackling of thorns under a pot, and the heat of the tumultuary rejoicing occasioned by it had exhaled and spent itself, I began to consider that the answer I had prepared (a good part of it being taken up in proving the pamphleteer tardy in several reports made by him in matters of fact, the knowledge whereof I conceived of slender edification, and the detection of him in such unworthy practices might be offensive to some of his friends whom I respected,) might in some respects rather cumber than benefit the world, in case it were published. And considering further, that the matters of real weight and consequence insisted upon in the answer, being handled only according to the exigency of the particulars of my charge, might with more advantage be discoursed in an entire treatise, I changed my intention of publishing the answer, into a resolution of declaring my judgment about the doctrinal imputations specified against me, more at large. This resolution continuing, seconded and strengthened with further light shining into my heart daily, from the Father of Lights, hath given life to the ensuing treatise."

This account is given by Mr. Goodwin in the preface to his "Redemption Redeemed," which bears the date of February 12th, 1650; and ascertains with sufficient exactness the time of his conversion to the Arminian system.

Though he declined to publish a formal answer to
Lane's book, he was not silent on the subject of which it
treats.   With regard to the accusation preferred against
him, as having asserted " That natural men may do things
whereunto God hath, by way of promise, annexed grace
and acceptation ; " he says, " A most dangerous error !
and of as sad consequence as that which was charged upon
Paul, when his adversaries accused him for teaching,
That they were no gods, which were made with hands.   For
doubtless men are natural before they are spiritual ; and
spiritual they cannot be made, but by believing ; and to
believing, we all confess, God hath promised grace and
acceptation.   But till I have an opportunity to give a
more full account to the world of my judgment about the
freedom, or bondage rather, of the will, and power of
nature in order to salvation ; I desire to publish this as my
belief in the point : *That no man since the fall ever did,
or ever will believe unto salvation, but only by the assistance
of the special grace of God.*   If this be an opinion heterodox,
I confess I am not orthodox in the point." *

The generality of people, being almost constantly
employed in secular business, and therefore unaccustomed
to deep and long-continued attention to subjects of
abstract speculation, have little conception either of the difficulties connected with many theological questions, or of
the mental exercises of learned and studious men.   Having formed their own religious opinions rather from cate-
chisms and the dogmas of their teachers, than from a
minute and critical study of the Holy Scriptures, and seldom or never inquiring into the reasons of things, they
naturally imagine that a change of religious sentiment
implies a reprehensible instability of character.   Such an
assumption, however, is a mere vulgar error ; since it sup-
poses that those who are entrusted with the education of
youth, never inculcate erroneous principles, and that no
man can be wiser in advanced age than he was in his boyish
days.   Besides, what, in all human probability, would have
been the present state of the Christian world, had Luther,

* Divine Authority of the Scriptures, p. 26, Edit. 1648.

and Melancthon, and Cranmer, and Knox, and Calvin, together with their noble co-adjutors, resolved through the whole period of their lives to entertain the same religious opinions? Convinced of the importance of divine truth, . and of their liability to error, these eminent men made a solemn appeal from the dogmas of Popery in which they had been nurtured, to the Inspired Writings; in consequence of which they openly renounced many of their former principles, and laboured to establish the faith they had endeavoured to destroy. The benefits arising to the cause of Christianity, and to society at large, from such a procedure in them, are important beyond conception, and have invested their names with unfading glory. The bare circumstance, therefore, of a man's renunciation of his former sentiments, implies no just reflection upon his character. When a man indeed neglects the Holy Scriptures, and is therefore "tossed about with every wind of doctrine," or when he changes his creed for temporal emolument or the gratification of his vanity, he sinks into merited disrespect: but when a minister, considering himself accountable to the Head of the Church for every position he advances in the pulpit, abandons any particular system of doctrine through a patient and conscientious study of the Bible, and this with the certain prospect of suffering the "loss of all things;" whatever may be thought of his creed, his integrity entitles him to general esteem. Such, precisely, was the case of Mr. Goodwin. Had he forsaken the doctrines of Calvin when Laud patronized the Arminian tenets, a suspicion might have existed, that he had changed sides for the sake of preferment. But he made no avowal of the Arminian system, till its adherents were left without a patron, and those of them who had enjoyed benefices in the church were driven from their pulpits, and persecuted with relentless severity. Free from every bias of secular interest, his conversion to Arminianism can be viewed in no other light, than as the result of deliberate inquiry, and an act of obedience to the high authority of conscience.

Instead however of paying him that respect which is due to every honest man, several of his contemporaries endeavoured to excite popular feeling against him, by an incessant repetition of the charge of instability; intimating that as he had been educated in the school of Calvinian theology, and had yielded to its doctrines the assent of his understanding, his arguments in favour of general redemption were unworthy of serious regard. In reference to this subject, he says, "I crave leave to add a few words concerning the change of my judgment in the great controversy about the death of Christ, (with the rest depending hereon,) by way of answer to those who represent my present judgment as little valuable, because it sometimes stood in a contrary way. Though I know nothing in the allegation subservient to the purpose mentioned, but rather much against it, yet let me say, (1.) That however sin and an evil conversation are just matter of shame, repentance and amendment are truly honourable. Nor do I know why it should be of any more a disparaging interpretation against any man, to reform his judgment than his life; neither of which can be done without a change. Nor (2.) can I resent any such conformity with my adored Saviour, which consists in an *increase of wisdom*, any matter of disparagement either to myself or any other man. Though He indeed was never prevented with error, yet was He post-enriched with many things. A man can hardly 'grow in grace, and in the knowledge of Jesus Christ our Lord,' without out-growing himself in judgment and understanding; without making straight many things in his mind, which were crooked before. (3.) That chosen vessel Paul never quitted himself like a man, never consulted peace and glory to himself, till he built up again that faith which he had destroyed. Nor was his authority in the Gospel a whit lighter upon the balance, because he had once been a Pharisee. (4.) I desire to ask the men who make the change of my judgment a spot of weakness or vileness in it, whether themselves were always in the same mind touching all things with themselves at present? If so, it plainly argues, that their thoughts and apprehensions now that they are men, are but such which are incident to children. And if, since their coming to riper years, they have always stood, and are resolved always to stand, by their first thoughts and apprehensions in all things, it is a sign that their judgments reside more in their wills, than their wills in their judgments, and that they are much more likely to judge according to appearance, than to judge righteous judgment. Yea, there are very few of those who call themselves ministers of the Gospel, but many times when they preach, within the compass of an hour, either change their judgments or deny them; their *doctrine* being Samaritan, when their *application* is a Jew. (5.) If to dig broken cisterns, with the forsaking of the Fountain of living water, be the committing of a double evil, how shall not a recoursing to the Fountain of living water, in conjunction with a forsaking of broken cisterns, be the practising of a double duty? To forsake an error is one duty, and to embrace truth is another: whereas to persist in the same mind, suppose it to be sound and good, is but a single duty. There is joy in heaven over one sinner that repenteth, more than over ninety and nine which need no repentance. That which is an occasion of multiplied rejoicing in heaven, why should it be matter of complaint, charge, or imputation upon earth? (6.) He is the most likely to give a right judgment between two countries, who hath been an inhabitant of both, and hath acquainted himself with the respective conditions of both. In like manner, it is so far from being a reason why a man's present judgment should be rejected, that he hath been of a contrary judgment formerly, that it rendereth it the more considerable, and competent to discern aright between the opinions with which it hath been thoroughly, and upon a conscientious engagement, acquainted. It is a true saying of the heathen philosopher, 'Every man is able to judge well of those things which he knoweth.' But when a man, having a long time known and professed an opinion, by the profession whereof he enjoyed peace, credit, wealth, love and respects from men of all sorts, and was in a fair way to lift up his head yet higher in the world, by con-

tinuance in the profession; shall, notwithstanding, relent
in his judgment, quit this opinion, and profess that which
is opposite to it, wherein he could not but conclude before-
hand, that he should lose credit, friends, all hopes of preferment,—when a man shall change his judgment upon
such terms as these, it is a strong argument that he
thoroughly understands the spiritual danger of that opinion
which he forsakes, as well as the truth and goodness of that
which he embraceth.   Therefore, (7.) as David replied to
Michal, when she upbraided him with a deportment by
which, as she apprehended, he made himself contemptible,
I will be yet more vile; so, the grace of God assisting me,
if the changing of my judgment upon such terms as I
have done, in the controversies mentioned, rendereth me
or my judgment contemptible, I am resolved, upon the
like occasion, to make both it and myself more contemptible, by cutting off from my soul error after error,
as fast as they shall be discovered, and by changing my
judgment as oft as I shall thoroughly understand, that
my spiritual interest doth require it.   It shall be one of
my chief exercises to diminish daily the number of my
errors, by making a frequent and diligent survey of my
judgment, and by separating the vile from the precious,
till no misprision at all of God, or of any of His things,
if it be possible, be found in me." *

In addition to these remarks, which display a mind more
in love with truth than with ease, or honour, or wealth,
it may not be improper to observe, that several of the
greatest divines that have adorned the different Protestant Churches, have undergone a change of sentiment
concerning the extent of the Divine philanthropy, similar
to that which was experienced by Mr. Goodwin.   Of this
number, among many others, were Melancthon, Arminius,
Tilenus, Dr. Thomas Jackson, Dr. Goad, Mr. Hoard, Dr.
Christopher Potter, the ever memorable Hales of Eton,
Dr. Thomas Pierce, Bishop Sanderson, and Archbishop
Usher: men of deep and various learning, accustomed to
read the Scriptures in their original languages, familiar

* Redemption Redeemed, Preface.

with the writings of the Christian fathers, well skilled in the laws of argumentation, and accurately acquainted with every scheme of predestination that had been previously advanced. To be associated with such characters, can be no dishonour to any man.

After the doctrines of Arminius had gained the assent of Mr. Goodwin's mind, he preached them to his people in the ordinary course of his ministry; but it does not appear that he distinctly announced them to the world as "the articles of his belief," till the year 1648, when he published his treatise entitled, "The Divine Authority of the Scriptures Asserted; and the Great Charter of the World's Blessedness Vindicated." In this singularly curious and valuable volume the author has embodied the substance of those arguments in proof of the divine authority of the Scriptures, which he had formerly advanced from the pulpit with eminent success. It contains many new and surprising thoughts, and ingenious and interesting remarks upon various passages of Holy Writ; and may be read with great advantage even by those who are conversant with the elaborate productions of our more modern apologists for revealed truth. Baxter, who had paid profound attention to the evidences of the Christian revelation, pronounces this an "excellent book," and repeatedly recommends the perusal of it to those who desire to have a thorough knowledge of the foundation upon which their faith is built.*

In this treatise Mr. Goodwin unequivocally asserts the glorious doctrine of general redemption, and the consequent salvability of all mankind; and contends, that the salvation of adult persons in every instance is conditional. "If a king," says he, "having caused a man's legs to be cut off, suppose he hath done it in a way of justice, yet if he should urge, press, and persuade such a man to run a race with those that are swift of foot, and promise him, with many expressions of love, exceeding great rewards if he would come as soon to the goal as they that run with

* Reasons of the Christian Religion, p. 453, Edit. 1667. Saints' Everlasting Rest, p. 267, Edit. 1609.

M 2

him ; this would be a carriage savouring more of unman-like insolency over the poor wretch in his misery, than of any real affection towards him, or any desire of his good. In like manner, to conceive that God applieth Himself with such moving and melting expressions of mercy, tenderness of bowels, love, grace, bounty, towards His creature man, as the Scripture emphatically asserts that He doth ; promising them life and glory if they will believe and turn to Him ; and yet to suppose that these men, to whom He maketh these rich applications of Himself, are destitute of all power to do what He requires of them, is to represent the glorious God, in His greatest expressions of mercy, grace, and love, rather as laughing the world to scorn in that great misery wherein it is plunged, than as a God truly desirous and intending to relieve it ; His professions of love, grace, and favour notwithstanding. Some indeed imagine, that they see such a face of God as this in the glass of the Gospel : but, God giving life and opportunity, we shall demonstratively prove in due time, that all such conceptions are most unworthy of God, and wholly inconsistent with those things which the Scriptures teach, as well concerning Him, as those gracious abilities which He hath indulgently conferred upon men through the Second Adam, notwithstanding their fall in the first."*

" God having received that obedience from the hand of Jesus Christ, which is every way as considerable in matter of glory to Him, as the sin of man was in dishonour and provocation ; He may, without the least disparagement to His holiness, wisdom, or any other attribute, offer terms of reconciliation and peace to him that hath provoked Him. Not as if God were bound presently to forgive men their sins, and to take them into special favour, because of what Christ hath suffered for them ; which seems to be the sense of many : Christ did not satisfy for any man's sins, in such a sense, or upon such terms. But Christ is said to have made an atonement for the sins of men, because He hath so far pacified and reconciled God to the world, that He is willing, notwithstanding their great sin, and affront put

* Page 169.

upon Him, to offer terms of life and peace; yet so, that they who will not condescend, or rather indeed that will not ascend to the terms offered by Him, that is, that will not Believe, shall have no further benefit by any thing He hath either done or suffered for them. Nor will it follow, that they for whose sins Christ hath satisfied, must needs, by virtue of that satisfaction, be presently justified and saved; or that God otherwise should be unjust, if, having received satisfaction, He should condemn men for those sins for which He hath been satisfied. The reason is, because, the satisfaction of Christ being an ordinance of God for the justification and salvation of men, MERELY ARBITRARY, AND DEPENDING UPON HIS WILL AND PLEASURE, as well in the operation as in the being of it, it cannot be conceived to extend any farther, nor to produce its effects upon any other terms, than His WILL and PLEASURE is that it should produce them. Now the Scriptures are very clear and pregnant in this, that the sufferings of Christ do not justify or save any man simply, or by themselves, but through a man's Believing. 'God so loved the world,' saith our Saviour, ' that He gave His only-begotten Son;' not simply that men should 'have everlasting life' by Him; but ' that whosoever Believeth in Him should not perish, but have everlasting life.' Notwithstanding the love of God, notwithstanding the gift of Christ unto the world, yet without Believing there is no escaping eternal death, no obtaining everlasting life. Why? Because the love of God and the gift of Christ, being both voluntary, they justify, they save, no further, upon no other terms, than the will and good pleasure of God is they should. Now the will of God touching salvation to man, is, that he should be saved by Christ through Believing. Fully consonant hereunto is that of the apostle, 'Being justified freely by His grace, through the redemption that is in Christ Jesus, whom God hath set forth to be a propitiation,' that is, an actual or personal propitiation, ' through faith in His blood.' Though justification be *free*, though through the *grace* of God, though through *the redemption which is in Christ Jesus;* yet no justification by any, nor by all of these, actually accrues to any man without Believing.

"Faith doth not add in the least to the nature, value, or efficacy of Christ's satisfaction; it only interesteth men in the value and efficacy of it; both which were in it in as ample and full measure before men believe, as they are after. The fire, whilst a man keeps at a distance from it, doth not warm him: when he comes near it, it doth: yet his coming near doth not make the fire any hotter than it was before; only it gives him interest and communion in the heat of it. Thus you see how men's sins may be said to be fully atoned by Christ, and yet men remain under the guilt of them, and perish everlastingly; and that without the least touch or shadow of disparagement to the justice of God. But we may have occasion to speak further to this point some other time; where we may further clear the difficulty,—How it may stand with the justice of God to accept Christ's satisfaction for the sins of men, and yet destroy men for them notwithstanding. It is a point well worth inquiring into; because generally we do not understand the counsel and mind of God in it aright. If we did, it would set us at perfect liberty from some of the most ensnaring entanglements in the Antinomian way, and quite break the credit thereof: and the truth is, that Antinomianism is nothing else but a system of the due and lawful consequences of their opinions who most fiercely oppose it.

"If God should offer and promise unto men life and peace and salvation, as we know He doth to thousands who never accept His offer, and so perish; and should press upon them with many expressions of love, tenderness, and great compassions, beseeching them that they would be reconciled to Him; having taken away, though justly, that power whereby they might have done themselves good by accepting those offers, *and should confer none other upon them in the stead;* this would be a dispensation towards poor miserable creatures, altogether unworthy that God, who is the Father of our Lord Jesus Christ, and in Him the Father of mercies, and the God of all consolation. As to that objection wherewith this opinion is burdened in the thoughts of many, that it is an Arminian doctrine, and maintains free-will, with the like ; we shall answer no more for the present but this : That if it be a doctrine asserted by Paul and Peter, as most assuredly it is, it ought to suffer no disparagement for being found amongst the tenets of Arminius. It is a faithful saying, and worthy of all acceptation, that Christ Jesus came into the world to save sinners; though it was in effect the saying of the devil, when he affirmed Jesus Christ to be the Holy One of God. It is a common Papistical trick, to nick-name truths and opinions which rise up against the interest and honour of the See of Rome, to bethink themselves of some heretic or other who asserted them. And I wish that too many of those who are called Protestants, and who as ambitiously as they affect the name of Orthodox, did not *praise such sayings* by a frequent imitation of them."*

Mr. Goodwin's anticipations of reproach and persecution, on his open avowal of these sentiments, were well founded. The affections of several of his friends were immediately alienated from him, and a violent outcry was raised against him as a most dangerous propagator of heresy. If he had actually held in his hand the wonder-working rod of Moses, and had threatened the country with a repetition of all the plagues of Egypt, some good men could scarcely have manifested greater alarm. A host of antagonists began to assail him with every species of weapon, and even those who possessed neither learning nor argument were employed in calling names. One noble champion of Genevan ortho-doxy attacked him in a pamphlet which he entitled, "HELL BROKE LOOSE ;" charging Mr. Goodwin in effect with over-throwing the divine authority of the Scriptures, denying original sin, asserting that the human soul when separated from the body is in a state of unconscious existence, and with opposing the imputation of Christ's righteousness to believers. His sentiments on the last subject were grossly misrepresented, and the other charges were not supported by even a shadow of legitimate proof.

* Page 195, &c.

But our author was not opposed and slandered by individuals only. The London clergy, of the Presbyterian denomination, were in the habit of holding weekly meetings at Sion College, to consult about ecclesiastical affairs. Having long invoked the parliament to suppress all the sectaries in the nation, and finding that their re-iterated request was not likely to be soon fulfilled, they resolved, (*since they could do no more!*) to unite in the publication of a tract, which they entitled, "A Testimony to the Truth of Jesus Christ, and to our Solemn League and Covenant; as also against the Errors, Heresies, and Blasphemies of these Times, and the Toleration of them; Subscribed by the Ministers of Christ within the Province of London, 1648." To this production the signatures of fifty-two clergymen are appended; among which are those of John Downame, Arthur Jackson, Samuel Clark, Francis Roberts, Christopher Love, Thomas Watson, Thomas Gataker, Daniel Cawdrey, Anthony Tuckney, Edmund Calamy, Simon Ash, Thomas Case, Lazarus Seaman, and Anthony Burgess. In this "Testimony" Mr. Goodwin is treated with flagrant injustice. He is not only associated with the heretics and blasphemers of the age, but is indirectly charged with abetting principles which he strenuously disavowed. His love of accuracy, and habit of correct thinking, had led him to make a distinction which these men attempted to turn to the worst possible account. He had remarked, that by "the Word of God" which is the foundation of the Christian religion, using that term in its sublimest sense, was rather to be understood the grand distinguishing Doctrines of Revelation, than the letter of Sacred Scripture: the latter having sustained some partial injury from the hands of copyists and printers; the former remaining through all ages as firm as the pillars of heaven. He nevertheless acknowledged that there is an important sense in which it may be said, that the Scriptures in their present form are both the Word of God and the foundation of Christianity. Whereas the authors of this "Testimony," putting a construction upon his words which he never designed them to bear, represent him as guilty of an absolute denial of both.

"If by the Scriptures," says he, "be meant the matter and substance of things contained in the Books of the Old and New Testament, I fully and with all my heart and soul believe them to be none other than the Word of God; and, God assisting, shall rather expose myself to a thousand deaths than deny them so to be. I absolutely believe that Jesus Christ is God, that He is the Son of God, was made man, died for the salvation of the world, rose again from the dead; that whosoever believes on Him shall be saved, that whosoever believes not shall be condemned; with a thousand more besides; all these assertions I fully believe not only to be truths, but truths of special revelation from God to the world.

"If by the Scriptures be meant, all the letters, syllables, words, phrases, expressed in the said books, whether translated, or in such Hebrew and Greek copies as are commonly used amongst us, I know no ground why I should believe that all the said syllables, letters, words, &c., were in any special way given by God to convey those truths and mysteries to the minds of men, which He hath been graciously pleased to reveal for their salvation. Concerning translations, the case is clear: there being none of these but which carry marks of human oscitancy and weakness in them. Concerning the Hebrew copies, I know no law that binds me to believe, that no transcriber of them out of their first originals, no printer of them out of these transcripts, ever miscarried after the manner of men, in these negotiations. I dare not say, but that in some of these copies there may be all things, even to words, syllables, and letters, of Divine inspiration; on the other hand, I cannot be confident that they are. As for the original Greek copies, it is generally known that there are many varieties of readings, and some of them considerable, between edition and edition. Now certain it is, that God did not direct His first penmen of the Scriptures, to publish different copies of those things which they were respectively appointed by Him to impart by writing to the world.

"Though I do not believe that any original exemplar of the Scriptures now extant is so purely the Word of God, but that it may have a tincture of the word of men in it; yet I confidently believe that the providence of God, and the love which He bears to His own glory, have so far interposed and watched over the great and gracious Revelation which He made of Himself by Jesus Christ to the world, that those books, wherein it was in all the particularities at first imparted to the world, neither have suffered, nor ever shall suffer, any such mutilation or falsification in any kind, but that they will be able abundantly to furnish men of all sorts and conditions with the knowledge of all things necessary to be known, either for their Christian deportment in this world, or their everlasting salvation in that which is to come.

" Concerning Translations, though I judge none of them to be the pure Word of God, without any embasement by that which is human; nor yet in such a sense as the original copies may be called the Word of God, which not only express the mind of God as translations, but hold them forth in that very language, and for the most part, if not altogether, in the self-same words and phrases, wherein God Himself directed the publication of them by writing; yet I judge them one of the greatest blessings that God ever vouchsafed to the Gentile part of the world; and conceive that though they do not, even the best of them, express the mind of God so entirely, or emphatically, as the originals do; yet even the worst of them that I know, express so much of the mind and will of God, by the true understanding whereof men may be brought to live godly, righteously, and soberly in the present world, and consequently to that immortal and undefiled inheritance reserved in the heavens for those that believe.

"Though I judge no translation whatsoever, either for gracefulness of language, significancy of terms, majesty of expression, to be equal to the original Hebrew and Greek; yet I conceive that there is no translation so disadvantageously compiled, but that carrieth somewhat differing, by way of excellency, from the manner of men, in the phrase and language thereof; yea that which is sufficient by the ordinary blessing of God upon a conscientious and intent reading, to evince the descent of the matter contained in it to be from God; as a seal of arms upon the outside of a letter is sufficient to discover from what person of honour the contents of the letter come.

" I conceive the matter of the Scriptures, I mean those divine truths, those holy and righteous commands, those great and precious promises, those astonishing and dreadful threatenings, expressed as well in translations as in the originals, to be of the greatest power to discover and assert their royal descent from God. There is such a brightness of divine excellency sitting as it were upon the face of the Gospel, that men who are not through the just judgment of God deprived of the use of their understandings about spiritual things, cannot but see and acknowledge manifest characters and impressions of the grace, holiness, love, and wisdom of God in it.

" The true and proper foundation of Christian religion is not ink and paper, not any books or writings whatsoever; but that substance of matter, those gracious counsels of God concerning the salvation of the world by Jesus Christ, which indeed are represented and declared, both in translations and originals, but are essentially distinct from both, and no ways for their natures and beings dependent upon either of them. A bargain agreed upon and concluded between two men, whether the tenor of it be ever drawn up in writing or no, is, for the nature of it and matter of transaction, a complete and true bargain: the writing, if any be made in reference to it, only declareth the nature of the bargain, which was in reality and completeness of being before the writing; and consequently the writing can be no part of it. In like manner, the good pleasure of God concerning the salvation of the world had, in all the particulars of it, completeness of being in God Himself, long before any branch of it was imparted to the world by any writing whatsoever. There was true religion in the world all along that great space of time, which had gone over the

head of the world before Moses was employed by God to
lay the corner-stone of that divine fabric of Scripture,
which hath been of a long time perfected.   Yea the
Gospel itself, and those rich discoveries which God reserved to be presented by Jesus Christ to the world at
His coming into it, were effectually preached, and believed
by many unto salvation, and Christian religion fully established in the world, before any part of the New Testament
was written.   The Evangelist Matthew is generally conceived, especially by ancient writers, to have been the
first penman that God was pleased to use in penning the
New Testament; and that it was about eight years after
Christ's ascension, before he put forth his hand to this
work.   And yet who doubts but that the foundation of
Christian religion was laid before this in the world; yea,
and much of this religion built upon it?" *

"What treasures of wisdom and knowledge the Scriptures brought at first out of the bosom of God, the same
they present to the world at this day.   God hath suffered
no man to rob them of their silver, or to give them tin or
dross instead of it.   The words they now speak, are the
same spirit and life, which they spake in the beginning.
It is true the holy God did not guide all the pens of the
transcribers of the Scriptures, with the same heavenly
infallibleness, with which He guided the pens and tongues
of His immediate secretaries, who wrote them from His
mouth.   This appears from that variety of readings which
is found in some words between copy and copy; which
difference   proceeded   from   the   ignorance,   or   negligence, or perhaps from a worse principle sometimes, in
those who were employed to transcribe them.   The native
sense of a scripture may, through a mistake, want, or
redundancy of a word in a false copy, be past finding out,
in respect of any light which the mistaken place affordeth;
yet by the help of other copies, by the series and carriage
of the context, by comparing other scriptures with it, the
sense which was lost one way may be saved another.   God
hath watched with that tender eye of providence over the

* Page 13, &c.

letter of the Scriptures, that there was no truth deducible from thence, at the first coming of them into the world, but that by an equal light of understanding, in conjunction with a like hand of diligence, and a like measure of assistance from God, may be deduced from them at this day."*

Such were Mr. Goodwin's views of the nature, importance, and value of Divine revelation. Where then must have been the consciences of the fifty-two "Ministers of Christ within the province of London," who could publicly stigmatize him, in the most solemn manner, as an abettor of "Errors *against* the Divine Authority of the Holy Scriptures?" They knew that he had recently preached many sermons in vindication of this momentous point; that by the instrumentality of his labours several persons had been convinced of this great truth; and they also held in their hands a volume on the same subject, just published by him, which was unquestionably the best defence of the Christian revelation that had then appeared in the English language. An attack of the same calumnious character was made a few years afterwards by Dr. Owen upon Dr. Brian Walton, the learned editor of the London Polyglot Bible; for which he was subjected to a severe castigation from that profound Orientalist.†

Equally unjust was the second charge which Mr. Goodwin's censors preferred against him. In their list of "Errors about natural man's free-will, and power to do good supernatural;" they repeat the accusation of Lane, concerning natural men doing that to which God has promised grace and acceptation; at the same time declining to take the slightest notice of Mr. Goodwin's explicit declaration respecting the absolute necessity of the promised aid of the Holy Spirit: thus intimating that he either denied original sin, or taught that men might correct and overcome the evil propensities of their nature, by their own unassisted efforts. This conduct was highly iniquitous. Where is the theological writer, however accurate, who may not be

* Page 258, &c.　　† See the Second Volume of Todd's *Memoirs of Bishop Walton*, 1821.

convicted of heresy, by a selection of isolated periods and half sentences from his works ; by a careful omission of his explanations ; and by a total disregard of the sense in which he designs to be understood ? Such was the "hard measure" that was awarded to Mr. Goodwin, and to some other persons, among whom was the excellent Dr. Henry Hammond. While those guardians of Genevan orthodoxy professed to discard the Popish doctrine of infallibility, they arrogated to themselves the high-sounding title of "THE Ministers of Christ," assumed authority to accuse, to condemn, and to traduce as heretics, men who were in every respect equal to themselves, in age, in ministerial diligence, in sound learning, in purity of conduct; and all this without condescending to hear what the accused had to say in their own defence, and without assigning any reason for censures so harsh and severe. The piety of these men has been extolled to the heavens ; but it is presumed, that if the New Testament be regarded as the standard of religious and moral excellence, the panegyrics of their admirers should be received with considerable abatement. Men who could make an open and deliberate attack upon the character of their brethren, by falsifying their opinions, for no other crime than that of differing from them in religious sentiment, and at the same time could express their regret that civil pains and penalties were not inflicted upon them, certainly did not excel in the exercise of that "charity" which "suffereth long and is kind, is not puffed up, and doth not behave itself unseemly ;" and, without which, even the most orthodox professors of Christianity are no more than "sounding brass and a tinkling cymbal."

Very dishonourable collusion was practised in obtaining signatures to this objectionable "Testimony." In the copy that was laid before Mr. John Downame, and to which he affixed his name, no mention was made either of Dr. Hammond or of Mr. Goodwin ; their reputed errors and heresies being foisted in afterwards. It happened unluckily, that Downame had licensed the Doctor's book for publication, and thus recommended it to general perusal. When he therefore found, that, by a manœuvre of his Presbyterian friends, he was made to condemn as heretical a work to which he had given his public sanction, he complained bitterly of their disingenuous conduct.* Others of the subscribers, one would hope for their own credit, were imposed upon in the same manner.

The author of the History of the Puritans, having noticed a few of the reputed errors against which these divines had borne their "testimony," observes in reference to Mr. Goodwin, that "he had published several large and learned books, as, The Divine Authority of the Scriptures—Redemption Redeemed—A Treatise of Justification, and An Exposition of the Ninth Chapter to the Romans, out of which the above-mentioned exceptions were taken. This divine, taking it amiss to be marked for a heretic, challenged any of the London clergy to a disputation; as thinking it a very unrighteous method to condemn opinions before they had been confuted."† This account reflects no honour either upon the accuracy or the candour of this celebrated historian. That Mr. Goodwin was the author of the "large and learned books" here ascribed to him, is true; but that he had "published" them at the time here referred to, is incorrect. The "Treatise of Justification," and "The Divine Authority of the Scriptures Asserted," are the only works here specified, which had then been presented to the world; and it was only from the latter of these, and from "The Scourge of the Saints Displayed," that these divines extracted passages which they denominated heretical. They could not "take exceptions" out of "large and learned books" that had no existence. That Mr. Goodwin should think it a very "unrighteous method to condemn opinions before they had been confuted," and should "take it amiss" under such circumstances "to be marked as a heretic," is not surprising; since these proceedings were a mean and despicable attack upon his personal character, designed to alienate his hearers from him, and to render his ministry inefficient. When Mr. Neal, however, states, that our

* Goodwin's Novice-Presbyter, Preface.   † Neal's Hist. Purit. vol. iii. p. 359, Edit. 1794.

heretic "challenged any of the London clergy to a disputation," he does not write history, but presents to his readers a mere sally of prejudice or of inattention. Mr. Goodwin was deeply injured, and therefore published a modest and temperate, yet firm and manly vindication of himself from the aspersions of his persecutors, without any of the vaunting levity imputed to him by the historian. This was his only means of redress, and he availed himself of it in a manner that was equally honourable to his understanding and temper. Like many other men who profess to write history, Neal is seldom to be trusted when speaking of persons whose theological principles he happened to dislike.

Goodwin's judges having dated their "Testimony" from Sion College, the place at which their self-constituted court was held, he entitled his reply, "Sion College Visited." In this excellent tract he says, "It was never well with Christian Religion, since the ministers of the Gospel cunningly vested that privilege of the church, of being the ground and pillar of truth, in themselves; claiming Nebuchadnezzar's prerogative amongst men, over the truths of God: 'Whom he would he slew, and whom he would he kept alive, and whom he would he set up, and whom he would he put down.'

"There came lately out of the press, a few pages styling themselves, A Testimony to the Truth of Jesus Christ, and pretending to a subscription by the ministers of Christ within the province of London. I wish for these ministers' sake, to whom I wish nothing but good, and for the truth's sake also, that I could conceive the boldness of any man so great, as to present them to the world for the authors of such a piece of weakness, without their consent. I should be able, by such an apprehension, to maintain those honourable thoughts of their persons, which (my witness is on high) I have always unfeignedly laboured to do.

"To scrapple together a few passages out of several books, without taking any notice of their true meaning; and some of these obvious truths; yea, to falsify sayings by leaving out some material words; and only to clamour,

'Horrid and prodigious opinions—Infamous and pernicious errors—The very dregs and spawn of those old accursed heresies—Anti-Scripturism—Popery—Arianism—Socinianism—Arminianism, &c.:' to pour floods of such reproachful and foul language as this upon men's opinions without one word of argument against them, is not only altogether irrelative to the extinction of errors and heresies, but very proper for the further propagation of them. For when men speak evil of that as an error or heresy, against which they have nothing of moment to oppose; the assertors may very reasonably suppose, that they speak evil of it, not out of judgment but affection.

"Brethren, give me leave to be serious with you. I believe you are straitened in your own bowels, in comparison of the enlargement you have in mine: though I fear you believe nothing less. I hear of many complaints and sad regrets from you, as that the ministers of Christ are much despised, and your auditories much depopulated, your respects with the people brought well nigh to a morsel of bread. I beseech you, consider! Hath he that puts his finger in the fire, any cause to complain, that the fire puts him to pain? Or is it any wonder if, when under a pretence of so much 'zeal for God's glory'—such 'integrity of heart' —such 'conscientiousness of appearing for God, His truth, and the cause of religion'—such 'detestation of all errors, heresies, and blasphemies'—with many such like glittering professions more, wherewith your 'Testimony' is garnished —you do, in the very face of these professions, stigmatize the truths of God with the odious names of 'infamous and pernicious errors and heresies'—set yourselves to pull down with both hands the names and reputations of the faithful servants of God, your brethren, and this without any cause at all given by them—report their sayings by halves, leaving out their explications, on purpose to defame them—represent such opinions as erroneous in them, which you allow for orthodox in yourselves—exasperate the sword of the civil magistrate against such as are peaceable and wish you no harm — foment divisions — multiply distractions — obstruct the composure and settlement of things in the land

N

—recompensing no degree of all this unworthiness with any proportionable or considerable good :—is it any marvel if, going thus to work, coupling such unworthy actions with such specious professions, you sink in the hearts of men daily more and more ?   Men will never be able to rise up before you, and call you blessed, unless they be holpen up by the hand of some visible worth in your ways.   Mean time, though I find the best of you no better than a brier to me, pursuing me with outcries, for a man of I know not how many errors ; yet there are four amongst your fifty-two, who have appeared against me to their deeper shame than others.   For what ?   They who publish books of errors,—they who recommend books of errors to be read, —can these men find in their hearts to lift up the heel against those who receive them at their hands ? Mr. Ash, Mr. Cawdrey, Mr. Calamy, Mr. Burgess ; how could these men anoint Mr. John Ball with oil, and salt me with fire, for only speaking what he speaketh, in that book of his which they recommend ?

"If any man ask, Why I could not be content to sit down by my charge, with the same patience wherein others, charged as well as I, possess their souls ? no man's pen moving against his accusers, but mine. I answer, Though I do not *sit down* by it in patience, I *rise up* with it, and bear it upon my shoulder, with more than patience ; even with joy and gladness ; as I stand charged from heaven to do : 'My brethren, count it all joy, when ye fall into divers temptations.' I trust that the tenor of my answer doth no ways imply, that the least hair of the head of my patience is fallen to the ground.

"But the chief motive which engaged me to this under-taking was, Because I look upon myself as the chief, if not the only person, for whose sake the fifty-two hands were drawn out of the bosom to smite the rest. I have reason to conceive, that this Court of Assize was called principally, if not only, for my sake ; and that no 'Testimony' had been given at this time, either to the 'Truth of Jesus Christ,' or against the 'errors and heresies' of other men, had not the two-and-fifty judged it expedient that my name should be blasted. My fellow-heretics are quickly dispatched; little being cited out of their books in comparison: I suppose, lest their errors should seem as large, as dangerous as mine.

"The subscribers, with many others of the same interest, are instant upon all occasions to declaim against me, as a friend to errors and heresies, and to cry out that I plead for a toleration of them all. I solemnly profess, that whoever they are, that bear the errors and wicked opinions of the times, as a burden of sorrow, I bear my share with them. Nor do I believe that any of them all, who seek to render me the hatred of men, by the imputation of such a delinquency, have run either faster or further, *in the way of God*, for pulling up those noisome weeds, than I have done. I have professedly engaged myself, in the course of my ministry, against four of those errors which are generally looked upon as most predominant amongst us, and to which all others whatsoever may easily be reduced: Antinomianism, Anabaptism, Anti-Scripturism, Querism. To which I might add a fifth, Manicheism; which, had it not the countenance which the other four want, would soon be found to be of as dangerous consequence to religion as they. I am a fool to boast myself; but wise men have compelled me, and wise men I hope will pardon me."

When Mr. Goodwin published his "Sion College Visited," Dr. Hammond also replied to the accusations preferred against him as a propagator of "errors, heresies, and blasphemies." His excellent pamphlet, which he entitled, "A View of some Exceptions to the Practical Catechism," is inserted in the first volume of the folio edition of his works. The Doctor and Mr. Goodwin both appear to infinite advantage, not only with regard to argument, but in respect of spirit and temper, when compared with their dogmatical and self-constituted judges. "Seeing it again appears," says the learned Doctor,.......... "that it is God's good pleasure to deliver me up to be evil spoken of, and accused, and to bear a yet deeper part of His bitter cup than many others of my brethren have done, I desire to bless and praise His name for this His goodness and mercy to me, and to embrace all those who have joined their hands to be instruments in this, as those whom by Christ's command... .... I am bound to love, to bless, to pray for, and not to think of any other way of return toward them. This, I thank God, I can most cheerfully do; and would satisfy myself to have done it in private, between God and my own soul, were there not another occasion which makes it a little necessary for me to say somewhat publicly; and that is, the vindication of the truth of Christ Jesus, which they who are willing to give 'testimony' to it, will, I hope, take from me in good part." *

On the appearance of Mr. Goodwin's "Sion College Visited," and of Dr. Hammond's "View," it was debated among the ministers who had signed the "Testimony" against these eminent men, Whether or not any answer to their publications should be prepared? and the question was finally determined in the negative: perhaps from a conviction that they had already overstepped the boundaries of truth and charity.† One of their fraternity, however, a warm young man of the name of William Jenkyn, less wise than his brethren, renewed the attack upon Mr. Goodwin; exasperated to find that he not only denied the assumed authority of his censors, but actually "visited" them with reproofs and expostulations. This abusive controversialist, whose tract was denominated "The Busy Bishop," was not only Mr. Goodwin's junior by many years, but vastly inferior to him in talents and learning. His conduct indeed would never have been tolerated among a people of refinement and delicacy. It was extremely indecorous for a comparatively young man, without any provocation, to make a boastful and insolent attack upon the character of an aged and laborious minister, who had suffered the loss of all things for conscience-sake; and to exhibit him before the world as an object of scorn and infamy. With a design of promoting the benefit of this antagonist, rather than of defending at large his own peculiar opinions, Mr. Goodwin published a reply to the production of Jenkyn, under the

* Hammond's Works, Vol. I. p. 199, Edit. 1684.   † Goodwin's Novice-Presbyter, Preface.

title of "The Youngling Elder; or, Novice-Presbyter."
In the composition of this pamphlet the author appears
desirous of raising a blush of ingenuous shame on the face
of his opponent. "The task whereunto I shall confine
myself in this undertaking," says he, "is to show my youth-
ful confidentiary more of himself than he understands; and
how far, even in those things wherein he most magnifies
himself, reason and truth are above him. I shall reduce
what I judge necessary to animadvert upon his book, to the
demonstration of these four capital defects in him:—In
point of conscience—of learning, or clerkship—of judgment, or apprehension,—of civility, and common ingenuity." At the conclusion of this work, Mr. Goodwin says,
" Though there be nothing in the preceding discourse, that
can justly offend any man; yet, considering partly the exigency of the season, which calleth upon all parties to join
heart and hand in order to the common safety; partly also,
the extreme weakness of many, who know not how to love,
where all their thoughts as well as persons are not loved
first, and adored for truth; I could easily have been so far
over-ruled as to have quietly borne awhile longer that burden of shame which Mr. Jenkyn hath laid upon me, and
accordingly have *forborne*, at least for a time, the publishing
of the treatise, had not an importune stickler in that cause
(having by sinister practices procured some of the sheets)
unseasonably published some part of it in a pamphlet;
wherein he labours to possess the world with prejudice
against it, whilst it was yet unborn. In consideration hereof
I was necessitated to a present publication of it; hoping
that neither a Christian apology for innocency and truth on
the one hand, nor a necessary reproof of error and undue
practices on the other, shall prove any obstruction in the
way of love, concord, and peace; but rather make way for
their advancement. No man shall go further with his
adversary to make peace than I. The most peaceable man
under heaven may draw his sword in his own defence, and
possibly wound his adversary, without the least reflection
upon that lovely disposition in him."

Mr. Goodwin's object in this pamphlet, so far as it refer-

red to his antagonist, was far from being realized. Instead
of being salutary in its operation upon the mind of Jenkyn,
it only stimulated him to a further attack upon the reputation of Mr. Goodwin, in a publication which he entitled,
"The Blind Guide." To this production it does not appear
that Mr. Goodwin wrote any reply. He had no hope of
promoting the moral improvement of his abusive assailant,
and therefore silently retired from the contest, submitting
his cause to "Him that judgeth righteously." It is but
justice to Jenkyn to add, that by a series of persecutions he
was afterwards softened into a more generous temper and
into more catholic principles. When his own party was
triumphant, he insulted Mr. Goodwin as a heretic and sec-
tarian, and loudly clamoured for the suppression of all who
called the dogmas of his friends in question ; little thinking
that a time would come at which the Episcopalians would
regain their power, and he should die in Newgate for non-
conformity to their established forms of religious worship.
"With what measure ye mete it shall be measured to you
again."

In his attempts to injure Mr. Goodwin's reputation,
Jenkyn was assisted by the noted John Vicars, "who could
out-scold the boldest face in Billingsgate;" * and whose
powers of railing stand unrivalled in the history of human
nature. The following is the title of the book which he
published against Mr. Goodwin, without having received
the slightest provocation : " Coleman Street Conclave Visited ; and that Grand Impostor, the Schismatics' Cheater
in Chief, (who hath long slily lurked therein,) truly and
duly Discovered : containing a most palpable and plain
Display of Mr. John Goodwin's Self-Conviction, (under his
own hand-writing,) and of the notorious Heresies, Errors,
Malice, Pride, and Hypocrisy of this most Huge Garagan-
tua in Falsely Pretended Piety; to the lamentable misleading of his too too credulous, soul-murdered Proselytes,
of Coleman Street, and elsewhere : collected principally out
of his own Big Braggadochia, Wave-like, Swelling, and
Swaggering Writings; full-fraught with Six-footed terms

* Foulis's Hist. of Plots, p. 179, Edit. 1674.

and Flashy, Rhetorical Phrases, far more than solid and sacred Truths; and may fitly serve, (if it be the Lord's will,) like Belshazzar's hand-writing upon the wall of his conscience, to strike Terror and Shame into his own Soul and shameless Face, and to Undeceive his most miserably Cheated and Enchanted, or Bewitched Followers, 1648."

Prefixed to this scandalous publication, as a frontispiece, is a portrait of Mr. Goodwin, with a windmill over his head, and a weather-cock upon it. On one side there is a figure of a human head, with distended cheeks, resting upon a cloud, and inscribed " Error," blowing the sails of the mill; and on the other side there is a similar figure, inscribed " Pride," blowing the weather-cock round on its pivot. In his left hand Mr. Goodwin holds a book bearing the inscription of " Hagio-Mastix;" the name of one of his tracts against religious coercion: on his right, a hand is stretched out presenting to him a book on which is written, " Moro-Mastix;" the title of an idle anonymous pamphlet which was published against him. An old decayed tree, stripped of its foliage and branches, stands on the left side of the venerable old man. At the top of this device are the following lines :—

> The cock my vain and various mind descries ;
> The mill my venting and inventing lies.

The following couplet is issuing from Mr. Goodwin's mouth :—

> In all the grists I grind in error's mill,
> Unhappy I, I am mistaken still.

Underneath this caricature are two sets of verses. The former of these, ascribed by Vicars to a "fawning flatterer," is taken from a fine portrait of Mr. Goodwin, engraven by Glover, and bearing the date of 1641. The following is a copy :—

> Thou seest not whom thou seest ; then do not say
> That this is he. Who calls a lump of clay,
> Without its soul, a man ? Thou seest no more ;
> Nay but a shadow of that lump. What store

Of gifts and graces, what perfections rare,
Among ten thousand persons scattered are,
Gather in one: imagine it to be
This shadow's substance, and then say 'tis he.   D. T.

These lines were written by Daniel Taylor, Esq., author of
the Letter to Mr. Vicars, mentioned in a preceding chapter. A very interesting character of this extraordinary
man will be found in a subsequent part of these memoirs.
In an opposite column, as a counterpart to this panegyric,
are the following lines by a "downright dealer, J. V."

I shame to see, what here I see, and say,
That this is he who fast and loose doth play
With piety. A soul full of deceit,
Clad in a lump of clay, the world to cheat:
In whom the scattered boils of errors base
Of full ten thousand sectaries take place,
Gather'd in one. And thus if you will see
Heresy's substance in a shade, 'tis he.

The abusive epithets which are crowded into the title of
this book, are a fair sample of those with which almost
every paragraph abounds. Yet many religionists of that
age seem to have thought, that the use of such language
was perfectly justifiable, and implied no violation of any
principle of Christian morals! The following letter to
Vicars, on the subject of his book, was written by one of
the parliamentary preachers; and very correctly displays
the spirit and manner of that class of theologians. It is
inserted in the preface to this calumnious publication.

"To my much esteemed friend, Master John Vicars.
"MY WORTHY FRIEND,

"IT is my loss, as well as grief, that I am not able
to peruse your manuscript. Surely I should have found
in it that zeal and wisdom, that quickness and meekness,
that conviction and clearness, that piety and reason,
that candid ingenuity in relating, and that solid modesty
in confuting, which would have well become yourself,
advanced truth, and have enervated specious errors. But
I am not well, and have been enforced lately to omit
preaching in my place, and am still indisposed to study.

Pray for me. Get the view to be supplied by a better eye; and be confident that I join with you, and all good men, against all heresies and blasphemies.

Sir, your truly assured friend is

Feb. 29, 1647. OBADIAH SEDGEWICK."

To this infamous production of Vicars, Mr. Goodwin, of course, published no reply. Indeed, who but a maniac would attempt to confute a work of this kind? The principles and spirit which could give birth to such a piece of wickedness and folly, are disgraceful to the human character, and merit universal execration. Mr. Goodwin just noticed it in the following manner : " As for Rabshakeh Vicars, with his pictures, poetry, and windmills, I conceive that he hath received already an answer meet for him, in the contempt of learned men—the neglect of wise men— the sorrow of good men—and the laughter of boys and children.

Ὡς ἀπόλοιτο καὶ ἄλλος, ὅστις τοιαῦτά γε ῥέζοι.
Such wages always let such workmen have.

I shall be no further troublesome to Mr. Vicars, except it be with the recommendation of a few words to him, for his Christian meditation : ' If any man among you seem to be religious, and bridleth not his tongue,' much more his pen, ' but deceiveth his own heart; this man's religion is vain.' Farewell, Mr. Vicars." *

The author of the History of the Puritans, who was attached to the Calvinian doctrines, which this book was designed to recommend, declined to give any account of it; and, for very obvious reasons, just intimates that it is " not worth remembering." In the last age, however, a clergyman of the Established Church intimated that its contents afforded him a high intellectual repast. The late Mr. Toplady speaks of Vicars in terms of admiration, and expresses himself as being delighted with what he calls, the "*facetious* title," and " exquisitely *laughable* frontispiece," of his book.† Such was the taste of this celebrated polemic.

* Novice-Presbyter, p. 120.   † Toplady's Works, Vol. I. p. 41, Edit. 1794.

CHAPTER VI.

END OF THE CIVIL WAR—DECAPITATION OF THE KING—GOODWIN'S ATTEMPT TO
JUSTIFY THE ACT—INEXCUSABLE SLANDER UPON HIM PUBLISHED BY BISHOP
BURNET.

In the investigation of Mr. Goodwin's personal history
thus far, we have found many things to admire and
applaud.   Had he confined his attention exclusively to
the duties of the Christian ministry, and left statesmen to
dispute about party politics ; or, (if he must have given
his opinion on questions of secular policy,) had he continued steadfast in his adherence to those sound constitutional principles avowed in his "Anti-Cavalierism," instead
of . suffering his mind to be unduly biassed by passing
occurrences, his conduct through the whole of his life
would have appeared to great advantage.   But, like several
other eminent men who flourished in that eventful age,
the very singular circumstances in which he saw the nation
placed, with regard to its government, led him unhappily
to declare his approbation of public measures which, whatever might be the design of those who adopted them, were
incapable of a just defence.   The part which he acted
with respect to those men in the army, who brought their
sovereign to the scaffold, has been frequently employed to
bring his general character into disrepute : and as partial
and exaggerated accounts concerning him have been often
repeated by different writers, we will endeavour to furnish
a faithful and circumstantial narrative of this part of his
conduct, freely censuring what we deem reprehensible,
and justifying him from such charges as have no foundation in truth.

The commencement of the war between the king and
the parliament has been already stated.   This momentous
contest was carried on with various success for several
years, till at length its fate was decided by the utter defeat

of the royalists at the battle of Naseby, which was fought on the 14th of June, 1645. The following year the king fled to the Scottish army before Newark, under the command of the Earl of Leven, by whom he was detained as a prisoner, and shortly after delivered to the commissioners of the parliament. By them he was conducted, Feb. 6th, 1646-7, to Holmby, or Holdenby House, in Northamptonshire; where he remained in easy if not honourable confinement, till he was seized in the following June by the army; and, after some removals, was placed in a state of delusive liberty and splendour at Hampton Court.

At this crisis he was presented with an opportunity of recovering his honours, and of replacing himself on his throne. The Presbyterians, now in the fulness of their power, with the parliament, the city of London, and the Scots at their command, openly avowed their hostility to a general Toleration in matters of religion; and the victorious army, composed of Independents, and of various classes of religionists, perceived that they had lavished their blood merely to substitute one tyranny for another, and had conquered only for their own ruin. In this exigence they preferred petitions and remonstrances to the parliament, and on the failure of these legal weapons, under the impulse of resentment and despair, resorted to violence, and destroyed the Presbyterian power, the government, and themselves. They became indeed the instruments of their superior officers, and were ultimately made the engine of Cromwell, by whom they, with the nation at large, were despoiled of their great political object, constitutional liberty, but were nevertheless gratified with their favourite toleration, though not in a perfect form.

These events, though just at hand, were not anticipated; Cromwell and Ireton, therefore, uncertain of their contest with the Presbyterians, made an offer to Charles, while he was in their power at Hampton Court, to reinstate him in his royalties on certain conditions, for which they stipulated on behalf of themselves and their friends. But the king, elated by an opinion of his own importance amidst the conflict of parties, rejected every proposal, and even offended those who made them, by his haughtiness, fluctuation, and duplicity. When they found, by his secret correspondence with the queen, that no reliance was to be placed on his good faith, Cromwell and Ireton determined on his de- struction : withdrawing therefore their protection, they compelled him, for his immediate preservation, to fly from Hampton Court in quest of another asylum. This he sought, but, instead of it, he unfortunately found a much more rigorous prison, in the Isle of Wight; where he endured a close confinement for twelve months in Caris- brooke Castle.

But even here, an opportunity was afforded him of regaining by treaty his liberty, and the exercise of his regal prerogatives. The persuasion which he entertained of his own importance, however, induced him to throw away the last means of safety. The negotiation between him and the parliament being protracted by the difficulties which he interposed, the army gained time to return from their victorious expedition against the Scots, and to concert measures against their common enemies, the Presbyterians and himself.* Having taken forcible possession of the House of Commons, and excluded those who were opposed to their schemes, the members who remained assumed authority to constitute what they called a " High Court of Justice." The captive monarch was then seized, and brought before this tribunal under a charge of high treason, for levying war against the parliament, and the people therein represented. After a trial of three days, during which he justly persisted in denying the authority of the Court, the king was con- demned to be beheaded. When this sentence had been pronounced, Mr. Goodwin, with some other divines, was directed to attend his majesty, and assist him in his devotions. With this order Mr. Goodwin reluctantly complied, and spent about an hour in the royal presence.† Their services, however, were declined by the king, who chose Dr. Juxon, bishop of London, as his attendant in his last hours.

Herbert, the king's faithful friend, says, " At this time,

* Symmons's Life of Milton, pp. 286–290. 1810.   † Obstructors of Justice, p. 96, Edit. 1649.

came to St. James's, Edmund Calamy, Richard Vines, Joseph Caryl, William Dell, and some other London ministers, who presented their duty to the king, with their humble desire to pray with him, and perform other offices of service, if his majesty would please to accept of them. The king returned them thanks for their love to his soul, hoping that they and all other good subjects would, in their addresses to God, be mindful of him; but in regard he had made choice of Dr. Juxon, whom for many years he had known to be a pious and learned divine, and able to administer ghostly comfort to his soul, suitable to his present condition, he would have none other. The ministers were no sooner gone, but John Goodwin, minister in Coleman Street, came likewise, upon the same account, to render his service; whom the King also thanked, and dismissed with the like friendly answer."[*]

A detailed account of his majesty's decapitation will not be expected in this place. It is of more importance to observe, that this catastrophe arose out of the faults of three distinct parties: those of the king, the parliament, and the army.

In enumerating the principal faults of Charles, it is impossible to pass over his love of arbitrary power. This, however, in him was a misfortune rather than a crime. He was an inheritor of the principles by which it was sanctioned, and partook of them in common with nearly all the kings who had preceded him, or who then occupied the thrones of the world. At that period a free government existed only in the pages of theoretical or fanciful writers. That the sceptre was a trust reposed in the hands of the monarch for the benefit of the people; that the people might lawfully be the watchful guardians of their own welfare; that the consent of the governed was, in any sense, the basis of government;—were at that time monstrous propositions in the eyes of monarchs, and generally considered as bordering upon rebellion and impiety. In the time

* Herbert's Memoirs of the two last Years of the Reign of King Charles I. p. 119, Edit. 1702.

of Charles, indeed, better views were propagated : but the throne was of course the last place to which they were likely to gain access. Without dwelling upon defects for which this unfortunate monarch was rather to be pitied than blamed, having derived them directly from his predecessors, and especially from his own father,—we proceed to notice certain faults in morals, which (as moral principles depend neither upon time, person, nor place) may justly be denominated crimes, in whatever individuals they may be found.*

One of these faults was, a want of fidelity to his engagements. "The sincerity of Charles's promises," says Dr. Warner, "has been called in question by many people;"— and "I apprehend that this charge is just. I do not say, indeed, ... that the king always made use of doubtful and ambiguous terms, reserving the explication of them as might best suit his purpose, which is not very consistent with good faith; but it appears to me, I must own, that he sometimes used this artifice with a studied intention to deceive the parliament. But however this might be, ... it is notorious that he broke his faith in confirming the Duke of Buckingham's false account of the Spanish treaty, in protecting and employing Papists, in compounding with recusants, and dispensing with the penal laws against them. Nor is it less notorious, that his majesty broke his faith to the parliament, in the petition of right; and notwithstanding his assurances to the Commons of his intention to maintain their privileges, that he violated them within a few days after."†

"Perhaps the most exceptional part of Charles the First's character," says Dr. Birch, "and what appears to have been the main source of his misfortunes, and occasion of his ruin, was his want of sincerity in all matters in which his power and prerogative were concerned. This is too clearly proved by many public facts, to be denied by any impartial person : and might have been still more strongly

* Christian Observer, Vol. XIII. p. 373.   † Ecclesiastical History, Vol. II. p. 575. Edit. 1769.

evinced if the friends of the king's memory had not taken an uncommon care to suppress such evidences, as would have discredited their panegyrics on him."*

Another fault of this monarch, of which the mischief was no less extensive, was his connivance at the licentious manners of his court, and even of his particular friends. This fact stands not only upon the assertions of his enemies, but the ackowledgment of his admirers and apologists. Many concur in lamenting the profligacy of the royal camps and courts. There indeed almost every loose cha-racter was to be found. "Never any good undertaking," says one of the king's zealous advocates, when speaking of the royal cause, "had so many unworthy attendants, such horrid blasphemers and wicked wretches, as ours hath had. I quake to think, much more to speak, what mine ears have heard from some of their lips." † And though the personal example of the king was by no means such as to sanction these excesses, yet the re-issuing of the infamous Book of Sports; the silence of the crown as to the general laxity of manners; the admission to his court, and even to his favour, of the most profligate individuals; the society placed immediately around the young princes;—all loudly proclaim the king's neutrality in the war of morals, and his neglect to spread the wing of authority over such prin-ciples and men as would have been the champions of his throne and of his life in the approaching struggle. The evils which were likely to result, and which actually did result, from this religious indifference, were almost incal-culable. It drove devout men from his side; it hedged him in with persons incapable either of advising him, or of calling forth, by their virtues, the better and loftier feelings of his wavering subjects: it created in his children those habits which dishonoured the life of the one, accelerated the ruin of the other, and finally transferred the crown to hands more worthy to possess it. The best buttresses of a throne are, under God, those which are supplied by

* Inquiry into the Share which Charles I. had in the Transactions of the Earl of Glamorgan, p. 336, Edit. 1756. † Symmons's Vindication of King Charles, p. 165, Edit. 1648.

the breasts of a godly people. When these cease to yield their support, it may, at least in a free country, be expected to fall. The devotional spirit and the pious magnanimity displayed by Charles in his last days, appear to have been induced by the divine blessing upon his misfortunes, and must not be considered as the general characteristics of his life.

The faults of the parliament are equally conspicuous. Whether their conduct in hastening to decide their contest with the king by the sword, after the concessions he had made, be justifiable or not, we leave to the general historian. Baxter states, that the " great distrust which the parliament had of the king," was one of the principal causes by which the war was hastened. " They were confident," says he, " that he was unmovable as to his judgment and affections, and that whatever he granted them, was but in design to get his advantage utterly to destroy them; and that he did but watch for such an opportunity. They supposed that he utterly abhorred the parliament, and their actions against his ship-money, his judges, bishops, &c.; and therefore whatever he promised them, they believed him not, nor durst take his word; which they were hardened in by those former actions of his, which they called the breach of his former promises."* Whether they were warranted in taking up arms under these impressions or not, they have been justly accused of speedily abandoning the general and national object, for the pursuit of their own private ends, and the establishment of their peculiar opinions. For a time their measures were worthy of high commendation; such as a nation had a right to expect from its representatives. But soon these boasted champions of freedom began to secure their own perpetuity; to reward their own exertions; to take measures for building the fabric of Presbyterianism out of the ruins of Episcopacy; and to restrain conscience by the enactment of penal laws. These proceedings throw a shade upon the motives which dictated their earlier and more praiseworthy proceedings. To exchange an arbitrary

* Reliq. Baxter. Part First, p. 27.

monarch for a perpetual parliament, was to exchange one tyrant for many. To make themselves the sole judges of their own deserts, and distributors of their own rewards, was to create a drain upon the national resources which nothing could satisfy. To establish Presbyterianism in the place of Episcopacy, was to force upon all the religion of a few; to take from the party who loved an establishment the only one they revered, and to force a detested establishment upon those who would endure none at all:* to interfere in the affairs of private conscience, so as to threaten men with pains and penalties if they should dare to use the Book of Common Prayer either in public or domestic worship, was presumptuously to usurp the authority of God, by a profane intrusion into the sanctities of individual devotion. The parliament began well, but speedily abandoned their meritorious course, indulging the conceit, that power was safe only in their own hands, that unlimited power is safe in any hands, that they were at liberty to overthrow the ecclesiastical constitution, and to set up their private views as the standard of religion to the whole nation. They threw society into a state of anarchy and confusion, by dissolving the connection between the king and his subjects, and thus made a breach which their subsequent efforts were unable to repair. They subverted the institutions of the country, and prepared the way for a military despotism; but it was reserved for men of greater wisdom and moderation to establish constitutional liberty. The parliament was the more censurable, in the adoption of the selfish and violent measures now specified, because it professed to redress every public grievance both in the church and the state.

The faults of the army were of equal magnitude. The dissolute character of the court, and the persecuting measures of the Episcopal clergy, induced the more devout part of the nation to join the parliament; whose military forces therefore comprised a considerable number of men who were sincerely religious. Many of these at length imbibed sentiments concerning church-government very

* Christian Observer, ut supra.

O

closely allied to republicanism, and thus became hostile to
monarchy.   They suffered their religion to degenerate into
mere mental excitement, unrestrained by good sense, or
the precepts of Christianity.   Cromwell fanned the flame
of their extravagances, and not unfrequently distinguished
himself among them, by extemporaneous preaching and
prayer; and thus gained their confidence and attachment.
When he therefore formed the design of bringing Charles
to the scaffold, and of seizing the supreme authority himself, to engage their co-operation, he pursued these ends
under the plea of religion.   Professing zeal for God, a
decided abhorrence of religious coercion, and an inflexible
regard for liberty of conscience; he prevailed upon them
freely to surrender themselves to his guidance, and to execute the revolutionary schemes devised by him and his son-
in-law Ireton.   The king was unhappily governed by principles and counsels which rendered him hostile both to
civil and religious liberty, and made his promises suspicious;
the parliament had become highly despotic, and, under
Presbyterian influence, execrably intolerant; and the army,
headed by Cromwell and Ireton, controlled the one, and
shed the blood of the other, without any authority except
that of the sword.

What views soever may be entertained respecting the
character of Charles, there can be but one opinion among
the intelligent and dispassionate concerning the absolute
illegality of his execution, and of the measures which
immediately led to it.   The delinquencies of his government
had indeed been great, and there was too much reason to
fear that he would resume his former conduct if a favourable opportunity should again occur; yet for a few military
men, of their own accord, to control the parliament, to put
the sovereign to death, and thus completely to overthrow
the civil constitution of the country, was an assumption of
power, which no concurrence of circumstances could possibly justify.   The life of any ruler can only be at the disposal of the constitution; or of that system of laws and
regulations by which his subjects are professedly governed.
If his life be taken away by any means but those provided

by the constitution, it is murder : no pretended or even proved acts of tyranny can justify his being put to death in any other way. And what constitution in the civilized world provides for the infliction of death upon the supreme magistrate? Every such infliction, either against law, or without its sanction, is murder, by whomsoever perpetrated.* Among the English regicides there were indeed honest patriots, who thought that they were applying a remedy to all the evils under which the nation had long groaned, and were establishing the liberties of their countrymen upon a solid and permanent base. But they ought to have recollected, that the principles upon which they proceeded were subversive of social order, and therefore of all rational freedom. What government could stand, if those who are at the head of the military forces of any nation, are permitted to place themselves above law, and to control the regularly constituted authorities? Revolutions in states, effected by such extreme measures, are contrary to the order of God; and their punishment is, that they subvert the liberty which they are designed to secure. A sage of elder times has justly said, " We ought, in the government of a......commonweal, to imitate and follow the great God of nature, who in all things proceedeth easily, and by little and little ; as by putting the spring betwixt winter and summer, and autumn betwixt summer and winter ; moderating the extremities of the times and seasons, with the self-same wisdom which He useth in other things also, and that in such sort, as that no violent force or course therein appeareth."†

Cromwell and his bold associates have been condemned by some as the most wicked of human beings, and by others eulogized and defended as the greatest benefactors of their country. The excellent Baxter, who had vindicated the parliament in taking up arms against the royalists decidedly disapproved of the king's decapitation, and never hesitated, on all proper occasions, to declaim against it as

* Dr. Adam Clarke's Commentary on Judges iii.   † The Six Bookes of a Commonweale, written by J. Bodin, Done into English by Richard Knolles, p. 475, Edit. 1606.

a crime : he nevertheless thought that it admitted of considerable extenuation, and was vastly different from private assassination, and from the Popish doctrine of deposing and putting to death heretical kings. "I leave it to posterity," says he, "having been myself a member of the army four years, or thereabouts, that it was utterly against the mind and thoughts of Protestants, and those that they called Puritans, to put the king to death;......it was the work of Papists, Libertines, Vanists, Anabaptists; and the Protestants deeply suffered for opposing it ....And yet, ...I must needs add, that every wise man sees that the case itself much differs from the Papists. If the body of a commonwealth, or those that have part in the legislative power, and so in the supremacy, should unwillingly be engaged in a war with the prince; and, after many years' blood and desolations, judicially take his life, as guilty of all this blood, and not to be trusted any more with government; and all this they do, not as private men, but as the remaining sovereign power, and say they do it according to the laws ;—undoubtedly this case doth very much differ from the Powder-plot, or Papists' murdering of kings, and teaching that it is lawful for a private hand to do it, if he be but an heretic, or be but deposed or excommunicated by the Pope. A war, and a treacherous murder, are not all one with a private hand, or foreign prelate pretending to a dominion over the lives and states of princes, and over the kingdoms of the world; and that the Vice-Christ, or Vice-God on earth." *

In defence of the principles upon which the army had acted, a learned and ingenious tract was published in the year 1649, under the fictitious signature of Eutactus Philodemius, dated from Gray's Inn, and entitled, "The Original and End of Civil Power." Dr. Owen, also, compared the proceedings of the Regicides to the valorous achievements of the Man after God's own heart, in subduing the enemies of his country, and in preparing the way for the national glory and prosperity by which the reign of Solomon was distinguished. Speaking of Ireton, who

* Baxter's Key for Catholics, p. 323, Edit. 1659.

was one of the king's judges, and signed the warrant for his execution, the Doctor says, "He was an eminent instrument in the hand of God, in as tremendous alterations, as such a spot of this world hath at any time received, since Daniel saw in general them all......As Daniel's visions were all terminated in the kingdom of Christ, so all his actions had the same aim and intendment. This was that which gave life and sweetness to all the most dismal and black engagements that at any time he was called out unto. It was all the vengeance of the Lord and His temple : a Davidical preparation of His paths in blood, that He might for ever reign in righteousness and peace." *

The army had also a warm advocate in John Canne, who has long been in high repute for his references to the Holy Scriptures. This learned man announced himself to the world as the author of "The Golden Rule : or, Justice Advanced, &c. ; being a clear and full Satisfaction to the whole Nation, in justification of the legal Proceedings of the High Court of Justice against Charles Steward, late King of England, 1649." But among the numerous advocates of this measure, the author of Paradise Lost was the most distinguished. This consummate genius and scholar contended, in various publications, that the conduct of the army was not only defensible, as being in accordance with the law of nature, but so highly meritorious as to entitle them to perpetual renown.

It has also been observed by a very sensible modern writer, in reference to the army, that, "If ruin was apprehended by these men to themselves or the kingdom; if their civil or religious rights, in their eyes, appeared as intended to be sacrificed, and the king and the priest, whether prelate or presbyter mattered not, were to reassume their wonted rule; and above all, if the king's character appeared such to them, that no reliance was to be put on his promises, declarations, or oaths, (all of which they seem strongly to affirm,) we are not to wonder at the

* The Labouring Saint's Dismission to Rest : A Sermon preached at the Funeral of the Right Honourable Henry Ireton. Collection of Sermons, p. 420, Edit. 1721.

deed. All men know the force of necessity and self-preservation, and know also that they will operate more strongly than law or reason."* These considerations go to extenuate the proceedings of the regicides, but not to justify them ; for, in no case can it be lawful to do evil that good may come.

It is deeply to be regretted, that the cruel treatment which Mr. Goodwin had received from the Presbyterians, and the outrageous assumptions and intolerance of that body, together with the singular exigency of the nation at that particular crisis, gave such a bias to his mind as induced him to take up his pen in defence of Cromwell and his daring fraternity. Such, however, was the fact. He wrote two pamphlets on that subject. The first of these, which is entitled "Right and Might well Met," was designed to justify the restraint which was put upon the parliament, and was published before the king was brought to trial. A reply to this tract was immediately drawn up by Mr. John Geree, under the title of "Might overcoming Right :" Sir Francis Nethersole also addressed a printed letter to our author on the same occasion, accusing him of advancing principles in his last publication opposite to those contained in his " Anti-Cavalierism :" to which Mr. Goodwin immediately replied in a small piece which he entitled, " The Unrighteous Judge." This pamphlet bears the date of Jan. 18th, 1648, ten days after the first assembling of the High Court of Justice.† Sir Francis pressed our author to declare his opinion concerning the " untouchableness of the lives of kings," particularly in reference to the principles laid down in the " Anti-Cavalierism," and the " Right and Might well Met ;" to which Mr. Goodwin says, " Such a thing is indeed easy to be done, but no way honourable or comely for me to do. He that shall, especially in public, deliver his judgment in matters of great weight, without a proportionable retirement of himself, for the exact casting up of all particular accounts relating to such an undertaking, runs a double hazard :

* Harris's Life of Cromwell, p. 197, Edit. 1814.   † Ludlow's Memoirs, Vol. I. p. 275, Edit. 1722. .

the one, of misleading others; the other, of dishonour to himself." * In this language of hesitation and reserve, he expressed himself only twelve days before the king was actually brought to the scaffold. Sir Francis also accused Mr. Goodwin of "seducing" the soldiery and the parliament; and of "leading them out of the road of their loyalty;" to which he replies, "The God on high, who must shortly judge me, knows, and both parliament-men and soldiers know, *that I never was the man from whose tongue or pen the least word or syllable, tending to the forming or directing any of their proceedings, ever came.* Only when I discerned, that, through better teaching than mine, they were engaged in ways of conscience and honour, likely to bless the nation, I considered myself obliged in duty to bring forth the righteousness of their cause into the clearest light I could, and to stop the mouths of gainsayers with my pen."† Let the reader then judge, what-credit is due to the assertion of Granger, that "no man more eagerly *promoted* the murder of the king."‡ Of this charge, we believe, there exists not the slightest proof. Granger is not the only man who has advanced criminal charges against Goodwin which are notoriously untrue.

After a lapse of four months Mr. Goodwin produced a tract in vindication of the High Court of Justice, in its conduct towards the king; "having," as he says, "with all diligence, and good conscience, surveyed that great transaction, in all the circumstances of it; and being willing to tax myself at so much time and pains as to draw up a report in writing of what I find in that survey."§ The title of this piece is, "The Obstructors of Justice; or, A Defence of the honourable Sentence passed upon the late King, 1649;" and the whole is a reply to three distinct publications: "The serious and faithful Representation of the Judgments of the Ministers of the Gospel within the Province of London, in a Letter from them to the General and his Council of War"—Dr. Hammond's "Humble Address to his Excellency and Council of War"—and

* P. 14.   † Unrighteous Judge, p. 5.   ‡ Biog. Hist. Eng. Vol. III. p. 42, Edit. 1804.   § Obstructors of Justice, Dedication.

Geree's " Might overcoming Right." The author of this last tract died a short time before Mr. Goodwin wrote : his memory is therefore respected, and even his arguments treated with forbearance. The Presbyterian ministers, who had signed the " Serious Representation," had rendered themselves particularly open to animadversion. They had been active promoters of hostility to the king, through the whole course of the war ; and now protested against a measure which was the result of their own conduct; and the very possibility of which could never have existed but for the doctrine of resistance which they had strenuously inculcated, till the king was, in point of fact, reduced to the situation of a subject. "The ministers," says our author, " deposed the king, and consequently exposed him to that trial whereunto he was brought, [and] to that sentence which passed upon him.—The ministers with their party clearly deposed the king when they denied subjection to him—withdrew their obedience from him—acknowledged a power superior to his—levied war against him as a traitor, rebel, and enemy to the kingdom—chased him up and down from place to place—confiscated his revenues—and at last imprisoned his person."*

Dr. Henry Hammond was an episcopal divine of great learning, of eminent piety, and of a holy and upright life. His attachment to his royal master, to whom he sustained the office of chaplain, was uniform and exemplary. He voluntarily submitted to lose all his preferments rather than betray the church of which he was a member, or renounce allegiance to his king. With a magnanimity worthy of his elevated character, he took upon himself individually to remonstrate with those who meditated the death of his sovereign. At the same time, it must be confessed, that his views of government were unfriendly to general liberty, as tending to encourage arbitrary sway in the chief magistrate. For the Doctor's erudition and integrity Mr. Goodwin had the highest respect, while he thought it his duty to controvert his political principles, and to justify himself against the charges which the Doctor had

* Obstructors of Justice, p. 53.

preferred against him, not only in his "Humble Address," but in some other publications. "I perceive," says he, "by some pieces published by this Doctor, since the late troubles in the land, that he hath some particular desire to engage me. I cannot account for such desire, considering that many others have taken up the bucklers against that cause which he maintaineth, as well as I ; and that I never in any of my writings either mentioned his name, or reflected upon him in the least. I have heard frequently of him : nor have I at any time heard any thing concerning him but well and worthy of a man, his judgment in the grand state-question of the times excepted: the disparagement whereof I was very willing to pass by, as judging it honestly covered with his other principles and regular deportments. But since he hath once and again lifted up the standard of his pen against me, I have at last taken the field, hoping to right myself at that weapon wherewith I have been assaulted."*

There are many passages in Mr. Goodwin's "Obstructors of Justice" which are written with great acuteness, and strength of reason; but these relate to subjects of a collateral description. What he has advanced on the main question of his book, is unworthy of his endowments, though often plausible, and, *in point of argument*, equal to any thing advanced on the same side either by Milton or by any of his contemporaries.

It is but justice to Mr. Goodwin to state, that in defending the army he was not influenced by any dislike of social order, or by any predilection for a republican government, as opposed to a limited monarchy. In the case of King Charles he was evidently misled by his passion for religious freedom. No man ever lived, who understood the rights of conscience better than he, or who was more tremblingly alive to their importance. All dominion over conscience he regarded as a usurpation of the Divine prerogative, and an encroachment upon the most sacred rights of human nature. Whereas the king "was careful" of episcopal "uniformity," † and the

* Obstructors of Justice, p. 133.   † Perrinchief's Life of King Charles the First, p. 240, Edit. 1684.

parliament had issued ordinances in restraint of religious
liberty sufficient to disgrace even a Spanish government,
and to wound the obduracy of a Bonner. Had the king
therefore been restored to the exercise of his regal
functions, when the parliament voted his concessions to
be a ground for a future settlement, the probability was,
according to the opinion of Mr. Goodwin and others, that
the Episcopalians or the Presbyterians, or perhaps both,
would enjoy the countenance and protection of the state;
and all other bodies of religious people, after a sacrifice
of their property, and an exposure of their lives in the
field, would be delivered up to a grinding tyranny, such
as the Puritans had endured in the time of Laud,
Servetus and Castellio in the time of Calvin, and the
Dutch Arminians after the Synod of Dort. These not
improbable anticipations doubtless made a strong impression upon Mr. Goodwin's mind, as well as the revenge
which he knew to be meditated by the royal party.
Under the impulse of those feelings, which such a situation of affairs was calculated to excite, he wrote his two
pamphlets in vindication of the army.* The political
principles inculcated in these publications, as well as in
those of his bold compeers, are dangerous and indefensible;
they are nevertheless the errors of an ardent and generous
mind, desirous, above everything besides, of restoring to
his species those rights which they had received from
their Maker, but of which they were in danger of being
wantonly deprived. His ears had long been stunned by
vociferous appeals to the civil power to put down all
sectaries, and establish Presbyterian uniformity by pains
and penalties; and what such uniformity meant he well
knew from what he had himself witnessed in England,
from what he had read of Calvin's doings in Geneva,
and of the doings of Calvin's followers in the Nether-
lands. To us these sad events may appear remote; but in
the time of Goodwin they were recent transactions, and
produced a deep impression on the minds of thoughtful
men. Yet before many years had passed away Goodwin

* Right and Might, p. 18.   Obstructors of Justice, p. 117.

perceived that in getting rid of the king, the nation had only exchanged one tyranny for another. Even religious liberty was secured only in an imperfect form, an attempt being made to force a Calvinistic ministry upon every parish in the land. So much for Cromwellian liberty!

To animadvert upon all the unjust reflections which have been cast upon Mr. Goodwin, and the misrepresentations of his political conduct advanced by different writers, would be an endless task. One or two instances, however, it is requisite to observe. The partiality of Mr. Neal has long been a subject of just complaint. The History of the Puritans, as a whole, is a work of great value. It is a vast collection of important ecclesiastical facts; and the zeal which it uniformly displays in favour of civil and religious liberty is worthy of high praise. At the same time it is notorious, that the author's representations are often incorrect; that he is frequently negligent in the examination of his authorities; and that, on almost all occasions, when the honour of his own party is concerned, he yields to the influence of prejudice. He is scarcely ever willing to do justice either to individuals or communities who happened to differ from him. The account given by him of the political writings of Milton and Mr. Goodwin is highly disingenuous. After giving the title of Milton's answer to Salmasius, he simply remarks, that it was "written in an elegant but severe style;" and then proceeds to state, that "To satisfy the English reader, Mr. John Goodwin published a small treatise, which he entitled, 'A Defence of the Sentence passed upon the late King, &c.,' a very weak and inconclusive performance! For, admitting our author's principles, that the original of government is from the people, and that magistrates are accountable to them for their administration, they are not applicable in the present case, because the officers of the army had neither the voice of the people, nor of their representatives in a free parliament; the House of Commons was purged, and the House of Peers dispersed, in order to make way for this outrage upon the constitution. Our author was so sensible of this objection, that, in order to evade it, he advances this ridiculous conclusion : That though the erecting of a High Court of Justice by the House of Commons alone be contrary to the letter, yet being for the people's good it is sufficient that it be agreeable to the spirit of the law. But who gave a few officers of the army authority to judge what was best for the people's good, or to act according to the spirit of the law, in contradiction to the letter?" *

That Mr. Goodwin was unsuccessful in the accomplishment of his design, it would be folly to deny. It is nevertheless the duty of an historian, like that of a witness in a court of justice, to declare " the whole truth," so far as it can be ascertained, without partiality. In the present instance Mr. Neal has not thought it expedient to do this; fearful, as it would seem, lest Mr. Goodwin should not appear to sufficient disadvantage. He has not given the slightest intimation of anything objectionable in the political writings of Milton, excepting " the severity of his style," which is counterbalanced by its acknowledged " elegance:" but, seizing upon a single expression in Mr. Goodwin's pamphlet, and disregarding the argument with which it stands connected, he sneers at the whole, as " weak," " ridiculous," and " inconclusive." To the question which Neal has specified, Goodwin has given an extended and elaborate answer; yet his censor unfairly intimates that he was silent on the subject. Besides it is a fact, of which Neal could not be ignorant, that every thing advanced by Milton in defence of the king's execution, and of the proceedings which immediately led to it, is open to the objection which he has urged with such an air of contempt against Mr. Goodwin. Both these eminent men argue in vindication of these measures upon precisely the same principle,—that they were indispensably necessary in order to the civil and religious liberty of British subjects. To Milton's " Tenure of Kings and Magistrates," which, every one knows, was also intended " to satisfy the English reader," Mr.

* Hist. Purit. Vol. III. p. 503.

Goodwin makes frequent reference in his "Obstructors of Justice," in confirmation of his different positions. Though Milton's political writings are enriched by classical facts and allusions, irradiated by the blaze of poetic genius, and contain frequent bursts of powerful and commanding eloquence,—yet they are disfigured by such grim satire, and personal abuse, as Mr. Goodwin never wrote. Milton was a stern republican, systematically hostile to monarchy, and he treats the memory of his decapitated sovereign with sarcastic and offensive levity. From both these faults Mr. Goodwin is completely free. The contemptuous reflections cast upon him, and that indirect praise of his coadjutor, when the historian had introduced them to his readers, is undoubtedly to be resolved into that difference of theological opinion which subsisted between Mr. Neal and the object of his animadversion. At all events, no fair and candid historian, when he meets with two delinquents, will studiously conceal the faults of the more notorious offender, and wreak all his official vengeance upon the other. Such petty arts, how common soever, are infinitely beneath the dignity of genuine history.

It is an easy matter for persons living in the present times and enjoying the full benefit of religious liberty, to point out the errors of such men as Milton and John Goodwin, and censure them for the part they took with respect to their unfortunate sovereign, who had drawn the sword against his subjects, and was known to be opposed to a general religious toleration; but whether those who are the most forward to condemn these patriotic but mistaken men would themselves have judged differently, had they been living at the time, and been duly alive to the religious rights of the people, may admit of a serious doubt. The sad fate of Charles the First, however it may be blamed and regretted, had certainly an important bearing upon the peaceful and happy revolution of 1688, when the liberties of Englishmen were settled upon a permanent foundation.

In Mr. Goodwin's day, there arose in various parts of

the nation a people who expected the immediate appearance of Jesus Christ in person, to establish on earth a
new monarchy or kingdom.   They were principally,
though not exclusively, of the Baptist denomination.*
As there were four great empires, which had successively
gained the dominion of the world; the Assyrian, the
Persian, the Grecian, and the Roman; so these men,
believing that the kingdom of Christ was to be the Fifth,
received the appellation of Fifth Monarchy Men.   They
imagined, that under this glorious dispensation there
would be no sovereign but Christ, nor any to govern in
subordination to Him but the saints. †   Under this impression, many of them endeavoured to effect the subversion of all human government, as being opposed to the
kingdom of Christ, and as preventing its erection.   Soon
after Cromwell's assumption of the Protectorate, they
were detected in the formation of a conspiracy, the object
of which was, to blow up Whitehall when he was present;
for which several of them were imprisoned.   On regaining
their liberty, they plotted the destruction of Oliver's
son; and a few months after the Restoration, raised an
insurrection in London, in which they killed several
people, vociferating through the streets, *No king but Christ!*
"The madness of these men," says Bishop Kennet,
"extended so far, as to believe that they, and the rest of
their judgment, were called by God to reform the world,
and make all the earthly powers, which they called
Babylon, subservient to the kingdom of King Jesus; and
in order thereunto, never to sheath the sword, till the
carnal powers of the world became a hissing and a curse:
and by a misguided zeal they were so confident of their
undertaking, that they were taught and believed, that
one should subdue a thousand; making account, when
they had led captivity captive in England, to go into
France, Spain, Germany, and other parts of the world,
there to prosecute their holy design." ‡

* Ivimey's History of the Baptists, p. 261.   † Hobbes's History of the
Civil Wars, p. 255, Edit. 1679.   Noble's Lives of the English Regicides,
Vol. I. p. 272, Edit. 1798.   ‡ Register and Chronicle, p. 355.

Bishop Burnet has represented Mr. Goodwin as the most active and zealous of these miserably deluded people. "The Fifth Monarchy Men," says he, "seemed to be really on expectation every day when Christ should appear. John Goodwin headed these, who first brought in Arminianism among the sectaries; for he was for liberty of all sorts—he filled all people with such an expectation of a glorious thousand years speedily to begin, that it looked like a madness possessing them."*

That Mr. Goodwin either "headed" the Fifth Monarchy Men, or held any of their peculiar opinions, cannot by any means be admitted without proof, not the least shadow of which was ever produced by the bishop, or by any of Mr. Goodwin's accusers. On the contrary, the most convincing proof exists, that in giving this representation of his principles and character the right reverend historian was entirely in the wrong. Every man of reading knows, that the bishop's assertions are often fabulous, his characters frequently distorted, and that scarcely any thing can be less certain than many of his hearsay reports. Whether the whole of his numerous inaccuracies are to be attributed to inadvertency, or simply a reflection upon his veracity, this is not the place to enquire.†

Burnet was a native of Edinburgh, and did not visit England till the year 1663, when he was only twenty years of age. Charles the Second was then restored, and the vagaries and murderous exploits of the Fifth Monarchy Men were at an end. Mr. Goodwin was then an old man and a sequestered minister; and our juvenile adventurer, who, at that time, stayed only six months in this country, was busily employed in visiting the two Universities, and in paying visits to the nobility and dignified clergy.‡ On this subject, therefore, Burnet does not speak from personal knowledge, but appears to have retailed one of the vague reports of the day, without ever

* History of his Own Times, Vol. I. p. 67, Edit. 1724.   † See Rose's Observations on Fox's Historical Work, Appendix; and Heywood's Vindication of Fox's History, passim.   ‡ Thomas Burnet's Life of Bishop Burnet, annexed to the History of his Own Time.

inquiring whether it was true or false. And when it is recollected, that Mr. Goodwin was an Independent, and had sided with the army, it will scarcely be supposed that his sentiments and conduct would be correctly represented by popular fame, especially among the associates of the prelate, after the Restoration had turned the tide of public opinion in favour of monarchy and of the episcopal church.

Besides, few writers have ever been in the habit of declaring their religious creed in a manner more ingenuous and unequivocal than Mr. Goodwin; and yet, in his numerous writings, not the slightest trace of attachment to the peculiar notions of the Fifth Monarchy Men is to be discovered. It must appear a singular circumstance, that he should have " filled all men with such an expectation of a glorious thousand years speedily to begin, till it looked like a madness possessing them," and yet should never have introduced the subject in any of his publications: and it must be passing strange, if he should have produced such a mighty effect in the nation without employing the press. Can it be imagined, that " all men " would so attend his ministry in Coleman Street, as to be wrought up to such a pitch of frenzy? The same remark will apply to the publications of his antagonists. Prynne indeed charged him with being an enemy to civil government; but it was only because he denied that magistrates have any legitimate authority in the affairs of private conscience. Edwards wrote various pamphlets for the avowed purpose of effecting Mr. Goodwin's ruin. For this end, he not only examined our author's writings, but employed spies to attend his ministry, and to furnish an account of every thing in his public prayers and sermons that might be deemed objectionable, and used to his disadvantage. He mentions the wild opinions of the Fifth Monarchy Men, among other " errors and heresies," but never gives the least intimation that they constituted any part of Mr. Goodwin's creed, or that he had any connection with the men by whom they were held. Now is it probable—is it possible—that he should have been the head of a multitude of atrocious fanatics, who aimed at the subversion of all government, ecclesiastical and civil; that he should have gained "all men" over to those despicable opinions mentioned by the bishop; and that Edwards and Prynne, in their malignant efforts to expose him to the vengeance of the civil power, should have maintained absolute silence on the subject?

After Cromwell was invested with the supreme power, the Fifth Monarchy Men were the most active and daring of all his enemies. It was therefore deemed necessary to employ spies to associate with them, and to discover their proceedings and intentions. These wily men obtained access to the nocturnal meetings of those incendiaries, and from time to time presented to Cromwell's secretary an account of the persons who were present, of the principal actors among them, and of their various revolutionary plans. The communications concerning them, thus obtained, are preserved in the State Papers of Thurlow; where it is said, "The chief and leader of them is one Venner, that was a wyne-cooper: "* but in these authentic documents, which contain the names of all the leading characters among them, no mention whatever is made of Mr. Goodwin: no mean proof of the inaccuracy of Burnet's account.

This is also further proved by the public avowals which Mr. Goodwin so frequently made, not only of his conscientious regard for civil magistracy in general, but of his fidelity to the parliament, and afterwards to the government of the commonwealth. A few of these it may not be improper to adduce, as they show the character of the man.

"It is the will of God," says he, "that there should be some government in every society of men. In this sense, all forms of government that are lawful and just, whether they be simple, as monarchy, aristocracy, democracy, or mixed, having somewhat of two or of all these simples in them, are equally or indifferently from God." †

* Thurlow's State Papers, Vol. VI. pp. 184-188.   † Anti-Cavalierism, p. 5, 1642.

"No lawful rule, authority, or power, are enemies to Christ, but are confederate with Him."*

"The constant tenour of my deportment, from the beginning of this parliament, hath been fully parliamentary. If I should boast, that, to my power, I have not been behind the very greatest of those that have built up the parliamentary cause with the highest hand and the loyalest heart, I should not be ashamed. Some of my adversaries themselves in place have given large testimony to my faithfulness and diligence in this kind."†

"We freely allow to all Christian kings and magistrates in the world any authority whatsoever, which will not claim a right to punish men for not being as wise, as learned, as far insighted into religion as themselves; or for such matters of fact as are occasioned merely by such defects as these. The weakness of men's judgments calls rather for instruction than punishment. We cannot judge, that the mistaking of a man's way in a dark controversy deserves a prison or any other stroke with the civil sword."‡

"There are two ordinances, by which the good pleasure of God is, to communicate of His goodness and love to His saints, during the present state of things. One is the ministry of the word, the other civil magistracy. The one intended for their calling out of this present world, and fitting them for future glory; the other for their protection, that under the shadow of it they may lead a quiet and peaceable life in all godliness and honesty. To attempt a deliverance from either, must needs be as a covering the sun with sackcloth, and a turning of the moon into blood. I look upon magistracy as the only preventive appointed by God, to keep the world from falling foul upon itself, and being destroyed by its own hand."§

"Concerning the power of the civil magistrate, I have not only argued and asserted the lawfulness of it, but the necessity also; yea, and showed the benefit and

* Danger of Fighting against God, p. 15, 1644.   † Innocency's Triumph, p. 3, 1645.   ‡ Innocency and Truth, p. 73, 1645.   § Scourge of the Saints, Preface, 1646.

blessing of it unto the world; and have endeavoured with all my might to convince the error and sin of those who refuse subjection to it." *

"The zeal of my loyalty to magistracy and government hath been abundantly testified, by the frequent contests of my pen against all the profanations and pollutions of the glory of them: whether injustice, tyranny, oppression, unfaithfulness in those called to them; or anarchical, disloyal, tumultuous, seditious strains, either in word or deed, in those a good part of whose calling is obedience and subjection to them."†

"Do not such persons sin against an express command of God, who, under what pretext soever, teach disobedience to the powers over them; animating and incensing the people against the powers which God, whether in judgment or mercy, hath appointed over them? Can the sin of resisting the powers be more dangerously perpetrated, than when those who ought to live in subjection are urged, yea, upon religious pretences conjured, to refuse subjection, and are borne in hand, that whilst they break so signal a command of God, they do Him worthy service?"‡

"The prosperity and peace, both of the parliament and present government, together with theirs who are entrusted with it, have been the great contest and strife of my soul, ever since the day wherein God laid the foundations of it; and this against disobligements not a few nor inconsiderable. That I speak the truth in this, and lie not, I have many witnesses."§

"It is sufficiently known to the world, that I have always been as zealous an assertor of their authority, as any of their best friends whatsoever: nor have I to this hour suffered the least alteration either in my judgment or affections."‖

It will be seen by the references in the margin, that these public appeals were made by Mr. Goodwin, and repeated at different times, from the commencement of the civil

* Divine Authority of the Scriptures, p. 29, 1648.   † Exposition of the Ninth Chapter to the Romans, Dedication, 1653.   ‡ Dissatisfaction Satisfied, p. 11, 1654.   § The Triers or Tormentors Tried and Cast, Preface, 1657.   ‖ Triumviri, Preface, 1658.

wars, till within a little while of the Restoration : nor
did his adversaries ever confront them, except by the
idle charge, that as he opposed the interference of magistrates in the affairs of conscience, he was an enemy to
their secular prerogatives.   They demonstrate the un-
truthfulness of Burnet's statement.   Goodwin was not
"for liberty of all sorts."   He was not for lawless liberty;
but for liberty under the guardianship of righteous government.   The last two of these appeals were made when the
Fifth Monarchy Men were the most active in giving efficiency to their revolutionary schemes ; and when several
of them had been taken into custody for their opposition to
the existing government.   Now allowing Mr. Goodwin to
have possessed the least share of common sense, surrounded
as he was by men whose tender mercies were cruel, and
who would have exulted in an opportunity of subjecting
him to a state prosecution, it is impossible that he should
so frequently have courted an investigation of his political
principles, and conduct had he been the head of the Fifth
Monarchy Men, or even a member of their miserable fraternity : to say nothing of the improbability, that a man
of his strong sense and sound learning should ever be the
dupe of such consummate folly.

It is also worthy of remark, that Burnet's account is
self-contradictory, and therefore destroys its own credi-
bility.   Speaking of the Fifth Monarchy Men, he says,
" It was *no easy thing* for Cromwell to satisfy those, when
he took the power into his own hands ; since that looked
like a step to kingship, which Goodwin had long represented as the GREAT ANTICHRIST, that hindered Christ's
being set upon His throne...... *With much ado*, he
managed these republican enthusiasts ; " and yet in reference to the protector, the bishop remarks, " None of the
preachers were so THOROUGHPACED *for him*, as to *temporal
matters*, as Goodwin was." *   Thus the bishop states, in
effect, with his characteristic gravity, that while Mr.
Goodwin taught people to regard Cromwell's political
measures as an approximation to the GREAT ANTICHRIST,

* Own Times, Vol. I. pp. 67, 68.

he was more eager and zealous, or, to use the prelate's own term, more THOROUGHPACED in DEFENCE *of those measures,* than any other minister of his age! And that, while he exceeded all his clerical contemporaries in *ardent attachment to the usurper,* he was the head of a band of ruffians, who not only meditated the *overthrow of his government,* but formed a plan for *his assassination!* Few historians besides Bishop Burnet would have the hardihood to publish such a palpable absurdity, expecting that his readers would believe it.

But we have evidence still more convincing, that Burnet's account is untrue. Mr. Goodwin was not only unconnected with the Fifth Monarchy Men, but repeatedly wrote against them, and strenuously opposed the very principle, of which the bishop declares him to have been an enthusiastic advocate. The Fifth Monarchy Men were generally rigid predestinarians, whose avowed belief was, that all events, and the times of their actual occurrence, are ordained by an unchangeable decree of the Almighty. In reference to these deluded men Mr. Goodwin inquires, " Is the time of setting up the Fifth Monarchy determined by God, so that no human endeavours are available to hasten this period, nor any human opposition able to retard it? If neither, why should men trouble the world about them, and abuse the simplicity of inconsiderate people by bearing them in hand, that if they were permitted to umpire the affairs of state, they would bring the Fifth Monarchy upon the world, even before the day thereof? Why should these men clamour against persons, who themselves acknowledge to be godly, as if they stood in Christ's way, and would not suffer Him to set up His kingdom, only because they cannot be satisfied about the truth of *their notions,* and refuse to steer a course *threatening* RUIN AND CONFUSION TO THE NATION? Is it not the *declared opinion of these men,* that the day wherein that great jubilee they speak of shall begin, is unalterably fixed by God?"*

In his "Peace Protected, and Discontent Disarmed,"

* Dissatisfaction Satisfied, p. 16, Edit. 1654.

Mr. Goodwin expresses himself to a similar e ffect. "There were some men in Paul's days," says he, "whotr oubled the minds of many with this notion, 'that the day of Christ was at hand.' (2 Thess. ii. 2.) Yet this was no testimony of Jesus proper for that generation, with what confidence soever it might be pretended to have been such. And to set a few people agog with a conceit, that if they might set up such and such persons in places of power, they would lay the foundation of a Fifth Monarchy, and suddenly bring in the kingdom of Christ upon the world, is no testimony of Jesus proper to this generation. For Jesus hath nowhere declared such a propriety as this to reside in such a doctrine."*

Mr. Goodwin expresses himself in still stronger language on this subject, in another of his publications. Addressing the members of his church, and warning them against the most dangerous sects then in existence, he says, "Amongst the persons known by the name of Fifth Monarchy Men, (not so much from their opinion touching the said Monarchy, as by that fierce and restless spirit which worketh in them, to bring it into the world by unhallowed methods,) you will learn to speak evil of those that are in dignity, to curse the ruler of your people, to entertain darkness instead of a vision, to advance yourselves with confidence into the things you have not seen, and to please yourselves most when you neither please God nor sober-minded people."†

To the improbable, unauthenticated, and self-contradictory charge of Burnet, so dishonourable to Mr. Goodwin, we oppose all that mass of counter evidence, now before the reader; leaving him to declare on which side the truth lies, and confidently anticipating a verdict in favour of the accused. The truth is, Bishop Burnet's account of John Goodwin is throughout a tissue of falsehood, adopted and published without examination. John Goodwin had no more connexion with the Fifth Monarchy Men than Burnet himself had; and the statement he has made, that Goodwin was the head and leader of that miserable frater-

* Page 47, Edit. 1654.   † Cata-Baptism, signat. I. 3.

nity, admits of no excuse. The writer of false history violates the first duty which he owes to his readers, and does what he can to deceive them in perpetuity. Of this unpardonable offence Bishop Burnet was unquestionably guilty so far as John Goodwin is concerned. Had he taken the trouble to read five pages of any one of Goodwin's publications, he would have seen that this much-injured man was not the fool that he has thoughtlessly described. For nearly two centuries Burnet succeeded in ruining the character of John Goodwin in the public estimation; and yet in no respect was he superior to the man whom he so deeply injured, except in ecclesiastical rank. He was, in truth, vastly inferior to John Goodwin as a theologue, as a biblical critic, as a general scholar, and a writer of English. Solomon was not the only man that "saw servants on horseback, and princes on foot."

It was singularly unfortunate for Goodwin, that about sixty years had elapsed from the time of his death, before the publication of Burnet's History; so that, as his frends, who were personally acquainted with him, had gone to "the house appointed for all living," he had no one to do justice to his character, when that important but gossiping work was presented to the world. The Nonconformists would not defend him, for they were Calvinists, and he was an Arminian; Episcopalians would not defend him, for he was an Independent, and had sided with the parliament and the army; and so Burnet's mis-statement remained uncontradicted, and an upright and learned man suffered a permanent injury.

For Mr. Goodwin's attachment to Cromwell, so often charged upon him as a crime, it is not difficult to assign reasons which imply no reflection upon his memory. When men properly estimate the value of religious liberty, protection from the dire grasp of persecution, come from what quarter it may, will inspire sentiments of gratitude. This protection was afforded by Cromwell, who effectually humbled the intolerant Presbyterians, and declared his readiness to spread the shield over all classes of religious people, who forbore to interfere with his political measures,

and conducted themselves in a peaceable and orderly
manner. Had it not been for Cromwell, in all probability,
Mr. Goodwin's opinions would have cost him his liberty,
if not his life. At the same time, it is undeniable that
Cromwell, although a usurper, made England and Protestantism to be respected throughout Europe; and but for
him, according to their avowed principles, the Presbyterians
would not have hesitated to shed Goodwin's blood, but
would rather have thought that by such an act they were
doing God service. He was just such an incorrigible
heretic as Samuel Rutherford and William Prynne thought
might be hanged, or even burnt alive, for the public benefit; and yet that he was more "thoroughpaced" in his
attachment to Cromwell than any other minister of the
time is more than Burnet knew. Was his attachment to
Cromwell stronger than that of Dr. Thomas Goodwin,
Cromwell's chaplain? or that of John Howe, one of the
greatest and best men of the age, who was Cromwell's
ecclesiastical adviser? or Dr. John Owen, whom Cromwell
raised to high dignity in the University of Oxford? This
Burnet might assert, but he could not prove.

To the enemies of Mr. Goodwin, Burnet's mendacious
account has been an occasion of noisy triumph; especially
to the late Rev. Augustus Toplady. The mind of this
theologian was so thoroughly saturated with the doctrines
of Calvinism, that they seemed to be incorporated with his
very being. He scorned to conceal his religious opinions,
and gloried in their open avowal and defence. Had he, in
doing this, conducted himself with the decorum of a gentleman and a Christian, whatever might have been thought
of his creed, his honesty would have entitled him to
universal respect. But he set himself to destroy the good
name of nearly all the eminent men, whose sentiments
concerning the extent of the Divine compassion were contrary to his own; and seems never to have imagined, that
an Anti-Calvinist, whether living or dead, was entitled to
either justice, truth, or mercy. Eager to criminate Mr.
Goodwin, and thus to get rid of his arguments, this celebrated polemic seized with exultation upon the statement

of Burnet; and though it contained a palpable contradiction on its very face, he adopted it as a basis of the most unfounded charges. Toplady has endeavoured to improve upon the bishop's account, by adding several circumstances of his own invention; all of which are perfectly gratuitous assumptions, unsupported by the slightest authority, and some of them are absolutely false. He has applied to the venerable old man the most reproachful epithets, boldly taxed him with crimes that he never committed, and, in the teeth of the strongest evidence to the contrary, has represented him as one of the most consummate hypocrites that ever disgraced the human form, or insulted the patience of heaven.* A formal refutation of such accusations is unnecessary. A simple negative is all the reply to which unauthorized assertions, the mere ebullitions of angry passion, are at all entitled. Besides, the practice of calling names, and of falsifying history, never fails, among the candid and intelligent, to defeat its own purpose. It requires little sagacity to perceive, that no system of religious doctrine, which requires for its support the sacrifice of truth and charity, can ever have emanated from that Being who is the unchangeable patron of both.

On taking leave of the civil troubles of this country, as connected with the personal history of Mr. Goodwin, we cannot forbear to adore that infinitely wise and gracious Providence which superintends the affairs of men, and which is especially displayed in educing good from evil. By that Power the deeds of violence now related have been overruled for the permanent advantage of this favoured land. The lawless republicans, with Cromwell and Ireton at their head, though they did not establish liberty, gave the death-blow to monarchical tyranny. The arbitrary and cruel policy of the Stuarts was indeed resumed by the Second Charles, whose persecuting reign, in open violation of his promise, and whose mean acceptance of French gold, have stamped his character with indelible infamy. But though monarchical tyranny lived, it could never recover

* Toplady's Historic Defence, Introduction.

from the wound it had received, but finally expired with
the abdication of James.*   Finding that his attempts to
render himself absolute, and to subvert the Protestant
religion, had alienated the affections of his subjects from
him, this monarch, recollecting the fate of his father,
" yielded an easy and a bloodless victory to his opponents,
and left them to settle the constitution amidst calm and
sober councils." Out of that chaos of confusion and disorder
into which society was thrown by the civil wars and the
commonwealth, and by the oppressive sway of the two
succeeding kings, an invisible but Divine hand guided
them in the formation of a system of civil polity, which,
affording protection to the lowest ranks of society, and
extending the control of law to the highest, is the glory of
Britain, and the admiration of the world.   Under the
auspices of this constitution, British subjects enjoy more
rational liberty, have more true religion, and are consequently more happy, than any other nation upon the
face of the earth.

After William Taylor had enjoyed Mr. Goodwin's benefice
in Coleman Street about four or five years, he fell under
the displeasure of the existing government, and was
expelled after the example of his injured predecessor.   On
this occasion urgent application was made by Mr. Goodwin's
friends in his behalf; and after considerable difficulty had
been surmounted, their request was obtained. Mr. Goodwin
found, however, on his restoration to his church, that a
great part of the revenue which he had formerly enjoyed,
was alienated from him.   The vicar's income arose, principally, from the voluntary contributions of the parishioners;
many of whom, favouring the principles of the Presbyterians, presented to Taylor their respective quotas.   The
loss sustained by Mr. Goodwin in consequence of his ejectment, in the space of nine years, he estimates at One
Thousand Pounds: a large sum in those times, the absence
of which must have been severely felt by him, considering
the largeness of his family.†

* Noble's Memoirs of the Protectorate House of Cromwell, Vol. II.
p. 320, Edit. 1784.   † Pence Protected, Preface.

CHAPTER VII.

AFTER his conversion to Arminianism, Mr. Goodwin was surrounded by men who regarded him as one of the most notorious heretics of the age, and who were resolved (if possible) to overwhelm him by popular clamour; he was therefore compelled to defend himself and his opinions in open disputations, as well as from the pulpit and the press. It has not indeed been unusual in different ages, for men of opposite sentiments to meet by appointment in some public place, for the purpose of arguing the points at issue between them. Thus Carolstadt and Eckius, soon after the commencement of the Reformation in Germany, held a public disputation at Leipsic, concerning the doctrine of Luther, in the presence of several of the first personages of the empire.* The celebrated Richard Baxter and Mr. Tombs engaged in a similar contest, in the parish church of Bewdley, in Worcestershire, respecting the subjects and mode of baptism.† Mr. Goodwin was thrice drawn into oral debate, before a vast concourse of people, in defence of the Arminian doctrines. In the first of these Vavasor Powell was his opponent; a minister of the Baptist denomination; a man of great zeal, and of equal indiscretion. He was employed for some time as an itinerant preacher in Wales, where his labours are said to have been eminently successful. Having imbibed the extravagant notions of the Fifth Monarchy Men, he was afterwards swallowed up in the vortex of secular politics. During the Commonwealth he used the pulpit as a vehicle of the most daring invective against the protector and his government; in consequence of which he was apprehended and sent to prison. He and

* Cox's Life of Melancthon, pp. 92, &c., Edit. 1817.   † Baxter's Plain Scripture-Proof, Preface.

his fellow-captives considered themselves sufferers for righteousness' sake; but Cromwell told them, that they suffered for being busy-bodies in other men's matters, and for not minding their own proper business.*

Some disagreement having taken place between a few of Mr. Goodwin's hearers, and their Calvinian neighbours, concerning the extent of redemption by Jesus Christ, for the satisfaction of these parties, he was urged by Powell to engage with him in a public dispute. To this proposal Mr. Goodwin acceded; and the requisite preliminaries being settled, these champions met in Coleman Street, on the 31st of December, 1649, in the presence of several ministers and a crowd of people. The question at issue between them was, Whether Jesus Christ died for the redemption of all mankind, or only for those who will be finally chosen to the enjoyment of eternal life? The text which Mr. Goodwin particularly insisted upon, in defence of general redemption, was John iii. 16 : *God so loved the world, that He gave His only begotten Son, that whosoever believeth in Him should not perish, but have everlasting life.* Powell contended, that by the term *world*, in this passage, was to be understood the "elect of God" only: to which Mr. Goodwin replied, "If by the 'world' is meant the elect of God only, then the sense of the place must run thus : ' So God loved the elect of God, that whosoever of these elect should believe, they should not perish, but have everlasting life : ' which clearly implies, that some of the elect will not believe, and so consequently may perish. This is to put nonsense upon the place, and to destroy the savour that is in it; and therefore cannot be the sense of it as taken in this argument. That which destroyeth the construction of the sentence, and the savour which is in it, (which alone is fit to feed the understanding of a man,) cannot be the sense of the place. To understand the word 'world,' in this place, of the elect only, makes the sense altogether unprofitable. *Ergo.*" Through the whole of this argument Mr. Goodwin had decidedly the advantage of his opponent, who had raised a ghost which he was

* Ivimey's Hist. of the Baptists, pp. 232, 261.

manifestly unable to lay. Powell was therefore glad to give place to four of his Calvinian brethren, Caryl, Drake, Simpson, and Venning, who stepped forward to his assistance, and, in his stead, successively attacked his powerful antagonist. At the close of the debate, Powell again rose, and said, " I shall make bold to speak one word. For my part, I bless God that our meeting hath been as it hath ; that there hath been no more contention or division amongst us; and I refer what hath been controverted to the congregation, and desire them to judge. And if Mr. Goodwin will engage further at another time, there will be some to oppose him." To these remarks, Simpson replied, " I will never undertake to dispute, unless every man shall be commanded silence, but the two disputants ; and the moderator to keep up the question. And Mr. Goodwin having at this time pressed his arguments, if now he will answer to the question, there shall be some ready still to oppose." Mr. Goodwin replied, " Though I conceive the laws of dispute in this kind will somewhat suffer, by the observation of these rules ; yet, if the truth will not be entertained, nor the dispute carried on, but upon that motion, I will stand to it."

According to this agreement, on the 14th of January, 1649-50, a disputation was held between Mr. Goodwin and Mr. John Simpson, in the church of Allhallows the Great, in Upper Thames Street. Simpson, like his friend Powell, was a Baptist, and a Fifth Monarchy Man. They both held the same political sentiments, and were afterwards companions in prison for delivering inflammatory harangues against Cromwell. Dr. Calamy states, that Simpson was "a great Antinomian." Be this as it may, he was a thorough Calvinist. "I desire liberty," says he, " to prove, that there are some particular persons hated of God from all eternity ; and that there are others loved of God from all eternity ; and that God did really intend the salvation of the one by the death of Christ, and not in good earnest the salvation of the other ; but rather the aggravation of their condemnation thereby."

To these and other peculiarities of his creed, this disciple of Calvin attached the greatest possible importance. "The point which we are upon," says he, "is of great concernment; a fundamental point in religion; the ground of faith : what it is that every man and woman must believe, that they may be saved." Such were the views of Mr. Goodwin's second opponent : a man apparently of stronger sense than Powell, but inferior to him in charity and meekness. For the better accommodation of the assembly, in regard to hearing, Mr. Goodwin took his station in the gallery, and Simpson in the pulpit. The latter of them opened the meeting by answering objections against disputations of that nature. Mr. Goodwin then added a few introductory remarks, in which he distinctly states, that while he attributed considerable importance to the doctrine of general redemption, he was far from regarding an acknowledgment of it as essential to salvation. He also avows his conviction, that whether men hold general or particular redemption, if they "truly and sincerely believe in Jesus Christ for salvation," they are in the way to a blessed immortality.

In respect of himself, Mr. Goodwin says, "I must profess before you all this day, though in part it will redound, it may be, to some shame and disparagement to myself; yet for the honour of Him for whom I was created, and for whom I should sacrifice all that I have or am, I am fully resolved herein, that I cannot be better disposed of, than in sacrificing upon the Lord Jesus Christ, who hath already been sacrificed upon the service of my soul, and of yours. This is that which I would signify unto you, that for many years together, ever since I was capable of understanding anything in the Gospel, I was of that judgment whereof it seems Mr. Simpson is at this day; and though I would not speak of myself, yet I crave leave to acquaint you with what others have said in this behalf, that I produced more arguments for the confirmation of that opinion, than others of my brethren in the ministry usually did. But since it pleased God to enlarge my understanding so far, as to go round about the controversy, and to see and ponder and weigh, with the greatest im-

partialness of judgment and conscience I was capable of;
going round about again and again, and telling the towers,
and viewing the strength, the arguments, evidences, and
mighty demonstrations of that opinion wherein I now
stand; I was not able by all the assistance I had from my
former discussions, wherein I had given out myself to the
utmost of that light and learning and strength which God
had given me; all these were of no value or consideration
at all, to stand up against that further light which came
upon me on the other hand, though I was conscientiously
and deeply engaged in it.

"I know it is the sense of the greatest part of you, that
in matters of faith there is nothing considerable to be
built upon any man's reason, or upon discussions which
are drawn from the Scriptures by the mediation of human
understanding: which supposed, let me say, that there is
no man who holds, that Christ died for some particular
persons, and not for all, but his faith in this point doth
stand merely upon the workings of reason. Whereas that
opinion which I maintain concerning the universality of
Christ's death for all, stands upon express Scriptures,
plain and clear terms, without the intervention of any
man's reason to make it out. As there is no place in all
the Scriptures that doth affirm, that He died for some
particular persons only, or denies that He died for all men,
but many that expressly affirm that He died for all;
therefore clear it is, at least thus far, that all those arguments which are brought from the Scriptures to prove the
contrary, must be founded upon the discussions, issuings,
and givings out of the reasons and apprehensions of men."

In the disputation of this day several subjects of great
importance occupied the attention of the combatants;
such as the extent of redemption by Jesus Christ, the
nature of God's decrees relating to the election and
reprobation of men, and the meaning of various passages
in the ninth chapter of the Epistle to the Romans.
Mr. Goodwin stated and defended his own views with
great precision and force of reasoning against the
principles of his antagonist, which were emphatically

Calvinistic. The arguments on both sides were in substance those which are usually employed in this controversy.

At the conclusion of this day's debate, Mr. Henry Jessey, a minister of the Baptist denomination, a man of liberal sentiments and of a catholic spirit, interfered, and "spake to this effect: 'I desire, because there are many weak Christians here present, that are apt to be troubled, and to despair within themselves, to hear such differences between godly and learned men, they will be ready to say, they know not what to believe, nor what religion to be of; therefore I shall only desire to inform them this one thing: That the difference between the two opinions is not so great, but that men, whether they believe the one or the other, may be saved through the grace of God in Jesus Christ.'" On hearing this, Simpson exclaimed, "Mr. Jessey! Mr. Jessey! no more of that! I conceive that they that hold general redemption, and free-will, in opposition to free grace, never had any experimental knowledge of the grace of God in Jesus Christ."—"I am sorry," replied Mr. Jessey, "to hear such words come from you."—"Then Mr. Powell prayed, and the congregation was dismissed."

These disputants met again in the same place on the 11th of February following; when Mr. Goodwin, after the introductory prayer, said, "Because I found some inconvenience in staying long the last time, being in years, I desire that we may first agree upon bounds and limits of time for disputation." "We will refer it," replied his antagonist, "to what time you shall please." To which Mr. Goodwin rejoined, "I shall be willing to stand as long as I am well able; about two hours, or somewhat more; till about twelve o'clock, or a little after; and longer I shall not be well able to stay." Mr. Goodwin then stated, that having been unjustly reflected upon at the conclusion of their last meeting, as holding free-will in opposition to free grace, he requested leave to refute the charge by an ingenuous declaration of his sentiments on these subjects. Twice he solicited permission to do this, and in both instances was refused, and completely borne

down by the clamours of his opponent, who had preferred
the accusation. Having, as he expressed it, had dirt
thrown in his face, and being peremptorily denied the
liberty of washing it off, Mr. Goodwin submitted, and
proceeded to the discussion of various topics connected
with the doctrine of General Redemption, especially the
salvability of the heathen, and the decrees of God relating
to the eternal states of men. In the whole debate of this
day, Mr. Goodwin displayed his characteristic acuteness
and good temper, together with his accurate knowledge
of the Scriptures and of the Calvinistic controversy.
Towards the conclusion of the contest he annoyed his
antagonist exceedingly by producing two extracts from
Calvinian publications, in which the doctrine of General
Redemption was manifestly implied. One of these was
taken from a sermon which Powell had recently published,
and the other from the " Testimony to the Truth of Jesus
Christ," of which mention has been made in a preceding
chapter, and to which the signatures of fifty-two Calvinist
ministers were annexed. With regard to this latter work,
Mr. Goodwin says, "A second instance which I would
read to you, is out of a small treatise, published by most
of the ministers in the city, out of a pretence to give
testimony to the truth of Jesus Christ, against errors and
heresies : page 32.—' *Thousands and tens of thousands of
poor souls, which Christ hath ransomed with His blood, shall
hereby be betrayed, seduced, and endangered to be undone to
all eternity.*' Here is the doctrine of universal redemption
fully asserted; inasmuch as they that are ransomed with
the blood of Christ, are said ' *to be in danger of being
undone to all eternity.*' For danger implies not a possibility
only, but a probability and likelihood of falling into, and
suffering what they are in danger of. Now if the
ransomed of Christ may be in danger of perishing; then
the ransomed are not the elect only, in your sense, but
they that perish, and consequently all men. I could
bring you twenty other instances besides these, which
assert, preach, and affirm, and that constantly, from day
to day, the same opinions and conclusions which now

Q

they quarrel with, and make such matter of error and heresy, and things of such a dangerous nature. They cannot preach without them, nor write without them.— Can a man be in *danger* of miscarrying in that, wherein there is no *possibility* of miscarrying?"

This disputation was continued till Mr. Goodwin complained of being injured with regard to his health, and at length ended in all probability where such contests are likely always to end,—in the confirmation of both parties in their own opinions. "The time is past," says Mr. Goodwin, "and I have spent myself, and I fear have incurred some inconvenience in my health. Yet, notwithstanding, I have been freely willing to give testimony to the truth of the Lord Jesus Christ, which will be witnessed at the great day of His appearing. Till then, I shall be willing to lie under what reproach either you or whosoever else shall cast upon me. I have stood here, and denied myself many ways, and shall now refer both my cause and yours to the righteous judgment of God who cannot be deceived." He also added, "I desire the people to take knowledge, that there is no election or reprobation from eternity, but decrees of election and reprobation only. There is no reprobation of persons, because it is impossible there should be any persons from eternity. But the decrees of God being nothing but God Himself, to deny such decrees from eternity, is to deny God. But this is that which I deny: That these decrees respect persons *personally* considered. They only respect *species* of men. The decree of election from eternity was, That whosoever believes should be saved; and, on the contrary, That whosoever lives and dies in unbelief, should be condemned: this is the decree of reprobation. This is that which I say, There is no other decree of election and reprobation from eternity but only this. And so I have done."

On the termination of this contest, a short-hand writer, of the name of John Weeks, published a quarto pamphlet, containing one hundred and eighteen pages, entitled, "Truth's Conflict with Error: or, Universal Redemption

Controverted, in three public Disputations: the first between Mr. John Goodwin and Mr. Vavasor Powell, in Coleman Street, London; the other two between Mr. John Goodwin and Mr. John Simpson, at Alhallows the Great, in Thames Street; in the presence of divers Ministers of the City of London, and some thousands of others, 1650." From this curious document the preceding account has been extracted. In an address to the reader prefixed to this tract, it is said, "What thou hast here presented to thy view, I nothing doubt thou didst either hear, or else hast heard of; the sound of it having gone forth both far and near; neither was it done in a corner."

In the course of the same year there appeared a very sensible and argumentative pamphlet, entitled, "Good News to all People: Glad Tidings to all Men: God Good unto all, and Christ the Saviour of the World: or, The General Point faithfully handled by way of Exercise: or, A Sermon preached at Buckingham upon the 25th of March, being (as so called) Easter Day. By William Hartley, 1650." To this well-written discourse is appended the following note: "Upon a Conference in London touching the contents of this treatise, I was rendered one of Mr. Goodwin's disciples, of whom I have no further cognisance, saving that I was, February 11th, present at a dispute betwixt Mr. Goodwin and Mr. Simpson, where (notwithstanding the prejudice offered by the moderators and Mr. Powell), the truth of Mr. Goodwin's position, and his abilities in the management thereof, was sufficiently demonstrated."

On the same occasion, Mr. Goodwin published a small pamphlet, which he entitled, "The Remedy of Unreasonableness: or, The Substance of a Speech intended at a Conference or Dispute, in Alhallows the Great, London, Feb. 11th, 1649; exhibiting the brief heads of Mr. John Goodwin's Judgment concerning the Freeness, Fulness, Effectualness of the Grace of God, 1650." In the preface to this publication, the author says, "At the former of the two late conferences held in Alhallows the Great, between Mr. J. Simpson and myself, he was pleased, upon no occasion at all given by me, to traduce me before the congregation there assembled, consisting of some thousands of people, as a man holding free will in opposition to free grace. At the latter of the said conferences, perceiving him not so knowing what my opinion was in the said points, and fearing the like of his friends, who made up a great part of the auditory; to free them from an unchristian surmise against their brother, who never injured any of them; I was desirous to have given an account of my faith, touching the said particulars, in the presence of those who were met to hear. But he that had the face to charge unduly, had not the heart either to stand by so unworthy an action, or to acknowledge the unworthiness of it. For when I desired leave, over and over, and that with much earnestness, to have given some brief account to the people of my judgment touching the things unjustly charged upon me, he peremptorily denied it; and as oft as I made offer to speak upon this account, he, in a very unseemly manner, and with much clamour, interrupted me, and suffered me not."

"Concerning the grace of God," continues our author, "I have, upon all occasions, constantly taught, That the whole plot or counsel of God concerning the salvation of the world is of free grace, of mere grace and goodness of will in God. That His purpose of election, or predestination of men to life and glory, is an act of free grace also; and that there was no obligation upon Him to predestinate any man as now He hath done. That the gift of Jesus Christ unto the world is an act of free grace, and that God was no ways obliged hereunto. That to confer justification, adoption, and salvation itself, upon believing in Jesus Christ, are acts of the pure and free grace of God. That to give power and means of believing to men, is an act of mere and free grace likewise. That it is of the free grace of God, and by the assistance thereof, that any man doth ever actually believe." "Concerning the extent of this grace, my doctrine hath been, that it is not imprisoned or confined within the narrow compass of a handful of men; but that, like the sun in the firmament of heaven, it compasseth the whole earth from one end of it to the other, and stretcheth itself unto all men. That it is exceeding full and comprehensive: that the good which God graciously intends unto men, is full, absolute, and complete blessedness, containing every desirable thing in it. And that the means which God graciously exhibiteth unto men to make them blessed are every way sufficient for such a purpose.

"Concerning the effectualness of this grace, I teach upon all occasions, that in the gift of a power whereby to believe or to be saved, it is simply irresistible, and that men cannot hinder this operation of it. That what good soever any man doth, he doth it through the assistance of the free grace of God, and is in no capacity so much as to conceive a good thought without it. And that when any man actually believeth, he is mightily strengthened and assisted by the special grace of God thereunto. So that the act of believing is to be ascribed to God, not only as the sole Giver of that power by which men believe, but as the sole supernatural Actor also of this power; and that man, when he doth believe, is so far from having any ground of boasting in himself, hath all the reason in the world to confess, that he is an unprofitable servant, and hath only done that which was his duty to do. Only I conceive, that men are not necessitated by this grace to believe, whether they will or no; nor yet made willing upon any such terms, but that there is a possibility left unto them of remaining unwilling to any point of time till the act of believing be produced.

"My opinion being truly compared with the opinion of those that dissent from me, appears to have much more in it for the exaltation of the grace of God than theirs, and theirs much more in it for the exaltation of the will of man. My opinion makes the grace of God so free as to enrich the whole world and all that is called man in it, and that without the least engagement upon God from men thereunto; whereas their opinion imprisons it within a narrow compass of men in comparison, and so bridles the freeness of it in that consideration. As in one branch of their opinion they stifle the glory of the freeness of it, so in another they destroy the very essence of it, and make it to be no grace at all. For that opinion which makes the grace of God the cause of no other actions in men, than such as God cannot according to the constant method of His remunerative bounty reward, destroys the very nature of grace. And that the opinion maintained by our opposers doth this, is evident: because that, making men to act necessarily and unavoidably, by means of the grace which is given unto them, it maketh them to act physically, or as mere natural agents; and so reduceth all they do by virtue of the grace of God, to the condition of mere natural actions; which, by the standing law of God's remunerative bounty, are not capable of reward.

"Again: That their opinion tends many thousand degrees more than mine to magnify the wills of men is evident thus: I affirm the will of man, even under the strongest and most effectual motions of grace whereof it is capable, (the nature and essential liberty of it only preserved,) to be in a capacity of doing that which is evil; which is the greatest abasement of the will that can well be imagined: whereas the other opinion maketh the wills of men, under the effectual motions of grace to that which is good, like unto the will of God Himself; I mean necessarily good, and free from all possibility of sinning; which is the highest exaltation of the will that can well be conceived. Besides, that opinion making men unable to do righteously, for want of the grace of God, when they do wickedly, takes off the shame and demerit of sinning from the wills of men, and either casts them upon God for denying His grace unto them, or else resolves them into nothing. Whereas the opinion asserted by me, that men, when they do wickedly, have sufficient means from God to refrain from sin and do righteously, resolves the shame and whole demerit of sinning into men themselves, and their wills, and so renders them inexcusable. Thus you see how unjustly, and with manifest untruth, I have been charged to hold free will against free grace, and that my accusers are the guilty persons themselves.

"Concerning my opinion about the death of Christ, which is, that He died for the salvation of all men, without exception of any; and consequently for the heathen; as well those who enjoy the oral ministry of the Gospel, as those that want it: I herein hold nothing but what was generally taught and received in the churches of Christ for three hundred years together, next after the times of the apostles; which, by all our modern Protestant divines, and by Calvin in special manner, are acknowledged for times wherein Christian religion reigned in her greatest purity and soundness of doctrine; as I am able to make substantial proof, by express testimonies, and these not a few, from the best records of those times. That God's predestination of men, or purpose of election, depends upon His foresight of their faith, (an opinion clearly confederate with that of universal redemption by Christ,) is both by Calvin and Beza themselves acknowledged to have been the judgment of many of the ancient fathers; and is proved by many particular instances, and express testimonies, by Gerard Vossius, in his Historia Pelagiana, Lib. vi. Thes. 8. Concerning some few sayings found in some of those authors, which seem to be of a contrary import, and are cited upon that account, the truth is, that they are but seemingly so. They speak not of the purchase, but of the application, of redemption by Christ."

These extracts are important, as displaying Mr. Goodwin's correct acquaintance with the doctrines of pure Arminianism at this period, as well as the strength of his conviction that they are the sacred truths of God. He now began to meditate the publication of a work in which the grand principles of the Arminian system should be distinctly developed and largely defended. The times were favourable to this project. The power of the Presbyterians was broken; and that great object of his desire, general liberty of conscience, obtained. He considered the glorious doctrine of human redemption by the Son of God, as delivered in the Scriptures, and embraced by the

Primitive Church, to be obscured and held in bondage
through the restrictions and limitations imposed upon it
by the theologians of the Genevan school; and therefore
gave to his book the significant title of "REDEMPTION
REDEEMED." *

The publication of this work, which is a folio volume,
and bears the date of 1651, was a singularly magnanimous
adventure, and shows the author's superiority to public
opinion and censure. He had indeed nothing to apprehend in the form of legal process, since the persecuting
ordinances of the Long Parliament, which had been issued
as the guardians of Calvinian orthodoxy, had now become
obsolete, and therefore harmless as lions in sculpture.
The doctrines of Calvin, however, had acquired more
general popularity in this country than at any former
period; and Mr. Goodwin's attack upon them in this work
was by far the most formidable that had ever appeared in
the English language. Most of the distinguishing doctrines of Arminianism indeed might be distinctly traced
in the writings of British Protestants from the commencement of the Reformation in the reign of Henry the Eighth,
and had been formally defended by Godwyn, Mountagu,
Hoard, and others : but, previously to the publication of
Mr. Goodwin's book, they had never been reduced, among
us, to any thing like system, viewed in their connexion
and dependencies, nor recommended by such a combination
of eloquence and argument. Our author therefore had
nothing to expect but opposition in its most formidable
shape. Of this he was fully aware; yet he anticipated the
most beneficial results from putting the Arminian doctrines into a train of public discussion. The feelings
with which he appeared before the world on this occasion
are admirably depicted in his dedicatory address to " Dr.
Benjamin Whichcote, Provost of King's College, and
Vice-Chancellor of the University of Cambridge ; together

* " The first is, the redeeming of a captivated truth." Hakewill's
Apology of the Power and Providence of God, p. 16, Edit. 1635. This expression of Hakewill in all probability suggested to Mr. Goodwin the very
significant title which he prefixed to his great work. That he had read
Hakewill's volume we formerly took occasion to observe.

with the rest of the Heads of Colleges and Students in Divinity, in that famous University." In this noble composition, which displays almost every characteristic mark of mental greatness, our author says,

"Reverend and right worthy Gentlemen, Friends and Brethren in Christ! The oracles consulted by me about this dedication were neither any undervaluing of you, nor overvaluing of myself, or of the piece here presented to you; nor any desire of drawing respects from you, either to my person or any thing that is mine: much less any malignancy of desire to cause you to drink of my cup, or to bring you under the same cloud of disparagement, which the world hath spread about me. Praise unto His grace, who hath taught me some weak rudiments of His heavenly art, of drawing light out of darkness, for mine own use. I have not been for so many years together trampled upon to so little purpose, as to remain ignorant of mine own vileness, and what element I am nearest allied to; nor so tender and querulous as either to complain of those who go over me as the stones of the street, or to project the sufferings of others in order to my own solace and relief. My long want of respects from men is now turned into an athletic habit, somewhat after the manner of those who by long fasting lose their appetites, and find a contentedness of nature to live with little meat afterwards. I can, from the dunghill whereon I sit, with much contentment and sufficient enjoyment of myself behold my brethren on thrones round about me.

"The prize that I run for in my applications to you is to engage those whom I judge the most able, and not the least willing among their brethren, to bless the world, labouring under its own vanity and folly, by bringing forth the glorious Creator, and ever-blessed Redeemer, out of their pavilions of darkness, into a clear and perfect light, to be beheld, reverenced, adored, in all their glory; to be possessed, enjoyed, delighted in, in all their beauty, sweetness, and desirableness, by the inhabitants of the earth. I know you have no need to be taught, but possibly you may have some need to consider, that your gifts, parts, learning, knowledge, wisdom, books, studies, opportunities, pleasant mansions, will all suddenly make company for that which is not, and never turn to any account of true greatness, nor of any interest worthy of truly considering men, unless they shall by a solemn act of consecration be consigned. over to that great service of God and men, whereby that blessed union between them shall be promoted, the foundations whereof have been by so high a hand of grace laid in the blood of Jesus Christ. You know the saying of the great Prophet of the world, 'He that gathereth not with Me, scattereth abroad.' Whatsoever shall not offer itself, to be taken and carried along by Jesus Christ, in that sublime motion wherein He moveth daily, according to the will of His Father, in a straight course for the saving of the world, will most certainly be dissipated and shattered all to nothing, by the irresistible dint and force thereof. Gifts, parts, reason, understanding, under means of being improved by study; learning, knowledge; if these do not make one shoulder with Jesus Christ, in lifting the world from the gates of death, will undoubtedly, above the rate of all other things, abound to the confusion and condemnation of men. When men of rich endowments give their strength to other studies and inquiries, suffering the minds of men to perish in their sad pollutions, through ignorance, or, which is worse, those disloyal and profane notions of God and Christ, which reign in the midst of them, without taking any compassion upon them, by searching out and discovering to them those most excellent things of God and Christ, the knowledge whereof would be to them as a resurrection from death unto life; they do but write their names in the dust, and buy vanity with that price which was put into their hands for a far more honourable purchase. And yet they are sons of greater folly, who, by suffering their judgments to be abused by sloth, or sinister respects, (for there is a far different consideration of those who miscarry at this point through mere human frailty,) bring forth

a strange God and a strange Christ into the world; such
as neither the Scriptures, nor reason unbewitched, know,
or own; and most imperiously charge the consciences
of men with the dread of Divine displeasure, and
the vengeance of hellfire, if they refuse to bow the knee
before the images and representations which they have
set up.

" Knowing the terror of the Lord, according to the measure of the light of the knowledge of Himself, which He
hath been graciously pleased to shine into my heart, I
have, in the ensuing discourse, lift up my soul to the
discovery of Him to the world, in the truth of His nature,
attributes, counsels, decrees, and dispensations; and that
with simplicity of intention to disencumber the minds of
men of such apprehensions concerning Him, which are evil
mediators between Him and His creature; fomenting that
enmity between them which hath been occasioned by
unworthy deportment on the creature's side. I confess
that, in some particulars, I have been led (I trust by the
Spirit of truth) out of the way more generally occupied by
those who, of later times, have travelled the same regions
of enquiry with me : but deeply pondering what Augustine
somewhere saith, that as nothing can be found out more
beneficial to the world, than something further of God
than is at present known, so nothing is attempted with
more danger; I have steered my course with all tenderness
and circumspection; arguing nothing, concluding nothing,
but either from the grammatical sense, or best known
signification of words and phrases in the Scripture, and
this with the express agreement of contexts, together with
the analogy of the Scriptures in other places, or from the
most universally received principles either in religion or
sound reason, and more particularly from such notions
concerning God and His attributes, which I find generally
subscribed with the names of all that are called orthodox
among us, and have written of such things. Nor have I
anywhere receded from the more general sense of interpreters, in the explication of any text of Scripture, but
only where the express signification of words, or the

urgency of the context, or some repugnancy to the Scripture elsewhere, or some pregnant inconsistency with clear principles of religion or sound reason necessitated me to it. I seldom, upon any of these accounts, leave the common road of interpreters, but I find that some or other of the more intelligent of them have trodden the same path before me. For the most part, Chrysostom among the ancient expositors, and Calvin among the moderns, are my companions in the paths of my greatest solitariness. The main doctrine avouched in the discourse, wherein the redemption of mankind by Jesus Christ, no particular person excepted, is asserted, I demonstrate, from the best records of antiquity, to have been the œcumenical sense of the Christian world in her primitive and purest times. Nor am I conscious of the least mistake, either in word or meaning, of any author cited throughout the whole discourse; nor of any omission in point of diligence and care, for the prevention of all mistakes.

" The discourse, such as it is, with all respects of honour and love, I present to you; not requiring any thing by way of countenance or approbation, otherwise than upon those equitable terms, on which Augustus recommended his children to the favour of the senate: *si meruerit.* Only as a lover of the truth, name, and glory of God, and of the peace, joy, and salvation of the world, I shall take leave to pour out my soul in this request; That you will confirm, by setting the royal signet of your approbation to the doctrine here maintained, if you judge it to be a truth, or else vouchsafe to deliver me, and many others, from the snare thereof, by taking away with a hand of light and potency of demonstration those weapons wherein we trust. Your *con*testation, upon these terms, will be with me more precious than your *at*testation, in case of your comport in judgment with me: though I ingenuously confess, that for the truth's sake, even in this also I shall greatly rejoice. Notwithstanding, I deem it much more richly conducing to my peace and safety, to be delivered from my errors, than to receive countenance and approbation in what I hold and teach.

" I shall not need to desire you, that in your answer, you will not rise up in your might against the weaker passages ; but that you will bend the strength of your reply against the strength of what you shall oppose. A field may be won, though many soldiers of the conquering side may fall or be wounded; so may a mountain remain unmoveable, though the looser earth about the sides of it should be taken up and scattered in the air. In like manner, the body of a discourse may stand entire in its solidity and strength, though many particular expressions, remote from the centre, should be detected of inconsiderateness, weakness, or untruth. In some cases, one argument may be so triumphantly commanding, that though many others of the same engagement should be defeated, yet the cause protected by it may laugh all opposition to scorn. I acknowledge there are some passages in the ensuing discourse, which upon the review I apprehend obnoxious enough to exception, and which, had my second thoughts been born in due time, should have been better secured. But I trust that ancient law of indulgence in such cases as mine, is of authority sufficient in your commonwealth to relieve me :

————Opere in longo fas est obrepere somnum.

Neither need I suspect any of that unmanlike learning among you, which teacheth men to confute opinions by vulgar votes and exclamations. ' We know that this sect (or heresy) is every where spoken against,' had no influence upon Paul to turn him out of the way of his heresy. And as for those mormolukes of Arminianism, Pelagianism, which serve to affright children in understanding out of the love of many important truths, I am not under any jealousy concerning you, that you should suffer any impressions from them. You know that that great enemy of men, who of old taught the enemies of God to put His saints into bears' skins, and into wolves' skins, so preparing them to be torn in pieces by dogs, hath, in these later times, prevailed with many of the children of God to put many of His truths, such as they like not, or comprehend not, into names of ignominy and reproach, to draw others into the same hatred of them with themselves. This method of suppressing opinions, against which men have no competent ground of eviction otherwise, was first invented by the subtle sons of the synagogue of Rome.

"The truth is, you have no such temptation upon you as private men have, to flee to any such polluted sanctuary. By the suffrage of your authority, your esteem amongst men being so predominant, you may slay what doctrines you please, and what you please you may keep alive. If you justify, who will not be afraid to condemn? If you condemn, who will justify? Only God's eldest daughter, Truth, hath One mightier than you on her side, who will justify her in due time, though you should condemn her; and will raise her up the third day in case you shall slay her.

"I shall discharge you from any further sufferings from my pen at present; only with my soul poured out before God in prayer for you, that He will make His face to shine upon you, in quickening your apprehensions, enlarging your understandings, balancing your judgments, strengthening your memories; in giving you ableness of body, willingness of mind, to labour in those rich mines of truth the Scriptures; in breaking up before you the fountains of those great depths of spiritual light and heavenly understanding; in assisting you mightily by His Spirit in the course of your studies; in lifting you up in the spirit of your minds, above the faces, fears, respects of men; in drawing out your hearts to relieve the extremities of the world round about you; in making you so many burning and shining lights in His temple, the glory and delight of your nation; in vouchsafing to you as much of all that is desirable in this world, as your spiritual interests will bear, and the reward of prophets respectively, in the glory and great things of the world to come."

Such was the eloquent and dignified manner in which Mr. Goodwin inscribed to his Alma Mater this elaborate and invaluable production; in the composition of which he has brought his accurate and extensive reading to bear, and exerted all the energies of his gigantic mind.

Nothing could be more opportune than the publication of this elaborate defence of the universal philanthropy of God, and the dedication of it to the University of Cambridge, at this particular period, when a body of men were about to appear in that famous seat of learning, distinguished alike by their scholarship, their intellectual power, their deep and enlightened piety, and their cordial belief of the redemption of all mankind. Of this honoured fraternity Dr. Henry More, Dr. Ralph Cudworth, and Mr. John Smith were among its most distinguished members. They were known by the name of Platonic Divines, and were succeeded by men of equal distinction, such as Barrow and Pearson, who entertained the same liberal views respecting the extent of human redemption.

Goodwin's important volume is divided into twenty chapters; in the first of which he proves that there is no created being or second cause, but what depends upon the first, which is God; and that in its operations as well as in its simple existence. His object in the second chapter is, to prove, that although there is as absolute and essential a dependence of second causes upon the first in point of operation as of simple existence; yet that the operations of second causes (at least ordinarily) are not so immediately determined by that dependence as their respective beings or existences are. The third chapter treats of the knowledge and fore-knowledge of God, and of the difference between these and His desires, purposes, intentions and decrees; and shows how these also are distinguished from each other. The subjects of discussion in the fourth chapter are, the perfection of God in His nature and being, His simplicity and actuality, together with the goodness of His decrees, as deducible from this perfection. The fifth, sixth, seventh, and eighth chapters are occupied in proving from the Scriptures the interesting doctrine of General Redemption. The ninth, tenth, and five following chapters are a digression, containing a connected chain of argumentation, deduced from the Scriptures, to prove that it is possible for a believer so to apostatize from God as to perish for ever. In the sixteenth chapter the author resumes the subject of General Redemption, and pursues the same theme through the remainder of his work. He contends that this doctrine is demonstrable from the Inspired Writings, was held by the Christian fathers in the purest ages of the Church, and that many of the most eminent of its opponents, in several instances, have contradicted their own creed, and paid homage to that system in which Jesus Christ is recognised as the Redeemer of all mankind.

Explaining the sense in which he held the doctrine of general redemption, Mr. Goodwin says, "When with the Scriptures we affirm, that Christ died for all men, we mean, That there was a reality of intention on God's part, that as there was a worth of merit in the death of Christ, fully sufficient for the ransom of all men, so it should be equally, and upon the same terms, applicable to all men in order to their redemption, without any difference, or special limitation of it to some more than others. That God did only antecedently intend the actual salvation of all men, by the death of Christ; but consequently the salvation only of those who believe. That there is a possibility, yea, a fair and gracious possibility, for all men, without exception, to obtain actual salvation by His death; so that in case any man perisheth, his destruction is altogether from himself; there being as much in the death of Christ towards procuring his salvation, as for any of those who come to be actually saved. That He not only put all men without exception into a capability of being saved by believing; but also took off from all men the guilt and condemnation brought upon all men by Adam's trangression; so that no man shall be condemned but upon his own personal account, and for such sins only which shall be voluntarily committed by him, or for omissions which it was in his power to have prevented. That He procured this favour with God for all men, that they should receive from Him sufficient strength and means to repent, to believe, and to persevere in both to the end. That Christ by His death purchased this transcendent grace also, for all men without exception, that upon their repentance and believing in Him they should be justified, and that upon their perseverance unto the end they should be eternally saved.

"The imputation, from the guilt whereof we desire in special manner to wash our hands by this explication, is that as we hold universal redemption, so we hold universal salvation, or that all men shall be saved by Christ. To me it seemed not a little strange, how any man professing subjection of judgment to the Scriptures should ever come to a confederacy with such an opinion. For with what frequency, and evidence of expression, do these rise up against it, ever and anon asserting on the one hand the paucity of those that will be saved; and on the other the everlastingness of the misery of those who perish! Nor do they give the least intimation of release from misery, to those who die in their sins."

In defence of this view of redemption Mr. Goodwin has produced an astonishing mass of Scriptural argument, and has confirmed it by testimonies from Augustine, Ambrose, Jerome, Chrysostom, Athanasius, Hilarius, Cyril of Jerusalem, Eusebius, Arnobius, Didymus, Basil the Great, Gregory Nyssen, Gregory Nazianzen, Epiphanius, Tertullian, Origen, Cyprian, Clemens of Alexandria, Justin Martyr, Irenæus, Prosper, Cyril of Alexandria, Theodoret, Leo the Great, Fulgentius, Primasius, Gregory the Great, Bede, Theophylact, Œcumenius, Anselm, Bernard, Melancthon, Chemnitius, Luther, Calvin, Peter Martyr, Bucer, Paræus, Gualter, Hemmingius, Ursine, Aretius, John Fox, Lavater, Chamier, Perkins, Zanchius, Bullinger, Grynæus, Davenant, Kimedontius.

"My intent," says Mr. Goodwin, "in citing Calvin, with those other late Protestant writers whom we have joined in the same suffrage in favour of the doctrine of general redemption, is not to persuade the reader, that the standing judgment either of him or of the greater part of the rest was whole and entire for the said doctrine, or stood in any great propension hereunto; much less to imply

that they never in any other places of their writings declared themselves against it ; but to show, *that the truth of
this doctrine is so near at hand, and the influence of it so
benign and accommodatious to other truths of religion, that
it is a hard matter for those that deal much in those affairs,
not to assert it ever and anon, and to argue many things
upon the authority of it ;* yea, though *extra casum necessitatis*
on the one hand, and *incogitantiæ* on the other, they
are wont to behold it, as God doth proud men, afar off."

The following recapitulation of the chapters in which
the subject of perseverance is discussed, will give the reader
some conception of our author's plan, in this part of his
work, and of the important topics upon which he has ex-
patiated. " It hath been clearly proved," says he, " that
the doctrine which maintains an absolute necessity of the
saints' perseverance in grace to the end, hath nothing
more in it for the real consolation of the saints, than that
which is contrary to it. Diligent and unpartial search
hath been made into those passages of Scripture, which the
greatest advocates of the said doctrine of perseverance
mainly insist upon ; none of which, it hath been made
fully to appear, holdeth any real correspondency with it.
The best and most substantial arguments upon which the
said doctrine is wont to be built, have been weighed in
the balance and found light. The doctrine which avoucheth
a possibility of the saints' declining, and this unto death,
hath been asserted by the express testimony and consent
of many Scriptures. This doctrine also hath received
further credit and confirmation from several principles, as
well of reason as religion, and these pregnant and
strong. The truth of this latter doctrine hath been further
ascertained by several examples of persons, who, by their
fallings, have caused the said doctrine to stand impregna-
ble. This doctrine hath been countenanced also by the
concurrent sense of all orthodox antiquity. It hath likewise received testimony from the generality of that learning
and religion, since the times of the Reformation, which
have commended themselves unto the world in the writings
of that party in the Protestant churches, which is

commonly known by the name of Lutheran. Substantial proof hath been made, that the professed adversaries of the doctrine we now speak of, even the most steady, grave, and best advised of them, have unawares given large and clear testimony to it; being not able, without the help of the spirit which speaketh in it, to manage their discursive affairs in other cases. Yea, the Synod of Dort itself, convening with a prejudice against it, and provoking one another to lay the honour of it in the dust for ever, hath, at several turns, and in divers expressions, according to the interpretation of their own most orthodox and learned friends, fully comported with it, asserting that in clearness and evidence of principle, which they deny with solemnity of protest, and with a religious abhorrency in conclusion."

In the last chapter of this inestimable volume, Mr. Goodwin lays down the plan of the second part of "Redemption Redeemed," which at that time he intended to prepare for the press. He specifies twenty-three objections against the doctrine of general redemption, every one of which he pledges himself to confute. Most of these objections are copied from the Acts of the Synod of Dort. "We shall also," says he, "launch forth into the deep of that great question, concerning personal election and reprobation, and soberly inquire, Whether the Scriptures teach any such decree of reprobation in God, from eternity, whereby the persons of such and such men, or of a determinate number of men, before any actual and voluntary sin perpetrated by them, and without respect had to such perpetrations, be left under an unavoidable necessity of perishing everlastingly? Here also we intend to inquire, What the Scriptures teach concerning the state of infants? and more particularly whether it can be substantially proved from them, that any infant, dying before the commission of actual sin, is adjudged by God to hell fire?

" I shall take occasion also to discuss the great question about universal grace: whether God vouchsafeth not to all men, without exception, a sufficiency of power and means whereby to be saved?

" And because the ninth chapter of the Epistle to the Romans is frequently brought upon the stage of these controversies, we intend a particular explication of this chapter: yea, I am under some present inclination to engage myself upon this in the first place, and to publish it by itself, before I put hand to the greater work."

On parting with his reader the author prefers the following requests : " That he will strive, by fervent and frequent prayer, to interest God Himself in the composure of the work intended ; that through much of His presence with me in the framing of it, (if yet His good pleasure shall be not to judge a proportion of life and health for the finishing of it too high a dignation for me,) all my insufficiency for so great an undertaking may be drowned, so as not to appear; and that I may be enabled to bring forth the truth in those high mysteries, out of that thick darkness which at present is spread by men round about them, into a clear and perfect light. My second request to the reader is, that he will make a covenant with his expectations and desires, so as not to look for the second part of this work, till after such time which may reasonably be judged competent for a man of slow genius in writing, and of almost continual diversions through bye employments, to raise and finish such a building, as that in reason may be presumed to be."

The talent, the learning, and the temper displayed in this work are honourable to Mr. Goodwin in a high degree. Almost every page displays pious and benevolent feeling, and the argumentation, generally speaking, is eminently perspicuous, cogent, convincing, and impressive. A few passages, as might have been expected in a work of such a nature and of such magnitude, are liable to exception ; especially in the introductory chapters, which are of a metaphysical character ; but viewed as a whole, it is an astonishing monument of genius and industry. It is the most ample, and unquestionably the best defence of general redemption, that ever issued from the British press. Its reasonings on this subject have been cavilled at, and despised, but never refuted. An Arminian reader, whose mind is duly alive to the importance of his creed, in the studious perusal of this volume, will find it to resemble a lofty tree, the numerous branches of which are widely spread in all directions, bending with rich and mellow fruit.

In favour of this great work perhaps the following testimonies may not be deemed impertinent: The Rev. Joseph Sutcliffe, who is well known by his translation of the seventh and eighth volumes of Saurin's Sermons, and by several excellent original publications, has said, "Goodwin's Redemption Redeemed is a work of amazing labour and vast instruction."*

Mr. Wilson also, the able and candid author of the "History and Antiquities of Dissenting Churches," though no admirer of Mr. Goodwin's Arminian sentiments, has remarked, that "The long title of this book will give the reader some idea of the important subjects upon which it treats; and it cannot be denied that he has discussed them with great learning and ingenuity. The quotations from ancient and modern authors are very numerous; and some persons will be surprised to find not only the most eminent fathers and reformers of the church, but even Calvin himself, represented as favouring the doctrine of general redemption." †

The Rev. Walter Sellon, speaking of Mr. Goodwin, with whose principal works he was well acquainted, expresses himself in still stronger language. "His Redemption Redeemed," says he, "will ever remain as a monument of his great reading, clear reasoning, and sound judgment." ‡

There are some peculiarities in this volume, and in all Mr. Goodwin's principal theological publications, which are worthy of special attention. In ascertaining the import of any passage of Scripture, he seldom lays much stress upon verbal criticism, but views the passage in connexion with the argument of which it constitutes a part. He was well aware that almost any doctrines may be de-

* Translation of Ostervald on the Christian Ministry, p. 77, Edit. 1804.
† Vol. II. p. 423.   ‡ Works, Vol. I. p. 376, Edit. 1814.

duced from the Holy Scriptures by a little dexterity in etymologies, and an aptitude in bringing together isolated texts, which bear some affinity to each other in sound. By such arts he knew that the unwary had often been deceived; but he durst not attach a meaning to the words of the Holy Spirit, which he had reason to believe that Spirit never intended. How often have divines of a certain school attempted to prove, that man is passive in the work of conversion, by urging the apostolic inquiry, "Who maketh thee to differ?" (1 Cor. iv. 7.) Whereas the slightest attention to the context will show, that St. Paul is not there speaking of gracious qualifications, but of ministerial gifts and endowments. In support of the necessary "perseverance of the saints," the following passage has often been quoted with an air of confidence and triumph: "If his children forsake My law, and walk not in My judgments; if they break My statutes, and keep not My commandments; then will I visit their transgressions with the rod, and their iniquity with stripes. Nevertheless My lovingkindness will I not utterly take from him, nor suffer My faithfulness to fail." (Psalm lxxxix. 30–33.) But the connexion in which these words stand, most clearly shows, they have no reference to "saints" in general, but to David and his posterity, and that they speak not of any such continuance in the Divine favour, as is necessarily connected with eternal life; but simply of the appointment of David and his sons to the regal office, through the successive ages of the Jewish commonwealth, and as introductory to the reign of the Messiah. These examples, with a hundred more that might be adduced, illustrate the importance of that rule of interpretation which Mr. Goodwin applied with admirable effect;—a rule which will always be adopted by those who are more in love with truth than with the peculiarities of men. As an expositor of Scripture, our author appears to incomparable advantage, when placed by the side of the greater part of his contemporaries and opponents.

It is also observable, that in Mr. Goodwin's creed there was no article of which he was at all ashamed, or which he was in any way desirous to extenuate or to conceal. He had the fullest conviction,. that his theological principles were not only true, but in every respect worthy of God, by whom he believed them to have been revealed, and adapted to promote the spiritual and moral improvement of mankind. He therefore avowed and defended them in a manner the most explicit and unequivocal; and even took a pleasure in tracing them in all their bearings, and tendencies, and results. The reverse of this, in various instances, has been the conduct of men holding sentiments opposite to his. Where is the minister who, after a distinct and open avowal of the doctrine of absolute reprobation or preterition, will even attempt to apply that doctrine to any practical or beneficial purpose in the individuals to whom it is supposed to relate? Not a few theologians of the Genevan school express themselves in phraseology so guarded, as to leave the attendants upon their ministry in doubt whether they hold general or particular redemption: and others hesitate, before mixed congregations, to give a prominence in their discourses even to the doctrine of absolute election to eternal life. Upon what ground such conduct can be justified, it is difficult to discover. If the peculiar doctrines of Calvinism are the "mysteries of God," Christian ministers, as "the stewards" of those mysteries, are officially bound to declare them. "It is required in stewards, that a man be found faithful." (1 Cor. iv. 2.) God's gracious election of men is a topic to which the inspired writers frequently advert; and if the Calvinian view of that subject be Scriptural, on what principle are men authorised to conceal it? In what a singular dilemma is that man placed, who is ashamed or afraid to inculcate, except in an indirect manner, doctrines which he believes to have emanated from the blessed God, but of whose moral tendency he has reason to doubt! Whether the tenets of Arminianism be true or false, certain it is, that their consistent adherents feel themselves at perfect liberty, without the slightest hesitation or reserve, to declare what they believe to be the whole counsel of God, and are not hampered in their ministrations as are many of their predestinarian brethren.

Mr. Goodwin regarded all the truths of revelation as being in perfect harmony and consistency with each other, and to trace their connexion and order he deemed one of the noblest exercises of the human intellect. That the decrees of God should be irreconcilable with the decla-- rations, the precepts, the invitations, and the promises of His word, appeared to him a monstrous proposition, and nothing less than a reflection upon the Divine veracity. From the notion of absolute predestination as held by Calvin, arises that of limited atonement, of necessi-- tating grace, of unconditional perseverance, and of the unavoidable hardening of the non-elect. But then the Holy Scriptures distinctly assert, in almost every form of ex- pression, that Jesus Christ died for all men; they contain innumerable warnings, expostulations, and conditional promises, all of which are addressed to men as free agents; they also represent the Lord Jesus as weeping over lost souls, and declaring that He would often have gathered them as a hen gathereth her brood under her wings, but that they would not; (Luke xiii., xix.;) they expressly de- clare, "that when the righteous turneth away from his righteousness, and committeth iniquity,........all his righteousness that he hath done shall not be mentioned: in his trespass that he hath trespassed, and in the sin that he hath sinned, in them shall he die;" (Ezek. xviii. 24;) they also introduce the blessed God as swearing by Himself, that He hath no pleasure in the death of the wicked; but that the wicked turn from his way and live. (Ezek. xxxiii. 11.) No human ingenuity has ever yet been able to reconcile these palpable inconsistencies. The Calvinian doctrine of absolute predestination, which Mr. Goodwin accounted a mere assumption, appeared to him to cast a shade over the moral perfections of the blessed God, and to contradict the obvious import of all those parts of sacred Scripture which speak of the extent of the Divine mercy, and of human redemption; as well as to render inefficient the arguments and exhortations of ministers, when calling upon "all men every where to repent," and inviting " all the ends of the earth " to look unto Christ as their merciful Saviour. The legitimate consequence of that doctrine, when explicitly inculcated, and applied by individuals to themselves, he thought, was to lead some to presumption and others to despair. The elect cannot perish: the reprobate cannot be saved.

" Some men," says he, " desirous to commend themselves to God, as men zealous for His glory more than others, invent notions of some Scripture expressions, to bestow upon Him in the name of prerogatives, which, upon due consideration, are found unworthy of Him, and of a broad inconsistency with His glory indeed. What savour of glory to God can there be, in bringing Him upon the great theatre of the world speaking thus : ' I will cast out of My favour, and devote to everlasting burnings, to torments endless, intolerable, insupportable, thousand thousands, and ten thousand times ten thousand of My creatures, men, women, and children, though they never offended Me otherwise than children may offend many thousands of years before they are born. Though I thus in the secret of My counsel intend to leave them irrecoverably to the most exquisite torments that can be endured, and these to be suffered by them to the days of eternity, without all possibility of escaping; yet will I, in words, speak to their hearts, proclaim Myself unto them to be a God merciful and gracious, long-suffering, and abundant in goodness and truth, keeping mercy for thousands, forgiving iniquity, trangression, and sin. I will intreat them with bowels and great compassions, and profess Myself aggrieved in soul because of their impenitency : I will allure them to repentance, with all My great and precious promises of pardon, life, and glory, and all the great things of the world to come. I will most solemnly protest, and swear unto them by the greatest oath that is, even by My own life and being, that I desire not their death.' Can men endued with understanding, or that know in the least what belongeth to matters of honour and glory, savour anything in such proceedings, worthy the name, glory, and super-transcendent holiness and excellency of God? Certain it is, that there is nothing in God, nothing that proceeds from Him, but what is, according to the principles of reason in the hearts and consciences of men, just matter of praise, honour and glory unto Him.

"That prerogative which God stands upon in the Scriptures, and claims to Himself as a royalty annexed to the crown of heaven and earth, in reference to the condemnation of His creature, standeth not in any liberty claimed by Him to leave what persons He pleaseth to inevitable ruin, only in consideration of Adam's sin, much less without any such consideration; but to make the terms and conditions, as of life so of death, as of salvation so of condemnation, and these equally respecting all men; and not such as men are apt to think meet for Him to do, but what Himself pleaseth: such as the counsel of His own will adviseth, and leadeth Him to. For He is said, not to work all things, or any one thing, simply according to His own will, but to work all things according to the *counsel* of His own will. So that in whatsoever God acteth, we are to look not only for will, but counsel; i. e. wisdom, and tendency unto ends worthy of Him; and these discernible enough by men to be such, if they were diligent and impartial in the consideration of them. For example: The Jews thought it most equal, and best becoming God, that He should ordain the observation of Moses's Law to be the Law of life and salvation to men, and the neglect of this Law to be the Law of condemnation and death. God here interposeth, and declares that His Will is otherwise, and that He constitutes Faith in His Son to be the law of justification and life, whether joined with the observation of Moses's law or without it; and Unbelief to be the law of condemnation and death, though in conjunction with the strictest observation of Moses's law. This prerogative God Himself asserts with majestic authority, speaking thus : ' I will have mercy upon whom I will have mercy, and I will have compassion upon whom I will have compassion.' As if He should say, ' Men shall not prescribe to Me terms of showing mercy. I will not be advised or obliged by them, what manner of persons I shall justify and save: I mean to follow the counsel of Mine own will, in these great and important affairs, which concern the life and death, the salvation and destruction of My creature.'

"Though it be not denied, that God hath an absolute sovereignty over His creature, i. e. a lawful power to dispose of it as He pleaseth; yet it is an horrible indignity and affront put upon Him, and no less than a constructive denial of His infinite grace, goodness, mercy, bounty, love, to affirm that He exerciseth this sovereignty upon the hardest terms that can be imagined, and no ways conducing to His own glory; which they affirm, in effect, who maintain, that from eternity He purposed to leave the greatest part of men to everlasting misery and ruin, without any possibility of escape. Suppose that God should grant an absolute power to parents over their children; as that, if they pleased, they might slay them, or dispose of them to be slain, or expose them as soon as they are born to suffer all the extremities that are incident to flesh and blood; can it be imagined, that persons of loving and tender dispositions would ever desire to have children that they might show their power over them, in disposing of them unto death, or exposing them unto misery, as soon as they should be born? Are such intentions or desires as these consistent with goodness and tenderness of disposition? How prodigiously then and portentously inconsistent must it needs be, with the grace, goodness, mercy, bounty, love of God, which are all infinite, to create millions of men, with a desire or intention to declare His prerogative over them, in leaving them irrecoverably, irrevocably, unavoidably, to the endless torments of hell!"*

About the time when Mr. Goodwin published his Redemption Redeemed, several other works against the peculiar doctrines of Calvinism issued from the British press. One of these was an able defence of General Redemption, in reply to Dr. Owen, who had begun to distinguish himself as an advocate of limited mercy and

* Redemption Redeemed, p. 66.

atonement. It was the production of Mr. John Horne of Lynn, in Norfolk, a very learned and pious man, and was entitled, "The Open Door for Man's Approach to God: or, A Vindication of the Record of God, concerning the Extent of the Death of Christ, 1650." To this work the Doctor never published any answer, affecting to regard it as beneath his notice : others, however, thought, that its argumentation was too powerful for him to confute. Horne was a deeply pious man, an accomplished divine, and an acute reasoner. He examined Owen's volume paragraph by paragraph, demonstrated its illogical and unscriptural character, yet avoiding every form of expression that was calculated to irritate, and maintaining a spirit of meekness and charity in perfect keeping with the doctrine which he undertook to defend. He was a voluminous writer on this and kindred subjects, confining himself to the simple testimony of Holy Scripture, and abstaining from those metaphysical speculations in which he thought his great contemporary Goodwin too often indulged.

Nearly at the same time was also published, "*Appello Evangelium* for the true Doctrine of Divine Predestination, concorded with the Orthodox Doctrine of God's Free Grace, and Man's Free Will; by John Plaifere, sometime Fellow of Sidney-Sussex College, in Cambridge, and late Rector of Debden in Suffolk, 1651." This was a posthumous publication; the author having been dead several years : but manuscript copies of his work had been preserved in the libraries of the curious. Plaifere has shown himself to have been a man of admirable moderation, of great ingenuity, of sound judgment, and of deep learning. He states, with clearness and precision, five schemes of predestination which had been held by different classes of Christians, points out the objections to which most of them are liable, and gives the preference to that which he conceived to be the opinion of the fathers who lived before Augustine, and was espoused by the learned Arminius. In this work are also comprised an able discussion of several questions connected with the subject of predestination, and an excellent analysis of the Seventeenth Article of the Church of England. To this volume is appended an interesting letter by Dr. Christopher Potter, containing an account of the steps by which he had been led to renounce the dogmas of Calvin, and embrace the doctrine of General Redemption. Plaifere's Appello was reprinted in a "Collection of Tracts concerning Predestination and Providence," from the Cambridge University Press, and published in the year 1719. It was also inserted by the late Rev. John Wesley in the first volume of the Arminian Magazine.

Another work of the same date was entitled, "Fur Prædestinatus: sive Dialogismus inter quendam ordinis prædicantium Calvinistam et Furem ad laqueum damnatum habitus, 1651." This is a feigned dialogue between a Thief condemned to immediate execution, and a Calvinistic Preacher, who attempts to move him to repentance for his crimes. The thief, although by his own acknowledgment he had lived in the commission of the worst enormities, is full of self-satisfaction; maintains that he could not possibly have acted any other part than he has done, as all men, being either elect or reprobate, are predestinated to happiness or misery; that the best actions, as they are reputed, partake of so much wickedness as to differ in no essential degree from the worst; that sinners fulfil the will of God as much as those who most comply with His outward commands; and that God, as working irresistibly in all men, is the cause of the worst sins which they commit. The dialogue is managed with great address and ability; and, what must have given it its greatest effect, the statements of the Calvinistic doctrines are made in the actual words of the principal writers of that persuasion, of whom not fewer than forty are quoted, and specially referred to in the course of the work. This is a frightful view of the principle of absolute predestination, when applied to practical purposes by men acting under the impulse of their depraved passions.

The "Fur Prædestinatus" was published anonymously, and has been ascribed to the pen of Archbishop Sancroft;

it is therefore made a prominent article in the Life of that distinguished prelate, published by Dr. D'Oyly. This, however, is a mistake. The tract was in existence many years before Sancroft was capable of producing such a composition. It was first printed and circulated in Holland, in the early part of the seventeenth century, when the controversy respecting predestination was warmly agitated between the Calvinists and Arminians in the United Provinces; and was generally thought to have been the production of Henry Slatius, a man of infamous notoriety in Holland.* Two translations of this dialogue into English have made their appearance : one in the year 1658, and another in 1814.†

Henry Hallam and Lord Macaulay, after the example of Dr. D'Oyly, ascribe the Predestinated Thief to the pen of Sancroft; but Hallam acknowledges that it is unlike every publication with which Sancroft connected his name. Lord Macaulay, however, has no doubt on the subject, and founds upon it his harshest censures upon the archbishop. Poets are said sometimes to nod over their compositions; and it is clear that divines and historians are liable to the same infirmity. Had Dr. D'Oyly and Lord Macaulay read the pamphlet with a due degree of attention, they would at once have perceived that it was not of English but of Dutch origin. The thief is a Dutchman; he is educated at one of the Dutch universities and at Geneva; in support of his opinions he quotes some forty divines and professors, nearly all of whom are Dutchmen, and only one of them English. An old copy of the tract now lies before me in the Dutch language, with a counter dialogue, in which an Arminian attempts to bring the thief to repentance, not by appealing to the opinions of supralapsarian divines, but to the sacred writers. We see then that not only Bishop Burnet, but Dr. D'Oyly and Lord Macaulay, sometimes wrote dreams when they thought they were writing history.

* Brandt's History of the Reformation, Vol. IV, pp. 212, 589, Edit. 1728.
† D'Oyly's Life of Archbishop Sancroft, Vol. I. pp. 66-71.

CHAPTER VIII.

ATTACKS UPON GOODWIN'S REDEMPTION REDEEMED BY DR. HILL—OBADIAH
HOWE—BAILIE—RESBURY—JEANS—PAWSON—DR. OWEN—DR. KENDALL, AND
LAMB—HIS AGREEMENT AND DISTANCE OF BRETHREN—AND EXPOSITION
OF ROM. IX.

WHILE the ability with which Mr. Goodwin's " Redemption Redeemed " was written, excited the admiration of
his friends, it rendered his book highly offensive to those
persons whose religious opinions it was intended to confute.
Scarcely was it therefore in circulation, before the pulpits
of the metropolis began afresh to ring with charges of
heresy against its author.   Among the preachers who were
distinguished by hostility to this publication, Dr. Thomas
Hill, Master of Trinity College, Cambridge, appears to
have engaged Mr. Goodwin's first attention.   This gentleman was one of the Assembly of Divines, a frequent
preacher before the Long Parliament, and a zealous advocate of the Calvinistic doctrines.   Being appointed to
preach at St. Paul's Church, before the Lord Mayor and
Aldermen of the City of London, he availed himself of the
opportunity then afforded to caution his civic auditory
against the volume of Mr. Goodwin, as a work replete
with the errors of Pelagius and Arminius.   In addition
to this he cast some severe reflections upon Mr. Goodwin's character, and charged him with having falsified some
of the numerous quotations contained in his book.   Considering the nature and publicity of this accusation, Mr.
Goodwin addressed a letter to the Doctor, complaining
of his conduct, proposing an interview with him, either
alone or in the presence of their friends ; and requesting
him to make some public acknowledgment of the injustice
of his charges.   Mr. Goodwin also stated, that in case
these proposals were rejected, he would publish his
letter, and thus appeal to the Christian world.   The Doctor
appears to have declined either to have an interview with

our Arminian heretic, or to make any apology for the rude attack upon his good name.   Mr. Goodwin therefore committed his epistle to the press, under the title of "Moses made Angry: A Letter written and sent to Dr. Hill, upon Occasion of some hard Passages that fell from him in a Sermon preached at Paul's, May 4th, 1651."

Addressing his accuser, Mr. Goodwin says, " Sir, you are a gentleman, to whom I never, to the best of my knowledge, gave the least offence.   If unwittingly I have done it, I am ready to make you all Christian satisfaction.   For your learning and knowledge, according to what grounds I had to make an estimate of them, I proportionably honoured you; and much more because I always conceived you chiefly employed them about that most honourable work of propagating the glorious Gospel of God in the world.   That testimony also which, time after time, I received concerning your goodness of spirit, blamelessness of conversation, &c., much advanced my esteem of you.   Notwithstanding, had you poured shame and contempt upon my head alone, had you ground to powder only me and my name, you might have done it without trouble or inconvenience to yourself; at least from me.   Such millers in black clothing I meet with daily, and let them pass quietly by me.   But inasmuch as you have magnified yourself against the truth, yea, several of the most important truths of the living God, it will neither stand with that loyalty of obedience which I owe to the command of God imposed on me in that behalf, nor with that love which I owe to yourself as a Christian brother, to suffer such a sin to rest upon you.   I delight not in contests.   I am for peace with all men, and for a quiet and retired pilgrimage on earth.   So that whensoever I contend with any man, I sacrifice the darling disposition of my soul upon the service of the truth.   Nor shall any man approve himself more easy to be entreated, upon any equitable or tolerable account, or more willing to receive satisfaction from him that hath offended him, than I. Therefore, Sir, I beseech you, trouble not yourself either with seeking out, or pretending to find, any other intent

of this address to you, than as a simple, plain-hearted,
and Christian application of myself to vindicate the just
right of the dearly beloved of my soul, and I trust of yours
also, truth.

" You reflected upon the author of that book, which so
torments those that dwell on the face of the earth, as if
he falsified, wrested, perverted authors: the very truth is,
that this, if it be comely to call a spade a spade, is a pure
calumny. The authors cited in the said book, at least the
far greater part of them, speak as directly to the heart of
the main doctrines maintained in the book, as the author
of the book himself. Nor are you, nor any other man,
able to prove the least touch of any falsifying thing or
perverting any author brought upon that stage. If there
be any thing mistaken, (as mistakes may be incident to
the most upright of men,) in any quotation, this only
proves the author to be a man, not a falsifier. There is
nothing asserted in the said book, especially in the two
main doctrines there contended for, but what, for substance and effect of matter, is plainly affirmed over and
over not only by the most orthodox fathers, Chrysostom,
Augustine, &c., but by the most orthodox writers of later
times, as Luther, Calvin, Musculus, and others. Yea yourselves, the preachers of this age, however by times you
appear in flames of fire against them, yet otherwhile, and
sometimes in one and the same sermon, you give testimony
unto them. There is sufficient proof made, page 561 of
the book decried by you, that a jury of fifty-two preachers,
and among these such as are counted pillars in and about
the City of London, in the same pamphlet wherein, as they
pretend, they give ' Testimony to the Truth of Jesus Christ,
against Errors and Heresies,' do clearly build up the
principal doctrine avouched in the said book, general
redemption by Christ. Yea yourself, in this very sermon,
wherein you set yourself with all the might of your indignation against it, gave the right hand of fellowship to it,
in granting, that had Judas believed, he should have been
saved by Christ. See (I desire it rather to your satisfaction than shame) the doctrine of general redemption

s

demonstratively proved from such a position as this, p. 113, &c., and p. 135, &c., of that truth-teaching book so often hinted. The Synod of Dort itself acknowledgeth, that 'If Redemption be not acknowledged as a common benefit bestowed on mankind, that general and promiscuous preaching of the Gospel committed to the apostles to be performed among all nations will have no true foundation.' Therefore whilst you clamour against general redemption, you not only cry down the glory of the unsearchable riches of the free grace of God, vouchsafed in Christ to the world, but also fight your best friends, as well as those whom you traduce under the name of Pelagians, Arminians, &c.; liveries of like cloth which the servants of truth have been compelled to wear in all ages. Yea, in your inconsiderate contests, you act as men divided against yourselves; and your sayings, like the children of Ammon and Moab, when they came forth to battle against Judah and Jehoshaphat, help to destroy one another.

"If I knew how to relieve those truths of God, which you desperately affronted, without making a breach upon your reputation, I should freely pass by mine own interest, and demand nothing of you for personal reparations; although I believe that you hardly know how to provoke at much a higher rate, than you practised provocation upon me: unless haply that be some allay, that you were ravished by some other man's spirit, far worse than your own, into such a splenetic ecstasy. For Dr. Hill hath formerly worn the crown of a meek, temperate, and Christian spirit. But we read that Moses, the meekest man on earth, was, at the waters of strife, provoked to speak unadvisedly with his lips; and I, with many others, believe that Dr. Hill was overshadowed with the spirit of some lion or other, (which probably I could point at among the herd.) when he conceived those 'devouring words' whereof he was delivered in the pulpit, May 4th, 1651. The ground of my conjecture is, partly because that which was born of him here had so little of his own likeness in it; partly because it had so much of the likeness of another man. But concerning myself, the best is, that neither you nor others can value me at any lower rate than I do myself. You trod but upon the earth, when you trampled me under your feet. If you pursue me to the grave, you cannot hinder my resurrection; the day whereof will be time enough for me to become any thing.

"I know the miscarriages of the best and wisest of men are too many; and far be it from me to make any man a delinquent above the tenour of his misactings; and these construed with as much favour as a good conscience will afford. If you can, and be willing to, disclaim any thing in the said particulars, I desire to hear speedily from you upon that account; otherwise I shall presume, that my informations touching the premises were authentic."

About the time at which Mr. Goodwin thus addressed himself to Dr. Hill, he sent the following letter to Mr. Joseph Caryl, well known as a Presbyterian divine of that age, and author of an immense commentary on the Book of Job. The epistle itself sufficiently explains the occasion on which it was written.

" My Christian and worthy friend and brother in Christ :

" I CAME, some few days since, to understand, that there is one passage in my late book, entitled Redemption Redeemed, (possibly among many others of less offence,) of so hard a resentment with you, that you judged it of very dangerous consequence, and have cautioned several persons (as some of themselves have reported, I know not how publicly, or unto how many) against the danger of it. Whether your intent was hereby to blast the credit of that one passage only, or to render the book itself as unsafe, or however of no good consequence for them to read, I shall not too narrowly inquire into, much less determine. I acknowledge it to be far above my line, in the composure of a book, to be able to apprehend or foresee, what notions or expressions may possibly provoke a spirit of prejudice; or to deliver my sense at every turn upon such terms, as to leave no place or possibility for sinister construction : but this I am able to avouch, as in the sight of God, who will shortly bring every secret thing into judgment, that in the penning of that book I was conscientiously studious and careful to decline, as well in matter as in words, whatsoever I apprehend likely to offend any man, further or otherwise than as the truth, even with the fairest and clearest delivery of it, is apt to offend those who are not disposed to receive it. And I now am, and I trust always shall be, willing and ready to do the best I can to heal every man's offence, taken at any saying or expression in that book, when I come particularly to understand the ground or occasion of it. I hear that within these few weeks there was another, whose name I shall spare at present, who very reasonlessly, and without the least cause given, stumbled in the University pulpit at Cambridge, at another passage in the said book, where I give an account of my judgment concerning the fulness, freeness, and effectualness of the grace of God. Nothwithstanding, I had in some particular and distinct explications of myself, immediately before, endeavoured to remove the stumbling-stone, such as it was, out of his way; and had showed him before this, how he might with a very good conscience, and with more honour to himself, have passed by that passage without lifting up his heel against it; but that I want such particularity of information about the carriage of the discourse, as I desire and hope in due time to obtain. As for him, who, Arch-Rabbi like, concluded at once, and without premises, all those without exception that hold the doctrines of general atonement by Christ, and of a possibility of a final declining in such who ever believed, to be men Godless, Christless, Spiritless, graceless, I shall at present only advise him to lay his heart close to those two sayings of a wise man, Prov. xxvi. 12, and Prov. xxix. 20. When I shall hear that he is thoroughly baptized into the spirit of these Scriptures, I shall judge him a person worthy a reproof when he offends. In the mean time, I judge, that he who told it amongst news from heaven unto the city, that Arminius's rotten posts were lately new painted, together with him who not long after, diurnal-wise, told the same story over again to the same audience, only in a more dismal metaphor, informing them that Arminius's ghost was lately started out of his grave and walked; neither of them meddling any further with the controversies; I judge, that these are wise men in their generation, and did well consider that the name of Arminius is the most forcible engine, though made of nothing but air and wind, to batter the walls of those opinions, which they so cordially wish in the dust; and that should they have engaged any Scripture or argument upon the design, they had run a hazard of losing all that ground, or more, which they had reason to hope they had won, by drawing the pedigree of the said opinions, though most untruly, from Arminius; it faring with their credulous hearers according to the proverb: *The blind swallow many a fly.*

"But, Sir, concerning that passage in my late book, upon the horn whereof you were pleased to tie a bunch of hay, by way of signal unto your friends and others, to take heed of it, and to keep at a distance from it; if my intelligence leadeth me to the right place, (as I suppose upon competent grounds it doth,) as far as I am able, with the most impartial eye I have, to see into it, it is so far from meriting the brand of ignominy wherewith you have stigmatized it, that, rightly understood and considered, it is as innocent and offenceless, as any saying that ever fell from your own mouth, in any of your sermons. The passage I presume is this: page 335 of the said book: I shall cite it verbatim: 'Yea, that which is yet more, I verily believe, that in case any such assurance of the unchangeableness of God's love were to be found in, or could regularly be deduced from the Scriptures, it were a just ground to any intelligent and considering man to question their authority, and whether they were from God or no.'

"The reason of this saying I immediately subjoin in these words, 'For that a God infinitely righteous and holy should irreversibly assure the immortal and undefiled inheritance of His grace and favour unto any creature whatsoever, so that though this creature should prove never so abominable in His sight, never so outrageously and desperately wicked and profane, He should not be at liberty to withhold this inheritance from him, is a saying, doubtless, too hard for any man who rightly understands and considers the nature of God to hear.' What there should be in either of these sayings so much as liable to any suspicion of an incomportance either with reason or with truth, cannot enter into my thoughts to imagine or conceive. The pile of the discourse is built, and I cannot but presume regularly enough, upon this foundation; that if any thing were found in those writings known by the name of Scriptures, whether in the letter of them, or in any expressness of consequence from them, (here justified or approved,) of any blasphemous import against God, or any of His attributes, it were a just ground at least to question, whether the said writings were from God or no. I suppose I shall not need to argue this principle, being so full of light in itself. The Holy Ghost Himself teacheth us, that God cannot deny Himself; and as certain it is, that He cannot blaspheme Himself; nor yet authorize, inspire, or teach any person or creature whatsoever to blaspheme Him: the blaspheming of Himself being nothing else but a constructive denying of Himself, as is evident. Therefore what book or writing soever contains any thing blasphemous against God, I do not mean as simply *reported* but as *asserted and maintained*, is not only just ground to question (which yet is all I affirm in the point) whether such a writing or book be of divine inspiration or no, but even positively to conclude against them that they are not. So then, if there be any thing dangerous, or of suspicious consequence, in either of the said passages, it must be this; that in the former of them I suppose, and in the latter constructively affirm, that such an unchangeableness of the love of God as is mentioned in the former, and described in part in the latter, is of a blasphemous import, and repugnant to those great attributes of righteousness and holiness in God. Though the latter of the said passages recited carrieth a sufficient light in it to satisfy any man, impartially considerate, concerning the truth of this assertion; yet the matter being of a high and sacred import, I am willing and shall endeavour to give, both unto yourself and others, somewhat a more full and distinct account hereof.

"First, then, evident it is, that that unchangeableness of the love of God, which these passages speak of, and without a supposal whereof the common doctrine of Perseverance, against which I here argue, cannot be maintained, in the formal and proper notion of it, supposeth, that if ever God once truly loveth a person, it is impossible that upon any occasion or interveniences whatsoever, He should hate him afterwards.

"Secondly, every whit as evident it is, that such a notion as this supposeth that in case a person hath once, or at any time, truly believed, suppose in his youth, (under which condition he must needs be beloved by God,) though the very next hour or day after his believing he should fall into the ways of sin, wickedness, disobedience, rebellion against God, and should, without repentance or remorse, continue in these abominations, adding drunkenness to thirst, from time to time, for ten, twenty, it may be, forty or fifty years together, yet God all this while truly loveth him, and remaineth unchanged in His affection towards him, and consequently loveth him with the same love; as great, as rich, as dear, under all these horrible pollutions, and most accursed abominations, as He either would or could have loved him with, in case he had all this while walked in the greatest innocency and uprightness of heart and life before Him. Now then this is that which I affirm: That to attribute such an unchangeableness of love unto God as this, which maketh Him to love an obstinate and obdurate sinner, a worker of all manner of abominations, with the same affection wherewith He loveth a just, holy, and good man, a worker of all righteousness, is of a blasphemous import to those glorious Attributes of His, His righteousness and holiness. For if the case were thus with God, should not the world have cause to demand, with those in Malachi, *Where is the God of judgment?* Or what is there, or can there be, of a more diametrical opposition unto holiness, than equally to respect and love the most unrighteous with those that are most righteous ?—or unto holiness, than to honour those that are most polluted and abominable, as much as those that are holy ?

" Nor can you here pretend, that I wrong your doctrine of Perseverance to the value of the least hair on your head, by making it a patroness and protectrix of such an unchangeableness of love in God, as that now represented : because evident it is, that without such an unchangeableness supposed, the said doctrine will neither have footing nor foundation to support it. For though you and others, patrons of this doctrine, understand yourselves, and befriend your doctrine better, than to express or represent it unto the world in those colours, wherewith I have now drawn the portraiture of it ; or to describe the unchangeableness of the love of God, which must be the basis and pillar of it, in such terms as it hath been described by me; yet there is nothing more pregnant and notorious, than that your soft and silken and most tender expressions of it, being regularly, and according to the exigency of truth, interpreted, and drawn out of those collusive involutions, amount every whit to as much in deformity and Atheologicalness of notion, as any expressions used by me import. For certain it is, (nor do I remember that I ever met with a denial of it, amongst the greatest defenders of your faith in the point of Perseverance,) that he that truly believeth may possibly fall, and that within a very short time after his believing, into the greatest and foulest sins that the nature of man is lightly incident to, as drunkenness, adultery, murder, envy, malice, covetousness, oppression, idolatry, &c., and from the time of his first falling into them may continue in the practice of them for many years together; yea, possibly, to the very approaches of death, without repentance. Only you teach indeed, but by human, not divine inspiration, that such persons, (I mean once believers,) in case they fall into such sins, as those now mentioned, or the like, yet never miscarry in the great business of salvation, but by a high hand of grace from God are always brought back unto repentance before their death. However, upon the former supposition, it clearly

follows, that your doctrine of Perseverance cannot stand
without the supposal of such an unchangeableness of love
in God, which is palpably, and in the eye of a very ordinary
understanding, of a highly disparaging and blasphemous
import to His righteousness and holiness.   In what sense
the Scriptures hold forth an unchangeableness in God, and
so in all His Attributes, and particularly in His love, I
declare once and again, upon occasion, in my late book of
Redemption, pages 63, 64, 278, 279, 205, 206, 318, 319,
and 330.   I demonstratively prove your doctrine of Perseverance to be at open and manifest defiance also with
another great Attribute of God, His Wisdom.   Yea, when
I look narrowly into the purport and tendencies of your
doctrine, I cannot overrule my thoughts, but that they
will be very jealous, that it is accessory to far the greatest
part of those abominations at this day raging amongst us :
Antinomianism, Enthusiasm, Familism, of the dangerous
and vile opinions and practices of those called Seekers, and
of those bred of the dregs of all these, the Ranters; and
generally of all the coolings, declinings, backslidings, and
of other foul and sad miscarriages amongst professors.

"Sir, I have looked upon you as the glory of the London ministry, and do still, notwithstanding the contest of
your judgment against mine, about the doctrine of Redemption, and the questions relating hereunto.   Yet, give him
leave, who is possibly looked upon by you, as by many
others, as the reproach and shame of this ministry, to say
this unto you, that those two opinions, the one of a peremptory personal Election from Eternity, the other of a peremptory and necessitated Perseverance of the Saints, genu-
inely interpreted, do, upon the matter, wholly dissolve the
usefulness and necessity of your ministry : the former in
relation to persons yet unconverted ; the latter in respect
of believers.   For the first, if there be a certain number of
men peremptorily designed by God to salvation, all others
as peremptorily excluded, what need either the one or the
other regard your ministry, or any other man's?   The
former shall be infallibly and irresistibly converted, saved,
whether you or any man preach the Gospel unto them or

no. If so, *Fortis ubi est Ajax?* where, or what is the necessity of the greatest preacher under heaven, in respect of them? The latter, notwithstanding all the possible relief that you by your ministry can afford them, will and must inevitably perish. Yea, all the good that you are capable of doing unto these by your ministry, is only to help them deeper into hell. If those who already believe shall certainly and against all possible interveniences persevere in faith unto the end, what if the ministry of the Gospel and they were quite parted? they should run no hazard of losing their crown thereby. This great truth, that your doctrine of Perseverance frustrates the ministry in reference unto the saints, I prove at large, and I suppose beyond all reasonable contradiction, page 301, 302, 339, &c. of the book formerly mentioned: where also I tear in pieces the fig-leaf of that pretence, that the ministry of the Gospel, notwithstanding the Perseverance of the Saints be supposed absolute and unfrustrable, is yet a means for the effecting or procuring of it.

" But, Sir, concerning the passage recited, wherein you pretend to find so much danger, that you judge it necessary to arm your friends with a religious caveat against it, I verily believe, that there is scarce any page in any of those books which either you have published in your own name, or licensed for others, but I could quarrel with somewhat therein, at as good a rate of ingenuity, if I judged the engagement worthy of me, as you have done at that passage of mine: yea, and wring every whit as bad blood out of the nose of it, as you have forced out of mine. But for oversights, hard expressions, or doubtful passages in other men's writings, otherwise than for the necessary defence of those truths which God hath stirred up my spirit to plead and protect, I have neither time nor mind to take any such cognizance of them. Concerning my own writings, so far as I find them justifiable for matter of truth, and defensible, I shall, God willing, *pro virili*, stand up to maintain them against all opposition and detraction, as fast as I shall come to understand that exceptions are taken against them. What shall reasonably and in a

Christian manner be excepted against any thing, I shall make no apology for, but with a spirit of meekness own the oversight, and only endeavour the rectifying. In case unjust opposers shall rise up too fast, or prove too many in number for me, I must then be content to edecimate, and turn myself only to those that are counted Pillars, and leave punies either to share with them in such answers, and satisfactions, which shall be given unto them, or otherwise to take their pleasure in flying upon the wings of their own wind. Sir, I cannot suspect a want of so much civility in you, as to deny water unto those for the washing of their faces, who are bemired, though casually, and by their friends : or that the publishing of these few harmless lines in order to my purgation will be matter of offence in the least unto you.

"Thus desiring that the Father of Lights will give to you and me, and all others that desire to serve Him faithfully in the Gospel of His dear Son, light and not darkness for our vision, I take my leave, and rest,

Yours with a perfect heart to serve you in our Great Redeemer,

JOHN GOODWIN."

To this letter Mr. Caryl returned the following answer :

" SIR,

" I SUPPOSE you printed and published your book with a willingness that it should be read and considered by all men; and knew also, that your opinion therein asserted concerning universal redemption, and falling from grace, hath been, as still it is, opposed by very many. For my own part, I plainly profess to you, that I have, according to my measure, held forth and maintained the contrary doctrines, not only before I saw your book, but before ever I saw your face; and so I judge myself bound to do, as I have opportunity, till I see ground to change my opinion; which as yet I do not, no not by what I have found in your book.

"As for that particular passage of it, which you say I have stigmatized with a brand of ignominy, as also cautioned my friends about it: what you mean by stigmatizing I apprehend not: all that I have said of it hath been but a manifestation of my dislike of it, or that it is an argument of your highest confidence, that the truth, in that point to which it relates, is on your side. Now truly, Sir, if you call this stigmatizing it with a brand of ignominy, I know not how to take it off, notwithstanding all that you have written in vindication of it in the letter you were pleased to send me.

"And whereas you intimate your purpose to print that letter; it shall I hope be no trouble to me, unless for your sake, if you do so. Only give me leave to caution you as a friend, to consider well both with yourself, and with your friends, whether it be so comely in you to discover such an eagerness in this cause, that you cannot contain yourself from publishing in print, what is spoken in private discourse among friends, concerning this or other passages in your book. The Lord lead us into all truth, and teach us how to walk in love!

Yours in truth to serve you, in all offices of Gospel love,

JOSEPH CARYL."

Mr. Goodwin perceived that the publication of his letter would be disagreeable to Caryl, for whom he entertained a sincere respect, and therefore abandoned that design. Several years afterwards, however, he was constrained to commit it to the press, to prevent the appearance of surreptitious and incorrect copies, which was meditated by some of the London booksellers. *

One argument urged by Mr. Goodwin in proof of General Redemption is, That all men are required to believe in Jesus Christ for salvation, on pain of everlasting misery. In opposition to what he had advanced on this subject, Dr. Thomas Barlow, afterwards Bishop of Lincoln, addressed a letter to him, in which he contends, that the obli-

* Fresh Discovery of the High Presbyterian Spirit. Preface, 1654.

gation and command to believe in Christ are not universal, but apply to those only to whom the Gospel is preached, and who possess a capacity to understand it.   The heathens, of course, according to his views, have nothing to do with that evangelical requisition.* In reply to this letter, Mr. Goodwin published a small tract, entitled, 'The Pagan's Debt and Dowry: or, a Brief Discussion of these Questions : Whether, how far, and in what sense, such Persons of Mankind, amongst whom the Letter of the Gospel never came, are, notwithstanding, said to Believe in Jesus Christ "

This pamphlet, which was written in great haste, and in the midst of numerous and pressing avocations, contains some able and ingenious reasoning respecting the mora obligations of the heathen, and in defence of their salvability : subjects on which crude and indigested speculations have been often advanced.   Some persons, laudably anxious to prove the necessity as well as the advantages of Revelation, against the assumptions of Infidelity ; and others, desirous of giving the greatest possible impulse to the cause of Christian Missions, have represented the salvation of men without the direct and perfect light of revealed truth as absolutely impossible.   But that millions of human beings, without any fault of their own, should be placed in circumstances which render their endless misery necessary and inevitable, Mr. Goodwin thought, could never be reconciled with those views of divine justice and equity which the Scriptures present, much less with the goodness and mercy of God.   There is indeed nothing in the doctrine of unconditional reprobation, as taught by Calvin himself, that is more revolting and objectionable than such an opinion.   On all subjects connected with the moral government of God, too much caution cannot be exercised lest sentiments injurious to the divine perfections should be advanced, even for the purpose of illustrating the value of truth, or of stimulating men to Christian duty.   Nor is there any necessity for resorting to principles of that desperate character.   The writings of the

* Barlow's Genuine Remains, p. 122, Edit. 1693.

Greek and Roman philosophers afford ample proof of the blindness of the human intellect, even in its highest state of cultivation, without the Revelation of God, and are sufficient for ever to confound the incoherent reasonings of Deism. And if men professing Christianity cannot be stimulated to Missionary enterprise by the solemn charge of Jesus Christ, that His Gospel should be preached to every creature, and by the melancholy and indubitable fact, that the whole heathen world is in a state of peculiar wretchedness and peril, no motives whatever will rouse them from their guilty supineness and indifference. With all submission to those who think otherwise, it is presumed that the necessary and unavoidable damnation of the heathen, as such, can never be successfully maintained in the teeth of the apostolic declaration, that God will render " glory, honour, and peace, to every man that worketh good, to the Jew first, and also to the Gentile." (Rom. ii. 10.)

As nearly all the men who had written against Mr. Goodwin, had treated him in a manner most abusive and indecorous, it excited his surprise on finding in Dr. Barlow an opponent who was disposed to exercise towards him candour and urbanity, and who actually spoke of his learning and talents in terms the most handsome and respectful. This generous conduct, so unusual among the polemics of that age, made a deep impression upon Mr. Goodwin's mind, and afforded him a welcome opportunity of indulging some of the best feelings of which the human heart is susceptible. The following sentences extracted from " The Pagan's Debt and Dowry," will serve to display the temper in which that ingenious tract was written : " I find you a man of a far better spirit, than any I have yet met with in any antagonist." — " I cannot but kindly resent * in you that worthy disposition to put honour where it was wanting ; and to help, with your respects, to fill up the pit which others have digged in the field of my reputation, to find the treasure of their own."—" I greatly

* " To RESENT; to be sensible of."—Phillips's New World of Words, Edit. 1706.

desire it at the hands of my God, both yours and mine."—
" You have writ not without grounds worthy a learned
man."—" I very much honour you, for those signal parts
of Christian worth and ingenuity, which, by the light of
your papers sent me, I sufficiently discern to be in you."
Language like this, in the controversial volumes of our
author's contemporaries, is extremely rare.

Dr. Barlow made no reply to Mr. Goodwin's tract, but
whether he was convinced by its reasonings, is uncertain.
The doctrine of the salvability of the heathen, which was
defended in this work, was not likely to pass uncensured
in an age of contradiction, when so many minds were
hardened in the school of absolute reprobation. No one,
therefore, who is acquainted with the theological history
of that period, will be surprised to learn, that this inoffensive publication was animadverted upon with great asperity
by Mr. Obadiah Howe, rector of Stickney, and minister of
Horncastle, in Lincolnshire. This gentleman sided with
the Puritans during the interregnum, but at the Restoration conformed to the Episcopal Church, and was presented
to the vicarage of Boston.* The work published by him
against Mr. Goodwin is entitled, " The Pagan Preacher
Silenced ; " to which our author replied in the preface to
his " Triumviri."

As Mr. Goodwin's " Redemption Redeemed " excited
general attention, so the books which were written against
it were considerable both in number and magnitude. Mr.
Robert Bailie, " minister of the Gospel at Glasgow," and
author of many bitter and intolerant pamphlets against
the Independents and Baptists, published a small volume
under the title of " A Scotch Antidote against the English
Infection of Arminianism : which Little book may be,
through God's blessing, very useful to preserve those that
are yet sound in the faith, from the infection of Mr. John
Goodwin's Great Book." Of this publication Mr. Goodwin does not appear to have taken any notice. Every
thing contained in it in the shape of argument is a bare
repetition of what had been advanced by preceding writers,

* Wood's Athenæ Oxonienses, Vol. II. col. 718.

and what, in Mr. Goodwin's apprehension, had been already confuted.

Another of Mr. Goodwin's assailants was Mr. Richard Resbury, vicar of Oundle in Northamptonshire. This gentleman had prepared for publication a small volume of Sermons, in defence of the distinguishing doctrines of Calvinism, nearly all the copies of which remained unsold for some years. On the appearance of Mr. Goodwin's "Redemption Redeemed," he seems to have thought that a favourable opportunity presented itself for giving an impulse to the sale of his book. He therefore drew up an invective against Mr. Goodwin by way of preface, and prefixed to his volume the following title, intimating that the whole was a reply to the work which then occupied so much attention : "Some Stop to the Gangrene of Arminianism, lately promoted by Mr. John Goodwin in his book entitled Redemption Redeemed : or, The Doctrine of Election and Reprobation in Six Sermons, opened and cleared from the old Pelagian and late Arminian Errors, 1651." Resbury was a thorough Calvinist. He contends strenuously for the doctrine of absolute reprobation, and attempts to prove the position, "That God decrees the being of sin in the world." In his preface he attacks Mr. Goodwin without ceremony. "In the first place," says he, "my hearty prayer is, *The Lord rebuke thee.*"

To this polemic Mr. Goodwin published an address, which he entitled, "Confidence dismounted : or, A Letter to Mr. Richard Resbury, of Oundle in Northamptonshire, &c., 1651." In this spirited pamphlet, Mr. Goodwin thus admonishes his opponent:

"Erasmus said, *Poor Luther made many rich :* meaning by occasion of his writings against the Pope, and such doctrines as were the pillars of his throne and kingdom ; which whosoever would undertake to oppose or confute, had great matters of preferment cast upon him. So I perceive that my poor writings are like occasionally to enrich many with credit, approbation, and applause from men ; and that as Caleb promised his daughter Achsah to wife to whomsoever should smite Kiriath-Sepher, and take it ;

so doth that spirit that is abroad amongst those that are called ministers of the Gospel, promise honour and applause unto any man that shall but offer to smite either my person or writings with his tongue or pen; though they speak or write neither truth, nor any thing to purpose against either. Mr. Resbury, it seems, hath hearkened unto the encouragement of this spirit, and by his title-page hath tempted the world to believe, that he hath done some worthy thing against my book of Redemption: whereas it cannot reasonably be thought, by any thing in his book, that ever he looked any argument or line of mine in the face: so far is he from answering any thing argued by me, either κατὰ πόδας or πόδα. Yet not content with the sound of his own trumpet in the frontispiece of his book, by which he would give the world to hope that he was preparing to battle against me, he, or some factor of his about the City, hath purchased the louder blasts of two trumpets more, to make the same sound, and hath bought of two of our common Diurnalists their respective outcries, or proclamarees, to call the world together, to be spectators of his learned valour. Indeed in his preface he supplies, in the most untrue and unchristian revilings of my person, that which in his discourse is wanting in weight and substance of matter for answer to my book. But the spirit I spake of suggested, it seems, this to him : ' If thou beest not able to grapple with his writings, lay on load of reproach upon his person. Thou shalt have a good reward for thy labour, as well in one kind as in the other; they shall prosper both alike in thy hand.'

"Sir, I beseech you, by the love you bear to the Lord Jesus Christ, with what conscience or face of ingenuity can you say, that ' *The main truths of God, concerning His Electing and Redeeming Grace, have by the daring hand of that unhappy man, Mr. John Goodwin, in his wretched Treatise, by him called (but miscalled) Redemption Redeemed, been so highly assaulted ;*' when you neither have showed, much less proved, nor are able to prove, that so much as any of these truths have been in the slightest manner assaulted by me in this treatise? I trust you will suffer the word of

T

Christian admonition from him who, God knoweth, and your own conscience may know, is no enemy to you, nor to your peace, nor to your honour or reputation; that such causeless aspersions and reproaches cast upon your Christian brethren, as these, will never make your face to shine with any true or permanent lustre, nor abound to your account in the great day. In terming me an *unhappy man* you speak truth enough in one sense, and little in another. It is my unhappiness, not to be believed when I speak the truth; and much more that my speaking the truth should prove a stumbling-stone to so many, and occasion their falling into the great and dangerous sin of hard speaking, reviling, persecuting with the tongue, opposing, calumniating the truth manifested to them. In all this, I confess, I am an unhappy man. But the Lord Jesus Christ Himself was, in all such respects as these, an unhappy man also, being set as well for the falling as for the rising of many in Israel. But that He was a sweet savour unto God, as well in those who perish, as in those that are saved by Him, He was a person thrice happy and blessed. And I should deny the signal goodness of God towards me, if I should not judge myself happy in those (not a few) who have been built up by my hand in the knowledge of God, in the grace of the Lord Jesus Christ, in the peace and joy of their souls; yea, and in the reproaches, hard sayings, and evil entreaties which I meet with from Mr. Resbury and others; inasmuch as these also work for me so much a better resurrection, and a far more exceeding and eternal weight of glory.

" Whereas you seem desirous to pick a quarrel against my hand, by terming it ' *daring* : ' I confess my hand and heart too are very daring, venturous, and bold in assaulting *error*, how strongly soever fortified by the judgments, affections, interests, pre-occupations, authorities, credits, writings of men. That clear, satisfying, and convincing light of the truth, which God hath graciously shined into my heart, teacheth my hand to war and my fingers to fight, against all that is lesser and lower than God in the quarrel and cause of truth. And if you count it a blemish or disparagement to my hand to be daring in this kind, it is a sign that your own hand hath little courage for the truth, nor that it dares lift up itself in defence of it, unless it hath a proud arm of flesh to stand by it, and second it in the engagement.

" Your subtle insinuation, to have yourself notioned like unto Michael the Archangel, and me unto the Devil, in this imprecatory prayer against me, *The Lord rebuke thee!* I perfectly resent. But, Sir, you should have done well to have considered, whether, in case the Archangel had had to do with a man as you have, (though as vile and sinful as you apprehend the man of your contest to be,) and not with the Devil, he would have prayed for him, *The Lord forgive thee,* and not *The Lord rebuke thee,* until his obstinacy had appeared. However, if I have so deeply sinned, as you deem me to have done, in judging me worthy to drink the Devil's cup after him, I shall join issue with you, in the words of your prayer against me, and pray, *The Lord rebuke me,* only with David's addition, *not in anger.*

" And, Sir, give me leave to doubt, whether you had the consent of your conscience in drawing up this charge against me, that *for the present I so seriously despise, and so boldly bid defiance to the peculiar grace of God.* Michael the Archangel durst not bring any railing, much less any forged or false accusation, against Satan himself, when he contended with him. If he had done this, he had fought with no better weapons than those which Satan himself useth in his battles. It is a thing of most deplorable consideration to me, that those who call themselves ministers of the Gospel, should so harden themselves against the fear of the Lord, as to speak and spread abroad at pleasure words of an infamous and disparaging import against their brethren, who never gave them the least cause of offence, and this without any colourable pretence of truth in them. For, Sir, I beseech you, what sentence can you, or any other of you, find either in my book of Redemption, or any other of my writings, wherein I make the least semblance, or give the slightest intimation, that I

T 2

at all, much less *so seriously* (as your charge advanceth), *despise the peculiar grace of God?* And yet your pen riseth much higher, and proclaims that I also *boldly bid defiance to it.* Well might the Apostle James complain that the tongue is a fire, a world of iniquity. I, especially in my treatise of Redemption, am so far from despising the peculiar grace of God, or from any bold bidding of defiance to it, that I magnify it upon all occasions with all my might, and demonstrate the peculiarity, i. e. the signal excellency and glory of it, to consist in this, that it encompasseth the whole world about, and particularly visiteth every creature of mankind, and this in order to their salvation. So that I make the grace of God, which is saving in the nature and tendency of it, never the less, but rather the more peculiar, by commending the rich diffusiveness of it to particular men. As for that grace of God, or rather that degree, or that operation of this 'grace, which is actually and eventually saving to men, I peculiarize it every whit as much, and, for aught I know to the contrary, upon the same terms, as Mr. Resbury himself and men of his judgment generally do. For my judgment clearly is, that no person is actually saved, but by such an assistance or operation of the grace of God, which no other person whatsoever partaketh of, or which is vouchsafed unto no other person but only unto those who are actually saved also. Only herein I may (I conceive) possibly dissent from them: they hold that this peculiar, actually-saving grace of God, is upon such terms decreed by God unto those that come to be saved by it, that there is an absolute necessity for them to embrace it and to be saved by it: whereas my sense is, that such grace is no otherwise decreed by God unto those who in time come to receive it, and *in fine* to be actually saved by it, than it is unto others, who never come to receive it; and that these might have received it, or come to be partakers of it, in the same way, and by the same means, by which those others, who are in conclusion saved by it, came to have part and fellowship in it. But this difference between Mr. Resbury and me, about the peculiar grace of

God, doth no whit more prove me to be a serious despiser
of it, or a bold bidder of defiance to it, than himself.
Therefore his charge against me in this point is merely
clamorous and aspersive, and such as a tender conscience
would have trembled so much as to demur upon; and how
much more to have published ?

" Concerning your charge of *wrested quotations,* I must
crave leave to tell you, that wrested quotations are
as far beneath me as I perceive speaking truth to be
above you. If you wrested the Scriptures no more than I
do authors, your notions about the counsels and dispensations of God would be much straighter than they are.
The truth maintained by me is able to stand upon her own
proper base, against all opposition, and hath no need at all
to be supported by the rotten props of wrested quotations;
no, nor yet by the credit or repute of any author or authors
whatsoever, though never so pertinently or candidly quoted
to her assistance. Nor do I mention or make use of
authors upon any such account, as if the doctrine I teach
were not able, without having any thing at all added to it
by men, to commend itself to the judgments and consciences of all considering men, and truly desirous of the
knowledge of the truth : but partly to remove that stone,
or straw rather, of offence, (at which people of effeminate
and weak apprehensions are so apt to stumble,) viz., That
the said doctrine wanteth an arm of flesh to stand by it;
was never held by orthodox or pious men : partly also to
demonstrate, that the greatest opposers of this doctrine
were not so consistent with themselves in their opposition
to it, but that ever and anon they fluctuated in their
judgments about it, and sometimes pulled down with one
hand what they had built up with the other. This is a
thing so manifest to those, that with judgment and observation are conversant in their writings, that to deny it is
in effect to deny that the sun is up at noon-day. Therefore
for him to wrest quotations, or pervert the sayings of men,
who hath no more need either of men or their sayings
than I, or the doctrine asserted by me, have, is to sacrifice
his name and conscience upon the service of a nut-shell,

or thing of nought. There was more wisdom than so, though not much honesty, in that saying of the heathen: *Si jus violandum est, regnandi gratiâ violandum est:* i. e.

Justice too sacred is to harm,
Unless a kingdom be the charm.

"One thing, before I close, I desire calmly to know of you : Why, or upon what account, you term the doctrine maintained by me in my treatise of Redemption, by the name of Arminianism? If it be simply because the said doctrine was, as you suppose, held by Arminius, I must crave leave to inform you, that unless the good figure of Synecdoche makes peace between your supposition and the truth, they will never agree. For the doctrine here taught by me was only in part held by Arminius: the main foundations on which I build, you will not find laid by him. Were it granted, that what I teach in that book was, for substance of matter, nothing but what is to be found in his writings, yet what reason is there why that which I teach in common with Arminius should be termed Arminianism, when you teach twenty times more upon the same terms, (I mean in common with Arminius,) and yet would be judged the freest man in the world from Arminianism?

"If you charge me with Arminianism, because the doctrine which I maintain was held by Arminius, with opposition or contrariety to the truth; I answer, (1.) Whether this be truth or no, *adhuc sub judice lis est,* is a case yet depending in the court of equity; and I believe, before many years have passed over the head of the world, all competent judges will pass sentence against you in the point. (2.) In case it were true, that Arminius did indeed maintain that doctrine in opposition to the truth, about which I make one in judgment with him, yet why should my doctrine be rather termed Arminianism, than either Calvinism, Musculism, Martyrism, or the like, considering that Calvin, Musculus, and others, reputed orthodox, did assert over and over, and this in terms every whit as significant and express as any found in Arminius, the very self-same doctrine; as I fully, and above all controversy and contradiction, prove by many testimonies cited from the writings of these men, in my treatise of Redemption? If you here plead, that these authors, elsewhere in their writings, declare their judgments in opposition to this doctrine: (1.) I make little question but that this may with as much truth be said concerning Arminius himself. (2.) If those other authors declare sometimes for the said doctrine, and other while against it, why should he, who teacheth contrary to what they deliver in one place be traduced as an opposer of their doctrine, rather than he who teacheth contrary to what they teach and deliver in another? Sir, I fear that when the Lord Jesus Christ (both yours and mine) shall come to umpire between you and me, your aspersing His truth with infamous and ignominious terms will turn to no good account unto you.

"Concerning your Treatise, or Sermons, if there be anything in them more material or weighty than what your great masters at the Synod of Dort have, upon the same account which you stand up to justify, afforded us in their synodical writings, it shall, God willing, be taken into consideration in due time. But I believe that when the oaks of Bashan shall be hewn down and fall, the shrubs and underwood will be broken down to the ground with them: and that when the horsemen are put to rout, the infantry will throw down their arms and quit the field. As to your decree of Absolute Reprobation, when you seek for it in the ninth to the Romans, you dig in a wrong field to find any such treasure; and the truth is, that you may as soon discover the element of fire at the bottom of the sea, as such a reprobation in that chapter, or in any other quarter of the Scriptures. Yea, yourself, in this very Epistle, making your ' *Elect ones, through weakness of judgment, and unskilfulness in the mystery of Christ, liable to be seduced by a spirit of error,*' do little less than shake the foundation of your absolute reprobation. If you speak of such a liableness to seduction, which endangereth not the salvation of the seduced, your zealous solicitousness for the suppression of error is to little purpose, at least in reference to such persons. For men, whether elect in your notion, or not elect, will be always liable to be thus far at least seduced, were all the errors at present on foot in the world never so thoroughly suppressed. Besides, according to your principles, all the sins which your elect shall at any time commit, shall work for good unto them, and not only be forgiven immediately upon the commission. Therefore your care of preventing their seducement, being truly interpreted, is only a care to keep them from that which would turn to a certain benefit to them, in case they were not kept from it. If you speak of a liableness to such a seduction, which may possibly end in the destruction of the seduced, then you clearly suppose a possibility of the perishing of your elect ones: and if your election staggers, how can your repro-bation stand? How impertinently you cite, and apply to your purpose, those words of the apostle, *The foundation of God standeth sure*, but that I am unworthy to teach, you might have learned from the 359 and 360 pages of my book of Redemption. But I shall, I trust, ere long, interruptory occasions not too numerously or importunely thronging me, vindicate the innocency of that ninth chapter to the Romans, from the scandalous imputation of holding correspondency with so monstrous and horrid a doctrine, as that which Mr. Resbury, with many others, led out of the way of truth by the same spirit of error and delusion, teach, under the notion of absolute repro-bation. In the mean time, hoping that, for the future, you will be more Christianly tender of the names and reputations of your brethren, at least until you know more evil by them, and this upon better terms than I am certain you yet know, or can know any by me, or I trust ever shall know; I take my leave; beseeching the God of all grace, with all fervency and effectualness of prayer and supplication, that He will vouchsafe to make both your anointing and mine, with the Spirit of revelation, much more rich and full than hitherto it hath been; that we may be more able to give the light of the knowledge of God in the face of Jesus Christ, unto men.

Your assured friend in Christ, above and against all unkindness or evil entreaties,

Oct. 15, 1651.   JOHN GOODWIN."

On the publication of this letter Resbury made a second attack upon Mr. Goodwin, in a work which he entitled, "The Lightless Star: or, Mr. John Goodwin discovered a Pelagio-Socinian, 1652." This work consists of remarks upon Mr. Goodwin's Letter, and upon the preface to his Redemption Redeemed; and the whole is designed to prove that the object of his animadversion, who held the total depravity of human nature and the necessity of Divine influence as distinctly as any minister of his age, was a *Pelagian;* and that, although he asserted the Godhead and atonement of Christ as strongly as any man that ever lived, he was nevertheless a *Socinian.* His spirit and manner of writing are worthy of his argument: malignant and abusive in the extreme. Had controversy always been conducted on the plan of Resbury, it would have been the bitterest curse that ever existed in the Christian Church.

It has been said that Resbury "was particularly honoured for what he wrote in opposition to Mr. John Goodwin in the Arminian controversy."* This is very probable. Many a person has been highly honoured, whose claims to that distinction were of a very equivocal nature. This was manifestly the case with Resbury. After disputing with his opponent at considerable length, he sometimes grants him all that he contends for; and, in cases of difficulty, to get rid of an argument, he interprets Scripture in a manner which, to say the least, reflects no honour upon his understanding. As a specimen, his explanation of the Parable of the Talents may be adduced. He contends that, by the Talents, the Doctrines of the Gospel are to be understood; and that Christian ministers are the servants to whom those talents are committed. This comment gave Mr. Goodwin an occasion to remark, with his characteristic

* Palmer's Nonconformists' Memorial, Vol. III. p. 44.

humour and acuteness, that upon these principles, " (1.) There must be five Gospels, or five doctrines of the Gospel, committed to some ministers, two to others, and but one to some. (2.) He that received five Gospels, or five doctrines of the Gospel, must be supposed to have made his five ten ; and he that received two doctrines, to have improved them into four. (3.) God should commend and reward ministers for multiplying Gospels, or doctrines of the Gospel, above the number of what He committed to them. (4.) The doctrines of the 'Gospel committed to ministers that prove unfaithful, should be taken from them, and given to them that are most faithful. These exotic notions are the fruits which grow upon the tree of Mr. Resbury's interpretation of the Talents."*

A tract containing an attack upon Mr. Goodwin was also published by Mr. Henry Jeanes, Rector of Chedsey, in Somersetshire, under the title of "A Vindication of Dr. Twisse, from the Exceptions of Mr. John Goodwin." This production was appended to the folio work of Dr. Twisse, entitled, "The Riches of God's Love unto the Vessels of Mercy, consistent with his Absolute Hatred or Reprobation of the Vessels of Wrath ;" and was intended to prove that Mr. Goodwin, in his "Redemption Redeemed," had given an incorrect representation of Dr. Twisse's opinions concerning the permissive decrees of God. To the animadversions of this gentleman Mr. Goodwin afterwards replied, in the preface to his "Triumviri."

Mr. John Pawson was another of those writers who were distinguished by their opposition to Mr. Goodwin's "Redemption Redeemed." Being appointed to preach in St. Paul's Church before the Lord Mayor and Aldermen of the City of London, a few weeks after Dr. Hill had occupied that honourable situation, he undertook to disprove the doctrine of General Redemption as asserted in Mr. Goodwin's work. His auditors, covered with civic honours, apparently desirous to prove their orthodoxy in the Genevan sense of that term, requested that the sermon might be published. With this request Pawson complied ; and to

* Triumviri, p. 14.

his discourse, which was designed to show that immense
multitudes of the human race were not redeemed by Jesus
Christ, but left under a fatal necessity of perishing for ever,
gave the title of " A Vindication of Free Grace." Reply-
ing to this inefficient publication, Mr. Goodwin remarks,
that "If Mr. Pawson would have given a title to his sermon
according to the matter, rather than his desire to make his
copies more plausible, he might rather have entitled it, A
Revenge upon, than a Vindication of Free Grace. For
what hath he in a manner attempted, but to make a nullity
of the most glorious and triumphant grace of God, which
magnifieth itself against the sin of Adam, in the whole
extent of it, and rejoiceth over all flesh, with a desire to
beautify it with salvation; and instead hereof, obtrudeth
upon the world a notion of a grace which is asthmatical,
and narrow-chested; or like unto that 'bed' in Isaiah,
' shorter than that a man can stretch himself on it, and
the covering narrower than that a man can wrap himself
in it;' a grace commensurable with the hearts of men,
but altogether unworthy Him, whose ways are as much
higher than the ways of men, and His thoughts than their
thoughts, as the heavens are higher than the earth? If a
painter should paint the sun in an eclipse, darkened ten
or eleven degrees of twelve, and then write over it, THE
SUN IN HIS MIGHT, it would be a very natural emblem of
Mr. Pawson's sermon and title compared."*

Mr. Goodwin's great work was not opposed merely by
single sermons and small tracts : the digression which it
contains respecting the Perseverance of the Saints, drew
from Dr. Owen a folio volume of more than four hundred
and forty pages, exclusive of a large preface, in defence of
the Calvinian view of that subject. The Doctor was then
in the height of his popularity, enjoying the Vice-Chancellorship of the University of Oxford, under the patronage
of Cromwell; to whom his book is dedicated, as " His
Highness Oliver Lord Protecter of the Commonwealth of
England, Scotland, and Ireland, with the Dominions
thereof." In this laudatory address, the Protector is re-
minded of his own personal interest in the doctrine of the

* Triumviri, p. 30.

unavoidable perseverance of the saints, being himself one
of the number.

Dr. Owen was a man of unquestionable piety, of great
diligence and application, and of high repute for theological learning; but was vastly inferior to Mr. Goodwin in
openness of temper, and perspicuity of argumentation. In
several of his controversial pieces there is a leaven of sourness, accompanied by an air of obscurity and reserve. To
ascertain his meaning, even on subjects sufficiently plain
in themselves, often requires more attention than the generality of readers are prepared to afford. He never seems
to disclose his whole heart to his opponent, nor to enjoy
an opportunity of yielding to the impulse of kind and
benevolent feelings towards such as called his dogmas in
question. Like most of his brethren, while writing against
Mr. Goodwin's opinions, he directed a blow at his personal
character. In the preface of his work, when speaking of
Mr. Goodwin, he says, " Whether from his own genius and
acrimony of spirit, or from the provocations of others,
with whom he hath had to do, many of his treatises have
been sprinkled with sarcasms, and contemptuous rebukes
of the persons with whom he hath had to do.—Much
indeed of his irregularity in this kind, I cannot but ascribe
to that prompt facility he hath, in putting abroad every
passion of his mind, and all his conceptions, not only de-
cently clothed in language of a choice significancy, but
also trimmed and adorned with all manner of signal im-
provements, that may render it keen or pleasant, according
to his intendment or desire. What the Latin Lyric said of
the Grecian Poet may be applied to him :

> Monte decurrens velut amnis imbres
> Quem super notas aluere ripas,
> Fervet, immensusque ruit profundo
>   Pindarus ore.''*

* Pindar, like some fierce torrent swoll'n with show'rs,
   Or sudden cataracts of melting snow,
  Which from the Alps its headlong deluge pours,
   And foams and thunders o'er the vales below,
 With desultory fury borne along,
 Rolls his impetuous, vast, unfathomable song.

                       WEST.

This insinuation concerning Mr. Goodwin, as if he were a man of an "acrimonious spirit," was neither just in itself nor generous as coming from the learned Doctor. Basking in the beams of affluence and honour, it was easy for him to say many fine things about good temper in controversialists, and to cast reflections upon a man who was pining in adversity, pointed at by the finger of scorn, and goaded by persecution. The Doctor should have recollected, that men who avowed their belief in the same theological creed with himself had deprived Mr. Goodwin of his living, and done every thing in their power to ruin his character, to deprive his children of bread, and to expose him to the vengeance of the civil magistrate. Vexed by such treatment during a series of years, he might have addressed his *good-natured* accusers in the language of another celebrated sufferer: "I also could speak as ye do: if your soul were in my soul's stead, I could heap up words against you, and shake mine head at you." (Job xvi. 4.) To be plundered of his property, traduced as a heretic, and then exhibited to the world as a man of an "acrimonious spirit," was the hard fate of our Arminian. But when the whole of his polemical treatises have been carefully investigated, in reference to the "spirit" they display, and fairly compared with those of Dr. Owen, or of any other contemporary writer, Mr. Goodwin will not appear to any disadvantage; especially if the circumstances under which the different authors wrote be taken into the account.

It has been said, that in "the whole" of his book against Mr. Goodwin, Dr. Owen "has given the world an example of a rare Christian temper in the management of controversy:"* but this is to be received rather as the compliment of a friend and admirer, than as the verdict of an impartial judge. The Doctor does not indeed treat his antagonist in that vulgar and abusive manner in which some others had done; but he never manifests a disposition to do him justice in any respect. When he mentions the high esteem in which Mr. Goodwin was held by many,

* Memoirs of Dr. Owen, prefixed to his Sermons, p. 12, Edit. 1721.

because of his talents and general character, he coldly remarks, " To interpose my judgment in the crowd, on the one side or the other, I know neither warrant nor sufficient cause." Through the whole of his work he affects to despise Mr. Goodwin's mode of reasoning; and never expresses the slightest respect for a man who had chosen rather to suffer the loss of all things than to violate his conscience : a man, too, who had been distinguished above all his contemporaries, as the friend and advocate of religious liberty; and to whom it is highly probable the Doctor himself was indebted for his best thoughts on that interesting subject. Besides, the "temper" which could furnish just occasion for the following complaint is certainly not entitled to very exalted praise : " Dr. Owen," says Mr. Goodwin, " will needs have me to hold, whether I will or no, that perseverance is to be obtained by ' manly considerations,' and by the exercise and improvement of a man's own abilities, without any assistance of the grace of God. By the authority of this supposition, he stigmatizeth my doctrine of perseverance with this brand of infamy : 'That my maintaining of the saints' perseverance is as bad, if not worse, than my maintaining their apostasy.' Certainly the Doctor's ingenuity and conscience were both withdrawn, when his enemy and mine tempted him to make so sad a breach upon his honour, as to charge me with saying, that the saints may persevere by any means whatsoever, without the grace of God; my avowed doctrine being, *That what good thing soever any man doth, he doth it through the assistance of the free grace of God ; and is in no capacity so much as to conceive a good thought without it.* These are my words, published to the world; and if the Doctor can produce any sentence of mine, contrary to the import of the words now recited, I shall provide him more honour in my thoughts, than yet I am able to do. Excepting mere oversights, which are not contrary in the least to honesty, faithfulness, and truth, I abominate the Doctor's insinuative charge : looking upon it as beneath the dignity of his function, parts, and learning to exhibit; and as much beneath my

principles and spirit to stand under, with the least obnox-
iousness of guilt or merit." *

With regard to the Doctor's mode of reasoning, Mr.
Goodwin says, "He seldom engageth against any argument, whether levied from some text of Scripture, or from
the clearest principles of reason, but first he vilifieth it;
and when he hath made it soft and tender, by steeping it
in this liquor, an answer of straw will serve to thrust it
through, and lay it for dead. The very transcription of
passages of this character out of his book would, I verily
believe, amount to a competent volume. I speak the truth
with all ingenuity and clearness of spirit: many of his
strains in arguing, many of his principles in answering,
are as uncouth and exotic to my understanding, as if his
intellectuals and mine had not been cast in the same
mould, nor he and I made creatures of the same kind.
His demonstrations are not so much as dialectical or
topical proofs to me; and for many of his fundamentals in
the fabric of his disputation for his notion of perseverance,
my soul knoweth not how to take pleasure in them. Yea,
when he doth not strictly argue, but only speak orator-
like, as in his epistles prefixed to his book, his sense oft
times is so retired, that, reading some periods twice or thrice
over, with a very great desire to communicate with him in
his thought, I suffered disappointment, and was not
able to reach him. At some turns I thought his printer
might be accessory to my sufferings in this kind; but
at others I could observe no symptoms of such a cause."†

The late Robert Hall entertained a very low opinion of
Dr. Owen as a logician. Thus he spoke of him in conversation with a brother minister:—"As a reasoner, Dr.
Owen is most illogical; for he almost always takes for
granted what he ought to prove; while he is always proving what he ought to take for granted; and after a long
digression he concludes very properly with, 'This is not
our concernment,' and returns to enter on something still
farther from the point."‡

* Triumviri, Preface.   † Ibid.   ‡ Works of Robert Hall, Vol. I.
p 164, Edit. 1856.

Messrs. Bogue and Bennett have informed the Christian
world, that "Dr. Owen, who had been brought into notice,
and raised to the highest posts of literary honour by his
attack upon Arminianism, triumphantly confuted Goodwin's Redemption Redeemed, in a treatise on the Perseverance of the Saints."* This is only a very slight specimen
of that loose and incorrect mode of writing, which these
reverend historians have adopted on almost all occasions
in which Arminianism is concerned. Indeed, a considerable part of what they have advanced on this subject, is a
mere tissue of sarcastic' levity, and unblushing misrepresentation. Their assertions not unfrequently betray either
a pitiful want of information, or a flagrant disregard of
that strict and unbending veracity without which historical
narration loses all its value, and becomes only a medium
of deception. Mr. Goodwin's work, as we have already
seen, is comprised in twenty chapters; the principal subject
of which is, as its title intimates, General Redemption;
including a digression concerning the Perseverance of the
Saints. The latter topic occupies seven chapters, and no
more. Against these chapters only, Dr. Owen's book was
written; and therefore cannot contain a triumphant confutation of Goodwin's Redemption Redeemed. Were it
admitted that the Doctor was perfectly successful in
the establishment of his thesis, and that he rendered
nugatory every objection of his antagonist, (a point which
will not be conceded,) even in this case, it could not
be said, that his volume contains a confutation of one
half of Mr. Goodwin's work. That a learned and argumentative treatise should be "triumphantly confuted"
by an attack upon a mere digression, while thirteen
chapters, in which the principal subject is discussed,
are passed over in total silence, involves a mystery
which these gentlemen have not even attempted to explain. Dr. Owen had no such opinion of his work
when he said, "What hath been, or may yet further
be done, by others, who have made, or shall make it
their business to draw the saw of this controversy to and

* History of the Dissenters, Vol. IV. p. 228, Edit. 1812.

fro with Mr. Goodwin, I hope will give satisfaction, as in other things, SO IN THE PARTICULARS BY ME OMITTED." *

The divine who was most distinguished by his writings against Mr. Goodwin's book was Mr. George Kendall, rector of Blisland, near Bodmin in Cornwall. This gentleman, who was afterwards created D.D., resigned his rectory, and took up his residence in London, purposely that he might watch Mr. Goodwin's movements, and "be in a better capacity to oppose him and his doctrine." † Kendall, like his friend Dr. Owen, wrote also with great warmth and eagerness against Mr. Baxter; whom he affected to despise, and whose theological opinions he was disingenuous enough to identify with those of Mr. Goodwin. He was the mere tool of a party, and would descend to any trick for the purpose of turning the laugh against his antagonists, and of exposing them to public contempt. "Dr. Kendall," says Baxter, "was a little quick-spirited man, of great ostentation, and a considerable orator and scholar. He was driven on farther by others, than his own inclinations would have led him. He thought to get an advantage to his reputation, by a triumph over John Goodwin and me: for those who set him on work, would needs have him conjoin us both together, to intimate that I was an Arminian." ‡ Baxter further describes him as a "bold man," "self-conceited," "superciliously scornful," and possessed of a "Cretian pen;" § that is, a pen addicted to lying. (Titus i. 12.)

In opposition to Mr. Goodwin's Redemption Redeemed this writer published two folio volumes. In the first he attempts to prove, that Jesus Christ did NOT "taste death for every man," and that the Lord did NOT "lay upon him the iniquity of us all;" and in the second he contends, with respect to those who have once been sanctified, that nothing can either deprive them of the Holy Spirit, or prevent their final salvation. His general mode of writing on these subjects is reprehensible in a high degree. He

---

* Epistle Dedicatory.   † Athenæ Oxonienses, Vol. II. col. 326
‡ Reliquiæ Baxterianæ, Part First, p. 110.   § Saints' Everlasting Rest, p. 828, Edit. 1669.

U

labours alu.ost incessantly to make his opponent appear
contemptible. For this purpose he has selected from Mr.
Goodwin's work a considerable number of passages in
which the author's meaning is not fully expressed, and
which, in consequence of their separation from their
respective connexions, appear weak and paradoxical. To
many of these passages he has annexed a comment, which
he knew to be directly opposed to the sense of his author.
By a liberal use of these mean expedients, he has represented the object of his animadversion as a consummate
fool. At the same time he indulges himself in low jokes,
and dull attempts at wit, when discussing subjects which
ought never to be touched but with fear and trembling.
He makes himself merry when speaking of the perfections
of God, and endeavouring to unravel " the counsel of His
will," respecting the endless happiness and misery of men.
Such conduct is not only a violation of good taste, but is
exceedingly pernicious in its influence. There is such an
awful sanctity connected with the doctrines of Revelation,
especially those which relate to the Divine nature, and to
the eternal states of men, that even mistakes concerning
them should be treated in a reverent manner. For that
levity which pervades his writings Kendall found no
example in the work which he professes to answer: the
whole of it, according to his own confession, being remarkable for " sobriety."

One example of Kendall's dishonourable conduct towards
his opponent will afford a sufficient specimen of his mode
of writing. Mr. Goodwin had asserted, after the example
of the most enlightened divines both in ancient and in
modern times, that when knowledge is predicated of God,
it is to be understood as existing eminently in Him, and
not properly, or formally, as in the imperfect minds of men.
"Knowledge in the creature," says he, " is a principle
essentially distinct from the soul where it resideth, and is
capable of augmentation and diminution therein, and of
separation from it. Whereas that which is called knowledge in God neither differs really or essentially from His
nature, or from Himself; but is one and the same thing

with Him : nor is it capable of growth, of decay, or of separation." * His disingenuous antagonist, having selected the following six words from different parts of a paragraph, " Knowledge not properly attributable to God," makes these remarks upon what he represents as Mr. Goodwin's doctrine : " And yet it [i. e. knowledge] is surely [properly attributable] to Mr. Goodwin in *a high degree*, and in *a low one* to every one of his weak brethren, who are not capable of *his profound speculations*. The silliest of us are not ignorant of all things : only God properly knoweth nothing." † Before an opponent who is capable of descending to the use of such contemptible expedients, it is impossible for any author to stand. And yet this writer of Calvinistic folios was encouraged and recommended by the Vice-Chancellor of the University of Oxford !

Describing his own manner of writing, Kendall says, " Though sometimes I *sneer*, I never *snarl*, much less do I bite." ‡ His readers soon find that his " sneers " are almost perpetual in their recurrence ; and as they proceed in the perusal of his volumes, they soon perceive that the reason why he does not *bite* is sufficiently obvious. He had no teeth. He possessed talents and industry, but was no match for Goodwin, either in argumentation, or in biblical learning.

What Messrs. Bogue and Bennett have said concerning Dr. Owen's book, had been previously asserted by the late Rev. Augustus Toplady in reference to the publications of Kendall. By these, said he, Goodwin's " Redemption Redeemed was effectually answered." " If it was," says Mr. Sellon, " I will eat it, as tough a morsel as it is. Has Mr. Kendall proved, that the Scriptures do not say what they do, in favour of general redemption, and the possibility of falling from grace ? Or has he proved, that the writers he quotes in favour of those doctrines, do not say what they do ? Or that those writers and those Scriptures do not mean what they say ? Or has

---

* Redemption Redeemed, p. 30.   † Vindication of the Doctrine commonly received in the Reformed Churches : Request to the Reader
‡ Common Doctrine of the Perseverance of the Saints, Preface.

he proved, that the plain passages of Scripture are to be explained by the figurative; and such as are easy, and of undoubted sense, by such as are more difficult and doubtful? If he has not proved these things, which it is impossible he should, he has not ' effectually answered ' John Goodwin's Redemption Redeemed."*

In the rear of those antagonists who appeared against Mr. Goodwin on this occasion, was Mr. Thomas Lamb, who styles himself a " Servant of Christ, dwelling at the sign of the Tun, in Norton-Fallgate, London." This polemic, according to Edwards, was originally a soap-boiler, and afterwards a minister among the Baptists. He was a man of great zeal, activity, and courage; and acquired considerable celebrity by frequent imprisonment; having, at one time or another, been confined in nearly all the jails in London and its vicinity. His book against Mr. Goodwin bears the following title: "Absolute Freedom from Sin, by Christ's Death for the World, as the Object of Faith, in opposition to Conditional, set forth by Mr. John Goodwin in his book entitled Redemption Redeemed; and the final Perseverance of .the Saints proceeding from Election by the Grace of God alone, maintained and sweetly reconciled with the aforesaid Doctrine: and the great Question of God's eternal Decree of Reprobating the unbelieving World, cleared from that Odium cast upon it by Mr. Goodwin, 1656." This work is dedicated to Oliver Cromwell, and copies of it were presented by the author to several of the most distinguished men in the nation. "The main pillar that bears up the fabric of his book," says Mr. Goodwin, "is that antinomish principle, which turns up the Gospel by the roots, viz.: That faith is no condition of the covenant of grace, upon which the salvation of men is by God suspended. The weak man, it seems, is not able to conceive how the covenant of grace should be absolutely and sovereignly free, in case faith, or any other service, should be required by God in the nature of a condition, for obtaining the good things covenanted therein, as justification, adoption, &c. And

* Sellon's Works, Vol. I. p. 376.

truly he that is not able to understand this, I can hardly look upon as a man that hath as yet attained the A B C of evangelical knowledge; much less as competent to engage in controversial divinity." Referring to the *fictitious* theology with which he considered the book of this illiterate wight, as well as the folios of his erudite opponents, to abound, Mr. Goodwin says, "Mr. Lamb may take Dr. Owen by the one hand, and Mr. Kendall by the other, and bespeak them thus:

> Scribimus indocti, doctique poëmata passim.
>
> Unlearn'd, and learn'd, we *poems* write amain." *

This man is not to be confounded with the Thomas Lamb who belonged to Goodwin's church, and of whom an account will be given in a subsequent part of these memoirs.

Mr. Goodwin's attempts to establish the doctrine of general redemption were not in every instance met by hostility. Several of his contemporaries regarded him as a magnanimous and successful champion of revealed truth, and presented to him their cordial thanks for his services. The subjoined letter is from a man of this class. It was published in the year 1653, under the title of "Sal Scylla: or, A Letter written from Scilly to Mr. John Goodwin, Minister of the Gospel in London." The writer says,—

"SCILLY, *May* 25, 1653.

"BROTHER,

"I DARE be bold so to call and esteem you, (considering what spirit you are of,) though I be but the least toe of that body whereof I believe you are an eye at the least, and Providence having brought your Book of Redemption to my hand, and given me time and opportunity to read it over once and again, as also seriously to ponder the full-mouthed authority of Scripture, reason, and the most godly learned, in vindication of that foundation of truth, the face whereof hath been, and still is, by most, almost

* Triumviri, Preface.

as much marred as was the face of the Lord and Master
of it, I should be injuriously unthankful to God and man,
if I should not acknowledge you so to be. For the light of
the body is the eye; and this light, which by reflection of
the true light hath enlightened your eye, doth from thence
again reflect upon many members, to guide their feet in
the way of grace, mercy, truth, and peace.

"About four or five years past, I met with two or three
small tracts upon the point, as L. S. Stooks, Horne *contra*
Owen. The first-mentioned, coming first to my hand, undermined my tabernacle, (as it might easily do, having but a
sandy foundation,) and blew up the whole fabric about
mine ears, spoiled all my goods which I had laid up for many
years, and I escaped only with my life, wounded and naked,
destitute of house or home, food, raiment, and medicine;
yet withal showed me a stone choice and precious, wherewith I might lay a more sure foundation for a better
house that could not be shaken : yet this stone was rough
and uneven, and I knew not as yet how to fit and square
it to build upon ; neither have I, or heard I, of any other
that could, till I found out Horne, who squared this stone
to my mind at that time : also he provided me with many
materials to build upon it. Having therefore so good
benefactors to bear the cost, I thanked God and them, and
fell to work. But having built two or three stones high, their
materials failed me. Wherefore my house being not yet
covered, and I weary of lying by the hedges, I made use
of some of the ruins of my old house to finish my new
building, and so patched it up as I could : but entering
into it, I found it every shower, like a contentious woman,
a continual dropping, until I met with your model, which
having thoroughly viewed within and without, I found
every stone so close compact and cemented, as if it had
been one entire rock; wherefore I pulled down so much as
was faulty, and built up again according to that last pattern. And now I thank my God, through the grace given
to you and me, I have a house wherein to shelter me from
all winds and weathers whatsoever; and not only so, but
which is well furnished with all things necessary for my

being and well-being.—I need not expound my parable; the moral, I believe, is obvious to the meanest member of your church.

"To relate the divers transactions between the Father, Son, Spirit, and my soul, from the twentieth to the forty-fifth year of my pilgrimage, would exceed the bounds of an epistle, and the limit of many sheets of paper. Therefore be pleased with this brief and general account: From the twentieth to the thirty-ninth year of mine age, I lived upon the husks of the common faith of election; yet did not then so account it, though since I have found it to be no better. In which time I was under many eclipses and re-lapses, and once even at the gate of despair: in this epilepsy, I made use of the common antidote, *Whom God loveth once, He loveth to the end: the gifts and callings of God are without repentance,* &c. But this was but a palliative cure, the cause still remaining, depending upon the common notion of election. During this time I was counted a Puritan, (except in my relapses, wherein I was only a scandal to those so called,) then I turned to the Presbyterian, after that to the Independent, thence to the Anabaptist, then to the Seeker; where seeking for that which could not be found, I had almost lost myself. Then I faced the Ranter, but found him to be set on fire of hell; and knowing by woeful experience, that the burnt child dreads the fire, I durst not come near. Here I was at a loss, and at as great a strait as the lepers before the gate of Samaria: If I stand here, I must perish; if I went back to any of the former dispensations, the famine was there. Therefore I resolved to yield· myself to the mercy of the Gentiles; which I did accordingly; where I continued the space of two years, not without hope, nor without God in the world, (though I had rejected the Scrip-ture, and all men's interpretation upon it,) the vision of all being to me as a book that was sealed, which neither learned nor unlearned could open or read; yet during this time I had hope in God, and committed my soul and body to my faithful Creator, who did speak peace to me in this strange land; and many times would lead me by His Spirit unto the Scriptures, where I should yet read with as little understanding as the Eunuch. At the end of this dispensation, I was led by the Spirit once more to the Scriptures; then opened He my understanding, and pressed me farther to search and try all things; which I did accordingly; and so by the grace of God I am what I am. And now, my Father, the Chariot and Horsemen of the Israel of God, ride on because of the Word of Truth : charge through all opposition : and Jesus Christ, who hath showed you so great things, as the despisers and wonderers of this world will not believe, though it be so plainly declared to them, shall show you yet greater things, that they may marvel. I know but two or three in all these west parts like-minded in this point; the rest, which are many and zealous, though they might know that the foolishness of God is wiser than men, and the weakness of God stronger than men, yet are so bewitched with tradition, that seeing the visions of God will not answer the visions of their own hearts, they will make the devil a seer, according to that of the poet :

Flectere si nequeo Superos, Acheronta movebo.

If the powers above I cannot bend,
I'll move the fiend some aid to send.

"And therefore they rejoice in, and boast of Master Kendall's answer: the word ' answer ' being I believe the strongest argument for the confirmation of their error, or the eviction of their truth.—Yet these, I bear them record, have all zeal for God, though not according to knowledge: for they being ignorant of the righteousness of God, and also of His love, goodness, mercy, wisdom, equity, and truth; and going about to establish His will and power alone; have not submitted to either. If your promise upon Rom. ix. be fulfilled, I pray send it down amongst us that the deceiving and deceived may, if possible, be undeceived. I pray also send us word, whether your Second Part to the same tune be finished, or when probably it may; when happily the grand objection, the want of means to them that never heard of Jesus Christ, may be convincingly answered, to the satisfaction of the most judicious of them who chiefly stumble at that stumbling-stone.

"I need make no apology for my boldness in thus writing; believing that your greatness is in being least, and servant unto all. Therefore follow ón, O man of God, to serve your God, and your generation, that you may finish the work which is given you to do, with joy, to the joy of many : and that both you and they may attain the end of your faith, even the salvation of your souls. For which the weakest and unworthiest of all the members of Christ shall cast in his mite of prayer into the treasury of the Almighty. My duty I commend to you, and all that love and wait for the appearing of our Lord Jesus Christ; which is by love to serve you all.

CHRISTOPHER SALTER,
Chirurgeon of the Islands and Garrison of Scilly."

It has been said by an acute observer of human nature, that few people care to understand what pretended heretics mean, and that fewer still have the courage to do them justice. The correctness of this remark was perhaps never more apparent than in the case of Mr. Goodwin. Many of the clergy in and about London undertook, in the course of their ministry, to confute what they called his errors and heresies : but the greater part of them, either through inattention or design, grossly misrepresented his opinions before their respective congregations; thus exposing him and his friends to popular reproach and clamour. Desirous of preventing their good from being evil spoken of, and of doing justice to the truth, Mr. Goodwin, in conjunction with his church, drew up a small quarto tract, which they published under the title of, " The Agreement and Distance of Brethren : or, A Brief Survey of the Judgment of Mr. John Goodwin, and the Church of God walking with him, touching these important heads of Doctrine ; Election and Reprobation ; the Death of Christ; the Grace of God in and about Conversion ; the Liberty of the Will ; the Perseverance of the Saints : declaring the particulars as well agreed upon as dissented in between them and their Christian

Brethren of opposite Judgment, 1652." In their prefatory address to the reader, these persecuted men remark, "The piece now in thy hand is only apologetical, and therefore we hope will not be offensive to any. It is lawful even for an offender, in case he be unduly assaulted, to rise up in his own defence : how much more for him that is conscious of no miscarriage, but knoweth that things are laid to his charge which he knoweth not ? Though the greater part of these papers be bestowed upon the justification of ourselves, in some tenets which we own, and for which we suffer, in many men's words and deportments, the penalty of persons deeply and dangerously erroneous; yet our design in drawing up [this] account [is] rather the washing of our hands in innocency of many enormous opinions, which some would fain thrust into the company of those tenets which we hold in opposition to them; hoping, by this means, to render them more obnoxious to jealousies and prejudice. For are there not some ministers, in and about the city, so far from all Christian ingenuity, as openly to declaim against us, as, in our doctrine of election, denying the Godhead of the Father, as Arius the Godhead of the Son ? as holding an election of qualities not of persons to salvation ? as exalting nature above grace ? as affirming that men, by their own strength, and without the special grace of God, may repent, believe, and be saved ? as denying a power in God to bring to pass His intentions ? to omit many others of like import which we abhor.

"To prevent the sin of slander in *others ;* who, through the suggestions of their teachers, may speak evil of us falsely ; and in *ourselves,* the sin of leaving a pit uncovered, into which men may very possibly fall, and receive much harm ; we have drawn up this brief model of our sense about the five heads of doctrine, which are solemnly controverted between us and our brethren, partakers, many of them, we question not, of like precious faith with us."

Mr. Goodwin and his friends also add, as the result of their own individual experience, " Truth delighteth little in the countenances of men, till she hath secured their judgments, and set up her throne in their understandings.

But this we can inform thee concerning her, that, well understood, she will bear any man's charges, that shall travel with her through the world: though we must confess, that many times her company is very costly. But what she spends in silver, she repays in gold; and with the rubbish of men's names, friends, and fortunes, builds up their consciences with that peace which passeth all understanding, and with that joy which is unspeakable and full of glory."

In this tract Mr. Goodwin lays before his readers the five points of doctrine, concerning which he and his Calvinian brethren entertained different opinions; shows how far he could agree with them on each subject; specifies the precise questions at issue between them; and then states some of the reasons which induced him to withhold his assent from their creed. This work was afterwards published in a duodecimo volume, of about one hundred and fifty pages; every paragraph of which, though composed amidst numerous provocations, is written in a strain of as pure charity, as perhaps ever emanated from a human mind. And it may be safely affirmed, that there is not, in the English language, any volume which, in as small a compass, contains so much information respecting the Calvinian controversy. The pamphlet of Mr. Wesley, entitled, "Predestination calmly Considered," comes nearer to it than any other, and contains more argument; but does not embrace so many topics as that of Mr. Goodwin.

To the first edition of the "Agreement and Distance of Brethren," was prefixed an excellent address to Oliver Cromwell, as "Lord General of the Forces of the Parliament of England;" who was well known to be strongly attached to the doctrines of Calvinism. This address is signed by Mr. Goodwin and thirteen members of his church, "in the name and by the consent" of the rest.

"Though God of His grace and goodness," say they, "hath endued us with some measure of strength from on high, to suffer for truth's sake, yet we are not well able to bear it that truth should suffer for ours. Out of this weakness, if yet weakness it be, we make this humble address to you, trusting that by the mediation hereof some part at least of those sufferings may be eased, which we cannot reasonably but judge and fear the truth suffers under the name of error, in the judgments and thoughts of many ; and this occasioned we confess in part by us, who have neglected, until now, the public rendering of some brief and plain account of such tenets which we hold and profess apart from the judgment of some other Christian churches amongst us, and from the more generally received sense of those who are called ministers of the Gospel in the nation. We can freely call God for a record upon our soul, that there is no spirit in us that lusteth after envy, or contention, or singularity of opinion, in the things of Jesus Christ : and we heartily wish that our brethren's doctrine were in all points such, that we might live and die in a thorough and complete unity of faith with them. We verily believe, that it was not more grievous to Abraham, to part with his son Ishmael and his mother out of his house, than it is unto us, to part company with our Christian brethren, (servants of the same God with us,) in any thing which concerns the common salvation. Nor shall we willingly give place unto any in endeavouring to keep the unity of the Spirit with all saints in the bond of peace. The ensuing lines, we hope, will abundantly testify the longing desire of our soul to go hand in hand with our brethren, as far as ever, by any construction, interpretation, mollification, qualification, restriction, proviso whatsoever, we are able to make any thing like unto truth of their doctrines and sayings. But when a voice out of our judgments and consciences, (which we cannot but judge to be the voice of God,) crieth aloud unto us, 'Take heed to yourselves ; go no further with them : the rest of their way is dark and slippery ; '—we look upon ourselves as warned from heaven to turn aside from them into those paths of doctrine which to us-ward are full of light and life and peace. And confident we are, that neither your lordship, nor any other person of Christian ingenuity, will turn it unto matter of reproach, or of the lightest blame unto us, that, having been so uprightly industrious and studious as we have been, (our consciences bearing us witness,) to inform our judgments of the truth, we should comport with them in our profession, and speak that upon occasion in the ears of men, which they assure us is of God. Nor can we doubt, but that, our judgments standing at that point of the compass, where the word of God, as conceived and understood by us, hath at present fixed them, you would impute unworthiness in the highest unto us, if, to please men, we should despise them, and profess or speak openly unto others things contrary to what they inwardly speak and avouch to us.

"Sir, that God whom we serve knoweth that no corrupt design hath beguiled us, or had the least influence upon our counsels, for making this dedication unto you. We are well able, through Christ strengthening us, not only to suffer still in the thoughts, sayings, and actings of men against us, for our judgments' and consciences' sake, (which we interpret to be for the truth's sake,) as we do; but even to rejoice in deeper sufferings than these, if God and men shall agree to call us to such a baptism. We are all thoughts made, that nothing that we are able, or can be made able, to do for the truth, will turn to any such blessed account to us, as our sufferings for the truth. The prize that we run for in this dedication, is not to receive from you either favour, countenance, or protection, either for our persons or opinions; these are the projectures of men that are fearful;—but to offer an opportunity to you of honouring yourself yet more, and of making your mountain so strong and sure that it may never be removed. For truth, with her children, being countenanced and protected by men, imitate the fruitful fields, *qui multo plus afferunt, quam acceperunt,* who return much more than they receive. And though truth, with those of her household and charge, require neither countenance nor protection of men, as if they stood in need of them, (for they know as well how to want as to abound,) yet men, especially men in eminency of place and power, stand in need of them, and of that protection and safety, the donation whereof is appropriate unto them; which yet they are in no steady capacity of

giving unto any, but unto their friends, and unto those
that shall stand by them in the day of their trial."

Mr. Wesley expressed a high opinion of Goodwin's
"Agreement and Distance of Brethren." He spoke of
it as an able and correct summary of the quinquarticular
controversy; and, as such, he revised the language,
omitting a few sentences, and wrote a brief recommendatory preface: but on some account or other he
did not commit it to the press.

Our author's next publication, relating to this controversy, was "An Exposition of the Ninth Chapter of the
Epistle to the Romans: wherein, by the tenor of the said
Chapter, from first to last, is proved, that the Apostle's
scope is to maintain his great doctrine of Justification by
Faith; and that he discourseth nothing at all concerning
any personal Election or Reprobation of Men from
Eternity, 1653." This book is dedicated to the lord
mayor and aldermen of the city of London; who, a few
months before, had requested Mr. Pawson to publish his
sermon against our author. Although they had already,
in effect, passed judgment in his case, Mr. Goodwin gave
them to understand, that he had much to say in defence
of his own sentiments; and modestly intimated, that
before they ventured in future to interfere between him
and his opponents, they ought at least to give both sides
a patient hearing.

In his address to the reader, Mr. Goodwin says, " I
find old age coming upon me liké an armed man, attended
with his accustomed retinue of infirmities, weaknesses,
and disablings from service, as well in the labour of the
mind, as of the outer man. Besides, the troublesome
importunity of some men in another way hath engaged
my thoughts to offer something in public, (and this with
as much expedition, as my slow pace, and other emergent
diversions, which are like to prove not a few, will afford,)
for the healing of it, if God shall graciously please to
stand by me in the cure. By reason hereof, my intentions
declared for drawing up a Second Part of my Book of
Redemption are set back for a time. Yea, whether God

will not, by the hand of death, discharge me from the service, before I shall be in a capacity to lift up a hand unto it, is beyond the ken of my understanding. However, He whose interest is a thousand times more concerned in such a service than mine, will, I am securely confident, awaken other instruments to the performance of it, though I shall fall asleep.

"If my brethren of hardest thoughts against me really knew, how little pleasure I take in declining their judgment, in the sense of this chapter, or in any point in religion; and how little offence I take at them, simply for their opposition in judgment to me, I suppose they could not be any otherwise affected towards me, than I am towards them; and that they would only pity and pray for me, as a man to whom the light of truth hath only in part shined, and not be continually shooting the arrows of bitter words against me, as if I were disaffected to them, or did not desire to speak the truth in love as well as they. However, if I could think that the measure which they mete out unto me, in hard sayings and otherwise, would turn to as good an account unto them, in the day of Jesus Christ, as I am certain they will unto me, I could count the temptation double joy. For the truth is, my reproaches are my best riches, and my mortality is more endeared to me, by my sufferings for the truth, than by any thing I have done, or am in a capacity of doing for it. My brethren need not fear, that I shall ever reciprocate either hard sayings or doings with them. Nature itself teacheth me not to reproach my benefactors."

Next to his Redemption Redeemed, and his treatise of Justification, this is the most valuable and important of all Mr. Goodwin's publications. It is indeed difficult to determine, whether the author excelled more in argument, or in the interpretation of Scripture. Various attempts have been made by learned men to explain the ninth chapter of the Epistle to the Romans; but the writer of these memoirs is ready to confess, that no commentary on that part of the sacred volume which he ever perused, has been so perfectly satisfactory to his mind as the Exposition of Mr. Goodwin; who contends that the apostle is not speaking of any irrespective appointment of men to eternal life and death, as some have supposed, but of the justification of sinners before God. He shows that God has an unquestionable right to determine in what particular manner He will confer His favours;—that He has constituted faith in His Son, as the grand condition of our justification before Him, to which all are therefore required to submit;—that the believing Gentiles, by submission to the Divine will in this respect, were made partakers of justifying grace;—and that the unbelieving Jews, notwithstanding their descent from Abraham, by seeking justification by the works of the law, not only fell short of that blessing, but were even deprived of all their national privileges. Mr. Goodwin shows, in a chain of connected and beautiful argumentation, that every part of that important chapter bears upon these subjects; and then proves, beyond all possibility of successful contradiction, that this is the apostle's meaning, from the last four verses; where the inspired author, stating the conclusion to which his premises conducted him, says, "What shall we say then? [What inference shall be deduced from these facts and observations?] That the Gentiles, which followed not after righteousness, have attained to righteousness, even the righteousness which is of faith; but Israel, which followed after the law of righteousness, hath not attained to the law of righteousness. Wherefore? [because they were absolute reprobates, and outcasts from the mercy of God? No:] Because they sought it not by faith, but as it were by the works of the law: for they stumbled at that stumbling-stone; as it is written, "Behold, I lay in Sion a stumbling-stone, and rock of offence: and whosoever believeth on Him shall not be ashamed." (Rom. ix. 30–33.)

"My witness is in heaven," says Mr. Goodwin, "and my record on high, that throughout my exposition I have not willingly wrested, or adulterously forced, any phrase, word, syllable, or letter; but have, with all simplicity of heart, without turning aside either to the right hand or to the left, followed the genuine ducture of the

context and scope of the place, consulting, without partiality, all circumstances which I could think of, in order
to a due steerage of my judgment in every thing."

Had Mr. Goodwin written an exposition of the Sacred
Books in general, judging from the specimen now before
us, it would have been one of the most valuable productions
of the kind ever presented to the Christian church. Great
use was made of this work, though without any mention of
the author's name, by Mr. Samuel Loveday, in a book published by him in the year 1676, entitled, "Personal Reprobation Reprobated;" and a very valuable extract from it
was inserted by Mr. Wesley in the third volume of the
Arminian Magazine.

The following arguments against the notion of Esau's
personal reprobation, in the Calvinian sense of that term,
will be read with interest, especially by Christian parents:
they form a part of our author's exposition of the 10th,
11th, and two succeeding verses of this important chapter:
"Nor to my best remembrance have I ever heard, that any
one of the learned fathers concluded from the passages in
hand, either Esau's reprobation from eternity, or his eternal condemnation in time. And yet more certain I am,
that neither could they, nor any other, have sufficient
ground from the said passages, to found such a conclusion
upon. Because,

"1. Esau is not here mentioned under any personal consideration; but only as the head and significator of his
posterity.

"2. It is the confession of those who are the most opposite in the doctrine of reprobation, and may be evinced
from the Scriptures, that all Esau's posterity were not
reprobated, in such a sense; as neither were all Jacob's
posterity elected.

"3. Neither doth that service, or subjection to Jacob,
which the oracle imposeth upon Esau, import such a reprobation; inasmuch as the servant may be elected, when
the master is in a state of reprobation. (1 Pet. ii. 18;
Philip. iv. 22, &c.)

"4. Were it granted, that servitude did import such a

x

reprobation as is contended for; yet, certain it is, that Esau in person never served Jacob.

"5. Neither doth that hatred of God against Esau, mentioned by Malachi, import any such reprobation of Esau; because it related not to Esau personally considered, as appears from that description which the prophet gives of the effects thereof: viz. 'Laying his mountains waste, throwing down when he should build,' &c., in which effect it never expressed itself against the person of Esau. These are not the proper effects of a hatred in God, which argueth a reprobation of men for eternity; unless we will say, that when Jerusalem was laid waste by the Chaldeans, all the persons that were sufferers in this calamity were reprobated by God from eternity. In case this could be proved, (the contrary whereof is evident from the Scriptures,) yet were it no sufficient proof, that all that deeply suffer in public desolations are therefore reprobated by God, or perish eternally.

"6. The drift of the apostle in the context doth no ways require a supposition, that Esau should be personally reprobated from eternity; but only, that in his posterity, and those sad events which according to the prediction were in after ages to befal them, he should prove a significant type of the spiritual and eternal misery of all those that should seek justification by the works of the law, or in a way of their own devising, and not submit to the counsel and good pleasure of God; who hath consecrated the way of Faith in Jesus Christ, as the only means whereby Justification is to be attained.

"7. His perfect reconcilement to his brother after that deep offence taken at him, is no light testimony of his own reconciliation with God. 'If ye forgive men their trespasses,' saith our Saviour, 'your heavenly Father will also forgive you.' Therefore unless it can be proved that Esau returned with the dog to his vomit, or continued in some course of impiety inconsistent with salvation, formerly practised, there can be no competent ground assigned of his damnation, much less of his personal reprobation from eternity.

" 8. If Isaac had understood the oracle delivered to his wife, ' The elder shall serve the younger,' as if it had imported, that his elder son had been reprobated from eternity, it is no ways probable that he could set his heart upon him as he did.   That terrible wrath of God revealed from heaven against the son in so signal a manner, could not but wholly quench all joy, pleasure, comfort, or contentment in the parent in relation to such a son.   Unless we shall judge Isaac to have been extremely sensual, and inordinately given to appetite, we cannot conceive that he could take any comfort in his son, or love him for his venison's sake, which the Scripture testifieth of him, if he had known that God had from eternity doomed him to the torments of eternal fire.

" 9. It is no ways probable, nor like one of the dispensations of God, that He should inform such parents, who were righteous and holy, who had found special favour in His sight, whose peace His heart was set to promote, that He had reprobated from eternity any of their children, and this whilst they were yet unborn.   A message of such a sad and horrid import, coming from the mouth of God immediately, to a weak and tender woman, whose hour of travail with two children was come, being likewise already sorely troubled and perplexed with the strangeness of her condition, could not but have endangered her life.   Certainly God did not intend to signify unto Rebecca, that she was ready to fall in travail of a reprobate; a child which He was peremptorily resolved to destroy with the dreadful vengeance of hell-fire.

" 10. If God should have signified to Rebecca, and by her to Isaac, that their elder son had been reprobated from eternity, and consequently that there was no possibility of his repentance or salvation, must not this have been a grand discouragement to them from lifting up so much as a prayer for him, and from all other endeavours in order to his conversion and salvation ?   And thus God must be supposed to have taught astorgy and unnaturalness to Isaac and Rebecca ; and taken them off from the performance of such duties on behalf of their child, which

x 2

He strictly and universally imposeth upon all other parents
without exception.

" 11. It was never known, or heard of, that God ever
made any discovery to the world of any man's final estate,
especially on the left hand, before he was born ; no, nor
before the perpetration of some grand and horrid sin.

" 12. There is no end imaginable, worthy the only wise
and most gracious God, why He should make known such
a thing concerning Esau, being yet unborn, as that He had
reprobated him from eternity.　Such a revelation cannot
well be supposed to be of any use, or edification to the
world ; but rather of evil tendency, and malignant influence
upon the hearts of men ; occasioning them to judge hardly
and most unworthily of God, as no faithful Creator, as
having no care, no love, no bowels of compassion towards
the workmanship of His hands ; not to mention that
dragon's tail, I mean the long bead-roll of enormous
notions and conceits, which attends the doctrine of personal
reprobation from eternity, the account whereof is to be
seen elsewhere.　Whereas if it be supposed, as according
to the evident scope of the context it ought, that by what
God revealed concerning Esau, or his posterity in him, He
signified unto the world, that they who should not submit
to His counsel and pleasure for their justification, and seek
it by faith in Jesus Christ, should be for ever excluded
from the heavenly inheritance : such a discovery as this is
apparently of rich and blessed consequence unto men."

CHAPTER IX.

CONTENDS FOR A COMPLETE TOLERATION IN OPPOSITION TO A LIMITED ONE PRO-
POSED BY THE INDEPENDENTS—THE FIFTH MONARCHY MEN—FRESH
ATTEMPT TO SUBJECT HIM TO A STATE PROSECUTION—A DIVISION IN HIS
CHURCH—HE ENGAGES IN THE BAPTISMAL CONTROVERSY—CHARACTER OF
DANIEL TAYLOR AND THOMAS LAMB.

WHEN the friends of Cromwell were investing him with
the protectorate, they drew up a scheme of polity, which
they entitled, "The Government of England;" and in
which it was specified, that all classes of people should
enjoy the free exercise of their religion, *who professed faith
in God by Jesus Chri·t*. After this, Cromwell called a
parliament, who, on the examination of that clause, pronounced it to signify, *All who held the fundamental doct·ines
of religion;* and accordingly appointed a committee further
to examine this subject, and to nominate a certain number
of divines, who were to draw up a list of such doctrines;
a professed belief of which was to be the test of toleration.
The committee consisted of about fourteen persons, who
named everyone his man. Archbishop Ussher was nominated
by Lord Broghill; but declined the service, on account of his
age and infirmities, and his unwillingness to wrangle with
the men who were to be associated with him. Mr. Baxter
was therefore appointed in his stead, and accordingly sent
for from Kidderminster to London. "But before I came,'
says he, "the rest had begun their work, and drawn up
some few of the propositions which they called fundamentals. The men that I found there were Mr. Marshall,
Mr. Reyner, Dr. Cheynell, Dr. Goodwin, Dr. Owen, Mr.
Nye, Mr. Sidrach Simpson, Mr. Vines, Mr. Manton, and
Mr. Jacomb."*

In settling the business for which they were convened,
these divines spent much time in learned strife and contention. Baxter, who was opposed to a general toleration,

* Reliquiæ Baxterianæ, Part Second, p. 197,

displayed greater liberality on this occasion than his col-
leagues generally. Possessing consummate acuteness and
subtlety, by his objections and remarks he gave some of
his brethren serious annoyance; and especially Dr. Owen,
whose principles and spirit in this debate excite no very
high opinion of his catholicism. "One merry passage,"
says Baxter, "I remember, occasioned laughter.   Mr.
Simpson caused them to make this a fundamental: 'He
that alloweth himself, or others, in any known sin, cannot
be saved.'   I pleaded against the word 'allowed;' and
told them that many a thousand lived in wilful sin, which
they could not be said to 'allow' themselves in, but confessed it to be sin, and went on against conscience, and
yet were impenitent and in a state of death; and that
there seemed a little contradiction between 'known' sin
and 'allowed:' so far as a man 'knoweth' that he sinneth,
he doth not 'allow,' that is, approve it.   Other exceptions
there were: but they would have their way, and my opposition did but heighten their resolution. At last I told them,
as stiff as they were in their opinion and way, I would
force them with one word to change or blot out all that
fundamental.   I urged them to take my wager: and they
would not believe me, but marvelled what I meant.   I
told them, that the parliament took the Independent way
of separation to be a sin; and when this article came
before them, they would say, 'By our brethren's judgment,
we are all damned men, if we allow the Independents, or
any other sectaries, in their sin.'   They gave me no
answer, but left out all that fundamental."*   It is scarcely
necessary to remark, that several of these divines were of
the Independent denomination, and that a majority of the
parliament were sticklers for Presbyterian uniformity.

That there are such doctrines of religion as those specified by the friends of Cromwell, a list of which these
divines were required to prepare, Mr. Goodwin was not
disposed to deny. No man was more deeply impressed
than he with the importance of revealed truth, and the
obligations of men to believe it upon the divine testimony.

* Reliquiæ Baxterianæ, Part Second, p. 199.

But in declaring to what doctrines individuals are required to yield their assent, upon pain of endless torment, he saw that regard should be had to their respective capacities, to their opportunities of obtaining religious knowledge, and to various other circumstances, concerning which God alone is competent to judge. At all events, he saw that this was a subject in which the civil magistrate had no legitimate authority to interfere; and that therefore the parliamentary committee, and the disputatious divines convened by their authority, might both suspend their idle toil. The just limits of the civil and ecclesiastical powers, in the knowledge of which Milton has represented the younger Vane as an eminent proficient, Mr. Goodwin understood above most men of that age.

> To know
> Both spiritual pow'r and civil, what each means,
> What severs each, thou hast learn'd, which few have done.

If Dr. Owen possessed those correct views on this subject, which his friends have so often ascribed to him, his acceptance of the office allotted him by the parliamentary committee reflects no honour upon his character. Why did he not rather inform his masters, that they were exceeding their just powers? This would have been much more creditable to him, as an advocate of religious liberty, than to be the tool of men who, either through ignorance or presumption, were taking upon themselves to usurp a prerogative totally unconnected with the civil office which they sustained. Christian truth is to be supported by Christian evidence, and not by whips, thumbscrews, prisons, and other appliances of the same kind.

While Cromwell's parliament were endeavouring to ascertain what doctrines of religion British subjects should believe as a qualification for the enjoyment of civil rights and privileges, they meditated the appointment of a few individuals, as the Triers of all candidates for the ministerial function. To these men it was proposed to give authority to prevent whom they pleased from entering into the church, or at least from possessing any of its revenues.

Under the oppressive measures of the Long Parliament
Mr. Goodwin had manfully defended universal liberty of
conscience ; and under the sway of the Protector, he could
not be an indifferent spectator, when arrangements were
in progress to invade the right of private judgment. With
him it was a principle, to which he always conscientiously
adhered, never to attempt by any means whatsoever to
bring into disrepute any government under which he was
actually placed. If he discovered any thing in its measures,
which he deemed unjust, he declared his opinion, and the
reasons upon which it was founded, with a firm and manly
tone, but always in language decorous and respectful. In
reference to the proposal of Cromwell's friends, that all
who professed faith in God by Jesus Christ should enjoy
the benefits of toleration; and that an inconsiderable
number of men should be appointed as the guardians of
the national pulpit, he drew up a very able pamphlet,
which he published under the title of "Thirty Queries,
modestly propounded, in order to a discovery of the
truth and mind of God in that Question, or Case of
Conscience : Whether the Civil Magistrate stands bound,
by way of duty, to interpose his Power or Authority in
matters of Religion and Worship of God ? 1653." He asks,

"Whether did not the Lord Christ rebuke His disciples, and that somewhat roundly, who desired a commission from Him to call for fire from heaven, as Elias
formerly had done, to consume those who refused to
receive Him? Did He not sharply reprove them in
saying, 'Ye know not what manner of spirit ye are of?'
meaning that they did not consider the nature of the
Gospel, and what lenity ought to be showed towards
sinners, in order to the propagation thereof, above what
the severity of the law admitted. And doth not the
reason which He immediately subjoined plainly show this
to have been His meaning ; *For the Son of Man is not
come to destroy men's lives, but to save them ?* As if He had
said, One great end of My coming into the world was not
that any man's life should be taken from him for My
sake ; but that I might mediate, persuade, and prevail

with those who otherwise are severe against offenders, as you are, to exercise all lenity and patience towards them, and to be tender over their lives, in order to the salvation of their souls?

"Whether the ancient saying amongst the fathers, *Sanguis Martyrum, semen Ecclesiæ,* i.e. 'The blood of the Martyrs was the seed of the Church,' be not altogether as true, and this upon the same account in reason, and experimented accordingly in all ages, that *Sanguis Hæreticorum, semen Hæreseos;* 'The blood of Heretics is the seed of Heresy?' And is not that saying of Tacitus, *Punitis ingeniis gliscit authoritas;* 'Punishment doth but make the authority and credit of any man's wit or parts to shine, and prevail the more;' altogether as true in matters of an ecclesiastical or Christian, as of a politic or civil import?

"Whether had not an Uzzah an honest and upright intention to accommodate the ark, and to preserve it from harm by shaking, when he put forth his hand to keep it steady by holding it? Or was the ark of God in any real danger of suffering inconvenience by the shaking of the oxen, in case Uzzah had not intermeddled to prevent it?

"Whether might Paul have been lawfully punished by the civil magistrate in Ephesus, for that sedition or tumult, which was occasioned in this city by his preaching the Gospel; and particularly of this doctrine, 'That they be no gods that are made with hands?' If not, whether may such ministers, upon occasion of whose preaching tumults are frequently raised by rude and inconsiderate people, be punished by the Christian magistrate upon this account? Or ought not rather the principals in such tumults to be inquired out and punished?

"Whether are any two, four, or six persons, suppose all of them godly, learned, and competently (yea, let it be, if you please, excellently) qualified for the ministry of the Gospel, competent judges of the gifts, parts, and ministerial abilities of many thousands of their brethren? Or

is it Christian, to set up Nebuchadnezzars in the church
of Christ? persons, I mean, who will ecclesiastically slay
whom they will, and whom they will keep alive; set up
whom they will, and whom they will put down? Or in
case it shall be judged expedient, that any such number
of persons be invested with such a prodigiousness of
power; who are competent judges of the meetness of
persons to be entrusted herewith? Especially where there
are so many thousands (as this nation through the
abundant blessing of God upon it affordeth) of very excellent abilities and endowments; amongst whom it is next
to an impossibility for men to single out any two, four, or
six persons, to whose worth and abilities all the rest shall
by any law of God, or of equity and reason, stand bound
to stoop or do homage? Or is it not a solecism in reason
and conscience, that greater parts, learning, and worth,
should be compelled to go on foot, whilst those that are
meaner and more servile are made to ride on horses?

"Whether, in case any two, four, or six persons shall
be advanced to that power and interest now mentioned,
are not they like to be the men who *wear soft raiment, and
live in kings' houses;* I mean, whose applications have been
to the greatness of this world; who by artifices and compli-
ances have insinuated themselves into the familiarity and
friendship of the *anointed cherubs* of the earth,—and are
able to give gifts unto men? And are such persons as
these, who cannot but be judged great lovers of this
present world, meet to be entrusted with that high umpirage
specified in the affairs of Jesus Christ?

"Whether, since the days of Christ and His apostles,
can it be proved, or is it at all probable, that ever any
person who preached the Gospel, how faithful and serviceable soever to God and men, was wholly free from error,
or universally orthodox? Or can it reasonably be thought
either pleasing to God, or profitable unto men, or advanta-
geous to the Gospel, that no man should be admitted to the
preaching of it, but only those who shall be adjudged by a
few men, (and these in some things, without all doubt,
possibly in many things, weak and erroneous themselves;)

to be throughout the whole circumference of their faith unspotted with error, and in all their tenets and opinions unquestionably orthodox and sound? Or in case some heterodox or unsound opinions may be tolerated in those who shall be permitted to preach the Gospel, what, or of what nature, or to what degree dangerous, may these opinions be? Or who, according to the word of God, shall be judged meet to umpire in this great and difficult affair?

" Whether it is meet or Christian, for any man, or number of men, (especially for any smaller or inconsiderable number,) to presume so far of their own abilities, wisdom, learning, knowledge, insight into the Scriptures, &c., as to judge themselves worthy to prescribe authoritatively, and to the exposing of those whom they shall make delinquents to civil penalties or inconveniences, unto the gifts, parts, learning, and knowledge of other men, and these probably no ways inferior, possibly superior, to themselves in all such qualifications and endowments? Or is it Christian or reasonable, either to tempt men into such a conceit, or to indulge men under such a conceit, of themselves, by delegating such a power or authority unto them?

" Whether, is not *the manifestation of the Spirit*, (as the apostle termeth the manifest gifts of the Spirit,) *given to every man to profit withal?* If so, who can with a good conscience inhibit such from publishing the Gospel, upon pretence of an unsoundness in some disputable opinions, or for want of that which some men call ordination ; whose abilities for that work are at least competent, and the exercise of them desired by many for their edification ?

" Whether did those Christians who, upon a great persecution raised against the church at Jerusalem, being *scattered abroad, went every where preaching the word*, pass any test of their abilities, or sufficiency for the work, before they put forth their hand unto it? Or is their fact in preaching the Gospel upon such terms, and before any public approbation, any way censurable by the Word of God?

" Whether are not all men bound to *pray that the Lord would send forth labourers into His harvest;* and if their prayer in this behalf be, as it may and ought to be, effectually fervent, whether shall it not prevail, and consequently will not the Lord of the harvest Himself send forth labourers hereinto? If so, are not such persons, who shall be commissioned with power to elect and reprobate whom they please, amongst those whose hearts shall stir them up to labour in this harvest, more like to refuse or keep back those (at least some of them) whom the Lord shall send forth (i. e. stir up their hearts to go) into this harvest, than any ways to accommodate him in his way, or to promote the harvest-work itself?"

On the appearance of Mr. Goodwin's " Queries," two anonymous pamphlets were immediately published against him. One of these was a formal defence of the coercive power of the magistrate in the affairs of conscience; and was entitled, "Master John Goodwin's Queries Questioned, concerning the Power of the Civil Magistrate in matters of Religion, by One Query opposed to his Thirty. Query: Whether the Fourth Commandment doth not sufficiently justify and enjoin the Power of the Civil Magistrate in matters of Religion? 1653." The other pamphlet is a sort of satirical vindication of Mr. Goodwin, who had, previously to the publication of his " Queries," given his signature to an address to the government, recommending some regulations of an ecclesiastical nature. This piece was entitled, "An Apology for Mr. John Goodwin; who, having subscribed Proposals to the Magistrate concerning matters of Religion, after that, makes Thirty Queries, Whether it be the Magistrate's Duty to interpose his Authority in matters of Religion. 1653."

To both these nameless assailants Mr. Goodwin drew up a reply, which he published under the title of "The Apologist Condemned: or, A Vindication of the Thirty Queries, together with their Author, &c., by way of Answer to a scurrilous pamphlet, published, as it seems, by a Proposalist, under the mock title of an Apology for

Mr. John Goodwin; together with a brief touch upon another pamphlet, entitled, Mr. J. Goodwin's Queries Questioned. 1653."

In answer to the man who assumed the character of an advocate, Mr. Goodwin says,

" The Gentleman, the Apologist, being, as I understand, a graceling of the greatness of this world, can have, in my understanding, no reasonable ground for taking sanctuary behind the curtain, but only some consciousness, that his pamphlet is beneath him, and that it would rather take from than add to him, if his name were known. He seems to be of that race of men, whose conscience will allow them to do evil, but their prudence will not allow them to bear the shame belonging to it, if they know how to help it.

" It is obvious to every eye that looks into the mock-apology, that the main projecture of it was the propounding of this main query and wonder, as the author terms it, ' How the same hand could subscribe the Ministers' Proposals for the Advancement of Religion, to the supreme magistrate; and yet propose this question, whether the magistrate stands bound, by way of duty, to interpose his authority in matters of religion.' He seems to promise unto himself the present downfall of the credit and esteem of the Querist, and consequently of his Queries, upon the sound of this ram's horn,—the bare proposal of his Query.

" But suppose the hand he speaks of had subscribed the said proposals, upon the terms insinuated, (which will be found to be an undue insinuation,) is it such a wonder, how Peter, that had denied his Lord and Master before a damsel, should yet confess Him with so much courage as he did, before a council afterwards? Or is it such a wonder, how he that doth weakly once, should at any time after do more wisely? Nay, questionless, of the two, it is the greater wonder, that he who hath stumbled and fallen to the earth should not rise and get up, than that he should not always lie upon the ground.

" But may not the Apologist bear the shame of being a false witness against the Querist, upon the like account on which they that witnessed against Christ, that He had said, 'I am able to destroy the temple of God, and to build it in three days,' are stigmatized by the Holy Ghost for false witnesses? For doth he not represent the subscription of the Querist to the Ministers' Proposals, as if he subscribed the reasonableness of the said Proposals, or the meetness of them to be put in execution; when he expressly declared, together with a friend of his, who subscribed at the same time, unto Mr. Nye, who importunately solicited our subscriptions, that he was not satisfied with the contents of the said Proposals, neither could he own or subscribe them, as meet to be put in practice? Hereupon Mr. Nye, affectionately pursuing his motion for our subscriptions, expressed himself to this effect: That though we were not satisfied touching the meetness of things contained in the said proposals, to be practised, yet we might lawfully subscribe them, as meet to be delivered unto, and to be taken into consideration by the committee. We, apprehending no snare, danger, or inconvenience in it, to subscribe them in such a notion, and with such a declaration of ourselves as this, and being desirous to go as far with our brethren of the ministry as ever our judgments and consciences would permit us, yielded accordingly, and subscribed. But to mention this by way of *Apology for Mr. John Goodwin*, had been to prevaricate with the design: and besides, to act at any rate of fairness is a strain of ingenuity higher, (I fear,) than the heart of a Proposalist is willing to be wound up unto. It is no marvel, that he hates the light: this, as our Saviour observeth, being the property of him that doeth evil. In the mean time, I find how hard a thing it is, so much only as to touch pitch, and not be defiled. I shall, I trust, from henceforth remember, that the generation of men with whom I had to do in this business,

> Fœnum habet in cornu : longe fugiam.
>
> A lock of hay tied to their horn they have :
> Far from them I shall flee, myself to save."

Mr. Goodwin's reply to the Apologist is explanatory

rather than otherwise; but his answer to his other opponent is argumentative, and contains a spirited and able defence of universal freedom in the affairs of private conscience. At the conclusion of his pamphlet, he says, " By the sense of this Antiquerist and Apologist, touching the interposure of the magistrate's power in matters of religion, it appeareth sufficiently, that if the land had a Phalaris king over it, there would be found more than one Perillus to make him brazen bulls for the tormenting of such Christians, who are either too weak or too wise to swim down the stream of a state-religion, or to call men Rabbi."

While Mr. Goodwin was thus laudably anxious to pre- serve the civil power from all unchristian interference in ecclesiastical affairs, he was equally desirous to establish its secular prerogatives, and to promote subjection to its authority. On the abolition of the regal power in England, and the transfer of the supreme authority to the Protector, many classes of people were inclined to insubordination and revolt. The royalists were vexed to see the sceptre in the hands of Cromwell, and longed to place the Prince of Wales on the throne of his ancestors. The republicans hated Cromwell for seizing a power which they thought no individual ought to possess, and for disappointing all those hopes of liberty which he himself had induced them to cherish : while others were impatient of all restraint, and desirous of bringing back " the reign of chaos and old night," as preparatory to the formation of one grand monarchy under the government of the Son of God. To soften the asperities of these disaffected persons, and in compliance with the urgent wishes of his friends, Mr. Goodwin published a small tract entitled, " Dissatisfaction Satisfied; in Seventeen sober and serious Queries, tending to allay the Discontents and satisfy the Scruples of per- sons dissatisfied about the late revolution in government, &c.; and to guide every man's feet in the way of his duty, and the public peace." In this inoffensive publication, which bears the date of 1654, he reminds the complainers, that there can be no moral evil in obeying just and equi-

table laws, by whomsoever enacted; that the apostolic
declaration, "The powers that *be* are ordained of God," is
the standing rule by which private Christians ought to
walk, and not those intricacies in point of title, of which
the generality of men are not competent judges; and that
it is a flagrant violation of the precepts of the Gospel, for
persons occupying no public station to attempt the subversion of government, or to bring it into disrepute by
popular clamour : positions which show the practical difficulties to which theoretical principles, on the subject of
civil government, directly lead.

An answer to these Queries was speedily drawn up by
one of the democratic levellers of that age, whose name
does not appear. "To this answer," says Mr. Goodwin,
"being delivered to me in manuscript, I judged myself
concerned to make some reply : which I accordingly did,
and published it."* This reply, which is entitled, " Peace
Protected, and Discontent Disarmed," was particularly
designed to moderate and to satisfy the Fifth Monarchy
Men. It is decidedly conciliatory and pacific in its character. In the preface the author remarks, that by some he
had been pronounced a " time-server," and a " worshipper
of the greatness of this world." To which he replies, " If
by time-serving they mean subjecting a man's self to
serve, with all diligence and faithfulness, the common
interest of the men of the times wherein he liveth, I plead
guilty to the indictment. I have, in this sense, been a time-
server well nigh ever since I was capable of the service.
But, if by time-serving be meant any unchristian or unmanlike compliance either with the head or tail of this
world, for secular accommodation, I can wash my hands
in the laver of David's innocency; and with an erect
conscience say, 'They lay to my charge things that I know
not.' And herein, I suppose, all those who have known
my principles and practice will be my compurgators."

In the year 1654, a fresh appeal to the civil power against
him was made, by a number of persons belonging to the
Presbyterian denomination. A small tract was drawn up

* Triumviri, Preface.

under the title of "A Second Beacon Fired;" consisting of extracts from various books, which were said to be heretical or blasphemous. In this pamphlet was inserted a quotation from Mr. Goodwin's "Redemption Redeemed," but so falsified in the transcription, as to bear a sense totally different from that which the author designed it to express. This piece was formally presented to Cromwell and to the parliament, accompanied by a petition for some legislative enactment to restrain the liberty of the press, and prevent the publication of such works as were not Calvinistically orthodox. The men who submitted to be the tools of a party in this dishonourable transaction, were six London booksellers; in reference to whom Mr. Goodwin published a very interesting and able pamphlet under the title of "A Fresh Discovery of the High Presbyterian Spirit: or, The Quenching of the Second Beacon Fired, 1654." This publication contains a letter addressed to those booksellers, in which the author complains of the injury done to him by the falsification of his words, argues at considerable length in defence of the liberty of the press, and urges them as Christians and gentlemen to make some acknowledgment of their misconduct. To this letter he received a scurrilous reply, which he has also published with notes and comments upon its several paragraphs. Those booksellers declared their design to give publicity to the two letters which had formerly passed between Mr. Goodwin and Mr. Caryl, concerning a passage in the "Redemption Redeemed:" Mr. Goodwin therefore inserted those documents in the work before us, that he might prevent the appearance of mutilated copies.

In his address to the reader, Mr. Goodwin says, "I shall not impose upon either thy time or patience at present: the brief of the story is this: Six London Booksellers, whose names thou wilt find mentioned in the superscription of the ensuing letter, and subscribed to the second, all as it should seem devout homagers to the Presbyterian fraternity of Sion College, not long after the first sitting of the present parliament, presented to the lord protector and the parliament a small pamphlet, entitled,

A Second Beacon Fired. In this pamphlet, amongst errors and blasphemies, by them so called, and some of them, in my judgment, too truly such, they cite some words of mine, out of a passage of my book of Redemption, leaving out others, which give the sense and import of the passage. These words, thus sycophantly and traducingly severed from their fellows in the same sentence, they present to the lord protector and parliament, as containing in them blasphemy and error. It was some while after the presentment of the pamphlet before I came to the sight or knowledge of it. At last, hearing that somewhat published by me was listed in their muster-roll of heresies and errors, to serve the design of their petition for the restraint of the press, as also of their no-Christian intendments against me otherwise; I purchased a sight of the pamphlet; and comparing the transcription, as they had mangled and misfigured it, with my words, I found myself most notoriously wronged and abused. Hereupon I wrote a letter to the said gentlemen booksellers, desiring Christian and equitable reparation of my name and repute, which they had not a little damnified by that egregious falsification of my words and meaning. These gentlemen, instead of giving me that satisfaction which Christianity and conscience required, return me such an answer to my letter as if they had taken unto themselves seven spirits worse than that by which they, or whosoever for them, indited the said pamphlet, and the falsifications thereof; and are so far from acknowledging any wrong done unto me, by misusing me and my words, that they justify themselves in that high misdemeanor, and seem to think that they do God service in straining the peg of that iniquity yet higher. Notwithstanding, I may, I suppose, fully acquit the said gentlemen booksellers from the guilt of drawing up the said responsatory writing: this I judge to be the froth of another spirit, which some years since leaped upon me, and attempted to rend and tear me:

Sic oculos, sic ille manus, sic ora ferebat.

Such eyes, such hands, such mouth, that spirit had.

Only the said gentlemen have involved themselves in the guilt of the unchristian contents of the said writing, by consent and subscription, and possibly by solicitation also; though I rather incline to think that the penman was chosen and requested to the work, not by men that use to *sell*, but by some who are more frequently wont to *buy* books. That motto in their title-page, *For Sion's sake we cannot hold our peace;* whose device soever it was, seems by the contents of the book, not to be meant of Sion, in the common acceptation of the word, as it signifies the· church of God, but rather of Sion College, in London. For certain it is, that the pamphlet is not calculated with any relation at all to the interests of the church of God; but most exactly for the interest of Sion College and her children. Doubtless whosoever was the enditer of the answer to my letter might have stood in the high priest's hall without any danger: his speech would never have betrayed him to have been of Galilee.

"Therefore as Paul, having received reproachful measure from men, and those failing in their duty who ought to have vindicated him, complains that he was compelled himself to appear in his own vindication, which otherwise he had rather should have been the work of others; in like manner, I am compelled once again to take hold of shield and buckler in mine own defence, and either to make or to keep those things concerning myself straight in the minds and thoughts of men, (if it may be,) which· men of most untrue suggestions have endeavoured to pervert and make crooked.

"And because the gentlemen booksellers, or rather the son of their right hand, their amanuensis, challenge me to print Mr. Caryl's letter about the passage of their falsification, sent unto me some years since, and threaten me that they may do it for me, if I will not, glorying over this letter, as if the publishing of it would confound me, and that the reasons therein against the said passage in my book were so satisfactory, that they did effectually silence me; I have therefore published both this letter of his to me, and mine also to him, which occasioned it. The truth is, I had printed both these letters presently upon their writing and sending, but only for a clause in Mr. Caryl's letter, wherein he insinuates his unwillingness to have passages of that nature made public. So that it was only out of my respects to Mr. Caryl, that I then forbare the printing of them, and should have done so still, had not these importune sons of High Presbytery thus reproachfully and triumphingly clamoured upon me to do it. But as for any reasons against the passage, either satisfactory or unsatisfactory, that letter mentioneth none, unless it be the asserting of the author's own judgment, and some other men's, in the point, in opposition unto mine, notwithstanding any thing offered by me in my book. If either the booksellers, or book-buyers, judge this a reason so *satisfactory as effectually to silence me for ever*, I cannot but judge them to be of the race and lineage of those who are over easy of satisfaction for their own advantage. Besides, of such a reason as this, I was not, nor lightly could be, ignorant, before Mr. Caryl's letter came to me.

" Such personal contests as these have always been the regret of my genius : and if I thought not that my reputation may be of more concernment unto others, than I judge it to be to myself, I should not move heart, hand, or foot, to pursue the rescue ; but abandon it to the lust and folly of those who have attempted to make a prey and spoil of it : but I remember a good saying of Austin : ' For ourselves, brethren, our conscience sufficeth ; but for you, our name also had need be excellent :'* and Jerome's advice was, that ' no man should sit still under a suspicion or charge of heresy.' †

" I trust this small piece may do some service unto the world in promoting and perfecting the discovery of the folly of those men, who resist that great evangelical truth (with its complices) which asserteth, That God, with His antecedent and primary intentions, intended the salvation of the whole world by Jesus Christ. Or however God, and the consciences of men, shall agree about the event and

---

* Nobis, fratres, sufficit conscientia nostra : sed propter vos etiam fama pollere debet.   † In suspicione Hereseos nolo quenquam esse patientem.

success of it, it here presents its services unto thee, good reader, together with the Christian respects and further service of thy cordially devoted friend and servant in Christ,

JOHN GOODWIN."

Mr. Goodwin's letter is addressed to his "Christian friends, Mr. Thomas Underhill, Mr. Samuel Gellibrand, Mr. John Rothwell, Mr. Luke Fawn, Mr. Joshua Kirton, Mr. Nathaniel Webb," to whom he says,

"GENTLEMEN,

"A FEW days since, an ill-conditioned pamphlet, entitled, '*A Second Beacon Fired,*' presented to the lord protector and parliament, fell into my hands. I find all your names printed to it; but know not whether your hearts be to it, and were consenting to the publishing and presentment of it; or whether some son of Belial, taking the advantage, it may be, of some of your known weaknesses, and desirous to disport himself with your disparagement, did not, without your consent, borrow your names, to father so hard-favoured a birth of his own. The reasons why I cannot but a little demur, whether the piece be yours or no, are, (1.) Because I find in it most unchristian falsification: even that which some would call forgery. (2.) Because I find in it, likewise, such counsels offered to the lord protector and parliament, under a pretext of godliness and zeal for Zion, which are obstructive to the sovereign interest of both. (3.) And lastly, there is a scent of such a spirit in the said pamphlet, which teacheth men to suppose that gain is godliness. I confess, that notwithstanding any personal knowledge of any of you, the pamphlet may be yours, under all the three characters of unworthiness now specified: for I know none of you beyond the face; and only one of you so far: yet report hath so far befriended some of you in my thoughts, that I am hardly able to conclude you all under the guilt of the shameful and unchristian enormities, which dare look the parliament and the world in the face out of those papers. For, (to touch the first in one instance only, not having opportunity of making proof of more at the present,)

"Page 4, of the said pamphlet, this absurd passage is charged upon me in my book of Redemption : 'In case any assurance of the unchangeableness ' of God's love were to be found in, or regularly deduced from, the Scriptures, it were a just ground to any intelligent man to question their authority, and whether they were from God or no.' Surely they who lay this saying to my charge may with as much honesty and conscience, and with as much appearance of truth, impeach David as guilty of saying, 'There is no God;' (Psalm xiv. 1;) or make the Apostle Paul to say, (Rom. x. 9,) 'If thou shalt confess with thy mouth the Lord Jesus, thou shalt be saved.' For though these words are to be found in these sacred authors, respectively, yet the sense they make, otherwise than in concert with the other words relating to them, was as far from their author's meaning as the heavens are from the earth. David was far enough from affirming, that there is no God, and Paul from saying, that if a man with his mouth confess the Lord Jesus, he shall be saved; yet the words of which both sayings consist are extant in their writings. In like manner the Beacon Fires, whoever they be, you or others, (for I shall not charge you with the folly, but upon better evidence,) commit the foul sin of forgery, in making me say, in their pretended transcription out of my book, that in case 'any assurance of the unchangeableness of God's love were to be found, or could regularly be deduced from the Scriptures,' &c. Whereas (besides several other words in the sentence) they leave out the characteristical word, *Such;* [any 'Such assurance of the unchangeableness,' &c.,] the word that is the heart and soul of the sentence; that gives a most rational and orthodox relish to the whole period, and without which the passage contains no more my judgment, than theirs who forged the transcription. For my opinion, which I argue and assert in several places, upon occasion, in my book of Redemption, is that the love of God, in all His counsels and decrees, is unchangeable; and consequently that an assurance of this unchangeableness is regularly enough deducible from the Scriptures, and this without any prejudice to their divine authority; yea, rather, to the establishment and confirmation hereof. So far am I, either from thinking or saying, that if in case any assurance of the unchangeableness of God's love were to be found in, or could regularly be deduced from the Scriptures, it were a just ground to any intelligent man to question their authority. Therefore they who have accused me, especially unto the parliament, of such a saying, have the greater sin. That kind of unchangeableness of God's love, the assurance of which I affirm, were it to be in the Scriptures, would be a just ground to an intelligent and considering man to question their authority, I had immediately before described, and sufficiently explained, in the reason of the said assertion; which I immediately subjoin in these words: 'For that a God, infinitely righteous and holy, should irreversibly assure the immortal and undefiled inheritance of His grace and favour unto any creature whatsoever, so that though this creature should prove never so abominable in His sight, never so outrageously and desperately wicked and profane, He should not be at liberty to withhold this inheritance from him, is a saying, doubtless, too hard for any man, who rightly understands and considers the nature of God, to bear.' From these words it plainly enough appears, that it is not *any assurance* of unchangeableness of God's love, as the Beacon Firers most unconscionably suggest to the parliament, and to the world, which I conceive to be a just ground to any intelligent and considering man to question the authority of the Scriptures, in case it could be found in them: but *such* an assurance hereof, by virtue of which, men turning aside from Christ, after Satan, from ways of righteousness and truth, to walk in ways of all manner of looseness and profaneness, may, notwithstanding, with secure confidence, promise salvation unto themselves, and that God will never take away His love from them. And whether such an assurance of the unchangeableness of God's love as this, were the Scriptures any ways confederate with it, (which far be it from every Christian soul to imagine,) would not be derogatory or prejudicial in the highest to their authority, let the Beacon Firers themselves, or any other persons, who make any conscience of putting a difference between God and the devil, determine.

"That pernicious counsel against the liberty of printing, and for the subjecting of the learning, parts, and abilities of all the men in the nation, unto the humour and conceit of a few, who, for their comporting with the religion of the times, shall be surnamed 'orthodox,' which the said Beacon Firers do, in effect, very passionately commend unto the parliament, and which, were it put in execution according to the terms of the suggestion, would certainly fire both city and country, as well as Beacons; should argue the *Second Beacon* not to be of your firing. For you are reputed friends unto Jesus Christ, and to the truth; and consequently who can imagine that you should give any advice, especially unto a parliament, which is of a threatening import, to the advancement and further discovery of Jesus Christ unto the world?

"What ground is there in the Word of God for the investing of Edmund, Arthur, and William, with a Nebuchadnezzarean power over the press, to stifle or slay what books they please, and what they please to keep alive, more than there is for the investing of Joshua, Peter, and Tobiah with the same? Or if the three latter be altogether as religious, judicious, learned, as the three former, by what rule of equity, reason, or conscience, shall they be more obnoxious in their writings, to the censure and disapprobation of these, than these in their writings unto them? Or by what rule delivered in the Word of God shall any man judge the three former, either more religious, learned, or judicious, and so more meet for the instrument under consideration, than the latter?

"Is not the granting of such a power over the press, as the Beacon Firers solicit the parliament to vest in a certain number of men, ill-consistent with the interest and benefit of a free commonwealth? Or may not the commonwealth deeply suffer by the exercise of such a power, in being thereby deprived of the benefit of the gifts and labours of many of her worthy members?

"If the supreme magistrate in a commonwealth be allowed to invest what persons he pleaseth with such a power over the press, is it not to be expected that only such persons shall be deputed to this trust by him, which are of his own judgment; and consequently shall comply with a state-religion? And are men of this character competent arbitrators, between persons of their own party and persuasion, and those who are contrary minded to them in their contests about truth and error? And in case the magistrate himself be unsound in the faith, (as men of his order have no privilege of exemption from error, more than other men,) shall not our press-masters be unsound also? and, consequently, shall we not have error countenanced and set at liberty, and truth imprisoned, and condemned to silence and obscurity?

"That great evil, the spreading of errors and heresies, the prevention whereof the advice given touching the press pretendeth unto, is not likely to be at all prevented, but promoted rather by it, should it be put in execution. For,

Quod licet ingratum est, quod non licet acrius urit.

And little question there is, but that, in case the liberty of the press shall be by any law restrained, they who otherwise would be but indifferent whether they published their weak, it may be their erroneous and wicked conceptions, will be hereby provoked to do it, though more secretly. Stolen waters are sweet.

"In case they shall, by any such law, be kept from venting their notions by the press, or by the masters of the press be prohibited the printing of them, they will be so much the more diligent and intent to propagate them privately; and probably gain many more disciples this way than by the other. The profane and vain babbling of Hymeneus and Philetus fretted like a canker, although they wanted the opportunity of the press for their propagation.

"The setting of watchmen with authority at the door

of the press, to keep errors and heresies out of the world, is as weak a project, as it would be to set a company of armed men about a house to keep darkness out of it in the night. For as the natural darkness cannot be prevented or dispelled, but by the presence of light, nor needeth there be any other thing, either for the preventing or dispelling it, but light only; so neither is it possible either to prevent or remove errors and heresies, which are spiritual darkness, but only by shining spiritual light in the hearts and understandings of men; neither needeth there any thing but this to effect either.

"Errors and heresies, the less they play in sight, are like to defend themselves upon terms of more advantage, and to lengthen out the days of their continuance amongst men for the longer time. For by this means they are kept from the clear and distinct knowledge of judicious and learned men, who otherwise being both able and willing to perform so worthy a service, would publicly detect and confute them. And I verily believe that the printing of J. Biddle's most enormous and hideous notions about the nature of God, and some other very weighty points in religion, will bring the judgment of bloody and deceitful men upon them; which, (according to David's award) is, not to live out half their days. (Psalm lv. 23.)"

In their abusive reply to our author's letter, these booksellers inquire of Mr. Goodwin, why he did not answer Dr. Kendall? to which he says, " Why do not you ask Dr. Owen, why he hath not all this while answered Mr. Horne? As charity, so discipline, begins at home. Yet I think I may in part excuse the Doctor at this turn. For, doubtless, Mr. Horne's *Open Door* is too hard to Dr. Owen to shut; and his most satisfactory answer would be, to acknowledge as much. If he should make this answer, he should deserve the commendation of a *recte respondes*. But my answer to your question is, that I have publicly engaged myself, (death, sickness, or other occasional intrusions not preventing me,) to answer more considerable men than he or his are. Besides, some of his own judgment in the controversies have no such opinion of what he hath written, as to think that it needs much answer. The reason hereof I conceive to be, because his answers, more generally, stand upon such odd, uncouth, wild, and reasonless principles, in which the generality of his own party can neither find sap nor savour, nor tell what to make of them. Yea, if all hear-says be orthodox, Mr. Vice-Chancellor himself, his co-adjutor against the truth, hath pulled in his horns again, which he put out to such a length in his quaint encomiastic of him, prefixed before his former book. But the consideration now mentioned, in reference to Dr. Kendall, is another reason why an answer to his book may be spared, without any great detriment or loss to the cause. Yea, upon the same account, an answer given to it, though never so satisfactory and full, would amount to no more than an answer *ad hominem:* others of his judgment would be as little satisfied, or convinced by it, because it would not reach their apprehensions."

The following accusations and replies illustrate the character of the parties at issue.

BOOKSELLERS: "You have been a trier these twenty years; and you have cause to fear, that you will be trying all things so long, that you will hold nothing at last. You are now about sixty years of age, and one of us remembering a verse,

Dum quid sis dubitas, jam potes esse nihil."

MR. GOODWIN: "You guess somewhat near the years of my earthly pilgrimage. I bless the God of Heaven, with my whole heart and soul, for sparing me so long, until I had thoroughly tried many of the doctrines of your teachers, and found them liars; and had opportunity to stigmatize them for such publicly, and to alarm the world concerning the danger of them. You see I hold several things too fast for your stoutest champions to wrest them from me. Therefore you shoot this arrow at a wrong mark."

BOOKSELLERS: "They that know you well, think you so proud, that they fear you have not as yet been with Jesus Christ to humble you."

GOODWIN: "You are much mistaken: there are none

but those that are strangers or enemies to me, that think thus of me. They that know me well are otherwise minded; and upon good grounds believe, that I would be willing and free, notwithstanding all your provocations, to carry your books after you; yea, to stoop to loose the latchet of the shoe of the meanest of you, had I any competent ground to judge, that such a service would turn to any spiritual or temporal advantage to you. But your tongues, it seems, are your own, and you think you are at liberty to say with them what you list."

BOOKSELLERS: "We have heard of a great Rabbi, who was converted from Cards and Sack-Possets to Errors and Blasphemies: but we spare you."

GOODWIN: "For the story of your Great Rabbi, it seems it is but a hear-say. If you had seven more as wise stories to join with it, I cannot imagine what service they would do you. Would they make you seem either more wise, or orthodox, or religious; or less unworthy, than you appear to be? Or if you intend to theatrize me under the fiction of your Great Rabbi, the conversion you speak of will not accommodate you with truth, in respect of either of the terms; either those *a quibus*, or those *ad quos*. First for Cards: there have now twenty years passed over my head since my coming to the city: of all this time I never spent so much as half a minute in the recreation: and for ten years at least together next before my coming, not a whit more. In my younger days, I confess, I did pass some of my precious hours in this vanity; yet without scandal, or any observation of inordinateness in my practice that way. As for *Sack-Possets*, counting from the first hour that I saw the light of the sun, I believe there are very few ministers about the City of London, though there be divers that have scarce lived half my days, but have fished as often in those ponds as I. If I be brought upon the stage by you, as a man of a servile appetite unto Sack-Possets, I believe I never came there before upon any such account.

"And for Errors and Heresies, whereunto your story, if it personates me, pretends that I have been converted, I confess I have been converted from Errors and Heresies truly so called, unto Errors and Heresies by you so called; that is, unto the acknowledgment of many worthy truths into the secret of which your souls, it seems, as yet never entered; which is the snare upon you to term them Errors and Heresies.

"For your sparing me, I could be content you should spare me less, upon condition you would not spare the truth so much."

To this vindication of himself against the six booksellers, who invoked the civil power to call him to an account for alleged heresy, which they professed to have found in his "Redemption Redeemed," these officious gentlemen offered no reply; feeling doubtless that they were better qualified to stand behind a counter, and sell the literary productions of other men, than to construct syllogisms against so acute and practised a reasoner as the man whom they had rashly assailed. An anonymous writer, however, undertook their defence; but him Mr. Goodwin effectually refuted in a quarto pamphlet of twenty-three pages, bearing the title of "The Six Booksellers' Proctor Nonsuited: wherein the Gross Falsifications and Untruths, together with the Inconsiderate and Weak Passages found in the Apology for the said Booksellers, are briefly noted and evicted, 1655."

The pugnacious booksellers and their nameless apologist were the mere organs of the Presbyterian party, who were anxious to secure the civil establishment of their system of theology and of church government, to the exclusion of every other, and were bitterly hostile to Goodwin because of the able and manful stand which he made against them on both these grounds; assailing as he did with unrivalled power and determination their theory of Limited Redemption, and with equal zeal and ability contending that all coercion in matters purely religious is essentially unjust and antichristian, inasmuch as every man must give an account of himself to God. His anonymous assailant said that religious Toleration was Goodwin's "Diana;" to which he smartly replied, that Diana was an idol, and therefore, according to Scripture, powerless alike both for good and evil: whereas toleration is a benefit, which the Presbyterian party themselves were glad to enjoy; but he saw no reason why other classes of Christians should be denied the same boon, liberty of conscience being the birthright of our common humanity.

While Mr. Goodwin was thus employed in repelling the calumnious attacks of violent men, he was called to witness a division in his own church: a circumstance which proved to him an occasion of exquisite pain and sorrow, and appears to have been one of the principal hindrances to the completion of his "Redemption Redeemed." Thomas Lamb and William Allen, men of exemplary piety and strong sense, who had stood by him amidst all his persecutions, and had adorned their Christian profession for several years, imbibed the sentiments of the Anti-Pædo-baptists, and withdrew from their spiritual pastor. About twenty other persons followed their example, and, with these at their head, formed themselves into a separate church; conceiving it to be unlawful to associate for religious worship, and to frequent the Lord's table, with people who had not been baptized by immersion in their adult age. The exclusive and intolerant temper of these men, was the great fault of the Baptists in that day, as it has often been in more modern times. The excellent Baxter, a man of truly catholic principles, says, "Many that are against Infant Baptism, think it a matter of so high moment, that whosoever is not baptized at age, you may not hear them preach, nor receive the Lord's Supper with them, nor be of the same church, nor pray with them in their families. O what abundance of my own acquaintance are of this opinion!" *

The spirit by which Lamb and his friends were actuated, "being a spirit of division, it was not satisfied," says Mr. Goodwin, "with separating one part of the body from the other by *water* only, (over which there had been opportunity enough for spiritual commerce,) but magnified itself further to divide them by *fire* also; inflaming its proselytes

* Plain Scripture Proof, p. 10. Edit. 1651.

with such a zeal over their new way, that they judged
themselves more holy than to incorporate in church communion with any person who goeth not wondering after
it; how full of faith and of the Holy Ghost soever: I
judged myself called upon by God to resist him, and with
the waters of the sanctuary to quench the fire which he
had kindled. By this troublesome spirit, I was drawn to a
double contest. First, I was engaged to stop the mouth
of that plea, wherein he pleaded the unlawfulness of conjunction between believers Dipped and believers Undipped.
Secondly, unless I would give way to him, and suffer him
to carry away the truth from my people, I was necessitated with the drawn sword of the Spirit, to oppose him in
his way wherein he was attempting to circumvent poor
children of that baptismal patrimony, which their Heavenly
Father had settled on them, and which their first feoffees
in trust, the primitive Christians, did constantly and
conscientiously exhibit unto them. This double encounter
entrenched very deeply upon my time."* This appears
to have been the " troublesome importunity " of which he
complains in the preface to his Exposition, as preventing
him from paying that attention to the Second Part of his
Redemption Redeemed which was necessary for the finishing
of that work.

On the Baptismal Controversy, which was then warmly
agitated, Mr. Goodwin published three tracts : the first of
these is entitled, "Philadelphia: or XL Queries peaceably
and inoffensively propounded, for the discovery of Truth
in this case of Conscience : Whether persons baptized, (as
themselves call Baptism,) after a profession of Faith, may
or may not lawfully hold communion with Churches who
judge themselves truly Baptized, though in Infancy, and
before such Profession ? 1653." Our author's second tract
on this subject is denominated, " Water-dipping no firm
footing for Church-Communion : or, Considerations proving it not simply Lawful, but Necessary also in point of
Duty, for persons baptized after the new mode of Dipping,
to continue Communion with those Churches, or embodied

* Triumviri, Preface.

Societies of Saints, of which they were Members before the said Dipping, 1653." The titles of these pamphlets explain with sufficient precision the topics of which they treat. The author contends that a difference of opinion and practice concerning the subjects and mode of baptism ought not to separate the members of Christian churches from each other. His principles are catholic, and his manner of writing affectionate and convincing. Speaking of those who had seceded from him, and for whose benefit he had taken up his pen, he says, "My conscience beareth me witness, that as I have been cordially and Christianly respectful and friendly to these men, as far as I have had opportunity to serve them; so I am still ready to bow down at the feet of the meanest of them for their temporal or spiritual accommodation."

Mr. Goodwin's third publication relating to this controversy is a quarto volume containing upwards of four hundred pages, and is entitled, "Cata-Baptism: or, New Baptism waxing Old, and ready to Vanish Away, 1655." This work is divided into two parts: the first contains "fifty-five Considerations, with their respective proofs and consectaries," designed to remove the scruples of those who would exclude the Children of believing Parents from the ordinance of Baptism: the second is an answer to a tract published by Allen, under the title of "Some Baptismal Abuses briefly Discovered." This work of Mr. Goodwin is every way worthy of his great powers. It is written in a spirit of truly Christian meekness and forbearance; and at the same time is thoroughly argumentative, and replete with original information on the subjects of which he treats. In the course of this volume he makes frequent reference to Baxter's book on Baptism, and repeatedly mentions that learned and pious author in terms of high respect.

Though Mr. Goodwin had studied the baptismal controversy with deep attention, it was with great reluctance that he was induced to take any part in it; because his mind was intent upon the completion of his favourite work on the extent of Redemption. "Verily," says he, "I have gone round about the whole body of that doctrine which so much magnifieth itself against Infant Baptism, and have narrowly and with an unprejudiced eye observed all the limbs and joints thereof, and cannot find so much as one sound member or clean joint in it. The whole structure of it stands upon foundations which either are sandy or irrelative to what is pretended to be built upon them, and so are no true foundations of this doctrine."

"I had rather be at the expense of seven years' labour in an expedition against those who will not suffer the Lord Jesus Christ to inherit the glory of His ever-blessed work of Redemption, in the just compass and extent of it; who presume to set bounds to the grace of God, which He never set; who preach this in effect for Gospel to the world, that God never bare any good-will to the greatest part of them, but decreed from eternity to torment them with the vengeance of eternal fire :—who preach also, that those whom they call Elect, though they prove the first-born sons of Belial, and provoke the God of heaven with the height of all abominations, may abide all this while in the love of Election, and are in no possibility of miscarrying in the high concernment of salvation,—with twenty things more of like confederacy with these, and reproach those who are otherwise minded with names of an odious import, as Arminians, Socinians, Pelagians, which the enemy of truth puts between their lips whilst they sleep with their mouths open : I had rather serve seven years' hard service against the conceits of these men, than so many weeks, though with more ease, against the lighter dreams of persons led aside by the baptismal spirit."

Mr. Goodwin considered himself to be providentially called to engage in this controversy. He not only regarded the subject to be important in itself, inasmuch as baptism is an ordinance of Jesus Christ, but he saw that many of those who had imbibed the principles of Anti-Pædobaptism, had also sustained great spiritual loss. They not only exerted themselves to make divisions in Christian churches, but imagined themselves to be elevated to such "a throne of glory and perfection," that they "beheld the whole

z

Christian world under them, walking but as shadows, and
the greatest of them not worthy to come under the roof of
the meanest of their sanctuaries." Addressing these men,
he inquires, "Whether a great number of those who have
done homage to your way have not been spiritual losers
by the change? sensibly declining in those Christian principles and dispositions, which at first they brought with
them unto your way; as if their new baptism had not been
into Christ, but into old Adam? This I have observed,
and must needs testify, that not any one of them, as far as
an estimate can be made by what is discernible in point
of conversation, hath gained so much as the making of one
hair white or black, by the exchange of his baptism; but
sundry of them have lost many degrees of that sweet
Christian savour and love, wherewith they excellently
adorned the Gospel before."

"If by the interposure of these papers between persons
drowned in Anabaptism, and those whose heads are yet
above water, I shall be able, through God, to preserve
these from sinking, though I be not able to work miracles
in recovering any of the other; yet shall I do service, acceptable to my Lord and Master Christ, and to many of His
churches. Or however God shall please to dispose of my
labour, as to matter of success, I have discharged my conscience. Notwithstanding, consulting with my own genius
and spirit, I am apt to think, that I should not have
appeared in these controversies, had there not been a fire
of Anabaptism kindled in that house of God, which He
hath committed to my charge, and this by one of the
household; a man of a sober and grave temper, but of
somewhat too passive a disposition, from melancholic and
superstitious impressions. So hard is it to watch Satan
so narrowly, but that, at one time or other, he will
insinuate himself, in the likeness of an angel of light, into
the temple of God."

Mr. Goodwin, however, was far from considering all the
Baptists of that age as equally faulty. "Amongst men
walking in the way of Presbytery," says he, "we find
ground for that distinction which divideth them into high

and low; the latter being a harmless generation, the other next to insupportable. So amongst those of the Anabaptismal persuasion, there are some the illness of whose temper teacheth them to make fire and sword of their persuasion; others again, the soberness and sweetness of whose spirit preserveth them from annoying the churches of Christ with any misuse of their opinion. This obvious difference between men and men of the same persuasion induceth me to believe, that the evils which so frequently attend it are not so much in the persuasion itself, as in the moral constitution of the greatest part of those who are entangled with it."

In addition to an excellent preface, Mr. Goodwin's " Cata-Baptism " is introduced by a fine dedicatory epistle to Christians of the Baptist denomination; in which, with great openness and candour, he explains the motives by which he was actuated in publicly opposing their peculiar sentiments, and states what he conceived to be reprehensible in their general proceedings. This epistle is succeeded by an admirable address, of considerable length, to the members of his own church; admonishing them of the evils they ought conscientiously to avoid, and pointing out to them the means by which they might adorn their Christian profession, and make their calling and election sure. The whole is eminently pastoral, and highly honourable to its learned and pious author.

Mr. Goodwin's tracts on baptism, together with some other publications on the same subject, made a deep impression upon the mind of Lamb. Grieved with the narrow and exclusive spirit of several of his brethren, who wantonly unchurched all who were not of their party, he began, according to his own account, to be " pressed much in spirit to consider the grounds of separating " from his former friends: and reading Baxter's Plain Scripture Proof of Infants' Church Membership, and " Mr. John Goodwin's and Horne's books of Baptism," he perceived that the practice of baptizing children was of much greater authority than he apprehended; and that, had it been otherwise, the rent made by him in Mr. Goodwin's church

z 2

was unwarrantable. Convinced that he had been misled, and wishful to retrace his steps, he wrote to Mr. Baxter for advice, and afterwards applied to Mr. Goodwin's church for re-admission to communion with them. "I have been at Mr. Goodwin's congregation," says he, "to acknowledge my sin in separating from them upon such silly grounds, and have offered myself to break bread with them if they pleased: but withal told the whole church that, for two reasons, I could not come so close to them as heretofore; because of my relation to the poor people I now serve, (being not yet well lodged in a safe place,) and because of some scruples in my mind, whether Independency did not infer schism in the church universal."

Mr. Goodwin was no bigot; and the result of Lamb's application was creditable to the parties concerned. In a letter to Mrs. Lamb, Baxter says, "I have strong hopes, that if I were in London, I could persuade such as your husband, and Mr. John Goodwin, and many an honest Presbyterian minister, as great a distance as seems to be between them all, to come yet together, and live in holy communion." Lamb also stated in his correspondence with Baxter, "In respect of Mr. Goodwin's church, with whom I was for several years joined, their principles are larger for communion than others."—"They have of their own accord made a vote to receive me, when my spirit should be free to return; and indeed have always manifested much love to me." Lamb also added, "My spirit is much set against gay apparel, and following fashions: but Mr. Goodwin's church is as sober as most, I think as any." *

Lamb and Allen both renounced the principles of Anti-Pædobaptism, and after the Restoration conformed to the Episcopal Church. Lamb used frequently to occupy Mr. Goodwin's pulpit during his connexion with him, having been ordained an elder with solemn fasting and prayer, and with the full approbation of all his brethren. Allen was a remarkable character. He was delivered out of the snare of Antinomianism, early in life, under the ministry

* Reliquiæ Baxterianæ, Part I. p. 180. Appendix, p. 51.

of Mr. Goodwin; and for more than twelve years was a
member of his church. He had not enjoyed the advantage
of a liberal education, and was devoted to secular business
till he was far advanced in life; yet such was his proficiency
in sacred knowledge under the pastoral care of Mr.
Goodwin, and the bias of his mind to biblical studies, that
he wrote several tracts of practical and didactic theology,
which would have done credit to a grave and learned
divine. Most of these were collected in the year 1707,
and reprinted in a folio volume of seven hundred and
fifty-four pages, including a general preface by the Bishop
of Chichester, and a sermon on the author's death by Dr.
Kidder, Bishop of Bath and Wells.

"He was a most diligent inquirer after truth," says the
Right Rev. preacher; "he sought wisdom as silver, and
searched for her as for hid treasures. Nor did his labour
prove in vain; for he did understand the fear of the Lord,
and find the knowledge of God. God had given him a
great and clear understanding, a solid judgment and
ability; and he improved his talent to a very great
purpose.

"He read the Holy Scriptures with wonderful care and
diligence, attained to great understanding of the more
abstruse parts of them; and though he had not the advantage of the learned languages to direct him, yet by
acquainting himself with those who had, and by indefatigable diligence, he did arrive to so great a measure of
knowledge of those things which they do contain, as would
be very commendable in a well-studied divine.

"He wrote several very excellent books, that need no
recommendation to the world. They are well known, and
well esteemed; and the greatest clerk will have no cause to
be ashamed to have them placed amongst other authors
with which he is furnished.

"His great knowledge did not puff him up. His
charity and humility and modesty held proportion to it.
He was far removed from a high conceit of himself, or contempt of others. He was far from being pert and talka-

tive : far from ostentation and show; from insulting over
his adversaries, or vaunting of his victories.

" He was exactly just to all men in his dealings and
trade. Of this there is no question : and those that knew
him well can tell, that in making up his accounts he was
scrupulously so ; and took great care that an error or mistake in his correspondent should not be to his prejudice.
He was greatly careful to do no wrong, and had learned
to forgive.

" In him we might behold great knowledge, and the
profoundest humility; an ability to teach others, and the
greatest docibility or readiness to learn ; the courage and
resolution of a confessor, and at the same time, the
humility of a little child; a great charity without vaunting, a great zeal without faction, and a diligent pursuit of
truth without dogmatizing or study of parties."

While Mr. Goodwin's mind was so painfully affected on
account of the division made among his flock by Allen and
Lamb, he was called to sympathize with one of his most
beloved and valuable friends on the bed of death, and to
follow his remains to the tomb. This friend was Mr.
Daniel Taylor, a merchant in London, and author of the
Letter to John Vicars, inserted in a former chapter of
these memoirs. At the interment of this excellent man,
Mr. Goodwin delivered a discourse, which he afterward
published under the title of, " Mercy in her Exaltation : or,
A Sovereign Antidote against the Fear of the Second
Death. A Sermon preached at the Funeral of Daniel
Taylor, Esq.; in St. Stephen's, Coleman Street, London,
on the twentieth day of April, 1655." This sermon is an
admirable specimen of his talents as a preacher. The
subject is Christian Mercy, in the constant and vigorous
exercise of which its possessor, according the constitution
of the Covenant of Grace, is able to rejoice in the prospect
of the general judgment, and the awards of eternity. The
sermon is of considerable length, and is learned, argumentative, eloquent, and impressive. In the preface the author
states, that some of his hearers had expressed their apprehension, that several of his positions " trenched very near

upon the Popish doctrine of justification by works. But certain I am," says he, " that I speak nothing in reference to justification, nor did the subject of my discourse lead me to treat little or much of justification, especially of that which consists of remission of sins. I am not more clear and better resolved in my judgment touching the truth of any one doctrine of Christian religion, than that all the good works in the world, were they performed by any man that had sinned in the least, would not be able to procure the pardon of his sins. Pardon of sin cannot be obtained by doing good, but by suffering evil; and this by a person that is sinless. ' Without SHEDDING OF BLOOD there is NO REMISSION.'

" That justification which consists in the Divine approbation of men, as, ' Well done, good and faithful servant,' ' Then shall every man have praise of God,'—of which that is to be understood, ' Not the hearers of the law are just before God, but the doers of the law shall be justified,'—this kind of justification, without which no man shall be saved, is to be obtained by good works; yet not so properly by the merit of these, as by virtue of the law of God's most gracious and bountiful acceptation. And yet, to say that there is nothing at all in these works, or nothing more than in others contrary to them, to commend any man to God, is to reflect upon His wisdom and righteousness in the establishment of that law by which they come to be approved and accepted upon such terms."

In the introduction of this sermon Mr. Goodwin says, " It is well known to a great part of you, who now hear me, that for several years past I have put from me the custom of funeral elogies and commendations; bequeathing this service to the works of the deceased, which have a commission from God to perform it, if there be cause; (Prov. xxi. 1;) whereas I have none that I know of, especially not to do it in consort with the work now in hand. But I have declined the practice, partly because of the offensiveness of it to many, who are weak; partly because of the offensive misuse of it by some, who seem otherwise strong. I confess, that it was the saying of one long since, 'If a dishonest practice be in any case tolerable, it is for the procurement of a kingdom; in all other cases, justice and right must take place.' So if a minister of God could be venially tempted to dispense with so good a resolution, as that which he hath taken up against blowing a trumpet in the pulpit before the dead, my standing at present is upon the ground of such an opportunity; being called to preach at the interment of a man of most exemplary and signal worth, in every kind, and whose life can hardly be remembered by those who have any knowledge of it, without falling into an agony of sorrow for his death. It was the saying of the poet, in respect of the enormous vices of the times and place wherein he lived, that it was a hard matter not to write satirically; so I may well say, on the other hand, in respect of so many things so highly commendable and Christian in him, upon the occasion of whose death I am now speaking to you, a man must resist a temptation to refrain from praising him.

"However, partly for my resolution's sake, which is not far from a vow, but more especially for your sakes, whom it much more concerns to be made praiseworthy yourselves, than to hear another praised before you, I shall leave the deceased to the good report of all men, which he purchased at a high rate of well-doing, and of the truth itself, (the Word of God, which giveth large testimony to him and to all like him,) and shall, in the name of God, and of the Lord Jesus Christ, by the opening and applying of the words read unto you, make an attempt upon you, to make you, if it may be, like unto him in that which was his glory whilst he lived, and his rejoicing at his death,—his goodness and mercy. Mercy enlarged his heart to rejoice against judgment: and O how happy shall you be, if you will be persuaded to cast in your lot with him, and suffer God to put into your heart by His Word and Spirit, which are now about to put you upon the trial, to take part and fellowship with him in that his rejoicing."

The sermon contains little information concerning Mr.

Goodwin's departed friend: but this deficiency is supplied in a very considerable degree, by an admirable dedication to "Mrs. Margaret Taylor, the late wife of Mr. Daniel Taylor, deceased; Mr. Edmond Taylor, Mr. Samuel Taylor, his brethren, together with the rest of his kindred, friends, and acquaintance." In this beautiful composition Mr. Goodwin says, with regard to his "dear friend," "He was religious not of custom, but of conscience; nobly disdaining to prostitute his judgment to any vulgar opinion in matters appertaining to God, simply upon the credit of other men's faith; and withal studiously scrupulous of receiving any tenet until he had caused it to pass through the fire of a strict examination, and found that it would not burn. Whilst the strength of his body was able to bear the exercises of devotion, he maintained a constant and close communion with God; and in the time of his last weakness, a few weeks before his change, amongst other savoury discourse, he bemoaned himself, that since the prevailing of his distemper he was deprived of his heart-breaking opportunities with God. His heart was very high in desires after knowledge of the truth, and this in the most profound questions controverted between men of the greatest judgments in these days. Books of divinity that were judiciously or accurately written, his delight was, at his spare hours,

Nocturná versare manu, versare diurná ;

'By night to read, and not to spare by day.'

"He put no difference between persons either for their concurrence with him, or dissent from him, in matters of opinion, or form of worship. That which commended any person to him, was his own opinion of his integrity, and goodness of heart towards God. His signal integrity, justness, and clearness in dealings, as well in the administration of the trust committed to him, as in his private occasions, are freely testified by all that had to do with him in either kind. The greatness of his estate made no breach at all upon the goodness of his disposition. He observed no distance made between himself and the meanest of his brethren, by his abundance: persons even of the lowest degree, by his affableness and humility, found access to him upon all occasions; and few, if any, came from him discontented. His carriage was composed and grave, yet without affectation; his discourse season-able and savoury, without offence. His native temper seemed to incline him to much reservedness: but by judgment and conscience he reduced that which was less desirable in his inclination. His habit and garb every ways comely; suitable rather to his profession than estate. Whatever savoured of ostentation or vanity, he left to be taken up by persons of looser and lighter spirits. The full cup which God gave unto him, he carried with an even and steady hand, without spilling; yet freely gave to every man that was athirst, and came in his way, to drink.

"His intellectual endowments were given him by the largest measure, which God in these days is wont to mete unto men. His understanding was large, and very com-prehensive: his apprehension quick and piercing: his judgment solid and mature: his memory fast and faithful: his elocution distinct and clear, elegant and fluent, yet not luxuriant and pedantic. He was more than of ordinary abilities to argue the most thorny and abstruse points in divinity; ready of discerning where the quick of the con-troversy lay; very expert in the word of righteousness; able to draw waters of life out of such wells of salvation, from whence many men of good understanding and learning had not wherewith to draw because of the depth of them. He had a singular dexterity to make the rough things of business smooth, to untie knots, and disentangle intricacies, in all manner of affairs that were brought unto him. I scarce know any man amongst those he hath left behind, of like felicity with him in giving advice in cases of difficulty and doubtful consideration. In sum, as well for parts of nature as of grace, he was a highly accom-plished man, adorned and set forth by God, for a pattern for others."

That such men as Allen and Taylor should have placed themselves under Mr. Goodwin's pastoral care, and that their characters should have been formed under his ministry, are circumstances which are highly honourable to all the parties concerned. According to Mr. Baxter, Lamb was also a man of an eminently vigorous mind, of deep piety, and of great purity and uprightness of conduct. Concerning the other members of Mr. Goodwin's church we have little or no information: but in Allen's address to them after his separation, he expresses his views of their character, and of the religious advantages he had enjoyed during his union with them, in terms of the highest respect. "There have now, dearly beloved," says he, "several years passed over our heads, since first I obtained that good opinion from you, as to be admitted into your society. And sure I am, I shall not flatter you in acknowledging, that if I have not in all this time improved my spiritual estate very much, it is not because I have not had opportunity so to do, but because I have not had a heart fully to improve this opportunity. And however mine own dulness and indisposition have obstructed much of that increase which was, as I believe, intended me on your part, yet this I must acknowledge, to the praise of that rich and abundant grace of God that hath uttered itself among you, and hath been declared by you, that your love, diligence, faithfulness, and zeal, and the grace of God in them, have made such impressions upon me, as by which you may well, as I doubt not but you will, stand much endeared to me all my days. As for those Christian respects I have received from you, they have so much exceeded what I could well expect, as that I have not been under any temptation of neglect this way, whereby the bond of my union with you should be loosened."*

The following paragraphs extracted from Mr. Goodwin's "Admonition to the remainder of the flock of Christ, yet under his hand and charge," will serve to illustrate his temper at this period of his life, and the views which he entertained of several of the sects then in existence. It is prefixed to his "Cata-Baptism."

"Dear souls, for whom I expect to be called, and this

* Some Baptismal Abuses Discovered, Dedication.

very shortly, to give an account to the great Shepherd of the sheep, for the time you have already been, and shall yet continue under my hand : that I may give this 'account with joy, and not with grief,' is the sum of all that either now, or ever hereafter, I shall desire of you. Nor do I desire this of you so much for mine own sake as for yours.

"Concerning myself, what my behaviour hath been among you, from the first day of your gathering under my hand, you well know : what my heart hath been towards you, my heart itself knoweth; but He that is greater than my heart knoweth much better, and will declare in due time. I have spent the best part of my days with you, and have endeavoured with all my might, human infirmities excepted, to train you up like saints, and heirs apparent to a heavenly kingdom. And now, not being like long to continue with you, the ' keepers of my house ' beginning to tremble, and they ' that look out at the windows to be darkened,' nor to publish many more books than this before my change ; I was desirous to take the present opportunity, whilst I am yet with you, of being your Remembrancer of some few things, a conscientious observing where of will do you Christian service, and help to bless you, when I am gone.

" Remember oft and seriously, that it is much more easy to begin in the Spirit, than to continue and be perfected in the Spirit : to run well for a time, than perseveringly to obey the truth : to interest yourselves in the love of Christ, than to continue in His love to the end. There were four several grounds that had good seed sown in them, and three of them bare profession ; but only one of them yielded perseverance. The Scriptures are full of fore-warnings, and examples of zealous professors for a time, who, in the progress of their course, turned aside, some into one by-way, some into another, and so lost the things which they had wrought, and perished eternally. How many of yourselves have, within the compass of a few years, turned aside, some on the right hand, and others on the left, into by-ways where the light of life either shineth not at all, or very malignantly, like unto a dusky twilight, wherein many travellers lose their way ? How many are there, not yet

separated from your body, whose spiritual pulse beats very
faintly, and concerning whom the ground of jealousy is
great, that they have fallen from their first love? What
between spiritual wickedness, (I mean sects and opinions
pretending to the truth,) and fleshly wickedness, (the love
of ease, pleasure, and the contentments of this world,) the
trees of Christ's forest, in His respective churches, are made
few, that a child may tell them. Therefore if you mean so
to run as to obtain, it mightily concerneth you not only to
take care how to believe, or to live holily, but how to do
both perseveringly. You must imitate those who, intending a long voyage by sea, freight their ship with provisions
accordingly. A little oil will serve to make your lamps
blaze for a while; but it must be a full vessel that will
keep them burning till midnight, or till the time of the
Bridegroom's coming.

"Beware of the notions of those who, to magnify the
inward teachings of the Spirit of God, vilify His ordinances,
and outward administrations; judging these to be but
impertinencies, and things which may with no spiritual
disadvantage be laid aside. For though 'neither he that
planteth be any thing, nor he that watereth;' yet he that
speaketh this, saith also to Philemon, that he owed unto
him even his own self; and gave thanks to God, who
always caused him to triumph in Christ, (meaning in the
success of his ministry in the conversion of men to Christ,)
and ascribeth to Timothy the saving of the souls of those
who should hear him. All which, with many more like
unto them, clearly assert a sovereign necessity of the
ministry. Where he that planteth and he that watereth
are despised, it is not God but the devil that giveth the
increase. For we read of no increase, ordinarily, given by
God, but upon the planting and watering by men. If there
were nothing but mere sacramentality in the preaching of
the Gospel, and other ordinances, the inspirations of God
cannot upon any competent ground be expected without
them; no more than Naaman had ground to expect a
cleansing from his leprosy, without washing seven times
in Jordan, or the Israelites, that the waters of the Red

Sea would be divided, had not Moses lift up his rod over them, as God had directed him.

" If you shall at any time be, by the providence of God, settled under a ministry, where the words of eternal life are preached with power, and in the demonstration of the Spirit, know that you cannot better yourselves by changing your station ; but you may, by such a change, endamage yourselves in the things of your eternal peace exceedingly. There is no going from before the face of the Gospel, where the glory of it shines out in the face of the inner man, but with imminent danger of spiritual loss in the remove. There are that are called preachers of the Gospel, in one form of profession or another, as there are preachers many, and teachers many; yet to those who have a true and lively taste of the Gospel, and of the Spirit thereof, the able and faithful preachers are very few. Nor can the practice of any carnal rite, one or more, least of all when even the lawfulness of them is matter of doubtful disputation, balance the loss that is like to be sustained by exchanging the sun for the moon : a spiritful and lively ministry, for that which is cloudy, flat, and of small execution.

" You can hardly enter into any of those new-devised forms of profession, which are at this day occupied by men pretending highly to religion amongst us, but there is signal cause of fear, that your spirits will receive some ill tincture even from the best of them, and that your hearts will be leavened with some unchristian impression.

" Amongst the Anabaptists, I mean those of the high form, you will be tempted to build upon the water, instead of the rock, and to rejoice in a thing of nought. You will be apt to learn pride, peremptoriness, turbulency of spirit, depising of those that are good; the magnifying of will-worship, above faith, love, holiness, humility, mortification, self-denial, fruitfulness in well-doing, and whatsoever doth most unquestionably commend men to God.

" Antinomianism is a school of lawless liberty ; wherein is taught how, without the least regret of conscience, to turn the grace of God unto wantonness; and where the impure elements of Ranting, the dregs of all sects, are plainly laid, under the names of most worthy truths, and such wherein the glory of the Gospel consisteth. A Ranter is nothing but an Antinomian sublimated.

"Those commonly known by the name of Seekers, are a generation who think they do God a choice service, in overlooking all that is written, upon pretence of looking for somewhat higher, more mysterious, and sacred: as if God, who hath spoken unto the world by His Son, intended to speak by these men somewhat of greater import! Amongst these, this snare of death will be spread in your way; you will be tempted to seek after another Jesus, with the neglect and contempt of Him, besides whom there is no Saviour.

"Amongst the Behemites, or Mysterialists, you will learn little but uncouth words and phrases, under which you may mean what you please, but nothing to the edification of any man, nor scarce of yourselves; together with an art to allegorize away the spirit, power, and authority of the Scriptures; and this under a pretence of teaching repentance, mortification, humility, &c., after a new and more excellent way than hath been formerly known. Here you shall meet with strange terms, in sufficient *number* to fill the world with notions such as the minds of men have been strangers to until now; yet will the whole Encyclopedia of this learning hardly enrich you with one distinct notion of truth which is not already abroad in the world amongst intelligent men, in a far more scientific garb of expression. Here you will be taught to comment upon the light with darkness.

"Contra-Remonstrancy, as it is commonly taught amongst us, is a model of divinity, drawn quite besides the pattern in the mount; I mean the mind of God revealed in the Scriptures. The appropriate principles of this way may reasonably be conceived to lead unto most if not all other sects, and those evils that are found in them. Amongst the sons of this divinity you will learn a faith which, instead of working by love, will work by carelessness and security, and which will give such large quarter to the flesh, that its own life and being will be sorely endangered, if not utterly overthrown : besides many most unworthy and hard thoughts of HIM who is grace, love, goodness, and bounty itsel ; and who is not willing that any should perish, but that all should come to repentance and be saved.

"Among the Arians, the life of godliness in you, if you carry any such thing with you to them, will be in danger of poisoning with dunghill conceits of God and Christ. Here the abominable idolatry of the old heathen, ' who changed the glory of the incorruptible God into an image made like to corruptible man,' which God most severely punished, is, in the clear and plain principles of it, taught, as a great and unquestionable truth. And He, whom the Holy Ghost styleth, ' God blessed for ever,' is allowed his Godhead in a diminutive sense only, and such which dissolveth the glory of the mystery of the Gospel, into a piece of odd and savourless projection, without any length or breadth, depth or height of wisdom in it. .

"Among the High Presbyterians, you must submit your faith to the test of men, and be content to be at a synodical allowance for what you believe. And yet, here you will be taught to sacrifice the peace, liberties, and comforts of other men, and these, it may be, better, more righteous, and sounder in the faith than yourselves, upon the service of such a faith, which is modelled by the fancies or weak understandings of men, and these superintended for the most part by some politic and corrupted interest.

"These are the principal sects at this day on foot amongst us, into which, if you be not established with the knowledge of the truth, and watchful in prayer to God, to keep you in the way of truth and peace, your foot will be in danger of sliding. A little consideration serves a man to make one in a multitude. Besides, there are reports abroad very credible, that there are emissaries of the Roman faction, Jesuits and others, who secretly insinuate themselves with all the prementioned sects amongst us. These being the most expert artists in the world in glosses and colours know how to allure the fancies of inconsiderate people unto them; their

most wicked and dangerous design being, to rend and
tear the nation into factions, that so they may upon
better terms of advantage commend the Romish Church
and Religion, for that unity which is found in them,
either to work the nation back again unto Rome, or to
bring the misery of confusion upon us.

"Take heed of falling in your esteem of any ordinances of God, and so of languishing in your zeal towards
the enjoyment of them. You can want none of them, if the
want be voluntary, but with certain loss in your spiritual
estate. They are like the pipes which, lying between
the full fountain and the empty cistern, join them together, and supply the emptiness of the one out of the
native fulness of the other. God is a fountain of grace,
goodness, light, life, strength, wisdom, and knowledge;
and His good pleasure is, to communicate of His fulness
in all these unto the poor, barren, indigent creature,
man. As they dissolve the communion between the fountain and the cistern, who cut off the pipe by which the
water is conveyed from one to the other, so do they estrange
themselves from God, who without necessity forsake His
ordinances. Certain it is, that He hath not appointed
them in vain : therefore they who forsake them sin against
their own mercies. The best means to preserve you in
honourable thoughts of them is to improve them conscientiously ; and upon every enjoyment of them, to take
a steady account what you have spiritually gained by them.
The loose and negligent use of them deprives men of the
benefit and blessing of them : and when men find themselves no ways blessed by them, they are at the next door
to despising them.

"You have opportunity of a fourfold variety of Christian
employment. You may meditate that which is good with
your heart: you may do that which is good with your hand:
you may speak that which is good with your tongue: you
may hear that which is good with your ears. It is pity
but that one or other of these ploughs should still be kept
going. You can hardly be cast under any such disadvantage at any time, but you may serve the interest of your

A A

souls, and better your accounts at the great day, by exercising yourselves in one or other of these engagements.

" Remember that all time lost, or misspent, though never so truly repented of, though never so fully pardoned by God, will turn to loss unto you all the days of eternity. For though God, upon the said supposition, will not punish you for your miscarriages, yet you cannot expect that He will reward them. The highest privilege that sin is capable of is pardon : reward is appropriate unto righteousness. Whereas, had the time which you misemploy been sown with the seed of righteousness, He that giveth to every seed its own body would have made your harvest of blessedness in the world to come so much the greater and more plentiful. Therefore be diligent and careful to improve the smallest shreds, or broken ends of time.

" And what shall I say more ? For the time would fail me to set before you all that is in my heart, for the comfortable and safe steerage of your course through the world. I trust that, without any recognition, through the grace of God that is given you, you retain in mind many things more of this blessed concernment, which God hath heretofore, at several times, given unto you by my doctrine ; and that, having so much heavenly light shining round about you, you will not venture your souls upon any loose presumption. Ye are in our heart to die and live together : and I trust I am not upon inferior terms in yours. My hope is rich concerning you, that you will fulfil my joy, in being ' likeminded, having the same love, being of one accord, and of one mind, doing nothing through strife or vain glory, but in lowliness of mind each esteeming others better than himself; looking not every man upon his own things, but every man also on the things of others.' If you continue walking in this way, you will find the issues of it life and peace : and the God of all grace shall dwell amongst you for ever. Farewell, my joy and crown of rejoicing in the presence of our Lord Jesus Christ at His coming, at whose right hand my hope is to meet you all at the great day."

A few brief notices concerning Thomas Lamb may with

propriety close this chapter. He received, as we have
seen, his early religious training under the ministry of
Mr. Goodwin, whose pulpit he occasionally occupied. At
the Restoration he conformed to the Established Church,
and it would appear worshipped to the end of his life in
the parish church of St. Stephen's, Coleman Street. He
died in 1686; and a sermon was preached at his funeral
on the 23rd of July in that year, by Richard Lucas, the
vicar. From this remarkable discourse we learn that
Lamb was not only a successful merchant, but a thoroughly
godly man, and one of the most distinguished philanthro-
pists of his age.

"His zeal in propagating the fear of God amongst
others was no less eminent in him than the piety of his
own demeanour. He never let slip an opportunity either
of reproving or discountenancing vice, or of preaching up
and recommending virtue; and this he did with that
gravity and authority, and with that goodness and charity,
with that evidence of Scripture, backed with strength of
reason and experience, that he seldom missed of doing
some good by it. He was extremely solicitous to instruct
youth in the principles of our religion : for which purpose
he had a Catechism of his own composing, containing the
grounds of our Christian faith, which he did industriously
imprint not only on the memories, but judgments and
hearts of young people."

"He was zealous for the observation of family duties,
and in all this was eminently exemplary himself. Nor can
it be unknown to many here how successful he was in this;
what a spirit of religion and goodness reigned in his
family, and what lasting impressions of both his endeavours
made in his children; and were it not that I should oppress
their modesty, and incur, it may be, an imputation of
flattery,—which I detest and scorn,—I would insist more
largely upon this topic, as a noble encouragement to the
watchfulness and industry of fathers and masters over
their children and families.".

"I may safely say, he did in some degree renounce his
own business and his own interests, that he might with

less distraction and better success attend the concerns of the poor and miserable. It is true, the charities he under-took and engaged himself in were too many and too great to be carried on upon his own single stock, or particular fund. He had therefore assistance many ways; and much from many good men, I believe, here present. But it is true, that he was not only a faithful steward and dispenser of other men's bounty, but also bountiful himself, even to the diminution of his estate. Several hundreds of prisoners were by him, with great travail and expense, set free. Nay, prisons themselves were set free from some oppres-sions and cheats that had obtained in them, and rendered more hospitable and tolerable to the miserable inhabitants; fees being reduced to a lower rate, and maintenance and provisions for prisoners much better settled. Many desolate orphans found in him the tenderness and com-passion of a father; and many desolate widows the care and protection of a husband. Such numbers of poor were relieved by him, that he was continually thronged by flocks of his clients, as he called them; and he could scarcely pass any street where the blessings of some one or other succoured by him did not light upon him. Nor did his charity exert itself only in the relief of the poor and needy, but also in ministering to every sort of necessity and misery of mankind. He comforted the afflicted, rescued the oppressed, advised and counselled the ignorant, and subdued the obstinate by the sweetness of his address, by the meekness of reason, and an extraordinary spirit of religion, which discovered itself in all his discourses.

" No sourness or churlishness of speech, no impatience or insolence of behaviour, did ever embitter his alms or relief to the needy. He would often hear not only tedious and impertinent, but also rude and passionate discourses with matchless patience and goodness, having regard to the miseries, not the frailties, of those who addressed them-selves to him. So intent was he upon the excellent works of charity, that he pursued them panting and almost breathless; and I have sometimes heard him regret the weakness and infirmity of his age, and express his fear lest he should live to those years wherein, through defect of strength, he might be utterly useless. Indeed, his decayed body was not at length able to undergo all the drudgery which so many and considerable designs of charity did require; and therefore, for several of his last years he maintained a servant on purpose to receive and execute his directions.

"He was often advised and pressed to go into the country for his health's sake. Against this he urged many scruples, which, though they appeared not to others of sufficient weight, yet he would never bring his mind to it. 'What shall my poor then do?' said he. 'It is even best for me to die in my station, and in my employment.'

"Shall I now, after all, add his justice, integrity, and diligence in all his dealings and undertakings? his simplicity and candour, his ingenuity, meekness, and humility in all his conversations? his plainness, sincerity, and zeal towards his friend, showing itself especially in his eternal interests? the sweetness and obligingness of his carriage, not towards his children only, but even towards the meanest that had any relation to him? Shall I add his Christian moderation, and comprehensive charity for all peaceful, humble, and upright Christians of every persuasion? Shall I insist upon his purity and heavenly-mindedness, not only to an indifference, but (I may almost say) even contempt for the things of this world,—wealth, power, honour, and the ostentation of life?

"Death was his meditation, death his expectation; and when he met it, he met it with a cheerful and serene soul. The last words I had from him, when I bade him my last farewell on Sunday, were, 'You and I shall meet again in another world. I do not question it at all.' Ah! that we could all live so as to have no fears, no doubts about our eternal life when we are come to die!"*

It is not every minister that has the honour and gratification of calling forth the mental energies and of forming the character of three such men as Daniel Taylor, William

* A Sermon preacht at the Funeral of Mr. Thomas Lamb, July 23, 1686. By Richard Lucas, M.A., Vicar of St. Stephen's, Coleman Street,

Allen, and Thomas Lamb, all of whom, especially in the early years of their religious course, belonged to the church of which John Goodwin sustained the pastoral charge. He succeeded in the course of his ministry so to fix their attention upon the truths of revelation as that they all became proficients in theological knowledge; and notwithstanding the controversies in which he spent so large a portion of his life, and the disputatious spirit of the age, they were all remarkable examples of Christian meekness, for the extent of their charities, and their practical observance of evangelical precepts. Indeed it is evident from the tenor of his pastoral admonitions, that his concern was, not only to give his people right opinions, but to render them examples of true religion; which, an illustrious contemporary says, " is a new nature informing the souls of men; a Godlike frame of spirit, discovering itself most of all in serene and clear minds, in deep humility, meekness, self-denial, universal love of God and all true goodness, without partiality, and without hypocrisy; whereby we are taught to know God, and knowing Him to love Him, and conform ourselves as much as may be to all that perfection which shines forth in Him."[*]

[*] Smith's Select Discourses.

CHAPTER X.

GOODWIN EXPOSES THE PROCEEDINGS OF CROMWELL'S TRIERS AND EJECTORS OF
MINISTERS—PUBLISHES HIS TRIUMVIRI—THE RESTORATION—DEBATE CON-
CERNING HIM IN PARLIAMENT—HIS DEATH—HIS WORK ON THE HOLY
SPIRIT.

On the abolition of Episcopacy in England, the approbation of all who entered upon the ministry so as to enjoy
ecclesiastical benefices, was claimed by the several Presbyteries in London and the country. But when Cromwell
gained the supreme authority, desirous of conciliating the
favour of other religious bodies, and of checking the power
of the Presbyterians, who might be supposed to admit
none but those of their own persuasion, he resolved to join
the different parties together in judging of ministerial
qualifications. Under his direction, therefore, a society of
clergymen and others, belonging to the Presbyterian, the
Independent, and the Baptist denominations, were appointed to sit at Whitehall under the name of Triers. The
Independents formed the majority, and were the most
active in the use of their delegated powers.* All
candidates for holy orders, and all ministers who were
presented to new livings, were required to undergo
a personal examination before these Commissioners, and
without their sanction none could be admitted. The
' Ordinance for the Approbation of Publique Preachers,"
investing the Triers with these formidable powers, bears
the date of March 20th, 1653.†

The appointment of the Triers was succeeded by an
Ordinance which the Protector issued, authorizing certain
persons, ministers and laymen, in the several counties of
England and Wales, to call before them any public
preachers, lecturers, parsons, vicars, curates, or school-
masters, "who are or shall be ignorant, scandalous,

* Calamy's Abridgment of Baxter's Life, p. 69.   † Scobell's Collection,
Part Second, pp. 279, 280.

insufficient, or negligent," and to eject them from their
livings.*

These classes of commissioners, generally speaking,
were both of them distinguished by strong aversion to
open profaneness, to prelacy, and to Arminianism. Baxter
therefore states, with respect to the Triers, that "they
saved many a congregation from ignorant, ungodly,
drunken teachers;" that they were "too lax in their admission of unlearned and erroneous men, that favoured Antinomianism or Anabaptism;" that "many of them were
partial for the Independents, Separatists, and Fifth
Monarchy Men;" and that they "were severe against all
Arminians," and against the Prelatists,† by whom, according to Dr. South, they were denominated "Cromwell's
Inquisition." When candidates for the ministry, or for
ecclesiastical preferment, appeared before them, " These
Triers," says Granger, "for the most part, brought the
test to a short issue. If a minister readily gave up the
five points of Arminius, embraced the tenets of Calvin, and
was *orthodox* in politics, he was generally qualified to hold
any benefice in the church."‡ But as there were several
learned and pious men in the nation, who were not
disposed to violate their consciences by making such concessions, the proceedings of the Triers were subject to
frequent animadversion. Mr. Sadler, afterwards created
D.D., who was presented to a living in Dorsetshire, and
rejected by the Triers, published a tract entitled, " Inquisitio Anglicana: or, The Disguise Discovered: shewing the
proceedings of the Commissioners at Whitehall, for the
approbation of Ministers, in the Examination of Anthony
Sadler, Clerk, Chaplain to the Right Honourable the
Lady Pagett, Dowager; whose Delay, Trial, Suspense,
and Wrong, presents itself for remedy to the Lord Protector, and the High Court of Parliament, and for information
to the Clergy, and all the People of the Nation, 1654."

Sadler declares himself to have been *inwardly* called by

* Walker's Sufferings of the Clergy, Part First, p. 178.   † Reliquiæ
Baxterianæ, First Part, p. 72.   ‡ Biog. Hist. Eng. Vol. III. p. 330. Edit.
1775.

the Spirit of God to preach the Gospel, and *outwardly* by the ordination of Dr. Corbet, Bishop of Oxford, in the year 1631. Being presented to the living of Compton-Hayway in Dorsetshire, on the 25th of May, 1654, he repaired to the Triers at Whitehall, for the purpose of obtaining their approbation; and presented to them his certificate, together with a recommendation from Dr Temple, and another from Lenthall, the Speaker of the House of Commons. After various delays, on the 3rd of July he underwent two separate examinations before the Triers, at which Philip Nye presided. Having been directed to withdraw, " I waited," says he, " to be called in again, according to custom, to hear the result: but was called for no more; insomuch that, when they rose, I followed Mr. Nye, and asked him of the issue of my examinations. He told me the Commissioners did not approve. I asked the reason why; but he seemed to slight me, and went away without speaking any farther to me." Sadler, however, was informed by Hugh Peters, that his case was still undecided. He therefore waited till the 14th of August, when he addressed a letter to Nye, in which he says, " If you please to approve me, as God and the world hath, by my meet gifts and lawful ordination, I shall, God willing, employ my talent to my utmost power, [and to] the best advantage. But if you are resolved to disapprove me, let it be, I pray you, upon record, and the reason why, that after times may know it as well as you." " Of this letter," continues our complainant, " I had no return: so that I am strangely kept, in an arbitrary way, under the hatches; and all this, to the loss of my time, living, and preferment, without any reason rendered me."

To this pamphlet are prefixed two petitions: one to Cromwell, and the other to the parliament. Addressing the former, the author says, " It is the comfortable hope, as well as the humble request, of your petitioner, that he shall be protected from the malignancy of prejudice, even the prejudice of Mr. Nye the Commissioner; against whose ever busy, partial, and injurious proceeding your petitioner doth humbly crave the benefit of that justice the law, rea-

son, and religion may or shall give unto your Highness'
most humble petitioner."

Several of the Baptist Churches also united in a public
protestation against the Triers : * and for the purpose of
exposing their religious principles and their partiality, Dr.
Lawrence Womack, who was raised to the Bishopric of
St. David's after the Restoration, wrote a very shrewd and
argumentative tract, entitled "The Examination of Tilenus
before the Triers, in order to his intended settlement as a
public Preacher in the Commonwealth of Utopia." To
this piece are annexed, "The Tenets of the Remonstrants,
touching the Five Articles which were voted, stated, and
imposed, but not disputed, at the Synod of Dort." Daniel
Tilenus, of whom a short notice will be found in the Appendix to these memoirs, wrote a small tract in French,
the object of which was to show the injurious tendency of
the Calvinian doctrine of absolute predestination, when
applied to practical purposes. This tract was translated
into English about the year 1629, by John L'Oiseau,
a French minister in London, and published under the
title of "The Doctrine of the Synods of Dort and Alez
brought to the proof of Practice." Dr. Womack adopted
this publication as the ground-work of his own, and therefore introduced himself to the world under the designation of "Tilenus Junior."

"The Examination of Tilenus" was animadverted
upon with some asperity by Mr. Baxter, in the preface
to his "Grotian Religion discovered;" and defended
with consummate ability and effect in a work entitled
"The Calvinists' Cabinet Unlocked;" written no doubt
by Womack himself. This writer was an acute logician,
and a complete master of the predestinarian controversy. He was well read in the works of the Dutch
Remonstrants, and in those of their adversaries both
in this country and abroad. Proceeding in the execution of his purpose, he soon after produced another
work, every way worthy of himself, entitled, "The Result
of False Principles : or, Error Convicted by its own

* Ivimey's Hist. of the Baptists, p. 230.

Evidence;" the design of which was to show, in a series
of dialogues, that the doctrine of absolute predestination is "not practicable in the exercise of the ministerial function—not serviceable to the interest of souls—
and not according to godliness." It does not appear that
any answer to these two latter works was ever presented
to the world; and little is hazarded when it is said, that
they never can be refuted. Womack died on the 12th of
March, 1685; having held the bishopric of St. David'ss
one year and four months, and displayed through all the
civil and ecclesiastical commotions of his age an exemplary attachment to his king and to the Episcopal Church
of which he was a member. His remains were interred in
the church of St. Margaret, Westminster.*

As a specimen of the proceedings of the Ejectors, and
of the encouragement given in those times to factious
individuals to harass and perplex the parochial clergy,
especially those of them who favoured monarchy and
episcopacy, the case of Dr. Edward Pocock may be fairly
adduced. This excellent man, who was one of the first
oriental and Biblical scholars of the age, was charged
with scandal before a court of Ejectors, by some of his
puritanical parishioners, and kept in a state of anxious
suspense for several months. When his adversaries found
themselves unable to substantiate their charge, they
accused him of *insufficiency*, and very nearly succeeded
in obtaining his ejectment on that account. No less than
four learned doctors deemed it necessary to appear on his
behalf, who with great difficulty succeeded in putting an
end to the prosecution. Whether they satisfied the
barbarians of the doctor's parish is uncertain: but they
prevailed upon his judges to dismiss the cause. "They
all laboured, with much earnestness, to convince those
men of the strange absurdity of what they were undertaking; particularly Dr. Owen, who endeavoured with
some warmth to make them sensible of the infinite contempt and reproach which would certainly fall upon

* Le Neve's Fasti, p. 514, Edit. 1716.—Goodwini Præsul. Angl. Com-
men. p. 518, Edit. 1743.

them, when it should be said, that they had turned out
a man for insufficiency, whom all the learned, not of
England only, but of all Europe, so justly admired for
his vast knowledge and extraordinary accomplishments.
And being himself one of the commissioners appointed
by the Act, he added, that he was now come to deliver
himself, as well as he could, from a share in such disgrace,
by protesting against a proceeding so strangely foolish
and unjust. The commissioners being very much mortified
at the remonstrances of so many eminent men, especially
of Dr. Owen, in whom they had a particular confidence,
thought it best for them wholly to put an end to the
matter, and so discharged Mr. Pocock from any further
attendance." *

Mr. Goodwin had little to fear either from the Triers
or Ejectors. His vicarage had scarcely any emolument
attached to it, and was therefore unlikely to be an object
of envy. But he was a decided friend of religious liberty,
and ready at any time to risk his life in that sacred cause.
He not only regarded the general proceedings of these
commissioners as intolerably partial and oppressive in a
free country, but contended that the authority with which
they were invested was an infringement upon the rights
of the Christian Church. He appears to have been
especially offended with the Independents, who, while
professing to believe that every congregation has a right
to appoint its own minister, presumed to come between
the people and the man of their choice, when they found
on examination that he was not sound in the faith of
John Calvin. Avowing therefore the highest respect for
the civil authority by which these commissioners were
employed, and disclaiming all personal malignity towards
the commissioners themselves, he made a spirited attack
upon their constitution and general conduct, in a pamphlet
which he published under the title of "The Triers, or
Tormentors, Tried and Cast, by the Laws both of God
and Men: or, Arguments and Grounds as well in Reason
as Religion evincing the Unlawfulness of those Com-

* Twells's Life of Pocock, prefixed to his Works, Vol. I. p. 41, Edit. 1740.

missions by which the Courts of Triers and Ejectors are established; together with the Unwarrantableness of the acceptation and exercise of the powers delegated by any man or company of men whatsoever, 1657."

This tract is admirably characteristic of the frankness and integrity of its author, and throws considerable light upon the ecclesiastical history of that period. " Being old and much stricken in years," says Mr. Goodwin, " and not far from that turning in the course of mortality, where Moses, the man of God, found, in his days, the ordinary period of the life of man; I am, by the high and dreadful concernment of my dissolution approaching, importuned to the uttermost to consider, what service I may do, whilst my tabernacle yet standeth, to my Lord and Master Jesus Christ, and for His sake to the world around me, which is likely to be of the choicest acceptance with Him, and will turn to the best account to myself, at my appearance before Him. In my thoughts upon this affair, I traversed much ground, and had a great variety of particulars presented to me, which all commended themselves to my conscience in both these respects. Amongst others, and with more rational importunity than the rest, some brief remonstrance against the two apocryphal orders of commissioned officers amongst us, (whether ecclesiastic or civil, can hardly be determined but by a *nemo scit,*) known by the names of Triers and Ejectors, much pressed and solicited me in this behalf. From the day that I heard of these commissions, my heart was troubled within me, and began to presage the many and great evils which they were likely to bring upon the Gospel in the ministry of it, and upon many godly, worthy, and well-deserving men. Of the truth of which presagements, myself, in part, with several others, are sad witnesses.

" Concerning the persons entrusted with the commissions I bear not the slightest grudge or ill-will against any of them; but from the heart wish them all prosperity and peace; and with all candour and clearness of spirit shall seek to promote them : only my soul hath no pleasure in their accepting the office, into which the commissions have tempted them; much less in the many strains in managing it. Those of them who are known to me I believe to be men of conscience and worth; fearing God, and lovers of truth: and for the rest, I charitably hope the same also. But, as one observed, some creatures that, being naturally fearful whilst alone, are daring and fierce in companies: so frequent experience showeth, that many men who, apart, are of a temper inclinable to honest, just, and good; in *consort*, prove boisterous and peremptory; apt to be led by oppressive counsels, and principles of much unworthiness. The reason whereof may be, the guilt and shame of unworthy doings, being divided amongst many, weigh but little upon the apprehensions and consciences of particulars. Concerning the persons by whose authority the commissions have been established, I have much less need to profess Christian loyalty, and entireness of respects, towards them, than the friendliness of my spirit towards the other.—But it hath been a fatal unhappiness incident to rulers professing Christianity, to think it their duty, and a service pleasing to God, to employ that authority which is vested in them for other purposes, about making, and enforcing by the sword, additional ordinances and decrees, to supply that which seems to them to be wanting in that system of orders and directions, which the Lord Christ hath drawn up and commended to be practised by those who profess the Gospel. Whereas, multiplications in this kind, and subtractions, are of the same demerit in the sight of God, and prohibited with the same breath by Him.

"To entrust an inconsiderable number of men with a negative vote, in the placing, displacing, and disposing of ministers over all the parochial congregations in a great nation, is an unheard-of prodigy, and must needs be of a sad portendance to the people, especially to the godly and well-affected. For, in case the Triers be froward, or bear a grudge against a parish, or judge him unsound in the faith whom the congregation desire, and can admit none that is contrary-minded, in these cases a congrega-

tion may never be permitted to enjoy a minister whom
they can cordially reverence ; but must be like sheep
scattered, or be in subjection to such a person as the
Triers obtrude upon them.

" The Commission is of a mischievous calculation, whensoever the patron, who has the right of presentation, shall
be found of differing judgment from the Triers. For in
case he be *orthodox* in the doctrines of universal atonement,
conditional perseverance, &c.; wherein it is sure enough
that the Triers are *heterodox;* he should not answer the
dictate of a good conscience, to present to the Triers a man
dissenting in such weighty points from himself; especially
when he knoweth a person likeminded, regularly capable
n all other respects, and willing to be presented. Very
possibly the conscience of a patron may, through mistake,
resent it as a thing unlawful, to present any man whom he
judgeth not sound in these great doctrines of the Gospel, or
that denieth the universal extent of Christ's death. In
this case, the people destitute of a minister are like to be
destitute still; and, for six months at least, to be exposed
like sheep not having a shepherd. And at the six months'
end, the patron being nonsuited in the plea of his privilege,
the people, if their sacerdotal demeans be considerable, are
like to have some favourite of the times wearing black,
instead of a minister, thrust upon them, or remain spiritually waste and desolate. The patron suffers an illegal
defeature of his just desire, on behalf of the worthy person
presented by him; and the person rejected, an unchristian
affront, and undeserved blot in his reputation.

" In the days of prelacy, in case the bishops, who were
then the Triers, were at any time sullen, or froward, so as
upon any illegal pretence to refuse to admit to a benefice
any clerk presented to them, there lay a *quare impedit*
against them, and they might be compelled by law to do
that which became them, to give their pass of institution
to those against whom there was no legal exception, though
never so much disrelished by their lordships. The Triers
of the last edition are mounted upon thrones of power and
authority far above the level of their forefathers, the bishops:

for these are plenipotentiary in the highest in their proceedings. They esteem all laws as Leviathan esteemeth iron and brass : ' He esteemeth iron as straw, and brass as rotten wood.' They laugh all appeals to scorn ; and, with the wild ass in Jeremy, being used to the wilderness, snuff up the wind at pleasure, and fear not to be turned away by any man. Never was there such a lawless generation of men set up in this nation over the Lord's people: never was there the like insufferable yoke of slavery fastened about the necks of the free-born people here, as the power given by commission unto, or at least claimed and exercised by, these men.

"Where there are great numbers of men in a nation, (and a great part of these considerable for piety, zeal, and abilities,) who are divided in judgment about many questions in religion, it is contrary to all approved principles of policy, to set up and arm one of these parties with power to judge the other; yea, to trample them down like mire in the streets, and this without remedy. For is not such a course as this of a manifest tendency to beget a spirit of insolency and oppression, in the party thus exorbitantly advanced ;˙and to engender and foment, in the party oppressed, a spirit of disaffection ? Are not the Commissions we speak of, of this calculation ? Do they not set up a generation of men to be judges over those that dissent from them in some weighty matters of faith ? Do not the men thus set up exercise a bloody dominion over their adversaries, only for dissenting from them ; (although they, nicknaming the same, call it dissenting from the truth ;) dooming them and theirs to be fed with the bread and water of affliction ; to suffer cold, hunger, nakedness, and all extremity, if God will not look upon them, and provide better for them ?

"To spread snares in the way of men's consciences, so as to expose them to danger, is not consistent with Christianity. Now whether the men armed with the authority of the two Commissions do not frequently perpetrate the said misdemeanor, I could be content to make themselves judges, if they would make their own proceedings the rule of their sentence. For is not the simple professing of those important truths, that Jesus Christ gave Himself a ransom for all,—that God reprobated no man under a personal consideration, nor intended so to reprobate any man, from eternity,—that He vouchsafeth a sufficiency of means unto all men, whereby to repent and be saved,—that He neither constraineth nor necessitateth any man to believe and be saved,—that those who truly believe may put away a good conscience, make shipwreck of their faith and perish,—Is not the professing of these truths a bar against all ecclesiastical promotion in the process of their consistory? Is it not their manner to screw and dive as deep as they know into the judgment of those that come before them, to discover whether there be not some touch, or tincture, some propension, or verging towards those opinions? If they answer tenderly, or whisper the least iota in favour of those opinions, they are lost and undone! They are condemned, they and theirs, by these consistorian judges, to the spade or flail, to cleanness of teeth, or begging their bread where they can find it. So that, when young men, who are fair for preferment, and want nothing but these men's goodwill in wax and paper, come before them, knowing that they are not likely to be supplied, but by a professed disowning of those truths, lately specified, let the regret in their consciences be never so strong, are they not under a sore temptation to dissemble both with God and man, in case they stand inwardly convinced of those truths? And may not such dissembling with God prove, yea, hath it not oft proved, of that sad consequence, to occasion such a breach between Him and His creature, as was never repaired? Woe to a generation of men, that spread such snares of death in their brethren's way!

"Certainly they who understand and believe, and are excellently qualified to teach, the just extent of the Free Grace of God in the Gospel of His Son; and so are uniform and consistent in their teachings; other endowments, as of meekness, humility, love, zeal, &c., concurring; are more competent for the work of the ministry, than those who, confining the grace of God within the sphere of their

own apprehensions, are inevitably entangled in their
ministry, so as ever and anon to pull down what even now
they built up, and to build up what a very little before
they pulled down. And yet such is the spirit of the men
now under censure, and they take themselves bound in
conscience, to admit the latter only; and to say unto the
former, You are not fit to serve at the altar, not fit to have
part in the ministry: you are not of our judgments, in all
points wherein we are infallible. Therefore we must smite
you with the rod of our power, that you may learn not
to *Remonstrate*, nor take up the truth in contestation
with us!

"When the trees of the forest went forth to anoint
a king over them, the olive, the fig-tree, and the vine,
refused the honour, alleging that if they should accept of
it, they must part with their several serviceablenesses
both to God and men; which, they pleaded, it was not
meet for them to do: only when the trees came to the
bramble, and made their motion to it, the bramble
accepted it; but withal enjoined them, prince-like, to
put their trust in his shadow; threatening them, that
if they should not, fire would come out of the bramble,
and devour the cedars of Lebanon. The honour which
is delegated by the commissions of Triers and Ejectors,
was not proper to be entertained by men who were
conscious of any usefulness in themselves, unless they
mean to part with it, and to take this in exchange.
Nor was it like to be accepted, but only by brambles,
who had a mind to rend and tear the flesh of those
who should come near them, and refuse to put their
trust in their shadow: I mean, in their learning and
judgment touching matters of faith. And there is a fire
gone out of those brambles, which hath devoured the
cedars of Lebanon. They have undone persons of eminent
growth in all Christian worth and excellency. Men of
sweet principles would have bethought themselves of better
opportunities for the exercise of them, than sitting upon
a consistorian throne, to the great grievance and offence
in a manner of a whole nation; and for the selling of their

brethren into the hands of poverty, disgrace, and misery, for no other crime than this conceit of their own, that their brethren's faith, in some points, is not so good and commendable as theirs. Men of modest and ingenuous spirits would never endure it, that their brethren, some of them, it may be, every way equal to the best of themselves, should take long, wearisome, and chargeable journies, from the remotest part of the land, to give attendance upon them, sitting upon their seats of honour; and with patience, reverence, and submission, to wait their leisure, I know not how long, for the dispatch of their occasions; yea, the leisure and pleasure of their underlings, whether register, clerks, or by what other name they call them.*

"No argument that hath yet been alleged for the establishment of the Triers is much considerable. For what reason can there be to exchange a method which is generally known, for another which, besides that it threatens a disturbance and discontent through the novelty of it, is not like to prevent those inconveniences that are sometimes found in the former? unless it be with introducing greater in their stead. If patrons of benefices, whether parochial congregations, or single persons, have sometimes preferred unworthy men to those places; have not the Triers been as great or greater delinquents in this? Have not they approved of, and given wings to birds of as unclean a feather, as any that were wont to fly from the other's hand? I always judged it beneath a spirit of ingenuity to hold intelligence with any man for information of the sinister practices of men, or to give encouragement to those who love to be messengers of such tidings; nor did I ever bestow the fourth part of an hour in following any report I have occasionally met with concerning the Triers, and their unhandsome and unhallowed doings in their way;

* "My delay was very troublesome, though not, it may be, chargeable, as that of Mr. Taylor's was; who came from York to London; and being called, examined, and approved at three weeks' end, was yet stayed seven weeks after, and, at the last, having spent above twenty pounds, was enforced to return without their Instrument; because, (as Mr. Nye told him, and he me,) *His certificate was not subscribed by hands they knew.*"
SADLER's *Inquisitio Anglicana*, p. 6.

although I have met with many in this kind; nor have I
kept a register, either with my pen or memory, of such
stories. Only I cannot but be sensible of the smart which
ever and anon I suffer, with having my ears beaten with
the loud complaints of their passports granted to the first-
born of undeserving men, and of their being denied to
persons excellently qualified and commended unto them
for that great work of the ministry. In this latter, they
are much more obnoxious than the other patrons we
spake of, even when they stumble at the stone of unworthy
presentations.   For though in these cases they behave
themselves amiss in helping chaplains, taken out of the
devil's school, to employment in God's house; yet do they
not, thus far, contumeliously entreat more deserving men,
nor obstruct their way to any preferment to which God
hath called them.   Therefore they are less peccant than
our commissioned Triers.   The truth is, that the generality of the Triers, being men bent in their dispositions to
promote a faction, under the pretence of countenancing
orthodox doctrine, and to suppress all of a contrary judgment to themselves, as erroneous men, corrupt and dangerous in their principles, &c.; it was none otherwise like,
from the beginning, but that they would steer that crooked
course which now they have steered; and that they would
countenance men of the greatest demerit otherwise, if they
were right for the design; especially if it should so fall
out, as I suppose it hath done, that men of more regular
behaviour should not come in unto them fast enough,
to complete the number of disciples, and augment the
party to their minds.

"If a trial of ministers before admission to a place of
public service be admitted as necessary, why should not
those who are authorized as competent for the ordination
of ministers, be judged competent for their trial? Is it
any good harmony in reason, that they who are judged
meet to be invested with the office of a minister, should
not, without a further trial, be entrusted with the work
of a minister? or that they who are judged meet to try
men in reference to the former, should not be as sufficient

to try them in the latter? What need was there then of
our new college of Triers? the erection whereof, together
with the irregular deportment of the masters of it, hath,
I dare say, more disaffected the generality of the nation,
and especially of the better party of it, to the present
government, than any other state transaction whatsoever.
Nor do I know any act whereby the government is more
like to commend itself to the people, especially the people
of God, than by plucking up by the roots that which hath
been so unhappily planted.

"If neither churches nor presbyteries be wood of which
to make the Mercury of Trying, why might not this image
have been carved in smoother timber, and of a better
grain, than that wherein it is now formed? Why should
the children of great assumings, who pretend their judgments be fairer than the moon, without spot or stain of
error; who cannot with a good conscience give the Lord
Christ in His servants any tolerable quarter, unless He
will declare for them and their opinions; who spread
snares of death in men's way, and tempt men to offer
violence to their own judgments and consciences, and so
to condemn themselves in that which they allow; who
count the crushing of godly men to be godliness, if they
understand more than themselves in the things of God;
why should men of this mould, rather than any other, be
the material of which to form the Trier? Is no vein of
men meet to make Triers, but they that can persecute
the innocent with a good conscience, and think they do
God service, when they keep out of His vineyard those
which He sends to labour in it; and who are like to make
the best and faithfullest labourers there?"

Mr. Goodwin was aware that he might incur personal
danger by thus exposing the proceedings of the Triers
and Ejectors, and the commissions by which they were
authorized. For this he was prepared; and therefore
says, "For myself, what trouble I shall gain, I think it
not worth putting to the account; being so near the line
beyond which there are no sufferings to them that love
God. Certain I am, that by giving my testimony against

so great evils, and damagers of the Gospel of Christ, and
sundry [of] His faithful servants, as the two commissions
against which I here contend, I shall gain a departure
in so much the more peace, whensoever my change shall
come."

The Triers and Ejectors, against whose appointment
and misdoings Goodwin bore this open and unflinching
testimony, stood high in the favour of Cromwell, who
now sustained the office and title of "His Highness the
Lord Protector of the Commonwealth of England." He
was unbounded in his attachment to the doctrine of
absolute predestination, and therefore wishful to make
it the national creed ; and these two classes of commissioners were labouring to introduce it into the pulpit
of every parish church in the land. He eulogized the
men in one of his parliamentary speeches,* and invited
the Triers, as a mark of special favour, to dine with him
at Whitehall, in the year 1655, when he appeared quite
at home in their company.† Yet we do not find that he
inflicted any penalty upon Goodwin. He knew him to be
loyal to the Protectorate, so far as its secular prerogatives
were concerned, and that no earthly power could impose
silence upon the sturdy Arminian of Coleman Street
when he saw the doctrine of general redemption assailed.
For that doctrine he was willing at any time to sacrifice
his reputation, his liberty, and even his life. In defending
this great truth he courted no man's favour and feared no
man's frown.

On the publication of Mr. Goodwin's tract concerning
these commissioners, Marchamont Nedham entered the
lists against him. This noted pamphleteer was at first a
favourite writer among the royalists : but fear of ruin, and
hope of gain, induced him to betray their cause. As the
reward of his perfidy, Cromwell allowed him a pension of
one hundred pounds per annum ; in consequence of which
he was distinguished during the Commonwealth as a writer
of news and of political squibs in favour of the Protector

* Cromwell's Letters and Speeches, by Carlyle, Vol. III. pp. 360-363,
Edit. 1846.   † Ibid. p. 130.

and his government.* He was bankrupt in character; so
that, having nothing to lose, he was a fit person to undertake the defence of any cause. In vindication of these
two classes of commissioners, he published a large pamphlet
entitled, "The great Accuser Cast Down : or, A Public
Trial of Mr. John Goodwin of Coleman Street, London,
at the Bar of Religion and Right Reason, 1657."

In the composition of this work, which was dedicated
with great formality to Cromwell, Mr. Goodwin had
reason to believe that Nedham was assisted by the famous
Philip Nye, of the Independent denomination, who appears to have been one of the most active and overbearing
of all the Triers. He therefore remarks, "The book hath
a double image visibly stamped upon it, like our Philip
and Mary coin : and there is aN Ey of Oxford learning, as
well as a mouth of Oxford railing, in the composition
of it."†

The appearance of this work was immediately succeeded
by "A Letter of Address to the Protector, occasioned by
Mr. Nedham's Reply to Mr. Goodwin's Book against the
Triers; by a Person of Quality." This is a very shrewd
and spirited publication; and contains several fine strokes
of satire upon Cromwell, and just animadversions upon
his pensioner. To Oliver the author says, "The occasion
that extorted this address was a scurrilous answer published by your Intelligencer, as a reply to Mr. Goodwin's
piece against the Triers, and dedicated with great solemnity
to your most *Serene Highness ;* not so much for Mr. Goodwin's vindication, as my own security, and all other your
Lordship's good subjects, still remaining unto you unde-
famed; that when any of us shall dare to peep out in print,
to look after the truth, or to see what is become of our
liberties, national and particular, and how they are
disposed of by your most *Serene Highness,* and the advice
of your council, for your use; we may not be flapt in the
face with the fox-tail of your Intelligencer, and be forced
for very shame to pull in our heads."

* Noble's Memoirs of the Protectorate House of Cromwell, Vol. I. p. 389,
Edit. 1784.   † Triumviri, Preface.

Speaking of the Triers, the author says, " They are the fittest to attempt the violation of other men's credit and repute, that have none of their own to lose. In this your honourable Committee were nothing great-minded, but base and cowardly ; having received a challenge from Mr. Goodwin to meet him in the field of truth and righteousness, there at the sharp of reason and God's word, to dispute the legality both of their delegated power and administration, to play him an Italian trick; entertain Nedham, that state-porter, that *venalis anima*, that mercenary soul, that for a handful of earth shall be hired to assassinate the greatest fame and reputation."

" My Lord, let him forbear hereafter to prefix your *Great Name* to his trivial papers: he may come in time to play with your band-strings : it will weaken your credit with Mazarine, Sweden, &c.; should they once come to know it. As for Mr. Goodwin, whose person he hath rather encountered than his arguments, it will little concern him ; having gained a deserved, though envied credit and repute, sufficient to bear him up in the estimation and valuation of knowing men, till time shall be no more."

This writer also speaks of Mr. Goodwin's controversial publications as having been conducive " to the great vindication of truth, advantage of state, conviction and consternation of his adversaries :" and adds, " If Mr. Goodwin have at any time, which is more than I know, taken the foil at the hands of any simple person, in the contest of truth and error, it is to let a person of the greatest intellectual abilities in the nation know, (I speak it without vanity, favour, or affection,) that he is not infallible and invincible."

It has been justly observed, that

> A keen reproach, with justice on its side,
> Is always grating;

and hence the Triers were so deeply mortified by Mr. Goodwin's attack upon them, that nothing which their apologists had to urge in their defence could avail to allay the perturbation of their minds. Stung with resentment that their proceedings were thus animadverted upon without reserve, and smarting under Mr. Goodwin's scourge, they selected a few sentences from his pamphlet, which they thought might be construed into reflections upon the existing government, and thus employed to his disadvantage. With these scraps they repaired to Cromwell's council, and presented their accusations against their courageous assailant. Goodwin was therefore cited to appear before Oliver's ministers of state, and reprimanded for presuming to attack their agents. " The testimony against the Triers, administered by my hand," says Mr. Goodwin, " occasioned such an overflowing of gall in the men, that no less than a double revenge upon me was sufficient to heal them. It was but half a cure, that they delivered me over to this tormentor, (Nedham,) to be scourged by him; they themselves afterwards turned informers, and accused me to the secular powers. The articles of my accusation were certain innocent passages transcribed out of my book, against which, notwithstanding, they had not a word to object whilst I was present. Only they had privately possessed some that were to be my judges, with an opinion that the said passages were reflexive upon their authority: whereas it is sufficiently known to the world, that I have always been as zealous an assertor of their authority as any of their friends whatsoever. Only I have so far comported with the light of reason and conscience, as to distinguish between the authority and the wills of persons in power. But my friends, the Triers, by the advantage of their interest in my judges, and daily opportunities of access to their ear, whereof I was wholly deprived, without proof of any miscarriage in me, obtained of them this gratification, To be admitted to stand by, and hear with what severity I should be reproved for their sakes. I will by no means say it, but only put it to consideration, Whether the proceedings against me, on behalf of the Triers, do not resemble those wherein it was acknowledged by the judge, that he found no fault in the man accused, and yet proffered this to satisfy his accusers, *I will chastise him and let him go ?* "

The Triers having failed in the attempt to substantiate

the charge of hostility to the government against Mr. Goodwin, he was at liberty to proceed in the defence of his theological tenets. His next work bearing on the Calvinian
controversy was his "Triumviri : or, The Genius, Spirit,
and Deportment of Mr. Richard Resbury, Mr. John Pawson,
and Mr. George Kendall, in their late Writings, &c. Together with some brief Touches in the Preface upon Dr.
John Owen, Mr. Thomas Lamb, Mr. Henry Jeanes, Mr.
Obadiah Howe, and Mr. Marchamont Nedham, in their
late Writings against the Author, 1658." This is a quarto
volume, containing upwards of five hundred pages. It had
been long expected, but was unavoidably delayed by the
author's other engagements, and by "a long weakness
and indisposition in body ; which," says Mr. Goodwin,
" in conjunction with the advice of friends, and physicians,
interdicting me the use of pen and paper, and sedentary
communion with my studies,.for a good part of the year,
made me all this while a servant to idleness." Although
this work was written amidst various interruptions and
infirmities, it displays all that mental vigour which the
author's earliest productions exhibit. In the preface, he
points out the " chief artifices " employed by his opponents,
especially by Dr. Owen and Mr. Kendall, to keep their
own opinions in countenance, and to expose his to disapprobation.

" First," says he, "they cover the native beauty of the said
doctrines with the odious epithets of Arminian, Pelagian,
Semi-Pelagian, Socinian, Pontifician, &c.; and then exasperate the weak and ignorant against them, as if they
were so many dangerous malefactors.—A second device is,
to affright vulgar spirits with the dismal consequences attending (as they pretend) the opinions of their adversaries :
as, That they are injurious to free grace,—exalt the creature,—deny the sovereignty of God,—make men their own
saviours,—suppose that Christ might have died and no man
have been saved,—that Christ might have been a Head
without a Body,—that the damned in hell owe as much to
God as those that are saved ; with others of like imperti-
nency.—A third method is, to pervert both the words and

sense of their adversaries; and one while to report their
opinions in words materially differing from their own;
otherwhile to argue against a sense put upon their words,
which they cannot but know to be far from that intended
by them.—A fourth stratagem oft made trial of is, to give
the point in question a close and slim *go by*, and pursue
another of some affinity with that depending, which they
pretend to refute; but which their adversaries do not
judge worthy of contest.—A fifth is, when the writings of
Luther, Calvin, Zuinglius, Melancthon, Musculus, Bucer,
Pareus, Gualter, with others of like character and repute,
are, with all clearness and expressness of sentence, cited
by the Remonstrants in favour of their cause; it is the constant practice of their adversaries to make these answers:
'Such passages are to be construed and understood by
others of a contrary tenor and import.' What is this,
but to reduce light into darkness? and to mediate reconciliation between palpable contradictions?—Sixthly, they
attempt to interest God in their quarrel, and make Him
a party, and themselves His advocates and friends; and with
height of confidence bear the world in hand, that they stand
by Him with all faithfulness, and He by them. With such
pretences as these they gain credit with men of light judgments, who buy their tenets with credulity.—Seventhly,
when they are hard beset with a stubborn argument
which they cannot handsomely turn, or give a plausible
answer to, they are wont to redeem themselves out of
the strait by pouring contempt upon it, slighting it as
weak, absurd, impertinent, not becoming a rational man,
unworthy him who urgeth it, &c. When they have thus
laid it low, any answer will do execution upon it. The
way of this retreat is sufficiently known to Mr. Kendall;
but it is worn bare and thread-bare with the feet of Dr.
Owen.—Lastly, they are ever and anon commending their
faith, that it attracts all or far the greatest part of holy
and good men, and leaves very few or none of these worthy
characters for the contrary doctrine; so that the proselytes hereof (a small remnant excepted) are but the refuse

of men." These several particulars Mr. Goodwin illustrates by apposite examples from the writings of his opponents.

The preface to the "Triumviri" is of considerable length, and contains spirited remarks upon five different works which had been published against him. In the body of this volume Mr. Kendall is the object of his principal attention; thirteen chapters being devoted exclusively to him. It is scarcely necessary to add, that when scrutinized by Mr. Goodwin with regard to his logic, his spirit, and his creed, this merry gentleman is frequently in a predicament which few people would envy. On dismissing him Mr. Goodwin says, "I have now done with Mr. K.; wishing from my soul, that Dr. K. may prove a better and wiser man. In the mean time I shall arm myself with Mr. Baxter's resolution, not to come any more so near him, until his breath be sweeter: until his language and tenor of discourse be changed from careless, light, and scurrilous, into that which is digested, grave, and serious, and such which becomes so majestic, so awful, so tremend a subject, as the unsearchable riches of the grace, love, and wisdom of God in the salvation of the world."*

Our author's attachment to the Arminian system was rather strengthened than otherwise by the books which were written in reply to his Redemption Redeemed. He thought that as the noble oak, when shaken by wintry storms, spreads its roots more widely, takes a firmer grasp of the surrounding soil, and bids defiance to the fiercest blast; so the genuine doctrines of Arminianism appear to greater advantage the more they are controverted and opposed. "Out of unfeigned love to all that are partakers of flesh and blood," says he, "I wish them from my heart communion with me in those great truths. I know them by those express characters of spirit and life that are in them, to be truths of God; nor have I met with any thing in the writings of all the three men of my present contest, which hath in the least shaken my confidence in this kind, or that for the least space of time put me to any stand. Their

* Triumviri, pp. 371, 372.

exceptions make little work for men competently versed in the controversies, to dissolve and scatter them."*

To this statement he added in the following year: "The truth is, that God hath so blessed me in the labour and travail of my soul, about those great points of election, reprobation, the intent or extent of the death of Christ, &c., wherein I have with some diligence, and with no less integrity and simplicity of heart, exercised myself for several years past; that before the coming forth of any thing printed by the three men against me, I was master of such principles and grounds, partly from the light of nature and common impressions found in the hearts and consciences of all men concerning God, partly from the writings of learned and worthy men, as well of the Contra-Remonstrant party, as Calvin, Beza, Musculus, &c., as the Remonstrant, but chiefly from the Scriptures, by which I was able to give myself satisfaction about any thing I met with objected in my way by any of those three men." †

In the preface to his " Triumviri, Mr. Goodwin also states, that notwithstanding the infirmities occasioned by sickness and by age, his heart was still set upon the completion of his favourite publication, Redemption Redeemed. "I shall not suffer the cause which I have undertaken," says he, "to sink under my hand; but while God shall please to supply life and health, with liberty and opportunities otherwise, shall go forward with the Second Part of my Redemption Redeemed, according to the model laid down; although I can hardly admit of any hope, that the days of my sojourning should hold out to the finishing of that work."

In the year 1659 Mr. Goodwin published a quarto pamphlet of considerable size, under the title of, "The Banner of Justification Displayed," in which he gives a comprehensive view of the means employed by Almighty God to invest mankind with that great blessing of the Gospel covenant; showing also that at the close of his studious and busy life he adhered with undeviating tenacity to the principles laid down in his treatise on that subject

* Triumviri, Preface.   † Preface to the Banner of Justification Display

which he published at the very beginning of his controversial career.   This valuable tract, with his " Exposition
of the Ninth Chapter of the Epistle to the Romans," and
his " Agreement and Distance of Brethren," was repub-
lished in the year 1835.

In the month of May, 1660, Charles the Second, having
been in exile from the death of his father, was placed upon
the throne of his royal ancestors. During this interval, a few
ingenious theorists, admirers of the Greek and Roman Republics, amused themselves and others with Utopian schemes of
public liberty. Those schemes, however, were not realized.
No acts of religious uniformity were indeed in force, yet the
nation groaned under a lawless tyranny, both in church
and state.   Cromwell was more absolute than Charles the
First with all his faults had ever been ; and the Triers and
Ejectors of ministers were invested with more formidable
powers in disposing of the clergy, than the bishops had
been wont to claim. Cromwell was now dead, and Richard,
his son and successor, had little aptitude for government,
having neither the sagacity nor the decision of his late
father. Hence the re-establishment of the ancient constitution of the country, in the restoration of monarchy,
was hailed with shouts of joy and triumph.   But amidst
the general exultation, those who had been in any way
concerned in the fate of Charles, soon began to anticipate
the effects of regal vengeance.   Amongst other men of
this class, the attention of the legislature was directed to
Mr. Goodwin and to his coadjutor Milton ; who were both
marked out as victims to be sacrificed to the manes of the
late king. On the 16th of June, the House of Commons
ordered, "That his Majesty be humbly moved,—that he
will please to issue his proclamation, for the calling in of
the two books written by John Milton ; the one entitled,
JOHANNIS MILTONI *Angli pro Populo Anglicano Defensio
contra Claudii Anonymi, alias Salmasii, Defensionem Regiam;*
and the other, in answer to a book entitled, *The Portraiture of his Sacred Majesty in his Solitudes and Sufferings ;* and also the book entitled, *The Obstructors of Justice,*
written in defence of the traitorous sentence against his

said late majesty, by JOHN GOODWIN ; and such other books as shall be presented to his majesty in a schedule from this House; and to order them to be burnt by the hand of the common hangman." The House of Commons also ordered, on the same occasion, "That Mr. Attorney General do cause effectual proceedings to be forthwith had by way of indictment or information against John Milton —and John Goodwin ;" and "that Mr. Milton and Mr. Goodwin be forthwith sent for in custody by the sergeant at arms attending this House." *

Agreeably to the request of the Commons, the king issued a proclamation, on the 13th of August following, charging, on pain of the royal displeasure, all persons who possessed any of these books to deliver them up within ten days, in order that they might be conveyed to the sheriffs of the different counties, for the purpose of being publicly burned at the ensuing assizes. In compliance with this mandate, several copies of these publications were resigned by their possessors, and committed to the flames with great formality at the Sessions House in the Old Bailey, on the 27th of the same month. The king's proclamation states, that " The said John Goodwin and John Milton are so fled, or so obscure themselves, that no endeavours for their apprehension can take effect." †

When this proclamation was issued, it was the avowed design of the legislature to bring Milton and Goodwin to " condign punishment ;" but by the prompt and urgent interference of their friends the danger was averted. They both became objects of the royal clemency, though not in an equal degree. To Milton, though incomparably the greater offender, were afterwards extended all the benefits of the Act of Oblivion ; a favour which was denied to Mr. Goodwin. In the House of Commons he appears to have had some decided enemies, and some powerful and zealous friends. The former contended for his blood, and the latter for his preservation. The debate concerning him lasted for several hours ; when it was finally determined

* Journals of the House of Commons, Vol. VIII. p. 66.   † Kennet's Register, pp. 189, 230, 239.   Toland's Life of Milton, p. 113, Edit. 1761.

that his life should be spared; but that he should be incapable of holding "any office, ecclesiastical, civil, or military, or any other public employment within this kingdom." Sixteen other persons, including Philip Nye and William Lenthall, the late speaker of the House of Commons, were subjected to the same incapacity.*

It is probable that Mr. Goodwin was indebted on this occasion to some of the leading men among the episcopal clergy, whose favour he had gained by the zeal and ability with which he had defended the Arminian doctrines: for nearly all the loyal clergy, whose influence with the government was great, were decided anti-Calvinists. Happily for Mr. Goodwin, it appears also to have been recollected in his favour, that the very spirited manner in which he had successively exposed the proceedings, and withstood the exorbitant claims, of the Presbyterians and the Independents, had contributed in no small degree to bring those domineering parties into disrepute, and, however undesigned, to hasten the return of the legitimate sovereign. That Milton should have been " distinguished from Goodwin with advantage," says Richardson, "will justly appear strange; for his vast merit as an honest man, a great scholar, and a most excellent writer, and his fame on that account, will hardly be thought the causes, especially when it is remembered Paradise Lost was not yet produced, and the writings on which his vast reputation stood were now accounted criminal, every one of them, and those most which were the main pillars of his fame. Goodwin was an inconsiderable offender compared with him." †

Mr. Goodwin had passed several years beyond the meridian of life when he espoused the doctrinal system of Arminius, and undertook its public recommendation and defence; and the opposition with which he had to contend was exceedingly formidable; yet he lived to see the reproach which was attached to that system in a great measure removed, and his wishes concerning it realized

---

* Wood's Athenæ Oxonienses, Vol. II. col. 504. Act of Free and General Pardon, Indempnity, and Oblivion, p. 33. † Life of Milton, p. 88. Edit. 1734.

to a considerable extent. Messrs. Bogue and Bennett, indeed, when speaking of the prevalence of Calvinism during the Commonwealth, state, that "John Goodwin must be mentioned as a *solitary*, but brilliant exception to the general character of those times."* But this is only an additional specimen of their fallacious mode of writing. That Calvinism should gain the ascendancy during this period, will excite the surprise of no one who considers the character of the Triers and Ejectors of ministers, and the lawless powers with which they were invested. They had, in fact, authority to control every parochial clergyman in the kingdom, and to dispose of every pulpit to which any revenue was attached by law. Nor will it be denied that Mr. Goodwin was a "brilliant exception" to the general complexion of those times; but that he was a "solitary" one, few persons, who have any knowledge of the theological history of that period, would have the hardihood to affirm. In the year 1654, when the Commonwealth and Calvinism were in the zenith of their glory, Dr. Owen lamented, "ARMINIANISM is crept into the BODIES OF SUNDRY CONGREGATIONS." † Mr. Goodwin also, speaking of the progress of Arminianism in England, from the publication of his Redemption Redeemed in 1651, till the year 1658, says, "I have ground to believe, that, in this nation alone, the doctrine unjustly defamed with her followers HATH GATHERED MANY THOUSANDS, greater than defamation; and that her competitress hath scattered of hers proportionably." ‡ It was also remarked by another writer, respecting the time of the Restoration, "That whereas, before the civil wars, one fire-brand towards the kindling of it was, to cast the odium of Arminianism upon the church, bishops, and clergy, as opening a door for Popery; the name of Arminian was not now so odious, nor so commonly imputed as a crime and scandal, to those who were offended at the rigid opinions of Calvin. For though the strict Presbyterians continued to take election and reprobation in the more absolute sense; yet

* History of the Dissenters, Vol. IV. p. 228.   † Doctrine of the Saints' Perseverance, Epistle Dedicatory.   ‡ Triumviri, Preface.

MANY OTHER PREACHERS, DURING THE DISSOLUTION OF THE CHURCH, HAD ESPOUSED AND DEFENDED THE CONTRARY PRINCIPLES."*

To the accomplishment of this change no man had contributed more than Mr. Goodwin. Not many months before the Restoration he said, in reference to one of his opponents, " I know it would be offensive to the gentleman, if I should relate how many letters and messages otherwise of thankful acknowledgment of the grace of God given unto me, for the clearing of those doctrines of election, reprobation, &c., and of Christian encouragements to proceed in my way, &c., I have received time after time from several persons of considerable worth for godliness and knowledge, inhabiting in several parts of the nation, some of them ministers of the Gospel, and others of them students of the University, &c.; but because such a story as this would, I presume, be a heavy burden to a tender and weak shoulder, I forbear it."†

This fact indeed is notorious. Notwithstanding the vigilance of the Triers and Ejectors, the doctrines of strict Calvinism were impugned on every side. To say nothing of the Quakers, the General Baptists, and of other classes of religious people, whose opposition to the theory of absolute predestination was unreserved; Mr. Baxter, Archbishop Ussher, and others, endeavoured to find a middle way between Calvin and Arminius; and, as they supposed, placed themselves at an equal distance from both. Among other eminent men who lived in those times, and were decidedly hostile to the peculiarities of Calvinism, the following distinguished characters may be mentioned: Mr. Samuel Hoard, Mr. Herbert Thorndike, Dr. John Bramhall, Dr. Henry Hammond, Dr. Jeremy Taylor, Dr. Edward Pocock, Dr. Henry More, Bishop Sanderson, Dr. Peter Heylin, Dr. Ralph Cudworth, Mr. John Smith, Dr. Brian Walton, Dr. Isaac Barrow, Dr. Lawrence Womack, Dr. Thomas Pierce, Mr. John Horne, Mr. George Lawson, Mr. Tobias Conyers. Many of these learned men, some

* Kennet's Register, p. 727.   † Preface to the Banner of Justification displayed.

of whom were severely persecuted, after the dissolution of monarchy, wrote with great zeal and ability against Calvin's doctrine of irrespective decrees. They did not all exactly agree in sentiment with Arminius; but they avowed their decided disapprobation of Calvin's theory of absolute and unconditional predestination; and their labours, in connexion with those of Mr. Goodwin, mightily contributed to turn the tide of public opinion in favour of General Redemption, and of the unnecessitated agency of man. The writings of Pierce and Womack on these subjects are far beyond all praise. Pierce, with consummate judgment and erudition, traced the errors of Calvinism to their source,—the doctrine of heathen fate; and Womack demonstrated their injurious effects when received as principles of action. Mr. Baxter, who has spoken of these two episcopal theologians with that harshness of language to which he was too much accustomed, acknowledges, that they were " the ablest men that party " had " in the whole land;" and that they were divines "of great diligence in study and reading, of excellent oratory, and of temperate lives."* This was no mean praise from a man who had been seriously baffled and perplexed by the writings of Pierce † and Womack against some of his favourite peculiarities. Thus it appears that Mr. Goodwin, though a star of the first magnitude, was not a "solitary" one in the Arminian firmament during the night of the Commonwealth; but belonged to a brilliant constellation, which shed the selectest influences upon the Calvinistic world.

Tobias Conyers, whom Doctor Calamy denominates "a very learned and extraordinary person," is entitled to special notice in these memoirs, as the bosom friend and warm admirer of Mr. Goodwin. He was sometime of Peter House, Cambridge, and afterwards minister of the church of St. Ethelbert's, London. He published, "The

---

* Reliquiæ Baxterianæ, Part First, p. 113.   † The following are the principal of Pierce's Works on the Calvinian controversy: A Correct Copy of some Notes concerning God's Decrees, 1665.—The Divine Purity Defended, 1657.—The Divine Philanthropy Defended, 1658.—The Self-Revenger Exemplified, 1658.—Self-Condemnation Exemplified, 1658.—Impartial Enquiry into the Nature of Sin, 1660.

Just Man's Defence, or the Royal Conquest; being the Declaration of the Judgment of James Arminius, Doctor and Professor of Divinity in the University of Leyden, concerning the principal Points of Religion, before the States of Holland and West Friezland: Translated for the Vindication of Truth, 1657."

Conyers was appointed to preach at St. Paul's church before the Lord Mayor and General Monk, on the 12th of February, 1659. The sermon delivered on that occasion was afterwards published under the title of "A Pattern of Mercy opened;" and in an advertisement prefixed to it, the author complains, that "aspersions were cast upon" him as being both "schismatical and heretical." In regard to these accusations, he says, "I crave leave to answer: That I am either schismatical or a sectary, I know not why any man should think me. It is true, I hold communion, and observe the laws of piety and holy charity, with that Christian people to whom Mr. John Goodwin is pastor.—If it be the Episcopal party that censures me for schism, I humbly crave leave to remonstrate, that I entered the ministry, when there was no church-government established, but every one did what was right in his own eyes. As I had no hand in pulling down that hierarchy, so will they not, I hope, blame me for joining with a people, that, I thought, espoused the interest of truth and holiness.—If it be the Presbyterian party: If I had made any schism, of all men, they had the least reason to take notice of it. For if little foxes or boars have entered, to root up and destroy the vineyard, it was by that schism or gap which themselves made. Therefore the brethren ot the Presbytery, remembering their own faults this day, will, I hope, exercise great lenity and grace towards those that are found in the same sin and transgression (if it be a sin and transgression) with themselves. To both parties (whom I wish may no more be called two but one) I shall only add this;—that when the fence is made up, which, how strong soever it may be, I wish may not be too strait, I must either keep out, or at my further peril.

"The second part of my accusation is error and heresy.

Erroneous I may be: *Humanum est errare.* Heretical I cannot be; because never censured by any lawful authority. I know not what brought me into suspicion with the city, unless it were my judgment about the Death of Christ, Election, and Reprobation, &c., wherein, I am sure, I hold nothing contrary to the doctrine of the Church of England, contained in her Thirty-Nine Articles, and interpreted according to her most learned and best beloved children; as Dr. Hammond, Dr. Taylor, Mr. Thorndike, Mr. Truscross, Mr. Gunning, Mr. Pierce."

The circumstance avowed by Conyers, that, although he was pastor of a separate congregation, he held church-communion with Mr. Goodwin and his flock, is remarkable, and affords a singular example of fraternal esteem and affection triumphing over selfishness and bigotry. This learned and liberal man was unhappily silenced by the Act of Uniformity.

Mr. John Horne, who was also contemporary with Mr. Goodwin, was minister of the church of Alhallows, in Lynn, from which he was ejected in the year 1662; though he continued his residence in that town till his death. He was a man of most exemplary piety, very ready in the Scriptures, excellently skilled in the oriental languages, and very laborious in the duties of his calling. After his ejectment, he was regular in his attendance upon the service of the church, and yet preached thrice at his own house every Lord's day; first in the morning, again after dinner, and in the evening. On other days of the week, besides delivering occasional lectures, he expounded the Scriptures in order every morning and evening to all that chose to hear him, as some always did. He was a man of great charity, commonly emptying his pocket among the poor whenever he went into the town. To the afflicted especially he was eminently compassionate; and was generally very much honoured and esteemed for his singular goodness both in Lynn and the surrounding country. He was a man of wonderful meekness, patience, and dispassionateness. In the point of Redemption he was a decided Arminian, contending earnestly, that Jesus Christ "gave Himself a ran-

som for all." At the same time he was equally careful to
exhibit and enforce the practical consequence of that animating truth. He taught, that Christ therefore " died for
all, that they which live should not henceforth live unto
themselves, but unto Him which died for them, and rose
again." This excellent man was the author of various
publications; two of which were replies to Dr. Kendall;
and a third is a decisive refutation of Dr. Owen's defence
of the doctrine of particular redemption. Horne died on
the 14th of December, 1676, aged sixty-one years.*

Of Mr. George Lawson, rector of More, in the county of
Salop, Mr. Baxter says, he was " the ablest man of almost
any I know in England; especially by the advantage of
his age, and very hard studies, and methodical head; but,
above all, by his great skill in politics, wherein he is most
exact, and which contributeth not a little to the understanding of divinity. He was near the Arminians, differing from them in the point of perseverance as to the confirmed, and some little matters more. He published an
excellent Sum of Divinity, called Theopolitica. He hath
written also animadversions on Hobbes, and a piece of
ecclesiastical and civil policy, according to the method of
politics : an excellent book, were it not that he seemeth to
justify the king's death, and meddle too boldly with the
political controversies of the times; though he be a Con-
formist. I must thankfully acknowledge, that I learned
more from Mr. Lawson, than from any divine that gave
me animadversions, or that ever I conversed with: especially his instigating me to the study of politics, in which he
lamented the ignorance of divines, did prove a singular
benefit to me. I confess it is long of my own uncapable-
ness, that I have received no more good from others; but
yet I must be so grateful as to confess, that my understanding hath made a better improvement, for the sudden,
sensible increase of my knowledge, of GROTIUS *de Satis-
factione Christi,* and of Mr. Lawson's manuscripts, than of
any thing else that ever I read; and they convinced me
how unfit we are to write about Christ's government and

* Palmer's Nonconformists' Memorial, Vol. III. p. 567.

laws and judgment, &c., while we understand not the true nature of government, laws, and judgment in general; and that he who is ignorant of politics, and of the law of nature, will be ignorant and erroneous in divinity and the Sacred Scriptures." *

As Mr. Goodwin was rendered incapable of holding any office in the church by the Act of Indemnity, he was of course compelled a second time to retire from his vicarage; accordingly a new presentation took place in the year 1661.† In the first instance of his expulsion, he was "persecuted for righteousness' sake;" but on the present occasion he was "buffeted for his faults," and therefore had no just ground of complaint. About two thousand of his clerical brethren were driven from their livings and their pulpits the following year, by the operation of the Act of Uniformity. Thus were several of the men who in the time of their prosperity had protested against the toleration of sectaries as unlawful and pernicious, themselves associated with persons of this obnoxious class, and reduced to the mortifying necessity of humbly soliciting that liberty of conscience which they had formerly opposed as one of the greatest of all evils! An instructive lesson to men invested with ecclesiastical power! Among the ejected ministers there were not a few who had obtained the benefices of episcopal clergymen that were still living, and whose property they had long been bound in honour and conscience to resign to its legal owners. Others of the ejected ministers, however, had not only obtained their preferment without any violation of justice, but were men whose tolerant spirit, personal piety, and ministerial abilities rendered them an ornament to the sacred office; and who, as Christian pastors, were scarcely inferior to any of whom the Church of God could ever boast. The exclusion of such men from the pulpits of the establishment was highly injurious to her best interests. Who can think of the silencing of such men as Baxter, and Howe, and Bates, without feelings of the liveliest regret? and even

* Reliquiæ Baxterianæ, Part First, pp. 107, 108.   † Newcourt's Repertorium, Vol. I. p. 537.

trembling for those who dared to incur the guilt of such a
measure? Mr. Goodwin lived to see the Puritan clergy
driven from the sanctuary, and to witness the commencement of those execrable persecutions by which they were
harassed during the irreligious reign of the Second
Charles. The episcopal clergy had been treated with
great cruelty and injustice during the dissolution of
monarchy, and, in their turn, resolved to take ample
vengeance upon their former supplanters. Dr. South,
who was one of the court preachers in those calamitous
times, says in a sermon delivered amidst scenes of clerical
ejectment and misery, " Toleration is the very pulling up
the floodgates, and breaking open the fountains of the
great deep, to pour in a deluge of wickedness, heresy, and
blasphemy upon the church." None of the religious
parties had sufficiently profited by those lessons concerning the rights of conscience which Mr. Goodwin had so
strenuously enforced. As the friend and advocate of
religious freedom, " his spirit was stirred in him " when
he saw some of the best men in the nation prohibited
from preaching, summoned before arbitrary tribunals, and
shut up in prisons among thieves and murderers; when he
saw congregations deprived of the ministry of men whom
they loved as their own souls, and irreligious men forced
upon them as their spiritual guides. Under the impulse
of feelings such as these measures were calculated to produce in a mind like his, he published a pamphlet entitled,
" Prelatic Preachers none of Christ's Teachers." This
was the last production of his pen, and was ushered into
the world without a name. Its design was to prove that
diocesan episcopacy was no institution of Jesus Christ, and
to call upon the professors of Christianity to discounte-
nance it as an innovation in the church of God.

Charles the Second was one of the worst kings that ever
disgraced a crown; yet one great benefit arose out of his
profligate, disastrous, and cruel reign, and that of his
moody brother: they effectually cured the English Puritans of their persecuting principles with respect to religion.
Under the Long Parliament, and during the Common-

wealth, the Presbyterians were all but frantic because they were not allowed to employ constables, jailers, magistrates, judges, and hangmen, in the enforcement of their system of ecclesiastical order; but when these formidable functionaries were employed against themselves, their views underwent a complete change, so that they became earnest converts to even John Goodwin's doctrine of universal toleration. Since then we believe the British Presbyterians have been as zealous advocates of religious liberty as any other class of their fellow-subjects. There was a time when their fathers would fain have hanged John Goodwin on account of his writings in defence of universal toleration; but the sons, having tasted the wormwood and the gall of religious coercion under the sway of the merry monarch and that of the infatuated James, freely confessed that Goodwin was in the right, and their fathers in error.

It should seem that Mr. Goodwin remained a nonconformist till the end of his life. According to the inscription accompanying a portrait of him, he died in the year 1665, and the seventy-third of his age. No account of his last days was furnished by his contemporaries, either in a funeral sermon, or in any other authentic document. This omission excites regret rather than surprise, when it is recollected that his death took place when London was an extended scene of consternation and disorder, arising from the ravages of the plague, by the contagion of which one hundred thousand persons are said to have been carried off in the short space of twelve months. Scarcely had this terrible calamity disappeared, when a considerable part of the city was consumed by fire. The Register of Burials belonging to the parish of St. Stephen, Coleman Street, contains the following entry; but whether it refers to the subject of these memoirs or not, is uncertain: " John Goodwin Jn whites Alley. vitler was buried the 3rd of September 1665." It was at this crisis that the distemper raged with the greatest violence. " Men did then no more die by tale and by number : they might put out a weekly bill, and call them seven or eight thousand, or what they pleased : tis certain they died by heaps, and were buried by heaps, that is to say, without account. If I might believe some people, ... there was (were) not less buried those first three weeks in September than twenty thousand per week."*

An intelligent and excellent man, who was preserved in those calamitous times, has also stated, " That most of the church-yards (though some of them large enough) were filled up with earth, or rather the congestion of dead bodies one on another for want of earth, even to the very top of the walls, and some above the walls, so as the churches seemed to be built in pits."†

If the entry in the register in Coleman Street just quoted relate to the subject of this narrative, it would appear that after his second ejectment he endeavoured to provide for his family by keeping an eating-house in the parish where he had long officiated as a learned and eloquent clergyman.

In the year 1670, a quarto volume, bearing the following title, was published in Mr. Goodwin's name : " A Being Filled with the Spirit : wherein it is proved, that it is a Duty incumbent upon All Men, especially of Believers, that they be filled with the Spirit of God." This posthumous publication did not receive the finishing hand of its accomplished author : it nevertheless displays the same pious and benevolent temper, acute and powerful argumentation, deep and familiar acquaintance with the Holy Scriptures, and singular facility in explaining their import, so strikingly manifest in his other theological works. He argues, "with strong commanding evidence," in proof of the Personality and Godhead of the Holy Ghost; and demonstrates the absolute necessity of His gracious operation on the minds of men, in order that they may be enabled to yield an obedient compliance with the requisition of the Gospel, in the exercise of repentance and of faith; be assured of their personal adoption into the family of God ; be renewed in holiness and righteousness after the Divine

* Journal of the Plague-Year, p. 274, Edit. 1722.　　† Memoirs of John Evelyn, Esq., F.R.S. Vol. I. pp. 309, 310, Edit. 1818.

image; be qualified for the service of God in this world, and for the perfect enjoyment of Him in a future state.

To this orthodox and useful book, Mr. Ralph Venning, a pious minister of the Calvinian persuasion, wrote an "epistle dedicatory;" in which he says, "I cannot but acknowledge to have profited by the perusal of it, and do heartily pray, that the Lord will teach all that read it to profit by it, and make it instrumental to their being filled with the Spirit.

"Though I confess myself not to be of the same opinion with the learned author in some other controverted points, yet I cannot but give my testimony concerning this piece, that I find an excellent spirit moving on the face of it, and acting in the heart of it, to promote the glory of God, the power of godliness, and consequently the good of men. Possibly an expression here and there may, as all human writings do, call for a grain of salt; but as to the tenor of the whole, and the tendency thereof, I judge it to be very inoffensive, and not a little, but very useful. The author, it is true, according to his wonted genius, doth often traverse a great deal of ground, and fetch some compasses, before he come to his journey's end; yet he makes it pleasant by such variety, and will thereby pay the reader for his pains in following him."

The publishers of this work, in their address to the reader, say, "The author himself, now at rest, having finished the work which God judged meet for him, and for which he was sent into the world, was a man whose heart was set within him to serve his generation with all faithfulness in the great work of the ministry; not much valuing the approbation or displeasure of men, when the interest of his Lord and Master, and the present peace and everlasting welfare of men, were concerned; being indeed very faithful and laborious in that great work. We may without vanity say of him, as our blessed Saviour said of John the Baptist, he was a burning and a shining light, and many did much rejoice, at least for a season, in his light; although at sometimes, in the faithful discharge of his duty, he met with the same measure that his great Lord and Master had measured out unto him in the days of His flesh. (John vi. 60–66.) "

With the exception of his "Redemption Redeemed," the volume on being filled with the Spirit is the largest of Goodwin's publications; and the sending of it forth within five years of his death, when the House of Commons had done its utmost to ruin his reputation, indicates a confidence that there were many persons still living who would welcome another production of his pen, though it had no respect to existing controversies. What sale it commanded at the time, we have no means of knowing; but it is a work of sterling value, remarkable for its originality and comprehensiveness, full of Scripture criticism and interpretation, and gives ample proof that no man, whether he be a minister or private member of the church, can ever rise to high attainments in personal godliness, or hope to be eminently useful in advancing the cause of Christ in the world, unless he be filled with the Spirit. The volume has been reprinted in Scotland within the last few years, along with several other Puritan works of great value.

While the editor and publishers of this treatise were disposed to hold up the author to public respect for his virtues and ministerial labours, there were others who contemplated his character and writings with sentiments of decided hostility. In the year 1683, the University of Oxford, wishful to display their loyalty, and to establish the divine right of kings, drew up twenty-seven political propositions, deduced from the writings of Buchanan, Knox, Milton, Owen, Baxter, Goodwin, and others, which they pronounced "damnable;" and in solemn convocation decreed, that the books containing them should be publicly burnt by their marshal in the School Quadrangle. A copy of these propositions and of the censure passed upon them was formally presented to the king, who was no doubt pleased with the doctrine designed to be supported, and probably laughed heartily when the parties had retired. The House of Commons afterwards returned the compliment to that learned body, by direct-

ing that the decree of the University should be committed
to the flames by the common hangman.*

With respect to the times in which John Goodwin
lived, it has been justly said, "The events of that
period are a most remarkable illustration of the maxim
which was laid down long ago by the most judicious
of the ancient philosophers, that any system cannot
be more effectually overthrown than by pressing it to
an unreasonable excess; and that the violent and in-
cautious advocates of any measure are taking the sure
means to defeat their own object. The supporters, he
says, of an oligarchical form of government, and those
of a democracy, destroy their respective constitutions,
if they carry the principles of them to an immoderate
length.† The candid and judicious reader may find these
truths strikingly exemplified in the history before us;
which exhibits the intemperate zeal of both parties producing results opposite to those which they respectively
aimed at. He may see how the bigoted advocates of
established abuses, and opposers of all amendments, contributed to bring about a complete revolution; while those
who were never satisfied without perpetual and total
changes, at length, by their restless turbulence, occasioned
the restoration of the original constitution. He will perceive how the most rash and violent supporters of the
Church Establishment were in fact aiding the efforts of
its enemies towards its entire overthrow; and how, on the
other hand, the Presbyterian party, the most intolerant
exactors of rigid uniformity, led the way, by their inveterate hostility to the Episcopal Church, to the predomi-
nance of the Independents; whose system annihilated all
establishment, and all uniformity, by erecting each congregation into a distinct and isolated church. Lastly, it
may be clearly perceived, that while the advisers and
abettors of the most violent and arbitrary measures, who
would have had no bounds set to the royal prerogative,

* Lord Somers's Collection of Tracts Vol. III. p. 223, Edit. 1748.
† Arist. Pol. et Rhet.

were the chief agents in producing the total overthrow of the monarchy itself, and the violent death of their unhappy Sovereign;—the intemperate advocates of the popular rights, who were not satisfied with any restrictions on regal power, and could brook no submission to any but a republican government, were in fact the means of establishing an absolute military despotism."*

* Whately's Use and Abuse of Party Feeling in Matters of Religion, pp. 306-308, Edit. 1833.

CHAPTER XI.

GENERAL VIEW OF HIS CHARACTER.

FROM the preceding narrative, it is presumed, a tolerably accurate view may be obtained of Mr. Goodwin's opinions and general character. Such of his contemporaries as Prynne, Edwards, Bastwick, and Vicars, would not acknowledge that he possessed either talent or moral excellence; but have represented him as a monstrous compound of folly, heresy, and wickedness: but their reproaches are the mere ebullitions of party spleen, advanced without proof, and therefore unworthy of serious regard. Several modern writers have been equally unjust to the memory of this great and singular man: not that they intended to mislead their readers, but being themselves misled by the scandalous mis-statement of Bishop Burnet, in which we have shown there is not a word of truth. Yet his libel has been read, believed, and repeated for two hundred years.

As a Christian minister, the conduct of Mr. Goodwin was highly exemplary. In the labours of the pulpit he was instant in season, out of season, refuting error, exposing vice, defending the doctrines, and enforcing the duties of Christianity. He did not insult the understandings of his hearers by an incessant repetition of common places, or of crude and indigested notions; but acquired ample stores of biblical and theological knowledge, that, like a scribe well instructed, he might bring forth things new and old for the edification of the souls committed to his care. For this purpose his application to study was intense and unremitted. His reading was accurate, and very extensive, notwithstanding his general poverty. With the works of the Christian Fathers, of the schoolmen, and of the most celebrated Protestant Divines, he was familiarly acquainted. Above all, he was an indefatigable and a successful student of the Holy Scriptures. He deliberately investigated all the facts and doctrines which they record, and made himself a com-

plete master of their phraseology ; inattention to which is
one principal source of error among theological students.
These qualifications gave to his public ministry a richness
and a variety, which afforded the highest delight to pious
and intelligent people, drew multitudes around his pulpit,
and fully account for that strong attachment to him which
his stated hearers so repeatedly expressed.

As an advocate of religious liberty, Mr. Goodwin was
equally entitled to commendation. He thoroughly understood the rights of conscience, and was their uniform and
zealous friend. When the whole Presbyterian world
clamoured for religious coercion,—when the British Parliament, engaged in war with the king, claimed dominion
over conscience, as one of its high prerogatives, and was
exceedingly jealous of its honours,—when scarcely any other
person dared openly to appear on the same side with him,
he contended with invincible courage, but without any
rudeness or indecorum, that

> Consciences and souls were made
> To be the Lord's alone.

To this grand principle he adhered, with the most laudable
firmness, amidst all the political changes the nation underwent; and never deviated from it a hair's breadth, from
the commencement of his authorship, to the end of his
life. For the establishment of this position, he exposed
himself to great personal danger, and sacrificed his property
and his reputation. It is highly honourable to him, that
he never defended religious liberty in the spirit of persecution. Strange as it may appear, such is the deceitfulness
of the human heart, that this has been often done. The
late Mr. Robinson of Cambridge seldom introduces the
subject of persecution, without a grin at the national
Church; many of whose clergy and private members are
as strongly averse to that evil as he himself ever was. And
surely those Christians who worship God in the use of a
Liturgy, and think it their duty to submit to episcopal
jurisdiction, are as much entitled to courtesy and respect,
as those who prefer extemporary worship and any other
form of church-government. If it be said, that several

dignitaries of the English Church were formerly distinguished by the spirit and practice of persecution; the
answer is: So were many Nonconformists, both in Great
Britain and America. But why, either in one case or the
other, should the sins of the fathers be visited upon the
children? Messrs. Bogue and Bennett, in their History of
the Dissenters, profess an extraordinary zeal for absolute
freedom in religion, and yet frequently pass beyond the line
of truth to fix a stigma upon persons who dissent from
Calvinism and Independency. But if liberty of conscience
is one of.the most sacred rights of human nature,—if it is
an act of injustice to injure any man in his person or property because he uses that right,—is it not also an act of injustice to injure him in his reputation on the same account?
The man who misrepresents the principles and character
of his fellow-Christians, because the creed which they conscientiously hold happens to differ from his own, let him
profess what he may, is a persecutor to all intents and
purposes; and takes his place among the Gardiners and
the Bonners of a former age. In the tracts written by Mr.
Goodwin against coercion in matters of faith, this mean
and intolerant spirit never appears, either under the garb
of liberality, or in any other form.

His patience of contradiction was very remarkable.
He openly avowed and strenuously defended the unbiassed
convictions of his mind concerning the doctrines of Divine
Revelation; but he was neither mortified nor offended
when he found that his brethren were not convinced by his
arguments. Several theological writers under such circumstances have suffered their passions to be irritated and
soured, and have rather displayed the querulousness of
children, than the moderation of Christian men. This
was the greatest defect in the character of Richard
Baxter. This extraordinary man imagined that God had
discovered to him a method, by which the followers of
Calvin and those of Arminius might be united in religious opinion. Delighted with the thought of terminating
one of the most perplexing controversies that had ever
agitated the Christian Church, he stated his plan, and

D D

assigned his reasons. A few persons entered into his views : but neither the Calvinists nor the Arminians were generally inclined to sacrifice those principles which his scheme required. Hence the good man was displeased, and applied to those bodies of Christians the most reproachful epithets ; such as, " Dogmatical word-warriors—incendiaries—corrupters of the Christian faith—subverters of their own souls—teaching to censure, backbite, slander, and prate against each other, for things which they never understood." The use of such language, in reference to men who in the spirit of meekness contend for what they religiously believe to be the truth of God, is in every respect unwarrantable ; since every man has an unquestionable right to follow the conscientious convictions of his own mind in the affairs of his salvation, and peaceably to communicate his sentiments to others. Of this Mr. Goodwin was fully aware ; and therefore never casts reflections upon his brethren because they thought his creed erroneous. "Far be it from us," he and his church say, "to obtrude our notions upon any man : neither shall it be any matter of discontent to us, that men cannot presently comport in judgment with us. We consider that as men's bodies must have competent time allowed them for removal from one place to another ; so must their minds also, for a regular and manlike quitting of a former opinion, held with any tolerable degree of probability, to take up another opposite to it. We ourselves were not suddenly, nor without many a looking back towards our former opinions, nor without many a going round about them, built up in that faith wherein we now stand ; and for the entertaining whereof, we have not only forsaken many of our brethren in the way of their judgments, but ourselves." *

As a writer, Mr. Goodwin repeatedly declares himself to have been slow in composition. And hence, his writings are less voluminous than those of many of his contemporaries ; and not a few of them are diminutive in size. He has faults which were common amongst the authors

* Agreement and Distance of Brethren, Preface.

of his time. In some of his later works his sentences are immeasurably long, and his style redundant : he multiplies words to satiety. Yet his meaning is generally clear, his language often forcible in a high degree, and his thoughts are original and impressive. There are passages in his writings, which, for sublimity of conception, and energy of expression, would not suffer by a comparison with the most admired productions of his age ; excepting only those of Milton, and of Jeremy Taylor. As a specimen the dedication and preface to his " Redemption Redeemed " might be confidently adduced. He was not deficient in imagination, and some of his illustrations are eminently beautiful. Of the Greek and Latin classics he appears to have been a passionate admirer, and hence his quotations from them are numerous, and often introduced with elegance and effect. But it is in perspicuity and strength of argumentation, in profound and striking views of evangelical truth, and in lucid expositions of different passages of Holy Writ, that his principal excellencies consist. As a logician he has seldom been equalled, and in a talent for illustrating Scripture he was perhaps never excelled. Various are the subjects upon which he employed his pen. His works comprehend several pieces of didactic and practical theology; a system of catechetical instruction; disquisitions on church-government; on the inspiration of the Holy Scriptures; on religious Toleration; on the subjects and mode of baptism; on church-fellowship between Pædo-Baptists and Antipædo-Baptists; on the quinquarticular controversy ; on the Deity, the personality, and the operation of the Holy Ghost ; on various political questions : and on all these topics, excepting the last, his writings are highly creditable to his learning, his judgment, and his moderation.

In the selection of terms he always aimed rather at strength than elegance. In one of his epistles " to the reader," he therefore says, " Trimness of style, and quaint-ness of invention, I know where thou mayest find, but not here. The bent of my study is, to provide for the con-sciences of men, though their fancies starve. And the truth is, that effeminateness and lightness of phrase doth but transmit the matter to the imagination : whereas a masculine and weighty expression carries it into the conscience, and makes it sink into the soul."*

It is especially to be regretted that Mr. Goodwin should have taken part with the men who were concerned in the fate of Charles. The two pamphlets which he wrote in their defence have left a blot upon his memory, and will never allow even those who admire his theological opinions and his general character to contemplate the whole of his conduct with unmingled approbation. That a man of his acuteness and penetration, a man who thought so correctly on almost every other subject, should have written these tracts, and have seriously thought that the measures which he defended would form a basis of national liberty, is a melancholy proof of the infirmity to which great minds are sometimes liable ; and can only be accounted for by recollecting the rude state in which political science then existed, and the peculiar condition of the country, when the very elements of the constitution were at war with each other. If we identify the present government of England, either in Church or State, with that under which Mr. Goodwin lived, we shall be unjust to him, and grossly impose upon ourselves. On every side he saw insulted parliaments, arbitrary taxation, illegal and sanguinary tribunals, corrupted and mercenary law, bigoted and desolating persecution.† By such enormities the nation was involved in the miseries of civil strife ; and when the principles of the king and of his advisers were considered, a recurrence of these evils was confidently anticipated in the event of his restoration to the throne. Speaking of the concessions of the parliament to the royal party as the ground of Charles's restoration to his regal prerogatives, Mr. Goodwin says, " What could such an encouragement, given to such men, but portend, either a re-embroiling of this miserably-wasted nation in wars and blood, or the necessity of patient and quiet subjection to the iron yoke of perpetual bondage, together with the certain ruin of

* God a Good Master.   † Symmon's Life of Milton, p. 586.

those who had showed most faithfulness in defence of the kingdom's liberties ?" *   Under these impressions he wrote his "Right and Might," and his "Obstructors of Justice," and not from any spirit of insubordination, or of hostility to the kingly office ; much less from any delight in blood, as is intimated in the pitiful account of him which is given in the "General Biographical Dictionary," published under the direction of Alexander Chalmers, Esq.   Such an insinuation could never have been made by any person who had the slightest knowledge of Mr. Goodwin's character.   He was deceived in the measures to which Cromwell and his associates resorted ; and his being deceived appears the more remarkable to us who know what followed in England during the Commonwealth, and the military despotism which arose out of similar proceedings in modern France: but Mr. Goodwin's errors were common to many eminent personages of that day.   They were the errors of Dr. John Owen, and they were the errors of John Milton, certainly one of the most accomplished scholars of his age, and one of the greatest geniuses that ever lived.

Amidst the political aberrations into which Mr. Goodwin was drawn in those days of confusion, he never acted the part either of a time-server, or of a parasite.   He wrote indeed in vindication of the Long Parliament, and of the Army ; but when they encroached upon the rights of private conscience, he did not hesitate with a firm and manly tone to declare his disapprobation of their unrighteous proceedings.   His religious sentiments rendered him offensive to the leading men both in the Parliament and the Commonwealth ; but such was his conviction of the truth and importance of those sentiments, that he would neither deny nor conceal them for any worldly accommodation whatever.   While other preachers and writers of far inferior ability were amply rewarded for their services to the government, he was treated with neglect and injustice. A bare protection from personal violence was the only remuneration he ever received for any of his political writings.   His continued attachment to the Long Parlia-

* Right and Might, p. 18.

ment and to the Protector was perfectly gratuitous, and
was manifested "against disobligements not a few nor
inconsiderable." The former party reduced him to indi-
gence by expelling him from his vicarage; the latter
restored him to it again, but with scarcely any revenue
attached to it. To enjoy the patronage of the great under
the Long Parliament he must have abandoned his doctrine
of religious liberty, and to acquire temporal honours and
emolument under the Commonwealth he must have sacrificed his Arminianism; but these lay too near his heart
to be resigned for anything "this short-enduring world
could give." There was in him a certain loftiness of spirit
which rendered him extremely averse to all crouching to
the rich and great for personal advantage. When accused
of flattering men in power, he says, "Luther professed
that for twenty years together he never felt the least
motion in his heart towards coveteousness : I may say, I
never found my heart tempting me to such a compliance
with any great person whatsoever. They who have known
me from my youth up will freely give this testimony of
me, that what other weakness soever they observed in me,
they never found me inclined to familiarities with great
men, much less to any adulatory comportments with
them."*

"Of all unchristian misbehaviours there is a peculiar
antipathy in my genius against the sin of flattery, and
unworthy compliance with great persons ; which principle,
though it hath kept me from honour and preferment, hath
abundantly recompensed that inconvenience otherwise:
nor do I intend to sell it, or to recede from it, at any rate
whatsoever. As for flattery, and undue applications to
the greatness of this world, all that know the manner of
my conversation will be my compurgators. But as there
is a great abhorrency in my temper from flattery, so there
is a strong propension to vindicate worthy actions, by
whomsoever performed, whether by shrubs or cedars. In
managing this principle it is very possible that my pen,
being warm, may rhetorize a little to the right hand;

* Peace Protected, p. 71.

which hath always been counted a venial delinquency by ingenuous men."[*]

" This I confess, that from first to last, I have stood by the Authority for the time being, and have contended for an universal subjection in all things lawful unto it. When there were two Authorities conflicting, that of the king, and the other of the parliament, I joined that which I judged best pleadable and most promissory of civil and RELIGIOUS HAPPINESS. To this Authority I have constantly adhered, not only in the lowest ebb thereof, when its competitress was ready to overwhelm it, but likewise under all those sad requitals wherewith it recompensed my service. For as I was a zealous asserter of this Authority, so was I faithful in declaring [its] just and lawful bounds; persuading it to contain itself within its own sphere; protesting that if it should prove like Jordan in the time of harvest, and overflow its banks, this would endanger the cutting off of the waters, and laying the channel of it dry. Men in authority can hardly be sufficiently jealous over themselves, lest they conceit their power to be more extensive than it is; or that in the exercise of it they intrench upon some of the appropriate royalties of God. But my faithfulness in endeavouring to preserve that Authority from destruction by its own exorbitancies was of so hard a resentment with it, that it did not only quench all remembrance of those other services wherein I sought to prevent the annoyance of it by other men, but kindled a spirit of unkindness, and of hard, that I say not unjust, proceedings against me. Upon this account I cannot but presume it was, that I was so frowned upon and smitten by this Authority : that I was, time after time, summoned before the Consistory, surnamed the Committee for Plundered Ministers ; and this by the procurement of some of the members of the Authority I speak of; that here I was coarsely handled, disgracefully entreated; my accusers, though but few and less considerable, countenanced; my friends, who appeared with me and for me, neglected ; and that at last I was compelled to drink the

* Obstructors of Justice, p. 141.

cup prepared only for Malignant Ministers; being not only sequestered from my living, but denied the liberty of preaching in my wonted place. Nor was there, as far as my memory is able to recollect, any reason given by the Committee, of so severe a sentence against me. I verily believe, that from the first to the last of the sitting of that parliament, there was no example of any minister in the land, who had so cordially, and with so much activeness in the promotion of their cause, adhered to them as I had done, and upon whom they had so little to charge otherwise, who received the like measure from their hand. I confess, that after several years' total sequestration, (between four and five, as I remember,) the Presbyterian interest somewhat damping, and the person gratified in my sequestration falling under some parliamentary dislike, I was, *with much ado,* restored to my place in Coleman Street. But, *jam seges est, ubi Troia fuit,* at my return I found only a piece of skeleton of those means, which at my departure I left a fair and full body. The chief men upon the place had transferred their devotion-benevolence, as well as their devotion itself, upon him who had served their turns and his own in my pulpit. So that if I should estimate the loss I sustained by my sequestration, (without valuing the disrepute accompanying it,) at five hundred pounds, I should, I believe, cut short the account by one half. Notwithstanding all these disobligements, yet did I not behave myself falteringly in that covenant of loyalty and service, wherein mine own judgment and conscience had engaged me, to the men who thus requited me.

"So that if I am a time-server, I have served very hard masters; from whom I never received any thing for my work, but in such coin wherein Paul five times received forty save one. Nor have I ever known, unless by hearsay, that the great men of the times have so much as the ninth part of a farthing, wherewith to reward those who have served them. But I know by experience, that they have scorpions wherewith to chastise their servants without a cause. Nor do I now write these things out of any querulous disposition, or desire that the masters of the present times should repair the breaches made upon me by their predecessors, but to stop the mouth of that unworthiness which is opened against me, as if I had thriven in the world so well by serving the times formerly, that I meant to follow the same occupation. The truth is, I am resolved, God assisting me, to serve the present times upon the same account on which I served the former; and judge myself bound in conscience so to do. There shall be no more wars in the land, nor bloodshed, nor tumults, nor plunderings, nor depopulations, in my days, nor in the days after me, as far as I shall be able to prevent them. I shall be free to serve men in authority, and in them the nation, and yet leave them at perfect liberty to dispose as well of their faces as of their places, to whom they please. I desire neither; and if they please to deny me both, I shall serve them as well as I can without them. My great design in giving unto Cæsar that which I know to be Cæsar's, is, that thereby I may purchase the more equitable liberty to deny unto Cæsar that which I know is not his, whensoever he assumes it. And if Cæsar, whoever he be, careth not to be served upon such an account, he must wait for relief till I am dead. For I am resolved to serve him, and yet not upon any other terms." *

This valuable extract gives an interesting view of the principles by which Mr. Goodwin was actuated in regard to his political conduct. On every occasion when conscience was concerned, he was firm and unyielding, free from every bias of secular interest. While we lament therefore the obliquity of his mind in the case of Charles, his honest integrity, and singular disinterestedness, will warrant the application to him of the solemn appeal of his illustrious coadjutor: "I invoke the Almighty to witness, that I never, at any time, wrote any thing which I did not think agreeable to truth, to justice, and to piety. Nor was I ever prompted to such exertions by the influence of ambition, by the lust of lucre or of praise; it was only the conviction of duty and the feeling

* Peace Protected, Preface.

of patriotism, a disinterested passion for civil and religious liberty."*

The part which Milton acted with respect to his unfortunate sovereign has been long since condoned by the people of England; and it is high time that the same favour should be extended to his fellow delinquent. He did not indeed write an epic poem, like Paradise Lost, so as to rival Homer and Virgil, and thus shed a permanent honour upon his country and its language; but he led the way in securing for the land of his birth, and for the world at large, a mightier benefit,—universal religious toleration, the doctrine of which he was one of the first clearly to unfold and manfully to defend. Compared with this grand achievement even the composition of Paradise Lost sinks into insignificance. The doctrine of universal toleration, of which Goodwin was the able, self-denying, zealous, and unwearied advocate, has given relief to the consciences of millions of upright Christians, is an element of prosperity to every nation that has adopted it, and will be everywhere acknowledged when the Church shall appear in her full millennial glory.

To Mr. Goodwin's abhorrence of persecution, as an outrage upon every thing sacred, and the scandalous intolerance of the Presbyterian party, his errors respecting the death of the king may be distinctly traced; nor can they be justly attributed to any other cause. It is also worthy of remark that the religious liberty for which he so strenuously contended has been fully realized in this country, since the glorious era of the Revolution in 1688; and especially since the accession of the house of Hanover to the British throne.

> O blissful days!
> When all men worship God as conscience wills.
> Far other times our fathers' grandsires knew!

Already the principles of universal Toleration are practically received not only in Great Britain, and in the United States of America; but also in Italy and Spain, where for ages the Inquisition inspired the people with terror, and prevented the spread of the Gospel. Were John

* Milton's Prose Works, Vol. VI. p. 388, Edit. 1806.

Goodwin now alive, he might say with truth to these nations, "The liberty of religious thought and worship which you all enjoy, I took out of the hand of the Amorite with my sword and with my bow."

When it is said that Mr. Goodwin was an Arminian, it is intended to use that word in its strict and proper sense. It is not unusual to find writers of considerable celebrity, either through prejudice or inattention, greatly injuring the learned and excellent Arminius by associating with his name sentiments which he openly disavowed. The doctrines espoused by him have been frequently identified with those of Arius and Pelagius. Of the same ungenerous treatment Mr. Goodwin had often occasion to complain. Whereas no theological writers whatever have more distinctly and strongly than they, asserted the absolute and universal depravity of human nature,—the proper divinity of Jesus Christ,—the reality of the atonement made by His death,—justification by faith in Him,—the absolute necessity of the Holy Spirit's operation in order to the commencement, the continuance, and the completion of personal sanctification; as well as in every act of Christian obedience. Several theologians have indeed contended for the universality of the Divine benevolence, and at .the same time have denied some of the doctrines here specified, especially those of original sin, and justification by faith. But to denominate such men Arminians is palpably disingenuous, and only calculated to mislead the uninformed. Could the pious and intelligent Arminius address such refiners upon the system which bears his name, he would bear an earnest testimony against them as corrupters of Divine truth.

In avoiding the doctrine of Necessity, Mr. Goodwin, like his great predecessor Arminius, never runs into the Pelagian quagmire. In his writings, Divine grace is always represented as taking the lead in every thing that conduces to the salvation of man. "Concerning the grace of God," says he, "and the freeness hereof, I hold nothing but what fully accords with these positions: That the original of the salvation of the world, and so of every person that comes to be saved, was from the free grace and good pleasure of God.—That the method, or system of counsels, according to which God effecteth the salvation of all that are saved did proceed entirely from the same grace and good pleasure.—That the gift of Jesus Christ for a Mediator, and so the grant of justification and salvation to men upon believing, issued solely from the same grace.—That men by nature, that is, considered under such a condition as they were brought unto by Adam, and wherein they should have subsisted, in case they had been born, had not the grace of God in Christ interposed to relieve them, have no power, not the least inclination or propension of will, to do any thing acceptable to God, or of a saving import.—That notwithstanding the healing of the natural condition of man by the free grace of God, there is not one of a thousand, possibly not one throughout the world, but so corrupts himself, that without a second relief, viz., in patience and long-suffering towards him, ever comes to repent, or believe, and so to be saved. —That it is from the undeserved grace of God, that any person is put into a capacity of believing, or hath power and means vouchsafed to him to enable him to believe.— That a man is put into this capacity of believing by an irresistible working of the free grace of God.—That when a man comes actually to believe, the exercise of this power proceeds also from the free grace of God ; so that no man ever believeth without present assistance from the free grace of God, over and above his ability to believe.—That the act of believing, whensoever it is performed, is at so low a rate of efficiency from a man's self, that, suppose the act could be divided into a thousand parts, nine hundred ninety and nine of them are to be ascribed unto the free grace of God, and only one unto man. Yea this one is no otherwise to be ascribed to man, than as supported, strengthened, and assisted by the free grace of God. I attribute as much as possibly can be to the grace of God in the act of believing, saving the attributableness of the action to man himself, in the lowest sense that can be conceived. For certain it is, that it is man, not the Spirit of

God, that believeth: and therefore there must be such a degree of efficiency about it left unto man, which may with truth give it the denomination of being his. They that go about to interest the grace of God in the act of believing upon any other terms, so that the act cannot truly be called the act of the creature, are injurious in the highest manner to the grace of God, at this main turn; rendering it altogether unprofitable to the poor creature; who by the verdict of such a notion shall be left in his sins. The law of Justification is expressly this: *He that believeth shall be justified.* Therefore if it be not man himself that believeth, it is impossible that he should be justified." *

In perfect accordance with these principles were Mr. Goodwin's views of predestination and election. "God is asserted," says he, "to have predestinated, or purposed, so many as should truly believe, unto Life and Glory; and all who should not believe, unto Destruction. Such a predestination of men from eternity as this, the Scriptures clearly hold forth: such a predestination is fully consistent with the glory of His Wisdom, and highly magnifies all His attributes, without the least disparagement of any. Whereas that doomful preterition, that blood which many wring out of the Scriptures instead of milk, hath no intelligible comport with any of them, but casts a kind of obscurity upon them all."†—"The tenor of God's decree of Election, which was from eternity, is this, Whosoever shall believe in My Son Jesus Christ, shall hereupon become a man of that species, sort, or kind of men, whom I have chosen from amongst all other men, and designed to salvation. Men cannot, in propriety of speech, be said to be elected from eternity, because they had no being from eternity: nothing having been from eternity but God alone."‡

"Neither God's election, nor His purpose according to election, can be said to proceed from faith foreseen; but from the mere grace and good pleasure of God. For though it be supposed that He decreeth to elect, and accordingly actually electeth, all that believe, and none other; yet this

———

, * Redemption Redeemed, Preface.   † Ibid. p. 68.   ‡ Ibid. p. 244.

at no hand proveth either that His purpose or the execution hereof proceed in their origination from the faith of such persons foreseen, no nor from the foresight of their faith : though this be more tolerable than the other. There is nothing in the nature of faith, nor in God's foresight of faith, in what persons soever, that hath in it any generative virtue of any such purpose in God. It is true, the incomprehensible wisdom of God, which mingleth itself with and steers all the motions of His will, led him to faith as the most proper foundation whereon to build His purpose of election, and accordingly His election itself: but this no more proveth that faith, either foreseen, or in what consideration soever, is the cause of God's purpose of election, than a good foundation is the cause of a man's desire or resolution to build a house. Doubtless the love of God to mankind, out of which He decreed the election and salvation of those that believe, was a most intimous principle in Him, flowing immediately from the essential goodness of His nature ; and not raised by any foreign influence or interposure whatever."*

Several persons appear to have no conception of controversy, except as associated with angry passions : and as Mr. Goodwin was frequently employed in logical warfare, attempts have been made on this ground to fix a stain upon his reputation. He has been represented as a sort of second Ishmael, whose hand was against every man, while every man's hand was against him. It is however manifest, that there is no moral evil in controversy, considered in itself; and that it only becomes such when managed with unfairness, or employed as a vehicle of slander. On the other hand, it may be a means of the greatest possible advantage to society and to religion. To the oral disputes of Jesus Christ with the Jewish sects, we are indebted for no inconsiderable part of the evangelical history ; some of the apostolical Epistles are unquestionably of a polemical nature ; and, judging from the practice of the Inspired Writers, there are occasions when it is perfectly lawful to adopt even an ironical style, in the exposure of error as well as of vice. The bare circumstance, therefore, of a man's being a contro-

* Exposition of the Ninth of Romans, p. 133.

versial writer implies no just imputation upon his character. Openly and zealously to oppose errors, and tyrannical impositions upon conscience, is no fault, but an imperative duty. It should also be remarked, that Mr. Goodwin considered it to be his misfortune, that he was so frequently engaged in disputation with his brethren; and often declares with considerable emotion, that nothing but a consciousness of duty, and an ardent love of liberty and truth, could induce him to submit to such a sacrifice of his personal feelings. He always enjoyed an opportunity of retiring from the rugged paths of controversy, to walk in the flowery meadows and among the delightful streams and fountains of exegetical and practical theology. " The great Searcher of the reins," says he, " knoweth, that if Himself would discharge me of the service of contradicting and opposing men, and dispose of me in a way of retirement, were it never so private and obscure, where I might only contest with mine own weakness and errors, He should give me one of the first-born desires of my soul. As for revenge, I have always, since I knew any thing of God, judged it not only an unchristian, but a most effeminate, base, and ignoble passion : yea, at this hour, my thoughts hardly suffer me to conceive of it as consisting with those things that accompany salvation. I wish it were as easy for others to forbear injuring me, as it is for me to neglect and pass it by, when they have done it. Whosoever burden me with the crimes of ambition and revenge, certain I am that they are strangers to my spirit and converse. As for ambition, unless to shape a course for the dust and dunghill ; for poverty, contempt, disgrace ; loss of estate, of friends, of whatsoever is called great in the world, be ambition ; the tenor of the course I have steered will be my compurgator, in the consciences of all those to whom it hath been known." *

Mr. Goodwin was naturally modest and unassuming : and hence, notwithstanding his talents and learning, he did not appear before the world as an author, till he was upwards of forty years of age. Many of his publications are of a

* Novice-Presbyter Instructed, p. 137.

practical nature; and nearly all his polemical works were
extorted from him by the misrepresentations and reproaches of his intolerant contemporaries. In the course
of his ministry he preached what he believed to be the
truth : but as his creed was not formed on the model of
Calvin's Institutes, and the Decrees of the Synod of Dort,
his brethren directed their discourses from the pulpit
against him, and filled the press with scandalous pamphlets,
the declared object of which was to effect his ruin. He
expostulated with his ungenerous assailants, expressed a
strong desire to live in peace, and for some time patiently
endured the most outrageous treatment. Now and then
he repelled an unprovoked attack, but suffered many such
to pass without any public notice. While he pursued these
gentle measures, he had reason almost daily to complain,
"How are they increased that trouble me !" Weary at
length of parrying the thrusts of his antagonists, and
having been long dared to the field, he buckled on his Arminian armour, carried the war into the camp of the
enemy, and maintained it there, with invincible magnanimity and surprising effect, during the remainder of his life.
"They who have known me," says he, "from my youth up,
until some few years past, very well know, that however
I was encompassed about with infirmities otherwise, yet
did I never either deserve or bear the blame of *boldness ;*
but always the contrary. Only since God was pleased to
call me out of the retirement of my unprofitable bashful-
ness, He hath made me, as Jeremy of old, an iron pillar and
brazen wall." *

In none of his public controversies, of a theological
nature, was Mr. Goodwin the original assailant. He
wrote nothing either in defence of his peculiar opinions
concerning justification, or in vindication of the Arminian
doctrines, till he had been openly impeached as a heretic,
and summoned to the bar of the public to answer for the
crime of perverting the truths of Christianity. It is true
that he commenced the attack upon the Triers and Ejectors
of ministers ; but this he regarded as a duty which he

* Triumviri, Preface.

owed to his country, and to the cause of religious freedom. "Considering," says he, "how enormous and insupportable the proceedings of the two newly-erected Consistories, the one of Triers, the other of Ejectors, grew from day to day, I had no rest in my spirit till I had answered the call of God in my conscience, to give testimony against them; and to declare the unjustifiableness of the power delegated to them; but especially that exercised by them; by clear principles in reason, but especially by the light that shines from heaven in the Scriptures." *

Mr. Goodwin's implicit submission to the decisions of Holy Writ, on all questions in divinity, is worthy of special notice. Some learned and speculative men have endeavoured to deduce the doctrines of religion from what they have called the Light of Nature; and have attempted to bend the Scriptures to them by elaborate criticisms and unnatural interpretations. Others have subjected the most sublime discoveries of Revelation to the test of mere human reason; and have resolved to yield the assent of their minds to no doctrine, the difficulties of which they could not solve upon rational principles. But our author was so deeply impressed with the conviction, that

> All truth is from the Sempiternal Source
> Of light Divine,

that, upon all occasions, he manifests a perfect willingness to bow to the authority of the Inspired Writings. "We ought not," said one of the greatest of men, "to attempt to draw down or submit the mysteries of God to our reason, but contrariwise, to raise and advance our reason to the divine truth."† In perfect accordance with this principle, it was the business of Mr. Goodwin's life to ascertain the meaning of the Sacred Oracles, and to form his creed according to what he believed to be the mind of the Holy Spirit. "I have not the least desire," says he, "to be wise above what is written in the book of God; nor have I the least hope of rising in wisdom to the height of what is written herein, whilst the encumbrance of flesh and blood hangeth on me. Only my desires are, that in my conscientious en-

* Triumviri, Preface. † Lord Bacon.

E E

deavours to ascend this mountain, I may neither be thrust down by those that are above me, nor be pulled backward by those that are beneath." *

To remain willingly ignorant, however, of what the blessed God hath seen good to reveal, Mr. Goodwin deemed equally criminal with a daring scrutiny into the divine secrets. He therefore set himself, by the use of every means in his power, to form an acquaintance with the "whole counsel of God," as declared in the Holy Scriptures. "If any man," says he, "advanceth himself into the things which he hath not seen, or above the proportion of his faith, let him suffer as a transgressor of the law of sobriety; I shall not be his advocate. I go no further than I feel the ground firm under me. If I come at any time to a place that is soft and tender, I tread light, and charge no great matter of weight upon it. Yet not to go up to the mount, when God calleth, and offereth the kisses of His mouth to us there, under a pretence of danger in climbing, is to reject the bounty of heaven, and betray the richest opportunities of making ourselves great in the sight of God, angels, and men. The things revealed in the Scriptures, as well those of the most sublime consideration, as things of a more obvious import, ' belong unto us and to our children,'—are our spiritual patrimony, which God our Father hath given us, to maintain ourselves honourably in faith and holiness. Every inch of such an inheritance is worth standing upon, and contending for."†

We hence perceive how it was that he attached such great importance to the doctrine of universal redemption, and spent so much time in defending it, and in recommending it to others: he did not regard the belief of it a necessary condition of salvation; yet he deemed it otherwise a matter of high importance. He thought that men ought to believe it because it is unequivocally revealed in the Holy Scriptures, while the opposite tenet is merely a matter of inference, being deduced from other doctrines, which are themselves matters of doubtful dispu-

---

* Divine Authority of the Scriptures, Dedication.   † Redemption Redeemed, Preface.

tation. He thought also that the opposite tenet, that of limited redemption, injurious in its influence upon the mind of every one who cordially embraces it, and allows it to influence his practice. Supposing him to be a minister, he is sent to preach salvation by Jesus Christ "to every creature." But while he is addressing a congregation upon this momentous theme, he does not know, upon his own principles, that any one of his hearers is redeemed by the blood of the cross; and if he tells them that they are thus redeemed, he may prove to be a false witness before God. How must this feeling check the ardour of his zeal!

Suppose one of his hearers to be convinced of his guilt and danger, as a sinner in the sight of God, and to inquire, "What must I do to be saved?" He is told that he must believe in the Lord Jesus Christ, who is the only Saviour of men, so as to trust in Him for pardon and eternal life. The anxious inquirer replies, "You told us that Christ died only for a part of mankind. How am I to know that He died for me?" What satisfactory answer can be given to this vital question, except that which is supplied by St. Paul? "He gave Himself a ransom for all;" and therefore gave Himself a ransom for *thee*. Faith comes by this doctrine, unbelief by its opposite.

Suppose the advocate of particular and limited redemption to be a father, to whom God has given a numerous family. He looks with yearning and tender affection upon his lovely children around him, for whom he offers his daily prayers, and whom he teaches the way of salvation by Jesus Christ; yet all this while he is in doubt whether Christ died for any one of them. He may hope the best; but his hope is necessarily connected with fear and painful misgiving; very different from the feeling of the man who believes that Christ died to redeem every soul of man. Hence he loves his family, and all mankind, not only as the creatures of God, but as the objects of redeeming mercy. In his estimation, therefore, there is a peculiar sacredness connected with every human being, however degraded by poverty, ignorance, and sin. The Son of God died to redeem him. No stumbling-blocks

2 E 2

should therefore be laid in his way; and every effort should be put forth to secure his salvation. In dealing with his parishioners Goodwin had long been hampered by his Calvinistic creed ; and greatly did he enjoy his liberty, when he could say with the apostle, " O ye Corinthians, our mouth is open; our heart is enlarged!"

Mr. Goodwin was fully aware of the necessity of divine assistance in order to the discovery and right apprehension of revealed truth ; and his views of the readiness of God to impart that assistance were very exalted. " The Spirit of God," says he, " hath such a great interest in the minds of men, that they cannot perform any of those operations that are proper to them, but by the loving interposure and help of the Spirit. The intellectual frame of the soul of man was, by the fall of Adam, brought to an absolute chaos of ignorance and darkness. So that if the understandings of men quit themselves in any due proportion to their peace, it must needs be by that gracious conjunction of the Spirit of God with them, which is a vouchsafement by Him who raised up the tabernacle of Adam, which was fallen, Jesus Christ, blessed for ever. What light of truth is, since the fall, to be found in any man, is an express fruit of the grace that is given unto the world upon the account of Jesus Christ, and is in the soul by the interposure of the Spirit of God ; the gift whereof, upon this account, is so highly magnified in the Scriptures."*

It has been remarked by Lord Bacon that Truth and Goodness differ from each other, but as the seal and the wax ; and that Truth, when duly received, imprints Goodness upon the human mind. The same sentiment occurs in several of Mr. Goodwin's publications. Erroneous conceptions concerning God, he regarded as the fruitful parent of superstition, of misery, and of sin. Hence he prayed to the Father of spirits for heavenly illumination and guidance,—divested himself of the prejudices of education, —rose above the fear of man,—and, with a mind eager for divine knowledge, studied the Bible through a series of years, availing himself of every help within his reach.

* Redemption Redeemed, Preface.

Having by these means found what he believed to be "God's eldest daughter, Truth," he became enamoured of her beauty, and made a solemn consecration of all his faculties to her service. Excepting the martyrs, few men have ever made greater sacrifices to truth and conscience. He re-signed personal ease and convenience, the friendship and esteem of his brethren, his reputation, his temporal emolu-ment, and became an object of general reproach ; a sort of scape-goat, on whose head were laid, by his Calvinistic brethren, nearly all the errors, heresies, and mental follies of human nature. The following language would have done honour to Martin Luther, or to the most distinguished of his contemporaries :—"The serpentine hissing of tongues and pens against me is now no strange thing, and so no great trial. From my youth up, I have conflicted with the viperous contradictions of men ; Truth having acted me in full opposition to my genius and spirit by making me a man of contention to the whole earth. But I can wil-lingly and freely say, Let Truth handle me as she pleaseth, deprive me of all things, yea, of that very being itself of which I am yet possessed, upon condition that she herself may reign."*

"I have given sufficient hostages unto the world that I shall never war upon it, or be troublesome to it, for neg-lecting me, or laying my honour in the dust. He who believeth that I was tempted into a way of schism by men's intemperate zeal against my Treatise of Justification,† is a stranger to me. But that which he calleth schism, is schism only so called, unless to separate from iniquity be schism. But the most intemperate zeal of men against my person, name, or books, is a temptation of a very faint influence upon me to turn me out of any way of truth, or to make me their enemy. Only when the truth is offended I con-fess I burn, and in case I find any strength in my hand to redress the injury done to it, I have no rest in my spirit

* Exposition, Preface.   † " Mr. John Goodwin—I believe was tempted into a way of schism, by men's intemperate zeal against his elaborate Treatise of Justification." Baxter's Plain Scripture Proof of Infants' Church-Membership, p. 193. Edit. 1651.

422 LIFE OF

until I have attempted the vindication. By truth I do not
mean mine own opinion ; for that which is no more than so
I shall neither trouble myself nor any other man about it ;
but I mean a doctrine or notion which I am able to demonstrate, either from the Scriptures or clear principles in
reason, to be agreeable to the mind of God." *

What was said by the ever-memorable Hales, of Eton,
may be justly applied to Mr. Goodwin : "The pursuit of
truth has been my only care ever since I knew the meaning of the word. For this I have forsaken all hopes, all
friends, all desires which might bias me, and hinder me
from driving right at what I aimed. For this I have spent
my money, my means, my youth, my age, and all that I
have. If, with all my cost and pains, my purchase is but
error, I may safely say, to err has cost me more than it
has many to find the truth; and truth shall give me this
testimony at last, that, if I have missed of her, it has not
been my fault, but my misfortune." †

When one of his opponents attempted to silence him by
urging the authority of Selden, Mr. Goodwin replied, " I
am most ready to comply with the learning and judgment
of a man many degrees inferior to Mr. Selden in the
honour which belongeth to learning, who shall teach me
that which I am able to comprehend, or to conceive at
least probable; but otherwise, angels from heaven, and
beetles from the dunghill, are teachers alike unto me ;
unless the light of reason showeth me a difference between
them, I have no more faith for the teachings of the one
than of the other. Were Mr. Selden Socrates, and my
apologist Plato, I must commend them, but not forsake
my ancient and fast friend, Truth, for their sakes." ‡

Mr. Goodwin was not less ingenuous and decided in the
open avowal of what he believed to be truth, than he was
diligent in the pursuit of it. The confession of the pusil-
lanimous Father Paul, " God hath not given me the spirit
of Luther," was not applicable to him. "I am re-

* Cata-Baptism, Preface.   † Hales's Works, Vol. I. p. 137, Edit. 1765.
‡ Apologist Condemned, p. 22.

solved," says he, "God assisting, not to be ashamed of any of Christ's words, nor to forbear upon occasion the freest utterance of them, before what generation soever; and hope that neither name, nor friends, nor estate, nor liberty, nor life itself, which have not betrayed me hitherto, will ever prove a snare of death to me, or hinder me from finishing my course with joy. If I fall in any of my standings up for the truth, the loss is already cast up by Luther's arithmetic: I had rather fall with Christ than stand with Cæsar."*

Speaking of himself, and of one of his coadjutors, in regard of whom an anonymous writer had inquired, "How dare these men so boldly and so deeply to traduce, calumniate, condemn, and post up a whole society of elders?" Mr. Goodwin says in another place, "The men he speaks of *dare not,* upon any terms whatsoever, traduce or calumniate any man, of what condition soever, much less a whole society of elders; they know that in so doing they should do the office of the grand accuser of the brethren. But I will tell you what they dare do: they dare, with the hand of truth, take lions by the beard. They dare, in vindication of the cause of God and of His servants, withstand His and their enemies, though never so formidable for number, rank, or other consideration, to their faces. They dare expose their names, estates, liberties, lives, to the wrath of men, for fulfilling the righteousness of God. These, and such things as these, they dare do."†

In the investigation of the doctrines of revelation the mind of Mr. Goodwin never dwells upon the surfaces of things. In the discussion of any theological question, he sees it in all its bearings, and has a distinct view of the end from the beginning. The grand principles concerning the extent of the Divine Philanthropy, which he was so anxious to establish and recommend, had not been hastily adopted, but had undergone a thorough investigation. They were not deduced, according to his apprehension, from a few isolated texts of Scripture, but from the general

* Postscript to the Scourge of the Saints Displayed.　　† Novice-Presbyter, p. 130.

tenor of the Inspired Volume : and the conviction of his own individual existence was not more strong, than his belief that JESUS CHRIST BY THE GRACE OF GOD TASTED DEATH FOR EVERY MAN. Most of his larger works, as his Treatise of Justification, his Redemption Redeemed, and his Exposition of the Ninth Chapter of the Epistle to the Romans, are written with singular closeness of thought, and evince such mental energy as is seldom displayed. It may be safely affirmed, that a student, whatever may be his religious persuasion, who wishes fully to understand the controversy on the five points, will not easily meet with an author who will give him more ample and correct information on the subject than Mr. Goodwin. His writings, and especially those just mentioned, are systematical: an advantage which some of Mr. Fletcher's best pieces do not possess. Indeed the extraordinary learning and talents of our author have been acknowledged both by enemies and friends. " I always find," says Dr. Barlow, " in the prosecution of your arguments, that perspicuity and acuteness which I often seek and seldom find in the writings of others."*—"I love and honour your person," says Mr. Jeans, "as in other respects, so for the good and great gifts and parts God hath bestowed on you."†— "His great learning, good sense, and extraordinary style for that day," says Job Orton, "render his works worth reading."‡—The authors of "General Biography" also remark, "His numerous writings display considerable learning, and very able polemical talents."§—" That Mr. Goodwin was a man of considerable learning," says Mr. Wilson, "is evident from his writings, as well as the testimony of learned men ; and he seems to have possessed a remarkable talent for disputation." ‖—Dr. Owen, whom no one will suspect of partiality to our author, or of a disposition to flatter an Anti-Calvinist, says of Mr. Goodwin, " My adversary is a person, whom his worth, pains, diligence, and opinions, and the contests wherein, on their account, he hath publicly engaged, have delivered him

* Genuine Remains, p. 122.   † Vindication of Dr. Twisse, p. 201.
‡ Palmer's Noncon. Mem. Vol. I. p. 198.   § Article Goodwin.   ‖ Hist. of Dissenting Churches, Vol. II. p. 424.

from being the object of any ordinary thoughts or expressions. Nothing not great, not considerable, not some way eminent, is by any spoken of him, either consenting with him or dissenting from him."* Archbishop Sancroft has also characterized him as "an able English divine."† Such was the man, according to the testimony of competent judges, whom Bishop Burnet, in sheer but voluntary ignorance, describes as a fanatic and a fool!

It has been frequently urged against Mr. Goodwin, that his temper was violent, and his general manner of treating his opponents indecorous and disrespectful. But this charge will be found on examination to be the result of prejudice, of inattention, or of something worse. "My conscience," says he, "beareth me witness, that I have not, to my knowledge, the least propension to be offensive to any man. I am able, with all singleness of heart, to say, that I am really interested in the design of the apostle, to please all men for their good : and better were it for me to die, than that any man should be able to make this myglorying void.

"Since I understood that exception was taken at some expressions in my writings as inclinable to sharpness, amongst others of my acquaintance, I desired the free and serious advisement of a grave, learned, and godly minister, (a good old Nonconformist of between forty and fifty years standing,) who had diligently perused all my controversial writings, upon the matter. His answer was, that he knew nothing in any of them that ministered any occasion of offence in that kind. Yet, not satisfying myself herewith, and putting off the relation of an author, I betook myself as a stranger and stander-by, to consider whether there be any passage in the said writings justly criminable : yea, I armed myself with prejudice, so that I might not be abused by partiality. Upon the survey, I am more than confident, that there is not any sentence in the said writings, but what, for matter of tartness, I am able to parallel either out of the Scriptures, or the writings of the gravest and most approved authors.

* Doctrine of the Saints' Perseverance, Dedication.   † D'Oyly
Life of Sancroft, Vol. II. p. 259, Edit. 1821.

" When men are much obnoxious, whether in corrupt-
ness of judgment, manners, or will, the weakness or sin-
fulness of this corruption being effectually represented, it
carries an appearance of sharpness, and truly hath that
which is offensive to the flesh.   It is the genius of truth,
especially when she goeth forth and meets men in the
face, armed with power of expression, to do severe execution upon delinquents; insomuch that, many times, by
reason hereof, she is taken for an enemy by those whom
she smiteth.

" That which causeth an appearance of more tartness
in my controversial writings, than is well justifiable, is, I
conceive, this: Though many plead the cause of truth,
both by reproof and argument, few make it any part
of their engagement either to represent the errors
or miscarriages against which they contest, according to what is erroneous in the one or sinful in the other;
or to seek out such expressions which are most proper to
carry the notion of the one and the other with the greatest
force of impression upon the understandings of men : both
which I endeavouring after in my writings, it makes them
seem to men accustomed to other styles, as if they were
seasoned with too much salt, or salted with fire. Whereas
all the saltness in them is but truth delivered with her
due advantage of expression. The best way to refute an
error, is by an argument which shows the absurdity of it.
Many are capable of a manifest absurdity, whose apprehensions cannot reach a closer demonstration.   As for
passion, I am not conscious of writing by it, unless haply
it be when I meet with Ignorance riding in triumph upon
Confidence's back; with which occurrency I have been
encountered in most of my controversial expeditions.—
Weakness, attended with humility, I can pass by, and
pity: confidence, supported by worth and truth, I can
bear: if at any time my pen turns into a rod, it is to give
correction to Confidence for keeping Weakness company;
or to nurture Weakness into more wisdom, than to suffer
Confidence to put her to open shame." *

* Inexcusableness of Antapologia, Preface.

"If our opinions know not how to live, without the disparagement of those who are of opposite judgment to us, it is a sore testimony against them, that they are not of the royal line of truth; who is able to maintain her legitimate offspring with her own native inheritance, without the unjust taxation of the reputations, practices, or opinions of her adversaries." *

It is not pretended, that in the warmth of dispute Mr Goodwin never lost the government of his temper, nor "spake unadvisedly with his lips;" or that he always exemplified "the meekness and gentleness of Christ." Had this been the case, considering the torrents of abuse which were poured upon him, both from the pulpit and the press, he must have been possessed of patience more than human. There were occasions on which he not only exposed the principles, but rebuked the insolence of his unfair and abusive antagonists; but he suffered many a scurrilous pamphlet against him to pass unnoticed, and in most cases returned good for evil. When he met with an opponent who possessed the spirit of a Christian, and the urbanity of a scholar and a gentleman, as in the case of Dr. Barlow, he not only treated him with politeness and respect, but his mind seemed to dissolve in the exercise of pure benevolence.

On this subject Sir Peter Pett has justly observed, that "Dr. Barlow's Letter and Mr. Goodwin's Answer may be, to such who write of controversial divinity, an useful specimen of two antagonists writing of the same with candour, and like gentlemen, as well as scholars and Christians; and the which was suitable to the natural tempers both of Dr. Barlow and Mr. Goodwin."†

The Rev. Walter Sellon has also observed in reference to our author, that, "There is hardly a controversial writer to be found, who has more strictly observed the rules of decency and modesty than he, notwithstanding the usage he met with from the Calvinistic party. Surely we cannot but have a high opinion of a man whom envy itself cannot but praise." ‡

* Calumny Arraigned, Preface.   † Barlow's Genuine Remains, p. 139.
‡ Works, Vol. I. pp. 376, 416, Octavo Edit.

"If I knew any thing justly offensive," says Mr. Goodwin himself, "in any of my writings, were it to the half, yea to the whole of any discourse, I am ready by a special act of reversal to cut off the relation; nor should it, by my consent, ever more be called mine. Reader, whosoever thou art, I authorize thee, whatsoever thou shalt meet with distasteful to thee, to take it and cast it into the errata. Unworthy is he of the name of a man, much more of a Christian, or to have so much place on earth as whereon to rest his foot, who takes pleasure in offending any man, otherwise than in order to his future joy. But glory, honour, and peace, be his portion, whose heart serves him to serve the world in the things of their peace, whilst they are making war against him with the weapons of unkindness; and will not accept any hard sayings, or evil entreaties, for a discharge from that love and faithfulness, wherewith he stands bound by the law of heaven to oppose them till he overcomes."*

Several years after writing this, having had to contend with such men as Edwards, Jenkyn, Kendall, and others of a similar spirit, Mr. Goodwin remarks, "The prophet Isaiah cried out, *Woe is me, for I am undone, because I am a man of unclean lips, and dwell in the midst of a people of unclean lips!*—implying, I conceive, that his daily conversing with people of unworthy language wrought a strong jealousy in him, that he had contracted somewhat of the same guilt. I confess I am under no small fears, lest so much scanning the writings of men of intemperate and unclean pens, as my conflicting with so many adversaries hath drawn me unto, hath taught my pen also many words of an uncomely character; and not being so strictly watchful over my spirit as I ought, I have not so well approved myself to God and good men, as it had been my wisdom to have done. But my God, who hath the greatest reason to be offended, I know hath pardoned my frailties in this kind; and good men, I trust, where He hath been gracious, will not be inexorable. For the future I shall, God willing, keep

* Inexcusableness of Antapologia, Preface.

myself from the temptation, and suffer men of provoking principles to write their pleasures without answering a word."*

Had Mr. Goodwin consented to study Christianity in the writings of Calvin, Beza, and other divines of the same school,—had he submitted to repeat their sayings under the name of *the* Gospel,—had he denominated all who held contrary opinions Heretics, Pelagians, &c., &c.,—and had he called upon the magistrate to punish all who dared to impugn Calvin's tenets,—in all probability he would have lived in credit among the ministers of his time, and have been esteemed by them as a worthy, reverend, and orthodox brother. By thus conforming to the fashionable creed and practice, he might have been a frequent preacher before the Long Parliament, and an honourable ecclesiastic during the Commonwealth; perhaps one of Cromwell's Triers, on whom candidates for the ministry, and for preferment, would have waited with all humility and deference. But of such conduct he was incapable. While studying the Holy Scriptures, he was fully convinced, THAT ALL COERCION IN MATTERS PURELY RELIGIOUS IS ANTICHRISTIAN,—THAT JESUS CHRIST DIED UPON THE CROSS FOR THE REDEMPTION OF EVERY HUMAN BEING,—AND THAT NO MAN IS EITHER ELECTED TO ETERNAL LIFE, OR REPROBATED TO ENDLESS MISERY, BY ANY DECREE OF GOD IRRESPECTIVE OF CHARACTER. Because he claimed the right, which he unquestionably possessed, of peaceably communicating these doctrines to the world, he was persecuted without mercy. Many of his contemporaries deemed it an intolerable hardship, that they were reduced to the distressing alternative of witnessing the prevalence of such *heresies,* or of confuting them by logical deductions. Fain would they have saved their midnight oil, and have prevented the exhaustion of their spirits, by employing the sword of the civil magistrate in the solution of their theological difficulties. By the mercy of heaven, however, this dangerous weapon was kept out of their hands. In endeavouring to supply the want of it, they palmed upon

* Triumviri, Preface.

Goodwin nearly all the monstrous opinions that have ever degraded the human understanding. They discharged against him the various epithets of reproach with which their minds were amply stored. They had recourse to caricature, and associated his portrait with ridiculous figures, for the base purpose of exposing him to public contempt. Regardless of truth, and in opposition to the strongest evidence, they represented him to the rulers of the nation as a sceptic who denied the inspiration of the Scriptures, and as an enemy to civil government. The pulpit rang with invectives against him, especially on public occasions, and the press poured forth floods of calumny. What has been said of a modern divine may with far greater justice be applied to him; he indeed

> Stood pilloried on infamy's high stage,
> And bore the pelting scorn of half an age;
> The very but of slander, and the blot
> For every dart that malice ever shot.
> The man that mentioned *him* at once dismissed
> All mercy from his lips, and sneered and hissed;
> His crimes were such as Sodom never knew,
> And perjury stood up to swear all true;
> His aim was mischief, and his zeal pretence,
> His speech rebellion against common sense;
> A knave when tried on honesty's plain rule,
> And when by that of reason a mere fool;
> The world's great comfort was, his doom was passed;
> Die when he might, he must be damned at last.

The magnanimity displayed by Mr. Goodwin under these circumstances, and which appears never to have forsaken him, proves him to have been a man of no ordinary firmness of character. This elevation of soul, this mental hardihood, was not constitutional insensibility, nor sullen indifference; for his mind was susceptible of the finest emotions; but it was produced and supported by Christian principles. The language in which he has described this temper, is worthy of being recorded in characters durable as time itself. "Loath I am," says he, "that men of hard language should fall softer anywhere, than upon me. For God having been graciously pleased to make the revilings of men such benefactors to

me, hath put a golden bridle into my lips, to keep me
from much sharpness of complaint. It had been a very
unseemly thing in Joseph, in the height of his honour in
Egypt, to have cried out of, or taken revenge upon, the
envy of his brethren in selling him ; which God had
sanctified as the means of his advancement. It is an easy
matter to forgive injuries, after God hath altered their
properties and turned them into blessings. Besides, my
hope is, that those who are zealous for supposed truths
will be zealous for truth indeed, when they come to see it.
In this case, I can freely set my hope against my experience,
and let my complaint fall. But as touching the hard
measure I have received from men, my best satisfaction
resteth in this consideration,—That God is both able to
pardon the offenders, and to recompense the sufferer." *

"As for personal revilings, I have lived so long under
these catadupes, that the noise of the cataracts very little
affects me, neither interrupting my sleep nor my meditations.—When first this yoke was put about my neck, it
was somewhat uneasy, it wrung and galled me. But after
I had been for a time accustomed to it, I looked upon it
as a chain of gold, weighing more in honour and peace
than in shame and sorrow. As Moses esteemed the reproach of Christ greater riches than the treasures of
Egypt, so is that hard measure which is daily measured
out to me, both in words and deeds, upon no other reason,
as far as I am conscious, but because I endeavour to make
men more like God than it seems they have a mind to be,—
that hard measure which I suffer in reproaches and disparagement, because of this, is of far richer contentment
to me, than ten times as many ' worthy sirs,' and 'reverend
sirs,' and other acclamations of honour would be."†

"Of any wrong done to myself I will not complain.
But I know a man who hath been forsaken of his friends,
found those of his own household to be his enemies ; who
hath been reviled, traduced, reproached ; waylaid by
tongues, by pens, by practices ; reported to have lost his wits,

* Treatise of Justification, Preface. † Inexcusableness of Antapologia, Preface.

abilities, parts ; suffered loss of his due and necessary subsistence, wrongfully detained from him, and for which he
hath laboured faithfully ; brought before rulers and magistrates ; represented to sovereign authority as a wilful and
presumptuous underminer of their undoubted privileges ;
besides twenty more hard sayings and practices against
him ; and all this for no other cause, but because he holds
a truth (as in all his heart and soul he is persuaded) which,
if entertained, is likely to bless the world. Of the injuries
offered to such a man I have cause to complain ; but for
any sufferings of mine own, I count it beneath my engagements to Him who strengtheneth me to do and suffer
all things, to stoop to take up any lamentation."*

"I know myself to be compassed about with as many
infirmities as the weakest of men, and my great unworthiness in many things is daily before me. Yet it hath
pleased my God, whom I serve in the Gospel of His Son, to
hide my nakedness from mine enemies, though many in
number, and diligent inquirers after it ; and so to dispose
of their ill-will against me, that the fiery darts of their accusations have hit where my breast-plate of righteousness
is most firm and best proof. It is too much to say of
myself, nor will I say it, but it would be a truth comely
enough in the mouths of others, that I am, if not the best,
yet none of the worst friends, which the Divine Authority
of the Scripture hath amongst men ; and that I have been
as diligent, as faithful, as laborious an assertor thereof, as
any of those who think themselves more worthy of the
crown. Notwithstanding, with what clamour have I been
traduced, not only to vulgar cognizance, but to Authority
itself, as an enemy of the Heavenly Original of the Scriptures, by some who, out of zeal for God, (for so they gloss
the practice,) neglect their own employments, and follow
Satan's in accusing the brethren !

" But that I daily fight with beasts at Ephesus, after the
manner of men, what advantageth it me if the Scriptures
be not the Word of God ? Or why have I bought so many
Scripture truths at such great rates as I have done, as with

* Innocency and Truth, Preface.

the loss of friends, credit, esteem with men, estate; yea all hope, that I say not *possibility* of bettering my condition in the world, low as it is, if I believe them not to be the Word of God? Why did I suffer an ejection out of my freehold, (the best means I had in the world for the support of myself, wife, and seven children,) for no other crime that I could ever hear of, but for endeavouring to go before others in a real reformation,—if I believe not the Scriptures to be the Word of God? If I did not believe them to be the Word of God, I would believe them as prudently as many others do; so as to keep fair quarter with soft raiment, great purses, full tables, and benches of honour; nor would I sacrifice my hope of rising in the world, upon the service of any thing contained in them. Did I not believe them to be the Word of God, I would not for the vindication of anything they say expose myself, as now I do, to the clamorous tongues of an ill-employed generation of informers,—God forgive them! I hope they know not what they do! I am neither Stoic nor Cynic: I had rather abound than be in want: I had rather have the good wills and the good words of my generation than their bad; and that the greatness of this world should rather smile than frown upon me. For the acquirement of all these I had as fair opportunities as others of my brethren in the ministry, and had a price in my hand as sufficient for the purchase, as many of those who have bought, possess, and enjoy; whose advancement I no ways emulate or envy. That which mainly separated between me and my desires in this kind was nothing else but my believing the Scriptures to be the Word of God. This principle was too stiff to bow at the feet of worldly accommodations: and these, on the other hand, thought themselves too good to subject themselves to this principle: and since they thus mutually resented the genius of one another, they have been strangers; and by this time scarcely know, remember, or take much care one for the other." *

" My God and my conscience have deeply engaged me.

* Scourge of the Saints Displayed, Appendix.

F F

in a warfare, very troublesome and costly; even to contend in a manner with the whole earth, and to attempt the
casting down of high things, which exalt themselves
against the knowledge of God. And daily experience
showeth that men's imaginations are their darlings, that
he who toucheth them touches the apple of their eye, and
appeareth in the shape of an enemy. To bear the hatred
and contradiction of the world is not pleasing to me: notwithstanding the vehemency of desire which possesseth my
heart, of doing some service in the world whilst I am a so-
journer in it, and leaving it at my departure upon somewhat
better terms for the peace and comfort of it, than I found
it at my coming, swallows up much of that offensiveness
and monstrousness of taste, wherewith otherwise the
measure I receive from many would affect my soul."*

"I have the advantage of old age, and of the sanctuary
of the grave near at hand, to despise all enemies and
avengers. I know that hard thoughts, and hard sayings,
and hard writings, and hard dealings, and frowns, and
pourings out of contempt and wrath, abide me. 'But
none of these things move me, neither count I my life dear
unto myself, so that I may finish my course with joy, and
the ministry which I have received of the Lord Jesus,
to testify the Gospel of the grace of God.' Farewell, good
reader, in the Lord; let him have a friend's portion in thy
prayers, who is willing to suffer the loss of all things for
thy sake, that the truth of the Gospel may come with
evidence and demonstration of the Spirit unto thee, and
remain with thee. If the embracing of the truth before
men keep thee from preferment on earth, it will most
assuredly recompense thee seven-fold, yea seventy times
seven-fold, in heaven."†

These extracts need no comment. They describe a state
of mind, in comparison of which, the most ample revenues,
and the highest literary honours, are less than nothing.
About fifty years before John Goodwin the great and good
Arminius advocated the same principles of universal
toleration, and of redeeming mercy, and with exactly the

* Cata-Baptism, Dedication.   † Exposition, Preface.

same results. But his spirit was tender and sensitive, so that he at length fairly sank under the cruel treatment of his Presbyterian contemporaries, the Dutch advocates of Calvinism and of persecution. Worn out, at length, by the incessant hostility of these men, he died in the flower of his age, with a blameless character, leaving a widow and nine young children to mourn his premature departure.* Happily for John Goodwin, he possessed as brave a heart as ever beat in a merely human breast, and a mind as robust as that of Luther himself; maintaining with unswerving tenacity, through good report, and through evil report, and under every form of government, the right and duty of every man to worship God according to the dictates of his own conscience; and that the sacrifice of the cross was offered by the will and appointment of God for every human being. John Goodwin was not the man he has been wantonly represented; but was worthy of a better age than that in which it was his misfortune to live. It was an age of revolutions both in the Church and the State; but every change proved to be nothing more than the substitution of one form of tyranny for another. He laboured hard for many years to introduce more Scriptural views of the mercy of God, and of the extent of human redemption, than generally prevailed among his Puritanic contemporaries, and to secure for all classes of religious people full toleration; but died without the sight. What he earnestly desired is now happily realized. The blessed doctrine of universal redemption is unequivocally preached in the length and breadth of the land; and Christians of every community worship God in their own sanctuaries under the guardianship of toleration laws. What our Saviour said to His disciples may now be said to every class of British Christians: " Other men have laboured, and ye have entered into their labours." It may be properly added, Cherish their memory; and preserve with unswerving fidelity the good deposit which they have placed in your hands.

* See the Works of Arminius, translated by my friend James Nichols, Volume First, *passim*.

2 F 2

CHRONOLOGICAL LIST

OF

MR. GOODWIN'S PUBLICATIONS.

1. The Saints' Interest in God, 1640.

2. God a Good Master and Protector to His People, 1641.

8. The Return of Mercies; or, The Saints' Advantage by Losses, 1641.

4. Animadversions upon some of the Looser and Fouler Passages in Mr. Walker's Discourse, 1641.

5. The Christian's Engagement for the Gospel, 1641.

6. Ireland's Advocate; or, A Sermon preached upon November 14th, 1641, to promote the Contributions by way of lending to the present Relief of the Protestant Party in Ireland. In the Parish Church of St. Stephen's, Coleman Street, London, by the Pastor there, 1641.

7. Arguments against Bowing at the Name of Jesus; composed about five Years since, by a Reverend Minister of the City of London for his own Defence, 1641.

8. A Defence of the True Sense and Meaning of the Words of the Holy Apostle, Rom. iv. 2, 5, 9. In answer to Sundry Arguments gathered from the forenamed Scriptures by Mr. John Goodwin; which Answer was first dispersed without the Author's name, but since acknowledged by Mr. George Walker. Together with a Reply to the former Answer, by John Goodwin, Pastor of Coleman Street, London, 1641.

9. Anti-Cavalierism; or, Truth Pleading as well the Necessity as Lawfulness of the Present War, 1642.

10. The Butcher's Blessing; or, The Bloody Intentions of the Romish Cavaliers against the City of London, 1642.

11. A Treatise of Justification, 1642.

12. The First Man; or, A Short Discourse of Adam's State, viz., 1. Of his being made a Living Soul. 2. Of the Manner of his Fall, by J. G., 1643.

13. Os Ossorianum ; or, A Bone for a Bishop to Pick, 1643.

14. Reply of Two of the Brethren to A. S., 1644.

15. The Grand Imprudence of Men Running the Hazard of Fighting against God, 1644.

16. Innocency's Triumph, 1645.

17. Innocency and Truth Triumphing Together, 1645.

18. Calumny Arraigned and Cast, 1645.

19. Some Modest and Humble Queries concerning a late Printed Paper, 1646.

20. The Scourge of the Saints Displayed in his Colours of Ignorance and Blood, 1646.

21. A Brief Answer to an Ulcerous Treatise, entitled Gangræna, 1646.

22. The Inexcusableness of that Grand Accusation of the Brethren, called Antapologia, 1646.

23. Twelve Serious Cautions necessary to be Observed in a Reformation according to the Word of God, 1646.

24. Sion College Visited, 1647.

25. The Novice-Presbyter Instructed, 1648.

26. The Divine Authority of the Scriptures Asserted, 1648.

27. Right and Might well Met, 1648.

28. The Unrighteous Judge : an answer to a Paper pretending to be a Letter to J. Goodwin, by Sir F. Nethersole, 1649.

29. The Obstructors of Justice, 1649.

30. The Remedy of Unreasonableness, 1650.

31. Redemption Redeemed, 1651.

32. Moses Made Angry : a Letter written and sent to Dr. Hill, 1651.

33. The Pagan's Debt and Dowry, 1651.

34. Confidence Dismounted: or, A Letter to Mr. Richard Resbury, of Oundle in Northamptonshire, 1651.

35. The Agreement and Distance of Brethren, 1652.

36. An Exposition of the Ninth Chapter of the Epistle to the Romans, 1653.

37. Forty Queries peaceably and inoffensively Propounded, 1653.

38. Water-Dipping no firm Footing for Church Communion, 1653.

39. Thirty Queries, modestly propounded in order to a discovery of the truth and mind of God, in that Case of Conscience : Whether the Civil Magistrate stands bound to interpose his Power in matters of Religion and Worship of God, 1653.

40. The Apologist Condemned : or, A Vindication of the Thirty Queries together with their Author, 1653.

41. Dissatisfaction Satisfied, 1654.

42. Peace Protected, and Discontent Disarmed, 1654.

43. A fresh Discovery of the High Presbyterian Spirit, 1654.

44. The Six Booksellers' Proctor Nonsuited : wherein the Gross Falsifications and Untruths, together with the Inconsiderate and Weak Passages found in the Apology for the said Booksellers, are Briefly Noted and Evicted, 1655.

45. Cata-Baptism : or, New Baptism waxing Old, and ready to Vanish Away, 1655.

46. Mercy in her Exaltation, 1655.

47. A Catechism : or, Principal Heads of the Christian Religion.

48. The Triers or Tormenters Tried and Cast, 1657.

49. Triumviri, 1658.

50. The Banner of Justification Displayed, 1659.

51. Prelatic Preachers none of Christ's Teachers, 1663.

52. A Being Filled with the Spirit, 1670.

In addition to these publications, Mr. Goodwin wrote Prefaces to the following works :

Ramsden's Gleaning of God's Harvest, 1639.

Fenner's Divine Message to the Elect Soul, 1645.

Satan's Stratagems, by Jacobus Acontius, 1648.

APPENDIX.

It is a fact, which is highly worthy of attention, that several of the greatest divines, who have adorned the different Protestant churches by their learning, talents, and virtue, were, in the early part of their lives, "straitened in their bowels" respecting the extent of CHRIST's REDEMPTION, and as they advanced in years and knowledge, they entertained enlarged views of the Divine Philanthropy. The following are some of the examples of this kind which may be specified:

MELANCTHON,

Luther's friend and coadjutor, was at first Luther's scholar, and drew from him his earliest religious opinions. But being a learned and dispassionate man, pursuing truth, he saw his errors and abandoned them; and espoused sentiments concerning the respectiveness of God's decrees, widely different from those he had formerly held. [A circumstance which is very conveniently passed over in silence by Dr. Cox, his late English biographer.]—*Pierce's* Divine Philanthropy Defended, p. 14, Edit. 1657.

LUTHER

Also went on long as he at first set out, with so little disguise, that whereas all parties had always pretended that they asserted the freedom of the will, he plainly spoke out, and said the will was not free, but enslaved. Yet, before he died, he is reported to have changed his mind on this and other kindred subjects: for though he never owned that, yet Melancthon, who had been of the same opinions, did; for which he was never blamed by Luther.—*Burnet* on the Seventeenth Article.

ARMINIUS

Himself was educated at Geneva, and in the early part of his life embraced those doctrines concerning predestination, which Calvin and Beza had taught in that city. Afterwards, however, when actually engaged in vindication of those doctrines, he was convinced that they were indefensible; and embraced the principles of those whose religious system extends the Divine benevolence and the merits of Jesus Christ to all man-kind.—*Mosheim's* Eccles. Hist. Vol. V. p. 440, Edit. 1806.

DANIEL TILENUS,

Professor of Divinity at Sedan, a man not less acute in judgment, than versed in all kinds of learning, distinguished himself by decided hostility to the sentiments of Arminius. Convinced at length by the arguments of his opponents, he changed sides; and proved the genuineness of his conversion by submitting to share with the Remonstrants in those severe persecutions which were inflicted upon them by the Dutch Calvinists.—*Brandt's* History of the Reformation, Vol. II. p. 137, Edit. 1721.

DR. THOMAS JACKSON,

President of Corpus Christi College, Oxford, is thus cha-racterized by the noted Prynne: "Dr. Jackson is a man of great abilities, and of a plausible, affable, courteous deportment.—Of late he hath been transported beyond himself with metaphysical contemplations.—The University of Oxford grieves for his defection" [from the doctrine of absolute pre-destination].—Anti-Arminianism, p. 270, Edit. 1630.

BISHOP ANDREWS

Is generally allowed to have been one of the most learned and pious men of the age in which he lived. Concerning him, Dr. Pierce observes, "That that inestimable bishop, in his most mature and ripest years, was very severe to those doctrines which are commonly called Calvinistical, is a thing so known, that I cannot think it will be denied."—Divine Purity Defended, p. 125, Edit. 1657.

DR. CHRISTOPHER POTTER,

Provost of Queen's College, Oxford, who was esteemed by all who knew him, as a divine of an amiable disposition, and of great probity, industry, and learning, has given a pleasing account of his conversion from Calvinism to the Arminian tenets; and the piety and meekness of temper displayed in the narrative add weight to his judgment, and are honourable to the cause for which he pleads.—Collection of Tracts on Predestination, p. 225, Cambridge, 1719.

DR. THOMAS PIERCE,

One of the ablest opponents of Calvinism that system has ever had, states concerning himself: "I was, in my childhood, of the opinions [concerning Election, Reprobation, &c.] Mr. Barlee doth now contend for. But, through the infinite mercy of God, I have obtained conversion: and being converted from the practice, as well as from the opinion, which I was of, I will, to my poor utmost, endeavour to confirm or convert my brethren."—Divine Philanthropy Defended,

THE EVER-MEMORABLE HALES, OF ETON,

Who was a Calvinist in his younger days, used frequently to say, that when he heard Episcopius argue in favour of General Redemption at the Synod of Dort, he "bade John Calvin good night."—*Hales's* Golden Remains, Preface.

MR. SAMUEL HOARD,

Author of a very able work entitled, "God's Love to Mankind Manifested,"—a work which produced a considerable effect among the national clergy, in the early part of the seventeenth century,—says, "I have sent you here my reasons which have moved me to change my opinion in some controversies, of late debated between the Remonstrants and their Opponents."— See the tract itself, p. 1, Edit. 1633. *Whiston's* Memoirs, Vol. I. p. 10, Edit. 1749.

DR. THOMAS GOAD

Was a person every way eminent, having the repute of a great and general scholar, exact critic and historian, a poet, orator, schoolman, and divine. He was a member of the Synod of Dort, and acquitted himself there with great applause, in opposition to the opinions of the Remonstrants. He at length saw cause to alter his judgment; and, in defence of those principles he had formerly opposed, wrote a very able work entitled, "A Disputation concerning the Necessity and Contingency of Events."—*Echard's* History of England, Vol. II. p. 122, Edit. 1718. Collection of Tracts on Predestination, Preface.

ARCHBISHOP USSHER,

Who is generally acknowledged to have been one of the most
learned men in Europe, in the early part of his life held the
doctrines of strict Calvinism; but as he advanced in years,
avowed his belief of General Redemption ; and is said, before
his death, to have expressed his dislike of the whole doctrine of
Geneva.—*Pierce's* Christian's Rescue from the Grand Error of
the Heathen, Appendix, Edit. 1658.—*Bird's* Fate and Destiny
Inconsistent with Christianity, p. 74, Edit. 1726.—*Parr's* Life
of Ussher, Appendix, p. 51, Edit. 1686.—*Wordsworth's* Ecclesiastical Biography, Vol. V. p. 504, Edit. 1810.

DR. ROBERT SANDERSON,

Professor of Divinity in the University of Oxford, and afterwards Bishop of Lincoln, has given an interesting account of
the progress of his mind, from the sublapsarian scheme, to the
mild sentiments of Melancthon and Arminius.—*Hammond's*
Pacific Discourse concerning God's Grace and Decrees, p. 8,
1660.

MR. RICHARD BAXTER,

At the commencement of his theological career, was eager in
his attachment to the peculiar doctrines of Calvin. But when
his judgment was more matured, though he still maintained
the absolute Election of some men to Life Eternal, he contended
strenuously for General Redemption, and for Universal Grace.
—*Baxter's* Catholick Theologie, Preface.

BISHOP DAVENANT

Appears to have undergone a change of sentiment similar to
that of Baxter. For Archbishop Ussher "freely declared himself for the doctrine of General Redemption, and owned that he
was the person who brought both Bishop Davenant and Dr.
Preston to acknowledge it."—*Calamy's* Abridgment of Baxter's
Life and Times, p. 405, Edit. 1713.

DR. DANIEL WHITBY

Says, " They who have known my education, may remember
that I was bred up seven years in the University, under men of
the Calvinistical persuasion ; and had once firmly entertained
all their doctrines." The zeal with which he afterwards opposed
those doctrines, in his Commentary on the New Testament

and in his Discourse concerning the Five Points, is universally known.—*Whitby* on the Five Points, Preface.

CALVIN

Himself, according to Dr. Watts, is entitled to a place among those divines whose attachment to the doctrines of limited mercy and partial redemption abated as they advanced in years. After noticing the difference between his sentiments as expressed in his Institutions and in his Commentaries, the Doctor says, "It may be proper to observe, that the most rigid and narrow limitations of grace to men are to be found chiefly in his Institutions, which were written in his youth. But his Comments on Scripture were the labour of his riper years, and maturer judgment."—Works, Vol. III. p. 472, Edit. 1800.

INDEX.